Praise for *A Happy Marriage*

"[*A Happy Marriage*] will break reader's hearts while at the same time renewing their faith in the value of the enduring institution of matrimony."

—Meghan Ward, *San Francisco Chronicle*

"A stunner."

—Michelle Green, *People* (3½ stars)

"The rawest depiction of longtime love in recent memory . . . A blood-and-guts foray into the nature of human intimacy."

—Megan O'Grady, Vogue.com

"Brave . . . instantly compelling . . . In prose that flexes with unflinching confidence, Yglesias parts the hospital curtain to show not just death's indignities . . . but also its tender comedy, small reprieves and surreal turns of fortune."

—Scott Muskin, *Minneapolis Star Tribune*

"Surprising and deeply affecting . . . A very brave book indeed."

—Nancy Connors, *The Cleveland Plain Dealer*

"Alive with passion and perception."

—Esther Hammer, *The Tampa Tribune*

"The protagonist recounts the triumphs and failures of a well-matched relationship with raw, often brutal honesty. Any twenty-one-year-old can rhapsodize over the curves of his beloved's cheekbones; it's the decades that follow—battered by infidelity, altered by age and circumstance, ravaged by disease—that reveal both the limits and transcendence of a true, lasting love."

—Leah Greenblatt, *Entertainment Weekly*

"Heart-wrenchingly honest . . . Enrique and Margaret's ups and downs will warm your heart and rip it out at the same time."

—DailyCandy

"By turns heartbreaking, amusing, depressing, and joyous . . . A beautiful story."

—*January Magazine*

"A profound, personal, and riveting read."

—*Berkshire Living*

"An honest and glorious examination of what it's like to be married . . . You'll come away with a better understanding of the deep-rooted, messy bonds of human relationships."

—*VIVmag*

"Rafael Yglesias's novel—long and graceful and written to display an intimacy wincingly believable—is about life, itself, not just one particular marriage. As the book alternates between past and present, we grow, along with the characters: as they jump boundaries, so do we; as they resign themselves to a sad inevitability, we feel viscerally cornered, too. It's a punch-in-the-stomach book, but the sharpness forces us to open our eyes wide. Impressive."

—Ann Beattie, author of *Walks With Men*

"Yglesias mixes passion and pain in this deep and searing story of love. With unflinching honesty, he reveals the resilience of the human spirit in the face of illness and loss."

—Jerome Groopman, author of *How Doctors Think*

A Happy Marriage

A Novel

RAFAEL YGLESIAS

SCRIBNER
New York   London   Toronto   Sydney

SCRIBNER
A Division of Simon & Schuster, Inc.
1230 Avenue of the Americas
New York, NY 10020

First Scribner trade paperback edition August 2010

SCRIBNER and design are registered trademarks of
The Gale Group, Inc., used under license by Simon & Schuster, Inc.,
the publisher of this work.

For information about special discounts for bulk purchases,
please contact Simon & Schuster Special Sales at
1-866-506-1949 or business@simonandschuster.com.

The Simon & Schuster Speakers Bureau can bring authors to your live event.
For more information or to book an event, contact the Simon & Schuster
Speakers Bureau at 1-866-248-3049 or visit our website at
www.simonspeakers.com.

DESIGNED BY KYOKO WATANABE
Text set in Garamond 3

Manufactured in the United States of America

1 3 5 7 9 10 8 6 4 2

Library of Congress Control Number: 2008051364

ISBN 978-1-4391-0230-5
ISBN 978-1-4391-0231-2 (pbk)
ISBN 978-1-4391-0981-6 (ebook)

For her

A Happy Marriage

chapter one

Take-out Girl

H E HAD ORDERED her in. While he waited for the start of *Saturday Night Live* on his new Trinitron (what vivid colors and definition, what bliss of technology!), he had ordered in the Dream Girl he didn't know he had dreamed until her great blue eyes, streaming tears from December's cold, examined him with a startled and amused stare.

The deliveryman was a close friend, the half-hated Bernard Weinstein who, with typical gracelessness, mumbled their names at the floor, "Enrique—Margaret. Margaret—Enrique," and rudely preceded her into the new studio apartment. New, that is, both to Enrique Sabas and to the world. The fifth-floor walk-up on Eighth Street in Greenwich Village had been gutted, and the renovations were completed two months ago to justify rebooting rent-controlled numbers to market level. Enrique had moved in a week after the last bathroom tile was caulked. So all was new in Enrique's life, from plumbing to TV, when this new girl entered, walked to the apartment's single luxury asset, a working fireplace, and released a burst of jet-black hair from the suppression of a red beret. She then turned her back on faded brick and pale marble mantel, kept her tearing searchlights on Enrique while she unzipped a black bubble down jacket, and revealed a fire engine red wool sweater tight to her trim, small-breasted figure. This bourgeois striptease shot a current through Enrique which felt as palpable as if he had ignored the posted warning, opened up the back of his new Trinitron, and stuck a finger where it shouldn't go.

Her wet blue eyes remained fixed on him while she dropped into a director's chair beside the fireplace, wriggled her skinny arms out of their down cases, and shrugged off the bubble's torso with a dainty lift and twist of her slim shoulders. She proceeded with a tomboy's physical confidence to sling a taut thigh over the chair's arm as if preparing to mount it; instead, she remained thus perched, her legs wide open, exposing the faded denim of her smooth pelvis. Enrique couldn't sustain a long investigation of that region. His eyes dropped involuntarily to what he would one day learn was a triple-A foot dangling in the space between them. He didn't know that her narrow size was very troublesome to a woman who loved shoes, or that the black suede boot swinging toward and away from him had been anguished over because of its high cost. To his male and ignorant twenty-one-year-old eyes, the delicate foot, thus encased, was merely provocative; not for its dainty dimension but for its restless kicks at him, as if they were intended to rouse him to do something to impress her: *Perform! Perform! Perform!*

He couldn't complain about this demanding presence because he had ordered her in, just like the take-out Chinese from Charlie Mom's whose remains were now stuffed into his red garbage pail under the stainless-steel sink. It would have remained stainless anyway because he had hardly cooked in the new kitchen that was one step up from but open to the narrow bedroom-living-working area of this apartment that he couldn't afford and that represented, although his third residence since leaving his parents' domain, his first true place all to himself, the previous two having had roommates—the first someone with whom he slept, the second not. He looked away to glum Bernard to obtain some sort of clarification because, yes, he had selected her from his friend's menu, but he hadn't expected noodles this spicy.

Although Bernard had proclaimed Margaret's extraordinary qualities, he had done so with characteristic and maddening vagueness. In his elaborate descriptions of Margaret, Bernard had failed to mention the extraordinary big and vivid blue eyes that rivaled the impact of Elizabeth Taylor's, or the ice cream smooth whiteness of her freckled skin. Nevertheless Bernard was a heterosexual male, and he might have mentioned that she had perfectly proportioned legs, that she was skinny without being flat-assed or flat-chested, and that for the brief moment Enrique allowed himself to look, the spread of those trim and yet rounded thighs was an invitation too overwhelming to contemplate without losing track of everything else and so merited, for God's sakes, some warning.

Enrique had dared Bernard to produce Margaret during one of their afternoon breakfasts at the Homer Coffee Shop when, once again, Bernard couldn't shut up about his remarkable female friend from Cornell, the amazing Margaret Cohen, but wouldn't agree to introduce her. (Margaret Cohen, Enrique complained, what kind of Jewish family names their daughter Margaret? A complaint which might have seemed more reasonable coming from someone other than a person named Enrique Sabas, who was himself Jewish, thanks to his Ashkenazi mother.) Bernard explained that he had a dread of intermingling friends from different ghettos of his life.

"Why?" Enrique demanded.

Bernard stonewalled him with a laconic shrug. "I'm neurotic."

"Bullshit," Enrique said. "You just don't want to blow all your carefully wrought observations at one dinner party."

"Dinner party?"

"Okay, bowl of chili. Anyway, by seeing all your friends separately you get to repeat one of your ideas seven times."

Bernard reacted with a wan smile. "No, I'm afraid if my friends meet they'll prefer each other to me."

"You're afraid you'll be a third wheel?"

"I'm afraid I won't be *any* wheel."

Enrique could well believe Bernard's explanation, but thanks to his own feelings of tortured self-love, he thought Bernard's paranoia applied solely to him because he was the novelist Bernard could only claim to be. By the unusually early age of twenty-one, Enrique had had two novels published, with a third soon to come, while Bernard at twenty-five possessed merely one endlessly rewritten manuscript to justify his also wearing Enrique's artistic uniform of black jeans and wrinkled work shirts. Proud Enrique believed that Bernard had kept him from meeting his other friends, particularly the women, because if the world were to see the two young novelists side by side, the pretender would be unmasked by the true crown prince of literature.

Still refusing to arrange an introduction, Bernard continued to extol unspecific glories of Margaret. "She's really, really extraordinary. I can't express it in mundane terms, but she's strong while being feminine, smart without being pretentious. In many ways she's like the heroines of 1930s American movies, particularly the noir films, but also the Sturges comedies," and so on, in a maddening drift of praise that surveyed every possible quality without settling on a particular trait. The messy description seemed to Enrique evidence of why Bernard was a bad novelist. Not one of his stories about Margaret came to a climax (sexual or other) or revealed her allegedly extraordinary character. After downing five cups of Homer's coffee on Monday of Thanksgiving week 1975, having endured nearly a year of dismal celibacy, Enrique hit on the strategy of insisting that she didn't exist. He declared her a construct, a punitive fantasy that Bernard had created to torment the lonely and horny Enrique.

Bernard blanched—something of a feat given his immobile and bloodless face. Bernard was five feet, eight inches tall and his frame slight, but his big head and halo of kinky black hair enlarged his presence, especially in a coffee shop booth. It bobbed for a moment before he protested that he wouldn't torture a comrade (meaning a fellow single male). "I'm sparing you."

"Sparing me what?"

"She'll never go out with you."

Judging this the Perry Mason confession he had been seeking, Enrique turned up a palm and gestured to an invisible jury, inadvertently summoning the attention of the Homer Coffee Shop waiter, who raised his rambling Greek eyebrows and asked, "Check?" Enrique shook his head and returned his attention to his infuriating friend. "You tell me about this beautiful—"

"—I didn't say she was beautiful," Bernard was quick to object.

"So she's ugly?"

"No!"

"She's plain?"

"It's not possible to describe her with clichés."

"But Bernard, I've got a clichéd mind, so use clichés with me. Is she tall? How are her tits? Is she fat? If she exists, you could tell me these things."

Bernard regarded Enrique with disdain. "That's silly. If she were a product of my imagination, I could easily make up those details."

"Could you?" Enrique shot back with unpleasant sarcasm. "I doubt it. I think imagining breast size may well be beyond your creative powers."

"Fuck you," Bernard said and meant it, too. In Bernard's rule book of their friendship, his potshots at Enrique's talent were amiable pokes, since Enrique had been published, while return fire was cruel and deadly.

"Well, fuck you for saying she would never go out with me," Enrique answered and meant it, because in his heart he feared no desirable girl would ever go out with him. This dread was exacerbated by his unusual combination of sexual experience and inexperience. He had already lived with a woman for three and a half years, having obtained a book contract and a live-in girlfriend at the same early age, sixteen. Before the start of his relationship with Sylvie, he had had intercourse once (the classic quick release of virginity, as brief and solemn as a late-night public service announcement on television), and since their breakup eighteen months ago, Enrique had found himself naked with only one other woman— with whom he had failed to consummate. Although he had made love many times, he had had only two sexual partners, tied with the number of books he had published.

What made him feel sexually doomed was that Sylvie had ended their relationship by having an affair. She told him that she was moving out for a few weeks so they could "take a break from living together." Enrique reacted by wildly accusing her of "fucking someone else." To his horror, she admitted that his guess was correct, but insisted that she still loved him as much as his rival; she claimed she needed time to figure out whom she loved more. Enrique was too half-Latin to agree to a competition and too half-Jewish to believe in Sylvie's assertion of ambivalence. He thought that she was unwilling to be their relationship's executioner, that she wanted him to do the dirty deed, which he promptly did, walking out of the apartment after shouting ultimatums ("It's me or him!") to sob alone on the streets of Little Italy.

It did not occur to Enrique that Sylvie might feel he didn't love her. He was exasperated when she asked whether he did, her face streaming confusing tears, fifteen minutes after confessing that she had cuckolded him. He gave no credit to her feelings of rejection since the news that she was cheating on him had made him wish to curl up and die. He didn't even bother to answer that he loved her because, considering the severity of his pain, it was obvious that he did and that he had loved her all the while they were together. He was the victim and she the killer, a distinction Enrique was young enough to believe had moral significance. She had lived with him for three and a half years, virtually all of his adult life assuming you could consider sixteen through twenty to be adult years; she had gotten to know him inside and out, and was now discarding him as inferior and outdated, like last year's black-and-white TV. In short, he had been dumped, and despite his public explanation that their breakup had been caused by intellectual and emotional incompatibility, in the dark night of his soul he believed she preferred the other guy's cock. Just as his second novel had garnered less attention than his first, and much poorer sales, his love life had suffered a steep decline that seemed to augur a desolate future.

"She doesn't exist, Bernard, that's why you can't describe her," the bleeding Enrique snarled from his corner of Homer's red vinyl booth. "You're so bad at making up characters you can't even invent the ideal woman."

Bernard's long, pasty white face stared without expression into the distance. This was his typical affect while listening and speaking, except for a slight curling of his upper lip when he declared the bankruptcy of traditional forms in the novel, such as realism, chronological structure, or third-person narrative. "Ideal woman," he mumbled contemptuously. "That's absurd. There's no ideal woman."

With five mugs of coffee in him, Enrique pounded the Formica, rattling number six. "It is not absurd!" he yelled. "I mean—ideal to me! Relatively ideal!"

Bernard sneered. "Relatively ideal. That's hilarious." Enrique knew, in some calmer and wiser part of himself, that he ought not to be so easily agitated by Bernard. He also knew that Bernard was preposterous, and believed that any reasonable person would agree with him. So it seemed unfair that, at the moment, he would have to admit that he had succeeded in topping Bernard at foolishness.

Bernard, pleased with his victory, removed an unopened pack of unfiltered Camels from his work shirt's pocket and began an elaborate ritual. He rapped the pack on the counter at least a dozen times, not once or twice, which was sufficient for Enrique to tamp down his unfiltered Camels. (They were riding the same express brand to lung cancer.) Then followed a slow ballet of Bernard's yellowed, tapered fingers unpeeling the cellophane cover. Not content with removing the strip which Philip Morris had marked with a red line to ease exposure of the pack's top, he stripped the package naked, which struck Enrique as so disgusting that he demanded: "Why do you take off the whole covering!"

Bernard replied in an overly patient and condescending modulation, "So I know this is *my* pack. We're both dromedary men." He nodded at Enrique's cellophane-encased Camels.

"Now I'm a moocher!" Enrique cried out, banging the table again. "You've made this Margaret up! That's why I didn't see you with her last month at the Riviera Café. Not 'cause you were on the other side of the restaurant! You were never there with her 'cause she doesn't fucking exist!"

Bernard put the cigarette between his thick, dry lips and let it hang there. "You're being childish," he mumbled, unlit Camel bouncing in the air.

Overwhelmed by caffeine and loathing both for himself and for Bernard, Enrique dug out his wallet from the back pocket of his black Levi's and removed its sole currency, a ten-dollar bill, easily four bucks more than his share of the breakfast plus tip. Latin pride held sway over thrift, or perhaps Jewish righteousness triumphed over socialism, or more likely a fondness for drama trumped the tedium of math and, with an awkward bang of knee on table, and a sweep of Army greatcoat across vinyl, and a stray sleeve upending the full ashtray, Enrique hurled his money at Bernard, shoving his right arm into the left arm's hole, and announced, "Breakfast's on me, you fucking liar." Although he had to walk out with his coat only half on—and backward at that—Enrique still thought he had made a good exit, and believed his judgment was confirmed when the following day, at the end of a call to confirm Bernard's attendance at that week's poker game hosted by Enrique, Bernard said, "Are you going to be home this Saturday?"

"Yes . . . ," Enrique said, drawing the word out warily.

"I'm having dinner with Margaret. I'll bring her by your place after. Around eleven? That a cool time?"

"I'll be home," Enrique said and held his laughter until after he hung up.

And so Enrique's charge of a fictionalized Margaret had been the perfect bait. She was certainly real, so terrifyingly real that although the suede-clad foot kept piercing his peripheral vision, he maintained focus on Bernard. His annoying friend had seated himself at the small, round butcher-block table to the right of the fireplace. He had kept on his too skimpy (for this weather) black leather jacket and now reached into its inner pocket to remove a fresh pack of cigarettes. He began the infuriating cigarette ritual, using the blond wood as a drum to beat out his Bartók concerto for unfiltered Camel and cellophane.

With his guests settled, Enrique sat on his bed-couch, currently in couch incarnation thanks to two long foam pillows with blue corduroy covers. He realized immediately that this position was untenable, since he would have to choose whether to look straight ahead at Margaret astride his director's chair or twist his neck to the right to see Bernard the modern nicotine composer, it being a wide-angle impossibility to keep both in his range of vision and disguise his real interest.

He bestirred himself as part of a maneuver to adjust his line of sight on his guests. "Need an ashtray?" he asked, moving behind Bernard and up the step to the kitchen area. He looked for the one made out of clear glass bought at Lamstons, around the corner on Sixth Avenue. He was pleased and proud of the relentless newness of everything in his apartment. He cherished the butcher-block kitchen table, and his long desk accommodated eight for poker, positioned under the studio's two windows facing noisy Eighth Street. He adored the Trinitron placed between it and the fireplace, and relished the kitchen's new and unused pots, pans, cutlery, plates, and bowls.

As he disappeared behind the kitchen's jutting three-foot wall, which housed his stove, it occurred to him that he was a host. "Anybody want something? Wine? Coke? Coffee?" And he added doubtfully, looking toward his garbage can, considering what could be rescued from the Chinese delivery and its supplementary offerings, "Tea?"

"Beer," Bernard said.

"Beer," Enrique repeated, opening his refrigerator. He looked inside although he knew the answer. "Sorry. No beer. Wine?" he reoffered since he possessed a bottle of Mateus, a cheap wine his ilk liked because its unconventionally shaped flask could be converted into a candleholder, dried wax forming a monstrous shawl down its slumped shoulders.

"Scotch," Bernard said as if that settled it.

"No scotch, Bernard. How about a vintage Mateus?"

"Mateus?" Margaret cried out in what could have been amazement or disdain.

Enrique leaned back from the fridge, reconnecting himself visually to his guests, to ask Margaret if that meant she wanted a glass. He was unsettled to discover that the blue eyed beauty had removed her right leg from its perch on the chair's arm, to shift ninety degrees leftward to observe his movements in the kitchen, incidentally making what appeared to be an uncomfortable cradle out of the director's chair. Her back was no longer resting on the canvas sling but leaning against the right arm; somewhat painfully, Enrique assumed, although the pine edge was cushioned by her down jacket. Her legs were draped over the left arm, pointing slim hips, cute butt, and smooth pelvis toward Enrique. In his feverish imagination, she was offering herself to him—though Bernard was between them in this configuration and could claim Margaret meant the invitation for him. She raised her right arm to idly tuck a pretty mass of tight black curls behind her perfectly formed ear. Her hair was straight everywhere but at her temples, he noticed, too unsophisticated in feminine ways to distinguish whether that was natural or not. Gazing at the girl spread across his chair in a posture which defied its design, Enrique couldn't remember what he had intended to ask her.

Margaret smiled broadly and fully exposed her teeth for the first time, revealing a flaw in her beauty. They were too small for her generous mouth and spaced apart, like a child's. "You really have a bottle of Mateus?" she said, her freckled cheeks full of merriment.

"Yes, it's a dirty job, but someone has to buy it," Enrique admitted, humiliated.

"No scotch? No Jack Daniel's?" she asked with a laugh.

"No hard liquor," Enrique confessed and hung his head in mock shame. "Just cheap wine."

"Told you," Bernard said to her.

Enrique shut the refrigerator door, perhaps a little too hard. "Told her what?" he demanded.

"You don't drink," Bernard said, an unlit cigarette bouncing like a conductor's baton between his lips. He positioned the phosphorescent tip of a match on the rough surface of the striker and lowered the book's cover over it. Enrique watched as Bernard drew the match out from this hiding place in a slow and graceful motion, igniting it safely in the air. A few months before, over one of their midafternoon breakfasts, Enrique had tried to duplicate Bernard's enviable method. He lit the match all right, and also the rest of the book, which flared into a fireball, soaring out of Enrique's startled hand up and away from their booth, terrifying two elderly patrons nearby, triggering a supercilious smile on Bernard's face, and enraging the waiter, who squashed it out and then cut off that day's free coffee refills at a drowsy two. Subsequent solo attempts at practicing Bernard's technique had similarly failed.

"How come you don't drink?" the brilliant blue eyes demanded.

"I drink," Enrique insisted, bringing an ashtray to his interrogators.

"He doesn't drink 'cause he didn't go to college," Bernard said, holding his burnt-out match high, a dismal Mr. Liberty, failing to light Enrique's way to the shores of the Ivy League.

"Right!" said Margaret, reaching back into one of her jacket pockets to produce a pack of Camel Lights. "Bernard told me you dropped out of college to write."

"I dropped out of *high school*," he said, back in possession of the trump suit's ace, "to write my first novel." He timed this play of the winning card with a gliding movement of white socks on glazed oak floor, arm and hand fully extended to offer Margaret the glass ashtray, a skinny, long-haired courtier in black jeans, asking the princess's restless suede boot: *Good enough? Good enough? Good enough?*

"You didn't finish high school?" she asked.

"Didn't finish tenth grade," he said, less prideful now, not sure if she was impressed by his reverse achievement.

"Well, at least you stayed long enough to learn how to smoke," Margaret commented drily, swinging her boots down to the floor and leaning forward to accept his glass gift—and that did it. That brought those depthless blue eyes within a foot, perhaps six inches, maybe even closer, and something happened inside Enrique, like a guitar string suddenly unstrung. There was a shock and a vibration in his heart, a palpable break inside the cavity of his chest. He had dropped out of high school and never took a class in anatomy, but he did know that the cardiovascular system wasn't supposed to react as if it were the source and center of feeling. And yet he would have sworn to all and sundry—not that he expected to admit it to anyone—that Margaret, or at least her bright blue eyes, had just snapped his brittle heart.

chapter two

Fatal Vision

E NRIQUE STUDIED HER sleeping profile, the heavy Ativan unconsciousness she hugged for security against the terror of what she faced alone. All alone, he had to admit, although he had tried hard, and succeeded with a grind's grade-grubbing anxiety, to be with Margaret for every examination, every CT scan and MRI, every infusion of chemo, fingers entwined for each of three surgeries until obliged to release her to the OR's whooshing doors. Even during those enforced separations he didn't separate, pacing in prominent view in the waiting area, afraid to break for a piss. He wanted to be the first face remembered out of anesthesia's woozy awakening, including the shivering agony before morphine drapes fell to hide her from the latest wounds. But that's fanciful, isn't it? he asked himself. The same drugs that cleared pain also wiped away the memory of his comforting words and kisses, although she seemed to know, always know, that he had been there.

Enrique was so diligent he would have suspected himself of insincerity except that he had missed once. Badly. Nearly three years ago, he had left it to her beloved friend Lily to walk the overnight hospital hall of terror after the urologist finally delivered to Margaret the diagnosis of bladder cancer that he had confided to Enrique two days before. Sure, Enrique had the excuse that their youngest, sixteen-year-old Max, was home alone, still ignorant of why his mother was staying in the hospital for a third night after what was supposed to have been an hour-long procedure. Sure, but he could have arranged something else, as he had done subsequently many times. His half sister, Rebecca; or Lily; or someone could have stayed with Max while Enrique attended to what was more urgent: to embrace Margaret's dread, to encourage and console her, to cheer and to love her although he was scared to the bone, sick to the soul with fear.

But all those desperate feelings were long ago, two years and eight months ago, one hundred and forty-seven days and nights in the hospital ago, three major surgeries, a half dozen minor surgeries, and fourteen months of chemo ago, two remissions and two recurrences ago. Looking back through the defeated glaze of fatigue, it seemed inevitable now that it would end like this, this inch-by-inch dying, this one-track terminus when hope had become a skeleton's grin.

Margaret seemed hardly to breathe or dream, small figure made smaller by the fetal hunch, and yet he didn't believe it was a peaceful sleep, or true sleep at all. The drugs dimmed her consciousness, but they did not let her forget the accumulating loss of pleasurable life, and certainly not the looming dead end ahead.

He looked out the window at a dense, rain-swollen sky lowering over the East River and sipped a Dean & Deluca's coffee. Any taste with the promise of energy, no matter how short-lived, was welcome to join the fight against pervasive fatigue. Yet despite two cups, he could feel his forehead, eyelids, cheeks all sag as if he'd been scalped and a mask of flesh was sloughing down to his chin. If Enrique let his eyes shut briefly to rest them from the burn of Sloan-Kettering's air-conditioning, in an instant the private room's carpeted floor fell away and he was afloat—until a nod, a voice, the vibration of his cell phone startled him back to a state of exhausted alertness. These days friends urged him to get more sleep and immediately withdrew the advice because of its evident impracticality. However, to silence his willfully dense half brother—who, in lieu of visiting Margaret at the hospital, insisted on inviting Enrique over to his apartment for dinner—he had to spell out the logic of his schedule: "I want to be at the hospital at night when she's most alone and I don't want to abandon Max so that means sleeping at Sloan, getting up at dawn—which, believe me, is no problem in a hospital—to get downtown to wake up Maxy to try to convince him to eat something and walk him to the subway and then take a shower, change my clothes and get back up to Sloan for morning rounds which I usually miss anyway, 'cause they do them early which doesn't matter since I can catch the doctors again in the afternoon just before I head down to dinner with Max."

He had talked like that since the earliest days of combat with Margaret's disease, in narrative spurts sorely in need of punctuation and editing, without proper endings or middles. It was a symptom of fatigue and an adaptive response to the way most people reacted to his wife's frightening illness: they interrogated Enrique intrusively about the logistics of Margaret's battle while carefully avoiding discussion of its denouement. Enrique had grown old—three weeks ago he had turned fifty—but he had not lost his youthful fondness for altering a famous quote to aggrandize his daily life. When he raised the subject of victory or defeat for Margaret, and friends were quick to end the conversation, he would intone to himself in a whisper: "I am become Death, the destroyer of chitchat."

Margaret's eyes opened just as he had decided to leave the tall chair beside her bed for a midmorning nap on the room's couch—although experience had taught him a daytime snooze accomplished little more than transforming grumpy and alert fatigue into despairing grogginess. It was hard to resist, however, the lure of the uncomfortable sofa bed, which had been restored to couch incarnation by an orderly while Enrique was downtown. Enrique had insisted on spending an exorbitant amount—after her third hospitalization, the cost had been assumed by her generous parents—for a room on Sloan-Kettering's nineteenth floor, because it provided a bed for him and he could stay with Margaret during the desolate and frightening nights at the hospital. On this so-called VIP floor, the rooms were decorated to resemble those of a luxury hotel and included a small desk, a comfortable armchair, a coffee table, and a foldout sofa, which had just seduced him when Margaret opened her great, sad eyes.

She didn't speak. She didn't ask about seeing Max off to take his class's high school graduation photo. She didn't volunteer whether the doctors had come back during Enrique's hour-and-a-half absence. She gazed as if they were in the midst of a lull in a long conversation and she was giving thoughtful consideration to his last remark. She seemed to absorb him with her brilliant eyes—as blue as the day they met and bigger than ever in a face narrowed by starvation.

They were upper-middle-class New Yorkers, rich by any reasonable standard, citizens of the wealthiest metropolis in the richest nation in the world, and Margaret had been starving for half a year. She hadn't been able to digest solid food or drink fluids since January because her stomach no longer emptied its contents into her intestines. This failure, elegantly named gastroparesis by science, had first been hopefully diagnosed as a side effect of chemotherapy's accumulating toxins—the premise being that it was theoretically reversible—until in time several of the specialists said that the more likely cause was her metastasized bladder cancer, growing and spreading on the outside of her intestines. Cancerous lesions, too small to be detected by CT scans, were stiffening the bowel's peristaltic action, stalling it, and preventing anything she swallowed from being digested; solids and fluids remained in her stomach until she threw them up, regurgitation provoked by overflow.

Back in February, one of Margaret's many doctors, a short, autocratic Jewish Iraqi émigré, had inserted a flexible plastic tube known as a PEG (an acronym of the medical term *percutaneous endoscopic gastrostomy*) through her skin and into her stomach to drain everything she swallowed into a bag outside her body. The drain was necessary even if Margaret took nothing by mouth. Enrique had vividly learned that when the intestines shut down and the stomach doesn't empty, green-black bile—digestive juice manufactured by the liver and passed into the gallbladder—finding itself with nowhere to go, backs up into the stomach and, in four hours, fills it.

A pint of that repulsive liquid had collected at the bottom of a bag hanging beside her bed, inches from where Enrique's foot kicked like a metronome to keep him awake. Near his other foot was a pump suspended on an IV pole that had been disconnected and pushed away last night. Its task was to circumvent her useless stomach by pushing a finely grained, beige-colored gruel, an easily digested nutritional substitute, not very different from the Enfamil formula they used to give their infant sons, into her small bowel through a second tube that had been surgically inserted ten days ago by a different doctor, an apologetic, ruddy-cheeked surgeon. This tube was called by a confusingly similar acronym, PEJ, the *J* standing for *jejunum*. It was intended to supply nutrition directly into her intestine, not to provide stomach drainage.

Margaret's team of doctors and nurses had been trying to nourish her through the PEJ for the past three nights, beginning at midnight with a goal of continuing until six. Each night they had failed to complete the enteric feeding. The first try had worked until five in the morning, the second until three-thirty, and last night it had flunked almost immediately. A little after one am, Enrique had been awakened by Margaret calling his name in exhausted distress, asking him to summon the nurse to turn off the pump because the fine gruel had backed up to the rear of her throat, giving her the terrifying feeling of being drowned by a meal she hadn't swallowed in the first place.

Margaret hadn't starved to death in January—it was now June—thanks to a system called TPN, an acronym for total parenteral nutrition, which provided all sustenance intravenously, avoiding her digestive system altogether. The necessary fats, proteins, and vitamins were delivered in liquid form through a port in her chest and absorbed by her blood system. At the hospital, the staff taught Enrique how to clean her port, mix the TPN, and connect her to its pump. With his new training, Enrique could treat Margaret at home.

It was cold and snowy, and Margaret had weighed one hundred fourteen pounds when they started. TPN had sustained her into the warmth of June, but it kept little else alive for her. It did not provide her with energy or the freedom to use it. The TPN, a sour-smelling, milky brew, required twelve hours daily to flow. Even if the process was started as late as ten at night, TPN would truncate evening plans and consume most of the morning. The nutritional system was also failing at its main task, as evidenced by Margaret's current weight of one hundred and three pounds.

This ebbing of her life force was painfully charted for Enrique by Max, who had been told the previous September that his mother was considered incurable, that she would live beyond nine months only if she responded to experimental drugs for which there was no proof of beneficial effect. Max, like his older brother, Gregory, shared his mother's keen affection for facts. He fixed on one in April. Margaret had been hospitalized to treat an infection. Max visited after school for an hour, lying quietly beside her in a Sloan-Kettering bed. When Enrique walked him out to the elevator, he asked, "Are they going to do something about Mom's weight?"

Enrique explained, in the gentle, reassuring tone he tried to maintain, although often what he had to say was neither gentle nor reassuring, that they would be upping her calories in the TPN from now on. Max interrupted, his blue eyes getting bigger. "Good," he announced. "Because her fat pads are gone."

Enrique had no idea what Max meant. Margaret's cancer had taught him that making assumptions or deductions could easily lead to error, that it was always prudent to ask questions, so he asked his baby boy what fat pads are. "Fat pads, Dad, like this one." Max grabbed a hunk of fat near his father's hip and lower back that Enrique hadn't realized was there. "Hers are gone," he said and frowned.

"Well she's always been thin—" Enrique began.

Max shook his head. "No, Dad. You're skinny and you have fat pads." Max pinched the lump of flesh again, painfully, and Enrique twisted away. "Sorry," Max apologized for hurting his father. "Fat pads are for storage, Dad. You only use them when you're starving. Mom doesn't have any left."

After that exchange, Enrique stopped wondering why Margaret's expeditions consisted of nothing more adventurous than a slow walk around the block. For a woman who had relished fast-paced hikes, hours of tennis or painting in her studio, a morning at the Met for inspiration, an afternoon at Costco for toilet paper and cans of tuna, a day of gossiping and volunteering with other mothers at her sons' former or current schools, for that energetic Margaret, who would hop on the balls of her feet with sheer pleasure if you proposed doing something entertaining, an out-of-breath stagger didn't seem like activity.

For Enrique, TPN felt like a full-time occupation. Supplies were delivered to their apartment building twice weekly, always on time, although Enrique waited for them with an anxious uncertainty, betrayed by the ferocity with which he immediately tore open the boxes to make sure everything was there. In their bedroom, the stuff lined a six-foot-long wall to a height of three feet. Enrique walked to Staples on Union Square and bought a half dozen stackable plastic file-storage units. He threw out the folders inside, using the units as bins to sort and store the bags of saline hydration, the requisite packages of sterile tubing, sterile gloves, sterile syringes, sterile caps for the plastic attachments to her chest port, the sterilizing sticks to clean its see-through adhesive bandage, and a dozen other bits of paraphernalia that produced two bags of garbage he carried to the hall chute each day. There were three bins for the TPN tubing and various bottles of antacid and vitamins that Enrique had to inject into large, translucent bags of nutrition. He stored them in a small refrigerator he bought at P.C. Richard on Fourteenth Street, nodding pleasantly at the salesman's assumption that Enrique was purchasing it for his son's NYU dorm. By then, their bedroom, with its IV pole and sterile packages, looked as much like a home as Sloan's imitation of a luxury suite resembled a hotel.

The labor of being a TPN nurse was both dull and terrifying for Enrique: the meticulous hand washing, the weird hot and slimy feel of the gloves, the care to make sure he didn't puncture the bag or himself when adding ingredients or attaching the tubing, the danger of contaminating something in the dozen or so steps that required sterility since Margaret could easily end up with a one-hundred-four-degree-plus fever. He was vigilant, although he no longer feared that a repeat of one of her infections would kill her, as he had in the early days of her fight, when cure was a real possibility. The end was inevitable and very near. She had to die of something because cancer does not kill alone. It kills with accomplices, so why not a sepsis? The reason he continued to dread an infection as the particular assassin was that he could not bear to watch her once again shiver and bake, eyes dulling, soft moans for rescue escaping as her brow broke into a fine sweat, her mind melting into delirium.

That was a death to be avoided, he thought, although what death to hope for he did not, and could not, imagine. That subject was as great a taboo as any Enrique had lived with in his fifty years. He didn't think about her dead; he didn't contemplate a future without Margaret. He understood that she would die, and die soon, but he also knew that he didn't truly believe her life could end. He had waited a year for his father to succumb to a terminal cancer, and he had learned from the surprise he felt at the event that no warning of the incredible fact of mortality could adequately prepare the primitive brain nature had given him to comprehend its finality.

Five months into the TPN routine, her days were spent lying on the living room couch watching *Law & Order* reruns, punctuated only by ventures to the bathroom, pushing the aluminum IV pole with its liter bag of hydration as if it were holding her up; nights she was plugged into the pump of milky fluid entering her veins. On May 10, Margaret greeted Enrique on his return from the supermarket with tears running down her face. He had bought frozen fruit bars so she could have the pleasure of tasting something sweet that wouldn't clog the narrow passage of her stomach

PEG. He had already opened the package to offer a choice of orange or strawberry, but he was silenced by the sight of her despair. Though her tears continued to flow, her voice rang with conviction: "I can't do this. I can't live like this. I can't go on being tethered to a bag for half the day. I can't stand not eating with you and the boys and our friends. I know it sounds so stupid, so trivial, so small, but I can't live like this."

He felt the box begin to drip on his jeans. He wanted to put the bars in the freezer because if they melted he didn't know if he could summon the energy to walk to the supermarket again. But he couldn't turn away from this statement. He had known for over a year, when her cancer returned in March, that she was almost certain to die. Last September, on hearing the news of her second recurrence and that there were no therapies with a promise of success, Margaret had decided to stop seeking experimental treatments, to try to enjoy whatever time she had left. He had agreed with her decision and felt a guilty relief that at least some of the horrors of the hospital could be skipped. There would be time, perhaps a few months, to commune with their sons, to sleep once more in their summer house on the Maine coast, to visit with friends somewhere other than waiting rooms. They tried to plan what final things to do; and then, on the sixth day, she changed her mind. She couldn't give up; to live without hope wasn't life. "I don't want to do a farewell tour," she said.

Enrique agreed instantly to this reversal, this time relieved that they wouldn't be passing up a chance for a miracle. In truth, he could find no comfortable place to sit in the company of her illness. He would feel guilt and shame no matter how he behaved. She was going to die and he was not; in the undeclared war of marriage, it was an appalling victory.

Since September he had lived with a modest hope: to assuage the keen awareness that she must let go of all the things and people she loved. Nothing grand, or as preposterous as the luminous conclusions of sentimental movies. His ambition since last fall had been to lift a single grain of the tonnage of her grief at saying good-bye to life. Listening to her while the red- and orange-colored frozen fruit bars melted onto his blue jeans, he knew he would fail.

She asked him to call her various doctors and push them to attempt something, no matter how dangerous, to restore her to normal eating.

Enrique made his rounds. Her urological surgeon, usually accommodating, begged off with the reasonable excuse that it wasn't his specialty. The Iraqi gastroenterologist refused to recommend anyone from his department, stating nothing could or should be done; he insisted she could survive on TPN indefinitely while they searched for a new drug to cure her. Her oncologist did consult with the appropriate specialist, but came back to report that the only possible procedure was unlikely to relieve her gastroparesis. The end-to-end anastomosis he cited certainly sounded like a desperate improvisation: attempting to circumvent her blocked digestive tract by taking a lower, cleared loop of bowel and hooking it up to her stomach. Besides, as each specialist implied with the sentence "It wouldn't be addressing her disease," what was the point of a risky surgery to restart her digestion when she would die whether or not they succeeded?

Margaret wore them down. For Enrique it was a grim amusement to watch her work her formidable will on men other than himself and his sons, especially to see these white-coated grandees of medicine, accustomed to patients accepting their rationalizations as incontestable, finally give way to her insistence on the value of the operation to her. "Even if it means I can have just one more meal with my husband," she explained, lying in a bed at Sloan a few days later. She was addressing the chief of oncology, a blood cancer specialist who had treated a celebrity friend of Enrique's. He had taken a fancy to Margaret two years ago, when they were introduced shortly after the start of her treatments, enjoying the apparent paradox of her cynical evaluations of the abilities of her various doctors with a sweet optimism that their treatments would succeed. He was an administrator powerful enough to make a Sloan-Kettering surgeon do almost anything. He listened to Margaret's plea, then turned to regard Enrique, squinting hard, as if peering through a microscope to discover what made having dinner with this bald, middle-aged writer worth enduring an abdominal surgery that was unlikely to work.

"I don't think having dinner with me is the crucial part," Enrique explained. "She'd be happy to have dinner with anyone."

Margaret laughed, although tears were running down her face, and added, "That's right. I don't care who you invite to dinner, I just want to have dinner."

The head of oncology told her that he and the Iraqi Jew would get her a surgeon, but first he had to provide cover for them all by bringing in the psychiatric department for a consult.

Enrique listened while she explained her desperate logic to a thoughtful shrink with a salt-and-pepper version of Bozo the Clown's hairdo. He nodded sympathetically as she said, "I had a life. I had a husband and children and friends. Now I lie in bed all day and I can't think. I can't even read a murder mystery. All I can do is watch stupid fucking episodes of *Law and Order*."

"There's nothing else on television," the somber Bozo said. After a silence, while Margaret wiped tears off her cheeks and blew her nose, the psychiatrist added, "I guess people like the show."

"Because it's about death with no emotion," Enrique mumbled. Used to her husband's cranky cultural observations, Margaret ignored him and repeated, "It's stupid. It's such a stupid life.

It's not living. I want my life back," she cried out and heaved with sobs. "I don't care if I die trying, I don't care how long it lasts. I don't care if it's only for one day. I want my life back."

The psychiatrist prescribed Zoloft and affirmed that she was of sound mind to make an informed decision. The chief of oncology and the Iraqi Jew persuaded the ruddy-cheeked colleague to perform the surgery—although in return for this concession they all insisted that Margaret also agree to the PEJ, inserting a tube into her small bowel, so that they could improve on TPN's intravenous method with an upgrade to enteric feeding if the rerouted plumbing of her stomach didn't work. Enrique wondered whether Dick Wolf, executive producer of all *Law & Orders*, would be bothered to learn that a team of medical experts had concurred with Margaret's judgment that watching his creations did not constitute having a life.

That's what had brought them back to Sloan in late May. The end-to-end anastomosis had failed. Using the PEJ for enteric feeding had also failed. Resuming TPN was her only option. She had lain these past three days, the first three of June, with Ativan's glazed eyes, pupils dilated, staring with an inconsolable sadness that he had never seen in her before. Not when she turned to him on their terrace two years and nine months ago as the first mushroom cloud from the World Trade Center blossomed in their direction and said, "We're watching thousands of people die." Not when she was first told that she had cancer, or that it had come back, or that it had come back again, or that there was nothing else to be done. There had been the flint of anger on those occasions, a willingness to engage and contend with the future. But this morning, this gloomy morning when she knew that her stomach would never work again, that there was nothing to do but lie there and die, her big blue eyes gazed at him from her narrow face and revealed a look of pure pain from deep in her soul, a nakedness more profound than flesh. "I need this to stop," she whispered to him without a hello or a preamble. "I can't do it anymore. I'm sorry, Puff," she said using the endearment she had invented for him in the first year of their love. "I can't do this anymore."

He knew what she meant, but pretended he didn't. "Yeah." He kicked at the pump and its narrow tubing filled with last night's backed-up gruel. "This is done. We'll go back to the TPN."

She shook her head. "You have to help me. Please." Tears fell without effort or interruption, as they did these days, water running from a faucet. "I want to die. You have to help me die."

He couldn't answer right away. And in that paralyzed silence, he realized there was something in his brain which—despite all the hours spent learning about survival rates and the nature of metastasis, despite closely watching his father die of prostate cancer—he hadn't known he would lose, this something in his head that had been present since Bernard Weinstein rang his doorbell twenty-nine years ago. In this silence of her silent, flowing tears, he realized that it was something essential which soon would be gone, and that it was more than simply the expectation that Margaret would stay alive. He had no word for it. A note of music, perhaps it was his name being called, something he didn't always enjoy, something he had grabbed for rescue, something he had possessed with pleasure, something he had resented with anger. In the carpeted silence of this luxury room of disease, he felt it depart for a moment, a preview of his robbed future, and he understood that this was real in a way nothing should ever be real, that their marriage was a mystery he was going to lose, despite twenty-seven years living inside it, before he understood who they were.

chapter three

Public School

I T OCCURRED TO Enrique, sometime around five in the morning, that although the package was enticing and in excellent condition, Bernard had failed miserably in his role as a deliveryman. He had failed in this crucial respect: by not departing. It was clear—at least to Enrique—that there was an almost palpable current of excitement running between himself and Margaret, that something had kept her talking long after *Saturday Night Live*. If that weren't enough of a clue, when they ran out of cigarettes and Mateus at four-forty-seven in the morning, and Margaret greeted Enrique's suggestion that they walk over to Sheridan Square for breakfast at Sandolino's with an enthusiastic, "Great idea! I can be decadent and have challah French toast," surely then it ought to have been clear to Bernard if he had any novelistic feeling at all for subtleties of character, that this woman, with whom Bernard had

had a handful of dinners since their graduation from college three years ago, all ending well before midnight, had been lured not by French toast, no matter how blessedly Jewish the bread, but by Enrique. Surely if Bernard had any grace he would excuse himself and let Enrique journey with Margaret to Sheridan Square as rosy-fingered dawn crept into lower Manhattan, casting Enrique, he hoped, in a romantic light.

But Bernard leapt at the opportunity for a predawn breakfast, and that made them a party of three   not that they had to wait for the scarred surface of one of Sandolino's pine tables at five-fifteen am. There were only six other customers present, although this twenty-four-hour comfort-food establishment was convenient to the pre-AIDS gay bars and clubs to the west, NYU students to the east, artists to the south, tourists to the north, and depressed writers from all directions.

Annoyed and disappointed that he had failed to jettison Bernard, Enrique nevertheless remained hopeful, having faith in his conversational endurance and especially comforted by the geographic logic of their eventual farewells. Their way home from Sandolino's put their apartments in this order: Bernard's first, at Eighth Street near Sixth, then Enrique's close by, but still somewhat farther east, at Eighth Street near MacDougal, and Margaret's last, at Ninth Street east of University Place. They would say good-bye to Bernard, whereupon Enrique would gallantly offer to escort the single girl to her door and make evident that his interest had gone well beyond establishing the mere existence of Margaret Cohen.

Enrique and Margaret kept up a lively dialogue while Bernard said little. When she had dispatched three-quarters of her challah French toast, she pushed the plate to the side and leaned forward to resume her mock interrogation, abandoned over five hours ago, about the extent of Enrique's education. She asked whether he had completed elementary school. Enrique triumphantly announced that he was a graduate of P.S. 173.

"What! Nooo!" Margaret shrieked, extending the *o* to indicate amazement while her delicate fingers touched the dark hairs on Enrique's left forearm, which rested on the distressed wood table between his coffee mug and hers. Her tips brushed his hairs lightly and remained hovering just above. Enrique felt as if each follicle was standing on end, pitifully pleading for continued and firmer contact. He looked down to see what was actually happening. This evaluating gaze caused Margaret to appear self-conscious about having touched him. She raised her eyes to look into his, and for the second time Enrique felt a shock of sensation, something more than sexual excitement. She must have misinterpreted his look, because she immediately withdrew as if he'd rebuked her. "That's impossible," she declared.

"Me going to P.S. 173 impossible?" Enrique wondered aloud. "Not only possible. Really easy. I lived across the street."

"But I went to P.S. 173!" Margaret declared, the elongated oval of her face framing the purer ovals of her astonished eyes. This was a look he would witness countless times, Margaret peering in wonderment at a fact which confounded or delighted.

Enrique said nothing for a moment. Margaret and Bernard had been in the same class at Cornell, which meant that she was three or four years older than precocious Enrique, who had left home at sixteen. He became friendly with people who were between four and eight years older than he because he had little choice; his contemporaries were in high school for at least two more years and away at college for another four. With more years of experience at living a so-called adult life, Enrique ought to have felt surer of himself; but he still possessed the skittish insecurities of an adolescent. Females were utterly strange to him, despite his having lived with a woman for over three years. He had read all of Balzac's novels, so he did know that no matter how young the woman, it was never correct to remind her that you were younger. He tried a neutral remark: "Um, so you were at 173 at the same time I was?"

"No!" Exasperated at not being understood, Margaret gave her head a firm toss, like a horse shaking off a fly. That too was a gesture he would come to know well. "In Queens. I grew up in Queens. I went to P.S. 173, but it was in Queens!"

"Uh-huh," Enrique said, confused by her annoyance. "Well, I guess we were fated to meet," he said, trying to turn a dull coincidence to romantic advantage.

"There can't be two P.S. 173s," Margaret declared and looked to Bernard for confirmation.

At last, after taking a conversational drubbing for hours, as each topic introduced seemed to enliven Margaret and Enrique while further whitening Bernard's pastiness and deepening the gloom of his sullen silence, Bernard brightened. He straightened his narrow, slumped shoulders to an artificial stiffness while his great head and unruly halo of tight curls wobbled. The impression this change of posture gave was of a puppeteer alerting the audience it was time for the dummy Bernard to speak. "Yeah, that can't be right. No way the city would have two 173s." His small brown eyes, bloodshot at the moment, fastened on Enrique disdainfully as he mumbled with certitude, "You must have your number wrong."

Enrique then revealed something to Margaret that he would rather not have, his short temper. "I don't have it wrong!" he snapped and tipped violently on the wooden chair. He grabbed the pine table for balance, sloshing coffee over the sides of their white mugs. An image of Guillermo, Enrique's father, a man too big in size for many rooms and too big in spirit for all, came into his mind while, out of the corner of his eye, he saw Margaret grab her coffee mug to prevent it from upending and reach for a napkin from the adjoining table to mop up the overflow. Her movements were an obvious warning that he was displaying too much anger to remain attractive to any woman, much less one so cheerful. Her good humor was remarkable. They had been talking for almost eight hours and she hadn't so much as frowned, a streak of pleasantness which was extraordinary considering that she wasn't an idiot. But fear of losing her admiration didn't restrain his vehemence: "Jesus, Bernard, I lived across the street from 173! I went there until sixth grade. I was the first student council president, for God's sakes. I haven't made a mistake about the number!"

Enrique had a deep and resonant voice, a lucky asset considering that although he was tall, six foot four, he weighed a Buchenwald one hundred and thirty pounds beneath his too long, straight black hair, which often fell across his face like a drape, narrowing it even more. It was hard to see past all that thinness, hair, and large tortoiseshell glasses, to his warm brown eyes, high cheekbones, strong chin, and full lips. The voice was his sole attractive feature that was also manly enough to excite. But when he was angry, its muscular pronunciation made him sound intimidating and full of contempt. It led Sylvie's list of what she didn't like about living with him. He apologized profusely for his verbal fits and proclaimed that he wanted to curb his temper, but the truth was that he remained essentially blind to how scary and excoriating he could be.

It baffled Enrique that his barbs drew blood. He felt his attacks were rare and always occasioned by self-defense. Perhaps if his victims had prior notice that the seemingly charming and agreeable Enrique was also armed and dangerous, they wouldn't have been so hurt. But warning was hard to come by when the attacker went to such pains to conceal his grievances.

Enrique took a deep breath to shut himself up and anxiously glanced at Margaret to check whether his flash of fury had revealed that he was the sort of angry man who could drive his live-in girl-friend into the arms of another. At the same time, Enrique was con-fident that if Margaret was provided the right information to challenge Sylvie's accusations of "adolescent rages," she would see the error of that characterization. He told himself that if Margaret had heard Sylvie state that Enrique was "too involved with his parents," Margaret would conclude, as he had, that his ex-girlfriend was repeating the canned wisdom of a bourgeois shrink. A shrink Sylvie needed, in Enrique's view, because her parents had divorced when she was six, permanently damaging her; and she was blocked as a painter, unable to produce a canvas for months on end, another proof to the prolific Enrique that her judgment of him was distorted. Yes, his carefully reasoned conclusion was that Sylvie and her friends had deserved each and every one of his denunciations; that, although he was intemperate, he was also correct.

Bernard identified Enrique's flammable condition and tried to light a match. He tipped backward in the uncomfortable Sandolino's pine chair until it hit the wall behind him, and he looked down his nose at Enrique with the same air he adopted at the poker table when he was about to turn over the winning hand. He smiled his version of a smile, a sneering curl of one side of his lip, as if he were a Jewish Elvis Presley. Then he mumbled, "Oh, I'm sure you're right, Ricky," he said, the anglicization signaling that Bernard felt secure about the likelihood of triumphing in this dispute. "After all, you're never wrong about anything." He glanced at Margaret and said in a confiding tone, "You don't know this about Ricky, but he's never ever wrong."

"What the hell does that mean?" Enrique shouted before he could remember not to. He tried to convince himself that all he had done was make use of his vocal resources, projecting like any good stage actor, and that was why six heads at the other tables had swung his way to stare at him.

But when he looked at Margaret, he quailed. Her shimmering blue eyes were drinking him in with a deep look of shock and an even deeper look of calculation. *She knows.* Enrique's thoughts collapsed into a black hole of self-loathing. *She knows I'm a crazy box of frightened tinder,* an assessment that, coming from anyone else, he would have considered a calumny.

After a moment of terrible suspense, during which he sat up straight and didn't draw a breath, Margaret said in a pleasant and relaxed tone, "But you have to be wrong."

In his turmoil Enrique forgot for a moment what the hell was in dispute. Was it the degradation of imperialism, the open wound of racism, whether the Knicks could win without a true center, or that Faulkner is impenetrable? At that moment he didn't care. Let the Vietnamese fry in their skins, let blacks languish as economic slaves, let the Celtics win eighteen more championships, let the pretentious insist that to be unreadable is genius. Let the deluge come, just so long as this delectable creature doesn't turn away from me. Admitting this to himself—that being right didn't matter compared to making love—managed to calm him down. Of course the dispute was beyond argument. He had attended P.S. 173 for a full six years. He had written 173 on every piece of homework, every test, every science project; as president of the student council he had put 173 on the telegram he sent to Senator Robert Kennedy inviting him to address their class graduation; and it appeared below Enrique Sabas's name on the return telegram from that glamorous and ultimately tragic political figure, a missive made no less thrilling by the text of its polite decline. P.S. 173, P.S. 173, P.S. 173—say it soft and it's almost like praying. It was more likely that he hadn't written his novels than that he had mistaken his elementary school's elegant name. Nevertheless, to ingratiate himself with this lively, good-humored beauty, he nodded thoughtfully while Margaret said, "New York can't have two 173s.

It would make a mess," she said, ostensibly to Enrique, but there was a special pleading in her manner and tone, as if she were addressing a higher authority who was always checking on her to make sure her thinking proceeded in an orderly fashion.

"A mess of what?" Enrique asked.

"A mess of . . ." She seemed to come to a complete blank. She stared at Bernard as if he had the answer.

Bernard, much to Enrique's dismay, did: "A mess of ordering school supplies."

"Right!" Margaret said, delighted. "One of the P.S. 173s would get all the number two pencils, and in the other the poor children would have nothing to write with."

Enrique's mood was lightened by her gaiety. He was happy to join her at this mystical place of make-believe reason. "Are you sure it *is* a citywide numbering system, and not borough by borough? They were pretty proud of us being in Manhattan. It said P.S. 173 Manhattan on everything. In fact, we had to write it on every piece of homework just like that, P.S. 173 Manhattan." Of course, making his case with deductions like that was silly. But he had intuited right about what might convince Margaret. She furrowed her brow and looked off while Bernard let his chair tip forward with a thud.

"You're making that up," Bernard complained. "I didn't write Queens below the name of my school."

"Well, that's because you went to a fancy Forest Hills school," Enrique said. He remembered that earlier Margaret had identified Bernard as having been raised in the "fancy" part of Queens as opposed to her "tiny and ridiculous part," an important distinction in the odd reverse snobbery of their antiwar, antimaterialist youth. Indeed, Bernard tried to squirm out of the characterization, claiming Forest Hills wasn't fancy. "Oh, yes it was," Margaret insisted with a mocking smile that made Bernard flinch. "My neighborhood in Queens is so dreary they don't even have a name for it. It's just called Adjacent," she said, one of many comments that Enrique found fascinating because they smacked to him of the sort of dispassionate and witty observation that a writer might make.

"Wait!" Margaret thrust her hand out as if she were a school traffic guard saving them from crossing on the red. She peered beyond Enrique while she remembered, "You're right. I wrote my name on the top line, then my class, and then below—'P.S. 173, Queens'! I wrote 'Queens.' I just thought . . ." And she stalled out, staring into the middle distance, as if someone had removed all her batteries.

Enrique found himself leaping in after that unspoken thought, trying to swim in her head, ". . . that it was borough pride and not an important distinction. P.S. 173 Queens, P.S. 173 Manhattan: that's why we both grew up with enough number two pencils."

Her eyes settled on his. She smiled, showing off those less than perfect teeth, too small and with gaps, undermining her otherwise commanding beauty just enough so that Enrique could manage to look at her without a gasp of awe. "Anyway," she added, "we had to buy our own pencils."

Bernard was unwilling to give up. "No," he said. "I don't believe it. The city isn't capable of that nicety. You made a mistake," he mumbled at Enrique, reaching for his decellophaned cigarette pack to begin a tapping concerto.

"About the name of the school I went to for six years?" Enrique said, catching Margaret's eye and lifting his brows to imply that they were in agreement about the idiocy of Bernard's logic, although he was perfectly aware that it had been her position. "I'll tell you what," Enrique offered. "We can hop on the IRT here at Sheridan Square, get out at 168th Street and Broadway, walk the six blocks to P.S. 173, and you can show me how wrong I am about this central fact of my childhood." There was a little too much anger in the final sarcastic phrase, "this central fact of my child-hood," the sort of prideful humor he had learned from his father, who would manage at once to mock himself for his grandiosity and let you know that, should you test his greatness, it would flatten you.

Margaret had had enough. She yawned. "Not me. No subway ride for me." Little tears had formed at the corners of her eyes and she picked one off with the tip of her index finger. "I have to go to bed. I'm too old to pull these all-nighters. I've got to crash."

This was gladdening news to Enrique, because his geographic calculations about their good-byes would now come to fruition. Spirit renewed, he copied his expansive father in a way that did not involve temper, although it did display Sabas pride, by picking up the check, which paralyzed Bernard and seemed to astound Margaret.

As he held the restaurant's massive double-width wood front door—a remnant of its origin as a carriage house stable—for Bernard and Margaret, he winced at the cold December sunlight. He was warmed, however, by the thought that when they said good-bye he would have his chance to obtain Margaret's phone number. He didn't think he would have the nerve to attempt, nor did the ménage-à-annoyance of the evening seem to warrant, a kiss. But the five-minute journey from Eighth and MacDougal to Ninth east of University would give him time to make his intentions clear with a lingering gaze and a sweeter tone than he dared in the Weinstein presence.

The fatigue of their all-nighter settled into their bones and lulled their walk into silence. The city was rising, although slowly on a Sunday. The streets were empty except for the odd dog walker, a deli owner cutting open bundled sections of the Sunday *Times* for rapid assembly by his son, and one old man in a black coat on his way to Saint Joseph's.

"I should get a *Times*," Bernard said.

"I get it delivered," Margaret said, adding, "By Alpert's," as if there was something magical about the service's name. Although Bernard whistled sarcastically, the silent Enrique was genuinely impressed. It delineated for him what until then had been a vague feeling, that there was something solidly bourgeois about this young woman, something grown-up about her underneath the girlishness that scared and excited him.

He didn't have long to reflect on her social class. The time to jettison Bernard was finally at hand. Margaret certainly seemed ready to let him go. As they approached the five painted black steps up Bernard's brownstone apartment, she pursed her lips to kiss him good-bye on the cheek. Enrique was too thrilled by the prospect of having her all to himself to bother to feel jealous when, instead of relishing the warmth of her lips on his frozen cheek, Bernard—that most lethargic of men—volunteered that he wasn't tired and would walk Margaret home.

Enrique couldn't catch himself from blurting out, "Don't worry about it. I'll walk her home. I'm going that way."

"You're going ten steps that way," Bernard said and knocked Enrique as he brushed past. That he made contact at all was unprecedented and irritated Enrique almost to the point of physical violence in response. Margaret let go of a laugh, a burst of amused sound that she released and immediately reeled back in, as if hoping no one had noticed. Her staccato of delighted laughter was truncated, it seemed to Enrique, by a supervisor's imposition of propriety and reserve, which seemed to contradict her bold stare, tomboyish body language, and teasing manner. It was as if a scolding voice offstage had cautioned her not to be loud and indiscreet. She said, "It's very sweet but nobody has to walk me home. I've been walking home alone since first grade."

They both insisted, however. They weren't concerned about

her safety but whom she was safe with. So this, Enrique's first attempt to have Margaret to himself, ended in failure. And for his pains he didn't even receive the cheek kiss Bernard had squandered. When they turned onto Ninth Street, a cold wind struck them. They were more exposed thanks to the unusual postwar apartment complex with a setback deep enough to allow something rarely seen in the city and especially rare in the Village— twenty feet of landscaping. All this elegance, only one block from the tawdry noise and cheap storefronts of Enrique's Eighth Street, confirmed the impression of comfort and bourgeois ease surrounding a woman who had her *Times* delivered. In December, however, this elegance increased the wind's bite. Margaret made a chattering sound and called out to them, "Thanks! Good night, boys. I mean, Good morning," as she rushed into her building, shouting back, "I'm freezing!"

Enrique said nothing to Bernard during their three-block return trip, mumbling a good night at his door, tramping up the five flights to his bed, and collapsing into sleep with neither the initiative nor the energy to masturbate. Four hours later, he staggered up from the defeat of his solitary twin bed, groggy and sullen and determined to win the next round. He had to do something about his longing to be with her. Although he couldn't remember a single image, he felt as if he had dreamed of nothing but Margaret. He paused long enough to brew a cup of coffee in his new Chemex pot and down it before calling Bernard. He said to the faint hello, "You awake?"

"Oh, I was up early. I couldn't sleep for long," Bernard answered in a pregnant tone, as if that fact were significant.

"Yeah, I feel like shit. Like I'm hungover."

"Fuck, you really can't drink," Bernard mumbled.

"No, I don't mean . . . Oh, forget it. I was calling for Margaret's number. What is it?"

There was a silence. Enrique was poised with a number two pencil (the irony amused him) and his favorite pad, a National brand notebook with lined, pale green pages. He looked at the lead tip and listened to the phone's quiet as if it were a code. "Bernard?"

"Why do you want it?"

Enrique didn't bother to consider why he was being asked so foolish a question. "I want to ask her out."

Another silence.

"Bernard?"

"Um . . . I . . ." Even for laconic Bernard, the pauses were remarkable. At last he finished in a rush, ". . . don't want to give it to you."

"What?" No response. "Why not?"

"I don't think you should date her," he said so matter-of-factly that Enrique hesitated to answer. He tried a laugh because it seemed to him a real possibility that Bernard was teasing him.

"Bernard?" he said in a singsong attempt to be light. "You're kidding. What's . . . ? Come on, what's her number?"

"I'm not kidding."

"You won't? You really won't give me her number?"

"No." There was a remarkable absence of emotion. A simple statement of fact.

"Why not?" Enrique whined, unmanned somehow by the confidence of Bernard's no. "Are you planning on dating her?"

"No. You know that. I explained my relationship to Margaret. We're friends."

"So what do you care?"

"You shouldn't go out with her. She's out of your league."

Enrique repeated each word as if he were learning a new language: "She—out—of—my—league?"

"Uh-huh. I have to go, Enrique. I'm writing. I'll see you at poker tonight, okay? Seven?"

"You won't give me her phone number, but you expect me to let you play poker at my house?"

"Uh-huh. See you later." And he hung up.

Enrique held the phone to his ear for a moment as if waiting for Bernard to get back on and say he was joking, then slammed the phone down so hard that the receiver bounced off the base, skidded on his desk, and dropped off the edge, leaving a black mark on the glossy sheen of the recently polyurethaned wood floor.

"Jesus fucking Christ!" he announced to the room and wondered how this could have happened to him. Four years ago he had been interviewed by *Time* magazine, and *The New York Review of Books* had declared his first novel to be one of the best on adolescence in literary history. How could a girl from Queens who did freelance work as a graphic designer be considered out of his league? And how could an unpublished slab of gray flesh make such a judgment? And since when were there leagues when it came to men and women? Is this nineteenth-century England? Am I Pip and she Estella? Bernard and Margaret, according to last night's conversation, were members of Students for a Democratic Society in college. Margaret said she supported the Black Panther takeover of the Straight at Cornell, at least their aims if not their methods, although she didn't flinch at the sight of their guns. She said they looked "scary and beautiful." What bothered her was that they declared the Panthers to be an all-black movement and threw out all the white SDS kids. How could this woman, who was radically committed to the principles of integration and equality, who wanted an end to American racism and imperialism, regard as beneath her the half-Jewish, all-published Enrique? And Bernard? That socialist? That decrier of materialism who believed in civil rights and self-determination for the Vietnamese? He didn't think Enrique Sabas should be permitted to date Margaret Cohen?

Enrique would have laughed at this grotesque hypocrisy, called everyone they knew in common to tell them the hilarity of it, if it weren't for the fact that in some place inside himself, and not very deep down, he agreed with Bernard's assessment. He was out of her league. She was beautiful, he was awkward. She was cheerful, he was in a rage. She was obviously sexually confident, he was secretly terrified. She was outgoing, self-assured, well-educated, and evidently had normal parents. She could parry with grace from her side of a conversation, although she didn't know how to tell a story as well as Enrique, but so what? That was what he worked at night and day. If he didn't best her at storytelling, he might as well put a bullet in his brain.

Yes, she was beyond his reach, Bernard was right. But agreement on that didn't persuade Enrique that Bernard's stated reason was the thwarted novelist's true motivation for withholding Margaret's number. Bernard wanted her, and knowing he would never have her, he wanted to be sure Enrique didn't either.

Although he was shyer than ever of women after his recent rejection by Sylvie and his failure at his sole one-night stand, Enrique's political outrage and competitive instinct overwhelmed modesty and fear of rejection. He knew Margaret lived on Ninth Street. He hadn't noticed her street address, but he could go look at it. In extremis, he could stand in her lobby and wait for her to appear, though he doubted he would have the gall for such a romantic vigil. From the lowest of his new shelves, he grabbed his new white pages, supplied by NYNEX's installer with his new phone and its new number, and looked up Cohen. He knew that single women in New York, to thwart heavy breathers and obscene talkers, either paid to have unlisted numbers or used the initials of their first names—although the latter precaution seemed likely to fool only the stupider breed of pervert. Her home delivery of the *Times* suggested to Enrique that Margaret might spring for the extra charge of being unlisted. So it was with trepidation that he ran his finger down the plentiful supply of Manhattan Cohens until he reached the *M*s, and by God! What joy! There were five M. Cohens, two on the Upper West Side, two on the Upper East Side, and one, a single lovely *M,* on Ninth Street. There she was, M. Cohen, 55 East Ninth Street.

He reached for the phone and felt his stomach slip all the way to the floor. He swallowed hard, but that didn't alleviate his queasiness. He dialed M. Cohen. He knew if he allowed himself to think, even for a second, he would quail.

She answered on the third ring, just as he was about to give up. Her voice was hoarse, presumably from their marathon of Camels and conversation; still, she sounded bright, eager to talk. He said, "Hello, Margaret, it's Enrique Sabas. We haven't spoken in so long I thought I'd call." Nervousness making him loud, he fairly shouted this unoriginal witticism, the best he could come up with in the aggrieved state of mind Bernard had provoked.

"That was crazy," she said in good cheer, as if *craziness* were a synonym for *fun.* "I haven't stayed up yakking like that since college. And believe it or not, I have to run out to a brunch at my friend's now for more talking. Can I call you back? What's your number?"

"Oh, sure. I was just hoping we could, uh, I don't know, go to a movie or—"

"I'm glad you called," she interrupted him. "I was going to ask Bernard for your number." Hearing this, Enrique's heart, a tiny, huddled creature in his skinny chest, leapt, but it instantly crumpled when she added, "I think I should try to have an orphans' holiday meal for everyone who can't be with their families. You inspired me with your complaint that your mom and dad and brother and sister deserted you."

"I was sort of kidding," Enrique said. In an attempt to be

interesting during the first hours of talk last night, he had exaggerated his mild disappointment into a wild grief over not having, for the first time in his life, a celebration of Thanksgiving and a Jewish Christmas with his half-and-half family and its half-sibling components.

"I know you weren't really complaining. But, you know, like you were saying, your parents are in England for Christmas, and my friend Phil Zucker's family is on a cruise, and there are at least two other friends who've told me they're alone for the holidays, so I thought I should have a dinner for all the orphans." Out came that staccato release of sudden laughter, and just as quickly it was reclaimed. "Is that crazy?"

"Sounds great," Enrique lied. And to be convincing, he added, "I'd love to come." Of course, it was the last thing he wanted, to be with Margaret and at least two or three other males.

"Oh my God, I'm late. I have to go. What's your number?" He told her with a sinking feeling, and then came the disaster: "I'll call you when I've figured out my Orphans' Dinner. Bye!"

And so he was alone again with the black receiver for a companion, stuck in his narrow studio with its narrow twin bed, waiting for a call that he felt certain would never come.

chapter four

Anhedonia

H E BROUGHT HER home from Memorial Sloan-Kettering for the last time. For so portentous a journey there was little fanfare. After nearly three years of treatments, it was as if they had acquired additional members of their family, including the inevitable relative they were no longer speaking to. Of those doctors with whom there was still friendly congress, three stopped by with farewells and one with an argument.

The autocratic Iraqi Jew was the first to appear, less than an hour after Enrique informed his office that Margaret wanted to end all treatments, transfer into the hospice program, and die at home. The small, proud specialist walked into Margaret's room alone and unannounced. That was unprecedented. His appearances had always been forewarned by his subordinates. When he did finally show up, it was with an entourage of fellow, intern, nurse-practitioner, and a pair of medical students who were probably the age of Margaret and Enrique's older son, Gregory, all of twenty-three. This solo performance heralded a new chapter, sadly limited to a single engagement, in their relationship.

He stood at the foot of her bed with a stern look, manicured hands at his sides. She peered up at him like a cowed and suspicious animal. He reminded Enrique of a conductor at Carnegie Hall, attempting to control a vast orchestra with little more than the force of his personality. He began with a concession, waving disgustedly at the feeding machine, evidence of the previous night's failure. "We're finished with that," he said.

He went on to insist that she return to TPN's intravenous method. He had already lost this argument a month ago. She had convinced the head of oncology and the Sloan psychiatrist that it wasn't a life worth living. There was no reason to expect she would agree to go back. Nevertheless he made the doomed charge. The handsome, dictatorial, and—Enrique could now see—softhearted man argued passionately, and against all the evidence. He abandoned his manner of preening arrogance and openly pleaded with great feeling. "There are new drugs all the time," he said. "You don't know how long you can live on TPN. I have patients who have lived for years with metastasized cancers worse than yours. The scans show your tumors aren't growing. We can find you a drug trial—"

Enrique knew that these statements were nonsense. Margaret had no tumor. Her bladder and its large invasive tumor had been removed two years ago. Her metastasis, found by accident during a surgery to relieve an intestinal blockage one year ago, was taking the form of small lesions, too small to be seen on CT scans, growing on the outside of her digestive tract. What could be observed was ascites, fluid filling her abdominal cavity, a sign of her cancer's robust and deadly life. Since January she had gone from being able to eat and drink to not being able to eat, to not being able to drink, proof that her cancer was advancing rapidly. While she lay in bed inactive, and TPN was pumping her full of two thousand, four hundred calories a day, she continued to lose weight and had no energy. She had had three serious infections within the last two months and had developed jaundice two weeks ago. As Margaret had observed about the friends she had made and lost in her advanced cancer support group, there seemed to be a tipping point with metastasized cancer. Everything indicated that she had begun her free fall. And yet. And yet Enrique found himself engaged by the specialist's irrational invocation of what had certainly died for Margaret, namely the belief that further struggle was worthwhile. Enrique kept his peace, but the Iraqi's words filled him with shame and doubt.

In September Enrique had supported Margaret's search for a miracle cure. Her condition then, although she was tired and subject to infections and intestinal blockages, still allowed her to socialize, to travel, to laugh. Trying desperate measures had also reassured all who knew her, especially her sons, her parents, and her siblings, that everything had been done to save her life.

But for Enrique there had been the cost of time, robbed from their farewell. While she was still fighting her disease, Enrique did not raise the subject of her death—of what she hoped and expected for him and their children in a future without her. Although Margaret wanted Enrique to be with her every waking minute and close at hand while she slept, their talk was reduced to the practicalities of the now. They did not discuss the end.

The struggle since September had been difficult and ugly. They had had to argue bitterly with her urological oncologist (the family member they were no longer speaking to) because she declined to enter a drug trial he recommended. He retaliated by resisting intense pressure from their friend, the head of oncology, to instead allow her to try off-protocol drugs. They had to find a new specialist outside of Sloan-Kettering who was willing to try off-protocol drugs. She endured long hours of treatment with two experimental chemos that didn't do her any good and made her feel worse. This time giving up wasn't surrender; it was acceptance. And yet hearing these irrational clichés of hope from a medical scientist, Enrique longed to believe.

Margaret answered the pleading doctor in utter despair. Tears flowed and her voice quaked while she curled up into a fetal position. She shrank from his words of optimism, wincing as if they were lashes of a whip. She pleaded, "I can't do this, I can't, I can't do it anymore. I can't go back to the TPN. I can't stand the smell. I smell like rotten milk all the time. I can't stand just lying here having it drip into me all day and all night just waiting to die. Please, please let me go . . ." She collapsed into body-racking sobs. Enrique fought his way past the hospital bed's bars and her IV lines to enfold her in his arms. As Enrique pressed his lips to the hollow of Margaret's smooth, almost translucent cheek, he saw the Iraqi wobble on his conductor's stand, unsure of himself. It reminded Enrique of the other time the self-confident doctor had been knocked off his perch by Margaret.

They had met him only four months ago, when Margaret had to maneuver awkwardly back into Sloan's service in order to be treated by this maestro. They had been told he was the best specialist in New York to fix her gastroparesis, the best to keep her nourished while they searched for a third or fourth or fifth experimental drug.

He had breezed in with an entourage of four, his white doctor's coat billowing on his short frame, to announce that he had delayed a surgery to see her on short notice because of the entreaties of his good friend the head of oncology. He demanded, without so much as a hello, to know why she had refused to enter the Phase 1 trial offered by the intractable urological oncologist.

Margaret had fixed herself up for this audition. She had worked meticulously on her wig to make its replica of her short black hairdo seem as natural as possible, and she had put on a pretty green floral skirt. She wore a white silk T-shirt smooth to her torso except for the bumps of the three access ports to the catheter installed above her right breast for TPN feedings and other intravenous medications. Her white teeth, bonded over twenty years ago into pretty and seamless proportions, shined a bold and cheerful smile at the Iraqi's stern countenance. "Because I was just being used as a guinea pig," she answered.

"So?" he scolded. "You have metastatic cancer. You're incurable. Your only chance to survive is to be a guinea pig."

"I don't mind being a guinea pig," she shot right back at him, aloft on an examination table, rocking her slim, pretty legs, like a girl on a swing, teasing the boys. "I mind being a guinea pig in a failed experiment."

"What do you mean—a failed experiment?" he said, pronouncing the phrase as if it were contemptible and possibly not English. "How *could* you know—?"

She interrupted him. "It was obvious. It was a terrible drug. I would have been the last patient to enter the trial. They already knew the drug didn't work. They needed one more guinea pig for their last cohort so they could finish the study and get the rest of their funding. The drug had only helped one patient live for six months, but she didn't even have my kind of cancer—she had ovarian cancer. Everyone else dropped out before completing three full cycles because they said the drug took away hedonia."

"Hedonia?" he mumbled, and now he seemed sure he was hearing something that wasn't English.

"All pleasure from living," Enrique explained softly. He had been told that if anyone could help Margaret out of this nightmare of vomiting every four hours with the regularity of an atomic clock, and keep her alive while they resumed treatment with the newest cancer drug available, Avastin, a drug that hadn't been shown to help bladder cancer but might (why not? why couldn't the unexpected happen?), it was this man. Enrique was sure these grandiose assertions about the Iraqi's skill were the requisite exaggerations made in the desperate world of terminal patients, and intensified by New York's culture, obsessed with celebrities to whom mythic abilities were ascribed. Although Margaret made fun of herself for believing in such claims, she was a devout. She was raised a nice Jewish girl from Queens, and in that enclave, having the best doctor was considered a basic necessity. She had been told by the powerful head of oncology to believe in this man, and warned that he was above being pressured by anyone. So Enrique did his best in tone and manner to appear submissive, especially because he was aware that, although Margaret respected authority, she was too brash, too demanding, too abrasive at times for men like this one, men who liked to walk astride the world, especially astride the female world. "Half the patients in the study stopped taking this drug before they got the full dosage," Enrique said. "It's called Epotholide, by the way. They stopped taking Epotholide because not only didn't it help their cancer but it took away all pleasure. Anhedonia, I think, is the term for the inability to feel any pleasure."

"Anhedonia," the great man's fellow repeated and wrote it down.

"Yes," Enrique confirmed and added, apparently just chatting, "You know, it's funny but that was the original title for *Annie Hall*. Woody Allen wanted to call it *Anhedonia*. Guess what? They didn't think that would sell tickets."

Margaret took Enrique's pass of the ball. She smiled apologetically at the Iraqi and said, "My husband is in the movie business."

That, of course, got the attention of the doctor's entourage. "Really, what do you do?" the fellow asked, and both medical students turned Enrique's way as if he had the answers to next week's test.

"I'm a screenwriter." Enrique shrugged as if it were embarrassing.

"He has a movie shooting right now," Margaret said. "They're in Toronto, but they're coming to New York soon, right?"

"Yeah, they'll be shooting down the block from here in three weeks," Enrique mumbled to the floor.

Margaret got as far as impressing them with the cast before the Iraqi interrupted. "Enough chitchat," he said to his team and then demanded of Margaret, "How do you know they only wanted you to fill out the last cohort?"

"I asked," Margaret said and released her loud and quickly retracted report of a laugh. "If you ask, they have to tell you."

The still frowning doctor turned on his heel and addressed Enrique. "You told her to ask?"

"No," Enrique said. "She read the disclosure documents and figured out to ask."

"You asked?" He whipped his head back to Margaret with an unexpected smile, a dawning of pleasure and illumination in his dark-eyed face. He regarded her with an attitude of admiration, long enough for Margaret, apparently unnerved by his look, to release another staccato laugh. "You are a smart woman," he declared at last.

Margaret beamed. "And I am a cooperative patient. I really am. I will be very obedient. I promise. I will do everything you tell me to."

"Good," he said with a comical and self-knowing nod of satisfaction. "You hear that?" he turned to his entourage. "That's what I like to hear."

"I will be obedient," Margaret continued, "but only if what you want me to do might actually help me."

His lean face broadened into a wide grin. "You will obey me if you agree with me, is that it?"

"Exactly," Margaret said, and the whole room laughed, with gratitude that somehow suffering and death had been mocked.

That was Margaret and Enrique's last tag team cancer triumph, their final seduction of a succession of healers. Having charmed her new doctor, Margaret abruptly excused herself to use the bathroom. She retched up the bile that had accumulated and the water she'd drunk during the past three hours. The sound could be heard clearly through the thin door of the examination room by the senior doctor and his team. The group paused their medical cross talk about how to proceed with her case to listen to the eerie lack of struggle as she vomited; Enrique knew, from two months of observation, that she was bent over, mouth open, fluid coming out like a fountain, apparently gallons of it. The Iraqi asked Enrique, "How often does she have to do that?"

"Every four hours. Her stomach doesn't empty at all. Here's the report." Enrique passed him the results of a grueling test a previous gastroenterologist had insisted she endure to prove that her vomiting every four hours wasn't a hypersensitive reaction to chemotherapy nausea. They fed her scrambled eggs that had been irradiated to make them visible on a CT, and then ran her through the scanner every hour to see whether any of it had left her stomach. After four and a half hours, while Margaret writhed and moaned from the effort to keep her nuclear breakfast down, the technician saw on the scan that it hadn't progressed at all, and let her throw it up. That was the end of two months of medical skepticism.

The specialist bowed his head to look at the test report and then announced, "We have to put the PEG in first thing tomorrow. She can't live like this. It's dangerous."

Four long months had passed since that grateful day of relief, months so grim that the previous years of treatment seemed cheerful by comparison. The bold, girlish, teasing manner that had charmed her star doctor was gone now. Margaret hid in Enrique's arms, in the fold of her crooked bed, without makeup, without wig, skin translucent from starvation, eyes bright and wide with despair and drugs, her hospital gown stained here with a brown splash of antiseptic and there with a drop of blood. This anhedonic Margaret was telling her doctor that despite her pluck, her nerve, her aggression, her flattery, and her compliance, she had nothing left. This Margaret who wanted to accept death was very different indeed.

"Okay, I'm going to leave you alone for now," he said, unwilling to admit defeat. "You're here for tonight. So we'll talk tomorrow—"

"No," Margaret cried out. "Please. I can't talk about this anymore." She buried her face in Enrique's arms and sobbed. "No more, no more, no more," she whimpered over and over in a hysteria of desolation.

The healer stepped off his conductor's stand and stumbled to the door. He caught Enrique's eye and said in a low but firm voice, "We'll talk."

Enrique had kept mum while the great man made his plea because Margaret was right and his case was unsupported by facts. But when she ceased sobbing and he handed her new tissues to replace the soggy ones, he couldn't restrain himself from asking, "Mugs, maybe there's something to what he says. You could stay on the TPN for just a month and try another dose of—"

She shrank from him, repelled, more terrified by these words than by anything he had ever said to her. "Puff!" she exclaimed in a whispered scream. "Puff! Puff!" she repeated, using the silliest, the most private, the sweetest of her nicknames for him. "You have to help me!" She gasped for air as if her feelings were strangling her. "I can't do this without you! I can't do this alone! I don't have the strength to argue! I need you to fight them for me! I need you to help me die! I'm sorry, I'm sorry, I'm sorry. I know it's not fair— I know I'm putting too much on you—"

And that was all he let her say, ashamed to have somehow managed the monstrous feat of provoking a woman who was dying in midlife to apologize to him for unfairness. He pressed her fragile, thin-haired head to his chest, pleading, "I'm sorry, I'm sorry, I didn't mean to say it, I'm sorry," and then a litany of I love yous.

She answered each of his declarations. "I love you *so* much. I love you *so* much," saying the "*so* much" as if it were a significant development, a furthering of her feeling for him that she had only recently understood.

Her sobs declined into sniffles, and she sighed into another motionless Ativan sleep. He lay beside her and occasionally kissed her forehead, as soft and moist as a baby's. He expected, when she woke up, that they would start talking in a way they never had, in a way they now must, about their marriage.

"And how are *you* doing?" he was asked at the end of almost every conversation with a friend or relative or doctor, as if they had all read the same manual. A few informed Enrique, in case he hadn't the wit to notice, that cancer could be as hard on the spouse as on the patient. They didn't accomplish their objective of letting him feel sympathy for himself. Inevitably, he felt obliged to point out that he was not dying and so it could never be as hard on him as on Margaret, that compared to most cancer victims and their families, he and Margaret were lucky. Their medical bills would be paid by Enrique's excellent insurance through the Writers Guild of America, the union of screenwriters. Other indulgences, such as the faux hotel suite at Sloan, were available to them thanks to the generosity of Dorothy and Leonard, Margaret's parents. Enrique was a writer and could either drop his work entirely or shift it to odd hours so as to be available to Margaret and to Max and Gregory. They had many friends who had rallied around them. They had both the intellect to negotiate the hierarchical world of medicine and sufficient contacts among the bullying powerful of New York with which to cajole doctors. He said it so often, he felt a little insincere, like a candidate making a stump speech, "This is a terrible piece of bad luck for Margaret, but compared to most families who have to deal with this, we're lucky." He meant every word. At age fifty, it seemed to Enrique that too much of his life had been wasted in a twisted shame of self-pity for what had been the petty frustrations and mistakes of his career. Faced with this, a true misfortune, he was surprised to find himself more often grateful for the allies and resources that he had been given to help him fight on Margaret's behalf than discouraged by an opponent who didn't even know he existed.

He could not and did not ask Margaret or his boys for comfort. His father was dead. His mother too old and too self-pitying to be a solace. His in-laws too frightened and too bereft themselves. His half brother, Leo, too anxious and too selfish. His male friends too distant from the realities and too uncomprehending of the experience. Margaret's best friend, Lily, too preoccupied comforting Margaret and herself. His half sister, Rebecca, who had been present and understanding and so great a help, could spell and reassure him, but she could not provide, no one could provide, what he had forsaken for nearly three years, what cancer had taken from him, and would soon take from him forever: Margaret's attention.

Lying beside her, waiting for the paperwork to bring her home for the last time, he expected that soon they would begin their final conversations, their farewell to each other. The struggle to live would no longer dominate. He was lucky even in this, he thought. She hadn't been incinerated by a terrorist's plane or shattered by an errant taxi. Even in her dying, he consoled himself, she was giving him something precious, a time for them to part with grace.

But he had miscalculated. Her decision to die brought a crowd.

chapter five

The Orphans' Dinner

H E TRIED TO be late. Not truly late, just the proper ten or fifteen minutes so he wouldn't be the first to arrive, which was odd, because he wanted more than anything to be alone with her.

He was dressed an hour and a half ahead of time. He wore black jeans and his sole white Brooks Brothers button-down shirt, which he ironed twice on a towel covering his butcher-block table. The second pass was necessary because the first left a crease on the collar that would symbolize something bad about him, he couldn't say what. Once all the creases were eliminated, he thoroughly concealed the white shirt underneath an equally white and very puffy hand-knit wool sweater. Looking at the total effect of this ensemble, few would have suspected how much thought had been put into it. It certainly wasn't flattering. The puffy sweater had been given to him as a Christmas gift by his Jewish mother and atheist father, purchased from a local craftswoman who lived near them in Maine. It would have worked best for a beer-guzzling bear of a man, concealing the overhang of his stomach and making great round thighs seem proportional. Instead, in this wad of white, Enrique resembled a pregnant anorexic, or perhaps an enormous cotton ball impaled on a pair of sticks.

He had a persistent suspicion that he looked silly in this outfit and anxiously checked and rechecked himself in the full-length mirror on the back of his bathroom door. His once roommate and bachelor best friend Sal Mingoti, who now lived, inconveniently, with a girlfriend of Sylvie's, had insisted that Enrique buy the looking glass at Lamstons. "The Women will need this," he assured Enrique as they awkwardly lugged the six-foot-tall glass up the five flights, and then Sal helped him drill and attach plastic holders to support its frame. That installation was a forbidding task for the literary Enrique but laughably easy for Sal, who had pioneered a dying manufacturing neighborhood soon to be known as SoHo. Sal, a broke, struggling sculptor, had learned to be plumber, electrician, carpenter, and tile layer en route to the coveted loft prize: a certificate of occupancy, or C of O.

Enrique had occupied the vast illegal space with Sal, or rather mostly slept for nearly a year after his breakup with Sylvie, and occasionally served as a holder of things that Sal drilled or glued or nailed. Sal had been kind about providing shelter for Enrique. He had refused all offers to help with the rent but also gently spurred Enrique to get his own place. In exchange, Enrique had inadvertently supplied Sal with a new inamorata. They were close and true friends despite the fact that Sal, unlike Bernard Weinstein, wasn't literary and had never read Enrique's novels. In fact, he hardly seemed to read at all, claiming to be dyslexic. Also unlike Bernard Weinstein, Sal was rooting for Enrique to succeed with Margaret (or any woman, really) and called about an hour before the dinner to ask, "Nervous?"

"No," Enrique not so much lied as deluded himself. "Just, you know, I don't like . . . dinner parties. I mean, what are they? You just sit and eat and talk."

"Oh yeah, Mr. E?" Sal said, using his affectionate name for Enrique. "You wish it was a dancing party?"

"No!"

"Yeah, that'd be a fucking nightmare. Dancing. It's sex with all of the work and no fun."

"All the potential for ridicule and none of the fun," Enrique amended.

Sal laughed, with the relaxed grace of a man who knows with whom and when he will next get laid. "Don't be nervous. She likes you, Mr. Ricky. It's obvious. She would have torn your clothes off if that bozo Bernard wasn't there. Women don't stay up all night talking 'cause they want to hear what men have to say."

"Then why a dinner party with all these other people?"

"Safety in numbers. She's a little scared of you. And that's good. That's really good. Just what you want."

Enrique loved Sal. He felt at ease with him, probably because Sal, precisely because he was neither a writer nor a reader, didn't resent Enrique's precocity. And the fact that Enrique almost never agreed with Sal's opinions and perceptions of the world (and thought his nonrepresentational shape-sculptures didn't qualify as decoration, much less art) only seemed to increase his feeling of trust. He knew that if he made a fool of himself with Margaret, Sal would not truly think less of him whereas, with the Bernard Weinsteins of the world, Enrique felt he was forever on probation, one misstep away from their permanent disdain.

Sal, the shaman of seduction, had a final word of advice. "Promise me one thing. Kiss her when you leave."

"What?"

"On the lips, Mr. E."

"In front of everybody!" Enrique fairly squealed with incredulity and horror.

"Yep."

"No!"

"I mean, no tongue. Don't ram it down her throat, but you know, move in, right up to her, pause for a sec, just one second, and then kiss her softly on the lips. She'll appreciate it. Believe me. The Women want men to make the move, you know? She's invited you to dinner with her old friends and you have to show her, you're not just another friend."

Sal's kiss order haunted Enrique. He knew he wasn't capable of so bold and public a gesture. With or without an audience, he might lack the nerve to kiss Margaret. Sal's suggestion caused him to forget to ask his friend if he ought to be wearing this huge, hot sweater on his bony frame. The thick wool felt especially close once he'd donned his green Army coat, trudged down the five flights, and pushed open the heavy metal door out onto dirty and frigid Eighth Street. He knew from the ice-cold mask of air that caused his eyes to wince and the tip of his nose to go numb that he ought not to be perspiring in this weather. He could already feel one particularly large and hot drop run down the washboard of his ribs to his bony hip. He paused to decide if he had time to run back upstairs, take another shower, and remove the tent of a sweater.

During this internal debate, his eyes drifted to the five black steps of Bernard Weinstein's building. He wondered, for perhaps the ten thousandth time, whether his nemesis was one of Margaret's guests this evening. Certainly Bernard was orphaned. More so than Enrique. Bernard's parents had divorced when he was a child, his mother had died while he was in college, and his father had long since remarried a woman who, Bernard claimed, hated him. Why don't I feel sorry for the scumbag? Enrique wondered. Whether he ought to or not, it seemed likely Margaret would take pity on Bernard and invite him to a dinner of holiday orphans. Enrique had been pretty sure he would have to contend with Bernard and his barbs since the day he got Margaret's call inviting him to join "a crazy group. I don't even know who's going to show up. I've invited everybody I could think of who's stuck in New York without family. And I have no idea what I'm going to make. We may starve."

That was his chance to ask if Bernard would be among them, but he was too paralyzed with pleasure and surprise that she had called him back. He had been unable to find a reply other than "Can I bring anything?" a question provoked by a memory of how his parents behaved. Of course what his mother could offer was a delicious salad made from her vegetable garden in Maine, or his father a signature blueberry pie, featuring a thin, crisp, and buttery crust, whereas Enrique could do no better than hand over a can of Campbell's soup. "How about a bottle of Mateus?" Margaret said and released her abbreviated shout of a laugh. "I'll bring a case," he said gamely and asked what time he should appear. "Sevenish," she said.

He hung up and felt humiliated, by what exactly he couldn't say. Replaying her joke about Mateus, he wondered if she was laughing at him, and had been laughing at him all along with her probes about his education. His mind reevaluated her cutoff laugh as a suppression of mockery rather than modesty, and he began to suspect that the role he was playing was a pathetic character in a Dostoyevsky novel: a lonely, hapless young man humiliating himself by pursuing a beautiful young woman obviously above his station; that he would eventually split Bernard Weinstein's skull with a hatchet, then Weinstein's unpublished manuscript would be posthumously hailed as a masterpiece, while Enrique's sole claim to fame would be as the envious monster who had robbed the world of a delicate genius.

It was in this hopeless frame of mind that he decided against going back to shower and remove the sauna of a sweater. He was certain to fail no matter what he wore, and so, perspiring in the cold, he marched toward Margaret's in a state of excited doom.

Having left his building at six-thirty, he arrived at his destination three blocks away at six-forty. Since he knew being early was tacky, he walked quickly past 55 East Ninth Street, spooked anyway by the doorman, who scowled at the double glass doors as if they were about to admit his greatest enemy.

For someone who had lived all but two years of his twenty-one in Manhattan, Enrique had little experience with doormen. In working-class Washington Heights, they didn't exist, particularly one in a starched gray uniform and possessed of a forbidding article of furniture—his lectern faced the entrance as if he were a Stalinist bureaucrat empowered to cast you into the gulag. Enrique rarely traveled to the Upper East Side precisely because up there they were ubiquitous. Not downtown—yet. This was 1975 Greenwich Village, one leg still in the bohemia of the fifties, the other sunk in the garbage and violence of the seventies.

Enrique's Village of Eighth Street displayed clear evidence of both. The washed-out red façade of the New York Studio School, looking vacant behind its dirty, blank windows, stood out from the otherwise commercial street of head shops and shoe stores. Home to a generation of Abstract Expressionists, it admitted through its scarred metal doors beautiful and moody young men and women day and night, as well as the middle-aged wrecks of their teachers, bald men in berets mostly. The artists moved unconcerned past the resentful and predatory gaze of the drug dealers and nodding off junkies in pools of urine. Turning off this street of art and degradation, and walking uptown a mere three blocks, was to time-travel forward to the thoroughly bourgeois Village of the second millennium.

When he and Bernard had walked Margaret home, Enrique had noted the unusually stately appearance of her street, beginning with an elegant prewar co-op on the corner of Ninth and University Place. Its unusual double-height windows provided glimpses of well-furnished rooms that looked European, as if the contents had been transported from Paris. The rest consisted of architecturally undistinguished postwar structures. Margaret's was especially blank, with its officelike array of identical size windows. He had also noted that her apartment faced a vast beige brick complex on the downtown side, which was saved from dullness by the rare setback garden—twenty feet or so of greenery. Even in December, there were half a dozen pine trees, gaily fitted with white Christmas lights, towering over dirty clumps of frozen snow.

There wasn't a single commercial building, or a tenement, or a dilapidated brownstone on Ninth Street stretching from Fifth to Broadway, although all the surrounding streets had plenty of them. It was a two-block oasis. Broadway was a hard-line border between it and the dangerous decay of the East Village. To cross Broadway in that direction, say to taste the spicy pastrami and steaming knishes of the Second Avenue Deli, was to step around the strewn upturned garbage cans of youth lost to drugs, to avert eyes from the homeless and the shattered ambitions of would-be artists and intellectuals stringing banners of futile political rage across the broken windows of abandoned tenements. Soon the neighborhood would have the romance of a modern *La Bohème,* and within half a decade the glory of gentrification, but what it meant to Enrique in 1975 was that he shouldn't walk east of Broadway after nine at night unless he was prepared to be mugged. Margaret's Ninth

Street, in Enrique's eyes, was a sole survivor of another time, the ruling classes of Henry James or a progressive Eleanor Roosevelt. He assumed it was a last gasp of a dying city, and in no way a harbinger of a post-2000 Manhattan filled with millionaires, oozing expensive condos to both rivers. He thought he was walking into the past while in fact he was seeing the future.

At Broadway, he turned uptown, struck by the delicate Gothic spires of Grace Church, once the most favored church of the powerful Episcopalian elite. From Tenth Street until Seventy-seventh, Broadway disobeyed the rule of the grid and cut its way on an angle through the heart of Manhattan. Enrique stood in admiration, the perspiration beneath his layers of Army coat and wool turning into a freezing sheen so that he was at once shivering and sweaty, an impressive feat of discomfort. He observed how the avenue's angle at Eleventh Street allowed a rare sight in New York, not a profile of a skyscraper, namely the Empire State Building twenty-odd blocks north, but an angled view of its rise above the city, as if it had rotated on the granite, to show off the details of its handsome façade. With nineteenth-century Grace in the foreground and the 1930s Empire State rising above uptown, lit against the black metallic sky, he felt small and unimportant. He really was an American Raskolnikov, too intelligent to be reconciled to his unimportance and helpless to escape it. He was in the city of his birth, the city of his childhood, the city of his adolescence, the city of his ambition, and he felt lost.

He also felt stupid. Killing twenty minutes on the street produced both tedium and anxiety. He walked to the Strand, the secondhand bookstore on Broadway and Twelfth, glad, as always, to see the familiar spines of the Modern Library editions of literary classics. He paused at the self-improving table with soaring piles of important nonfiction works, from Gibbon's *Decline and Fall of the Roman Empire* to Boswell's *Life of Johnson,* and guiltily maneuvered to the remainder shelves of modern fiction, furtively wending back to the *S*'s, where he found, as he did once a week, the same battered copy of his first novel (the spine was actually dented), a pair of his second, one without a jacket, and six copies of his mother's first novel. Of his father's eight books, only two were present. He paused on his way out at the newly published books obtained from the dozens of reviewers who lived nearby and enhanced their livings by illegally selling these free editions from publishers. Some were what the industry called advance readers' copies, with promotional copy citing advertising budgets and the like. Enrique glanced at a few and endured spasms of envy while reminding himself that he wasn't in a race, that readers did not ignore one writer because they liked another. After fifteen seconds of attempting to sustain this good fellowship with novelists everywhere, he once again failed to convince his spirit to be generous.

This circuit of the Strand and his journey of feelings—from nostalgia for the books that he grew up with on his parents' shelves, to intellectual inadequacy, to sorrow and pride over his family's impressive shelf of disappointments, to his tangle with jealousy of his betters—had lasted only ten minutes, and he still needed to kill at least ten more. He could have gone back and showered and discarded two or three sweaters in all this time. He felt stupider by the minute.

And yet, when he found himself half a block north of Ninth Street on Broadway, trying to make his steps as small as possible, he glanced at his Timex watch, saw that it was only five minutes before seven, and hurried, as if, with only half a block down and half a block across to go, he might somehow manage to be late.

When he finally confronted the sour-faced doorman, it was 6:58. He had to say his name twice. "Henry—what?" the doorman asked at the first hearing and retracted his head as if Enrique had just slapped him.

He repeated slowly and clearly, "En-ree-kay Sah-bus." Shame and the heat of his sweater caused his skin to release another misting underneath, and he felt utterly beaten. For a moment he wanted to flee.

He had fled from high school, of course, but Enrique had also several times come down with a last-minute flu to avoid a social occasion, including one at his editor's home that he absolutely ought to have attended if he cared at all about his career—and he cared very much. He'd been overcome then with a panic less severe than what he was feeling in Margaret's lobby, and he had canceled from a phone booth three blocks away, coughing unconvincingly like an inept actress playing Camille. "Are you sure you can't make it?" his editor asked with the tone of a teacher giving a pupil one last chance to avoid an F. "Everyone is very excited about meeting you. And there are important people here." But he made his voice weaker and added a fever to his symptoms, convinced that someone at his editor's party would make him ill indeed.

The doorman lifted a large, heavy black intercom receiver—it looked like something a Gestapo officer might use in *Casablanca*—and pressed a button embedded in a box attached to the lectern. Margaret's cheerful "Hi!" issued from the intercom's phone. The doorman said, "A Mr. Ricky Saybus is here to see you." He put an emphasis on the article *A* as if there were something fraudulent about the name that followed. Sure enough, Enrique heard Margaret exclaim with confusion, "A who?" and the doorman glanced at him with a self-satisfied smirk.

Enrique, bathed in sweat and misery and rage, spoke in his father's voice: resonant, commanding, and murderous. "Enrique!" he snapped. "Not Ricky. Enrique. Sabasss," he said, hissing his name with a snake's fury.

Say what his ex-girlfriend Sylvie might about anger, that did the trick. The doorman abandoned his sneering manner and pronounced the correct first name. Margaret responded clearly through the World War II device, "Oh, Enrique. Sure, sure. Send him up."

The elevator was too quick to allow him to fantasize about making a run for it. When it opened on the fourth floor, he stepped out to discover that he was facing the door to Apartment D, that it was ajar, and that he could see Margaret's profile as she said to someone inside, "I think two and a half boxes will be enough!" Then her cheerful face appeared, flushed from the heat of cooking. "You're incredibly on time!" she said. "This is hysterical. I can't believe how on time you are, and everything is a mess!" And that was followed—there it was again—by a truncated laugh, clearly at herself, pleased and embarrassed by her behavior all at once. It happened too fast—he had assumed an anxious walk down a long hall—and he found himself talking without thinking, without his buddy Raskolnikov sniping at every word.

"I know," Enrique confessed easily, "I'm hopelessly nuts. I arrive everywhere too early. It's humiliating."

Margaret swung the door fully open to reveal a sprite of a young woman in a bright red apron peering up at Enrique with an expression of delight. She was so short, little more than five feet, he guessed, that she made the smallish Margaret, at five-six, seem tall. She had a thick, curly mass of brown hair, warm brown eyes, and a welcoming smile full of correctly sized teeth. The rest of her was so far below Enrique's eye line that he had no idea of her figure, and anyway she distracted with this flattering pleas-antry. "You're on time! That's not humiliating. You're doing the right thing." She gestured as if calling up to an audience in the balcony for agreement. "Everyone else is late. They should be humiliated." And she stood there, arms spread to the ceiling, with a confidence that those on high would agree.

Margaret, meanwhile, was urging him in, waving a large metal spoon. She too was wearing an apron, hers suburban goofy, illustrated with a black-and-white drawing of a harassed father-chef at a backyard barbecue, talking to his concerned wife, concerned because he appears to be unaware of the fact that, although he hasn't succeeded in getting his grill hot, the plate of hamburgers on a table next to it has somehow caught fire and now threatens to immolate him. "Don't worry, dear. The coals will be ready in ten minutes," read the ballooned dialogue.

Enrique obeyed the spoon's directive and stepped into the parquet floor of the L-shaped studio while Margaret confirmed her friend's reassurance. "That's right. You're the well-behaved guest. The rest of them are dopey— Where is it?" she abruptly demanded. In one sweep he noticed that her closet-size kitchen was immediately behind the front door to the left, that within two steps he was already in the heart of her living room, that a long glass table by the row of windows at the far end of the box was set for what looked like too many people for Enrique's comfort, and that on the wall running from the front of the apartment to the windows was the exact same shelving he had had in his teenage bedroom in his parents' apartment. All along its length were adjustable brackets hooked onto metal strips screwed into the wall. They supported four-foot-long wood shelves, their heights varied to accommodate tall art books or stunted paperbacks. At one point she had created enough vertical space to fit in a phonograph and speakers and what looked like a couple dozen albums. The Beatles' *Revolver* peered out from the nearest end. His mind was busy trying to understand her demand, "Where is it?" while the red-aproned sprite offered a surprisingly large hand for so small a body, saying, "I'm Lily. Sorry. My hand is wet."

"I'm Enrique," he said.

"Oh I know *that,*" she responded with a funny emphasis as if he had accused her of gross stupidity.

"Sorry. I'm so rude," Margaret said. "Enrique Sabas, Lily Friedman. Where's the case?" Margaret continued, with a mischievous look on her face.

Enrique felt the floor wobble as it occurred to him what she meant. "The case of Mateus."

Lily trilled with laughter. "We were hoping you'd bring a different vintage, but—"

Margaret finished. "Not a case, that would be hysterical. But we don't have enough wine!" she exclaimed pointing to the table set for ten. "I just have two bottles. We need at least two more."

"Not that we're alcoholics or anything," Lily said and shook her head, making a mass of brown curls bounce.

"Good-bye," Enrique said and turned on his heel.

"No," Margaret cried out. "Don't be ridiculous."

"We're fine," Lily said and waved away all worries. "I've got to dry my hands," she added and ducked into the kitchen, one step away, to grab a paper towel.

"Red or white?" Enrique asked, a hand on the door. He had no idea how this confident man had suddenly taken possession of him, but the general who was now in charge didn't seem to mind that his foot soldier Enrique was a bundle of nerves with a propensity for making a fool of himself.

And the recently elected commander in chief had guessed right that Margaret didn't mean to absolve Enrique of the task so easily. "Red?" she said uncertainly toward Lily, who had dried her hands.

"Don't be silly," Lily said. "Someone will bring wine. Somebody always does."

"We're having shrimp in our pasta, but it's a red sauce, so I think that's red, right?" Margaret said, cocking her head at him.

"Mary McCarthy told my father," Enrique said, shamelessly dropping a name that he knew young women were sentimental about because of *The Group,* a book he had never read and never would, "that if the wine is really good, no matter what the color of the grape, it will go with any meal."

"I love that," Lily praised, another bright smile beaming out of her low frame. Margaret's big blues, however, stared through him as if he had spoken in a foreign language. Perhaps the name-dropping displeased her.

"My theory," Enrique said, moving his gaze away from that disturbing examination into the welcome of Lily's browns, "is that Dad had brought Mary McCarthy the wrong wine and she was being incredibly polite." He opened the door. "Screwing up the wine," he called out as he left. "It's a family tradition. I'll be back with two bottles of red."

He heard them laugh through the closed door, and he felt a satisfaction about himself that was unlike anything he had experienced except when he got his rave in the *New York Review.* He was still humiliated. He knew that when he finally removed his huge green Army coat, disaster awaited. He could tell, from the distinctive odor of wet wool wafting up from his damp neck, that his sweater had been penetrated by perspiration, so the shirt underneath must be sopping. He had no idea where to find a liquor store, he had no idea what kind of wine to buy, and he doubted that he had enough cash to pay for two good bottles. Yet he would go back. He knew he would go back to the Orphans' Dinner in this state of disarray, with bad wine if necessary, and if they laughed at him, and when they laughed at him, as long as those lively girls were doing the laughing, he knew he would feel no pain.

chapter six

The Last Schedule

H E TAPPED THE calendar icon on his color Treo (what a mar-
vel of compression, what bliss of technology!) as he talked
into a tiny microphone that dangled midair on a wire connected
to the base and to his left ear. The headset allowed him to check
the electronic organizer function while simultaneously discussing
with Bernard Weinstein's wife, Gertie, when he could schedule
them for their farewell to Margaret. They had made the cut, and
so would be allowed to say good-bye face-to-face, although they
were on the B-list, which meant a fifteen-minute afternoon audience. Those closest to her would enjoy a last supper.

Scheduling and restricting access to Margaret for her last two
weeks had been less troublesome than Enrique had expected. Not
all were eager to sit opposite death. Enrique could imagine the
rationalizations of those residing in the suburbs of Margaret's

affections. "We're friends but, you know, more friends through our kids," they reassured themselves. "I'm not sure we would have given each other the time of day if . . ." So they eliminated themselves.

Margaret had shortened the potential list anyway, lopping off acquaintances and a few good friends from her many incarnations: the butch girls of Kittatinny summer camp; the good Jewish girls of Francis Lewis High School; the Marxists and earnest feminists of her Cornell radicalism; the guilty working mothers she shared cabs with; the frustrated artists; her chatty Monday morning tennis foursome; and the shortest list, the advanced cancer support group. That Margaret eliminated most of her compatriots was not what Enrique had expected, because she had always preferred a gathering that included as many as possible, and yet it was consistent with the duality of her nature and the vulnerability of her current circumstance.

Despite her fearless and merry ability to introduce herself and chat up strangers in the most forbidding of situations, usually Margaret preferred to stay home and dine with their sons. Afterward, she was content for an evening to consist of reading a genteel English village murder mystery, glancing up from her cozy position on the couch at TV shows Enrique watched noisily, nodding with affectionate and polite boredom at the rant he delivered about this or that travesty of culture or politics or baseball mismanagement. She remained serene, lying in wait for sporadic appearances by her sons as they sought snacks and breaks from homework, ambushing them with interrogations or hugs.

In her cave of males, she could happily hibernate for weeks, but when Margaret roused herself to entertain, she preferred an event both large and casual. She had invited well over a hundred people to her fiftieth birthday, held six months before her diagnosis; a good portion of the guests were little better than acquaintances, a few she had met only once. She insisted that she, Enrique, Max, and Gregory do all the cooking and catering themselves; Enrique had had to browbeat her for a week to agree to hire a lone bartender. She had been the same about the party they hosted when their new house in Maine was finished. People appeared whom they knew only by sight, and Margaret lost sleep the night before learning how to make sushi, introducing a different kind of crab roll to Blue Hill Bay.

She was a mix of hermit and social butterfly, and if he had been asked before her illness how she would say good-bye to the world, Enrique would have guessed that she would want to see many representatives from her diverse constituencies. But he wasn't surprised when she restricted the number of final visitors, just as she had severely reduced her contacts when first diagnosed, and only resumed swimming in the Olympic pool of all her friendships during the year of her remission. Once she metastasized, she limited her socializing to intimates.

The whimsical and unpredictable choice of Bernard as the exception to this rule was more typical of her at her healthiest. She had never been close to Bernard. There had been a half dozen casual contacts in the previous two decades, and except for one phone call, Bernard had ignored them during her illness—and why not? They weren't friends, and anyway she had never taken Bernard seriously. He was, as she had put it, "a drip," and she hadn't revised her opinion upward now that the world regarded him as a gusher.

Bernard did not fulfill his ambition to be a novelist. In the past quarter of a century, he had evolved into one of the country's leading cultural critics, and certainly its most visible. He had reviewed books for the daily *New York Times* for ten years, movies for *The New Yorker* for five, was still a columnist for *Time* as well as the author of two bestsellers of general cultural musings. Ten years ago he had become a regular on *Oprah* as a sort of literary educator at large, and he had subsequently morphed into his current incarnation as host of a middlebrow weekly interview show of cultural icons, over whom, it seemed to Enrique, he merely fawned. "You're kidding," Margaret reacted when Enrique told her that Bernard had e-mailed, writing that he'd learned the terrible news and wanted to see her. So Enrique didn't reply. Within a day, Bernard's assistant left a message in a bored monotone on their home voice mail that Mr. Weinstein would be honored if Margaret had time to see him.

"Honored?" Margaret repeated in her faint, hoarse voice, wearing a crooked smile. She was en route from her bed to her closet, pushing her pole of hydration with profound weariness. She was hunched over, wigless, without makeup, looking like a frail old woman. To be seen in this state would have horrified her until recently, and did still dismay her. "I look like an old crone," she had said to Enrique two months ago while he helped her undress for bed. Although she kissed him and said, "Thank you," when he told her that she was still beautiful, he knew that she didn't believe him. Or rather, that it wasn't enough of a consolation. The mirror she looked into was the reflection that mattered.

Six months ago she would have worked for hours to make sure that no one, including Enrique, saw her so bereft of vanity. On this first day of her public dying, she had no energy for such niceties. All reserves were gone. It looked as if a breeze could kill her. She had to struggle to push the IV pole, albeit weighed down with a fresh bag of hydration and a smaller dose of liquid steroids. Those palliatives were new, prescribed by Natalie Ko, the hospice doctor who was supervising her home care, to boost her energy for her week of farewells. They hadn't kicked in yet. Margaret moved as if each step cost her a precious last bit of vitality. Every couple of minutes she paused to dab at her eyes and her nose with a balled-up tissue. After she'd started taking Taxotere the previous summer, she'd sniffed from a continually running nose and tearing eyes. For a while she had been prescribed various antihistamine remedies, implying the side effect was an allergy. But when Margaret became exasperated that they weren't drying her up, one of the residents at Sloan had finally explained that the tears were caused by the body expelling Taxotere's lingering toxins. He said they would finish leeching out three months after she stopped the drug. Her last dose was two months ago. These tears would outlive her.

"I'll tell Bernard we don't have time," Enrique said, too drained to make fun of his pompous request.

"No, no. Bernard can come," Margaret said. "Just for fifteen minutes. It'll be amusing."

"Why? Because he's famous?" Like most New York hostesses, Margaret liked to add a celebrity to her gatherings. Enrique had supplied a few of the famous, the odd movie star or director, for her parties over the years. Evidently Bernard had made such a shiny object of himself that now his pale slab of flesh was believed to brighten a room.

Margaret wasn't offended. She knew that Bernard's great success was an irritation to her husband, a man disappointed in his own career. That made Bernard's celebrity a joke of fate, as if God had stuck out his leg and was laughing at Enrique sprawled on the floor. "He introduced us," she said, shrugged, and blew her dripping nose delicately. "I don't know. Just seems . . . like . . . it makes sense, right, baby?" she appealed to Enrique, her chin quivering with memory. "He brought me to you."

There were times, this was one of them, when Enrique would not breathe or speak for a moment, afraid that he would shake with the sobs he sometimes indulged when he was alone. Overpowering sadness rose and crashed within him, a wave that thundered and drowned him, and soon disappeared without a trace on the flattened sand. He said in a voice that warbled from the troubled sea inside, "*I* made him bring you to me," he corrected. "If it were up to Bernard, I never would have seen you again."

"I know, baby," she said, attempted a soothing smile that came out slanted. "But if there's time, let him and Gertie come. Just for fifteen minutes. Okay?"

So Bernard was granted a precious fifteen minutes from the short supply that remained for Enrique. The schedule had been set the previous night, when Dr. Ko presented alternatives to the method and timing of Margaret's death.

"I'll give you steroids and full hydration, you know, potassium, all the basic nutrients, for as long as you feel you need to say your good-byes," the hospice doctor had explained. Dr. Natalie Ko was a nice Queens girl like Margaret, only her successful immigrant grandparents were Chinese. At least both had escaped the borough. Ko lived in Brooklyn Heights now. She arrived at their apartment at the end of a long day, wearing a brown suit over a plain white blouse. She was Margaret's age and, like Margaret, had a high school senior at home. They had several friends in common and had met socially once or twice in healthy days. Enrique noticed her glancing at the art books on the shelf above Margaret's desk, and then down to the photos of the boys. Several times during her examination of Margaret, she peered up at the large painting above the bed that Margaret had done of Gregory and Max: a seven-year-old boy and his three-year-old brother hugging each other in Superman pajamas. When she finished, she draped her stethoscope around her neck, adjusting the collar of her suit so it would cover the black rubber, and sat on the side of the bed, one hand gently resting on Margaret's leg through the thin white cotton blanket they used in summer. But for the stethoscope necklace, she could have been a friend from college days come to say farewell.

"A week," Margaret said, looking at Enrique. "A week is enough," she repeated in a tone that was nearly, but not quite, a question.

"Two weeks?" Enrique suggested. "A lot of people want to say good-bye." He averted his eyes from the doctor. Over the past two years and eight months, they had discussed everything about Margaret's body with medical personnel, including reconstructive surgery on her vagina. Her tumor had grown so large as to abut it, and routine precaution against metastasis had demanded that half of it go. Resection would make intercourse impossible or very painful, and Margaret was insistent, much to Enrique's surprise, that an alternative be found. He had not flinched or blushed during any of those discussions, but that he wanted to coax his wife to live longer did flush his cheeks and pull his eyes to the floor.

"Can I really be on steroids for two weeks?" Margaret asked.

"You can be on them as long as your body can stand it."

"Won't I get an infection?"

"Eventually, yes. That's one option of how to end it. If you develop an infection, we could leave it untreated—"

With a spasm of horror, Margaret said, "I don't want to die of an infection." Three times she had suffered through the shaking chills of one-hundred-and-five-degree temperatures. The doctors had claimed she wouldn't remember much of those delirious nights; some part of her seemed to remember clearly enough.

"Then a week of full steroids is probably about as long as you should go. But you would still have energy for another week, because I'll step you down gradually."

Margaret shook her head. "Do you have to?"

"No. We don't have to do anything you don't want us to. You're in charge." The doctor's eyes strayed again to the picture of a lively Margaret, blue eyes sparkling, surrounded by her men. Their doorman had taken the photo nine months ago, at Margaret's request, on the day they told their boys that she was terminal. They stood outside their building: a mother, her husband, and two grown sons. The young men looked straight at the camera without sorrow or tears, defiance or resignation. They seemed to be standing ready, come what may. Enrique's right arm draped down Margaret's left, his fingers caressing her wrist protectively, a forced smile on his face. She was also smiling, but without effort, a pleasant, patient, loving, and utterly convincing smile. An intelligent eye could spot that she was wearing a wig. Otherwise this prosperous, slim, handsome, middle-aged woman appeared content and untroubled.

"After I see everybody . . ." Margaret swallowed hard and reached for a glass of cranberry juice. Her mouth dried out frequently, despite sipping sweet liquids for the pleasure of their taste. The fluorescent, bright fluid appeared a moment or two later in the translucent bag at the end of the tube exiting her stomach. To spare her visitors the sight of the odd and disgusting mix of bright red juices and black-green bile, it was kept inside a small shopping bag from L'Occitane, resting on the floor. Enrique drained the bag every few hours into a white plastic pitcher that he carried and emptied into the toilet. Mouth moistened, she finished her sentence: "After that week, I want to stop everything." She gestured at the IV pole on the other side of her bed. Two bags were hanging, one for hydration, the other an antibiotic for her latest infection.

The thin line of Dr. Ko's eyebrows furrowed, and her lips pursed dubiously. "Everything at once?"

Margaret nodded. "Everything," she whispered firmly.

Natalie Ko seemed to ignore that request. "You have a couple of alternatives as to how you withdraw hydration. After the first week, I'll stop the extra nutrients, of course. But as for hydration itself, you're getting three bags now. The second week you can go down to two, then the third week one bag—" She stopped because Margaret was shaking her head from side to side, slowly but emphatically.

"No." Margaret had to blow her nose to clear a drip. "After this week, I want to stop everything. I don't want to linger. "

This was not news to Enrique. Nor was the description of how Margaret would deteriorate. A hospice social worker had pointed him to a reputable Internet site to learn about the process. He checked them off in his head while Dr. Ko explained aloud the stages of dying from dehydration. When all intravenous fluids ceased, Margaret would get weaker and weaker, sleep more and more, and pass into a coma after four or five days, six at the most. Once she was comatose, Margaret's breathing would become rapid, shallow, and irregular, sometimes ceasing for what might appear to be forever before resuming its rapid pace in a startling fashion. She might also make the guttural sound that literature fancifully called the death rattle but that was actually the result of accumulating secretions in the throat and did not necessarily signal that death was imminent. Without hydration, her heart would stop after seven days, eight at the outside. Other than a drying out of her mouth, nasal passages, and throat, the process was not painful, and anyway those discomforts wouldn't arise for Margaret until she was in a coma. Since all liquids she took by mouth were drained through her stomach PEG, she could drink freely while conscious and thoroughly alleviate the dryness without prolonging her life. If there were any discomfort, physical or psychological, she would be given painkillers or Ativan to hurry her into unconsciousness. "It will be very quick once we stop all hydration," the doctor repeated. "Just a few days before you become very sleepy. Is that how fast you want it to go?"

Margaret at last showed some impatience. "Yes! If this were Oregon, I'd just have you shoot me in the head."

The hospice doctor flinched. In a low voice, with a shy glance at Enrique, she said, "Actually, there are studies which show deliberate suicide, even in hopelessly terminal patients when death is imminent, is very hard on"—she met Margaret's eyes—"not you, but the family members."

For a moment, Margaret didn't move a muscle, eyes unblinking, expression blank, as if she didn't understand what she had just been told or was so struck by the information that she needed to think hard about it. Her great blue eyes remained fixed on Dr. Ko, who waited quietly for her patient to react. Enrique knew his wife was not considering what had been said. This silence and this stare were familiar. It was how Margaret reacted to her mother scolding or nagging her. It was how Margaret defied Enrique when he got angry, a resistance at once passive and unmovable. Gandhi would have envied it.

But this time Margaret surprised him. She turned to regard Enrique as if just noticing that he had come into the room. "I know it's terrible what I'm doing," she said. It wasn't clear if she was speaking to him, or to the doctor, or to God. "I'm putting it all on poor Endy," she said, using another of her nicknames for him. "But he's so strong." Water glistened in her eyes and he felt sure these were not chemo tears. "He can take it. Right, baby? You can do this for me?"

Natalie Ko didn't understand what Margaret was asking. She answered, "This is fine. This way is okay for families. This is a good way to do it."

Enrique understood. Margaret had realized that her practical need to die as easily and quickly as possible might feel to his heart like cruel abandonment. He moved to the bed and took her hand. "I'm okay, baby," he whispered. "We'll have time together and you'll be comfortable. This is good," he said and had to stop because tears were rising and he knew they both needed to be calm with this doctor. Margaret wanted to leave her life gracefully and at home in their bed. He was determined she get that wish.

While Enrique studied the calendar to find options to accommodate the great Bernard Weinstein's apparently very tight schedule, he knew, almost to the day, how much time was left. Seven days of steroids and full hydration for the good-byes, seven more until death. Fourteen days of Margaret.

Seven of those days and nights would go to others, unavailable to him for their final conversation. Of course Lily would come every day for a few hours all the way to the end. And Margaret's parents had announced, distressingly, that they intended to visit each day of the final fourteen, driving in from Great Neck, where they still lived for half the year, the rest spent in the obligatory last stop for their generation of Jews—Boca Raton, Florida. They had come yesterday for eight hours, but Enrique guessed they wouldn't keep that up. He had observed the slump of Leonard's shoulders, and the agitated, ceaseless motion of Dorothy, sitting on the edge of a chair in her alert military posture, popping up every few seconds to check on something she was heating, or to straighten some errant object, or to ask Max for the tenth time if he wanted to eat. The effort they were making to maintain a brave front—they didn't weep or yell or even permit their clothes to wrinkle—was too great to sustain day in and day out. In healthy times Margaret saw her parents sparingly, on Thanksgiving and Passover and another two dinners spread over the calendar, less than a week altogether each year. Enrique was fairly confident that during those last two or three days before coma cast Margaret into permanent silence she would mostly be his. He could lie beside her in their bed and have a summing-up. There would be, finally, a respite from the hurly-burly of disease, the mess of flowers and exams, the spikes of fever and hope, the tuneful jargon of science and the worrying chatter of life. They would gaze back across the horizon of their marriage, and see together in a single glance what they had lived.

"Enrique?" Gertie's voice buzzed in his ear as she returned from her consultation with some Greater Authority on Bernard Weinstein's schedule. The sound hurt. He pressed the side button on his Treo to lower the volume. Instead, in organizer mode, the effect was to jump his view of the second week of June into the first week of July. He pressed buttons frantically to get back to the relevant dates, while Gertie, her Brooklyn harshness made painful by the high setting, complained, "I checked with Marie—"

"Marie?" Enrique interrupted.

"Bernard's assistant. Normally she handles his schedule. I'm terrible at this. Sorry. Bernard can't Tuesday. He's got a premiere thing, but we will be in New York, so is Wednesday evening possible? Maybe for drinks? *Ha!*" she shrieked without warning or apparent cause. Enrique had to pull the earphone out. He did that so violently his half sister, Rebecca, paused on her way upstairs with a strawberry frozen fruit bar for Margaret. The easily processed treat reminded Enrique of another worry. Margaret could theoretically eat anything, since it would all be drained through the tube exiting her stomach, but bulky foods could cause, and had caused, blockages. Enrique was unsure how she was going to pass tomorrow's feast, a last brunch with her parents and brothers and their wives that, on Margaret's request, would come from the Second Avenue Deli. "I'll chew the dogs thoroughly," she had assured Enrique. "And the knish? That'll just be mush. Dr. Brown's black cherry soda will push it through," she'd asserted with a crooked smile.

Having lost contact with Gertie, Enrique shook his head to indicate to Rebecca that nothing was wrong and pressed the speaker button on the Treo. A compressed, still loud version of Gertie's voice blared to life in the room: "Ha! Listen to me!

Drinks. You must think we're all insane. You poor man," she said, with a quaver of emotion. That was unexpected, given that he hardly knew Gertie, and that she was defensive of her husband, whom she correctly suspected Enrique thought didn't deserve his success. "How about five-thirty or six?"

"No, I'm sorry," Enrique said in a profoundly sad voice. "Wednesday all day and evening belongs to Gregory, our older son—"

"Sure, sure," Gertie pleaded, to abort his painful explanation.

He persisted, to drive home the point that trying to make Margaret's schedule fit anyone else's was grotesque. "—He is coming up from D.C., where he lives and works, to spend one last day, all to himself, with his mother, and although by five it might be over—"

"Sure, I understand, I understand." Gertie begged for mercy.

Enrique was relentless. "I don't want to risk shortening her time with him by having anyone show up. So I've reserved all of Wednesday for Greg."

"Of course, of course." Gertie managed to sound gentle. For once, her voice was low and sweet. There was a silence he didn't understand until, when she spoke again, he heard her gulping back tears. "Tell me . . . when you can see us . . . and I'll make sure Bernie is free. Just tell me what time makes sense." Not to imply that pity had provoked a complete surrender, she added, "But not Tuesday. Tuesday's just impossible."

"How about Monday? Two or three o'clock?"

"Hang on. Can you hang on, Rickey?" she asked, committing the sin of Anglicizing his name.

He took this opportunity to reconnect to the headset, mumbling to himself, "My name is Enrique," in the singsong of a child introducing himself to the class on the first day of kindergarten. He restored the Treo to its calendar and thought back to the odd encounter with Dr. Ko. After the discussion with Margaret about how and when she would die, he'd escorted the doctor downstairs. Natalie paused en route to her raincoat draped over a chair—that summer almost every day in June seemed to be cloudy and threatening—her clever, angular face crinkling with distress. She sighed heavily. "She is a very, very brave woman." Enrique agreed. That had been brought home to him by Margaret's illness, and it had been a great surprise. Margaret had many flaws, in particular a form of passivity that sometimes seemed like cowardice. That had been misleading. In the face of a deadly challenge she had turned out to be an astonishingly brave person. "I have to ask you something," Dr. Ko continued. "Please understand: what she's doing is completely rational. I have no problem with the logic of her decision. She wouldn't last more than a month or two if she did everything to survive, and she'd be really, really sick. But most people let it happen that way. They let the disease take them. They want it to—"

"Mug them," Enrique finished for her, remembering his father's stumble into death.

"Yes." She nodded, looked back upstairs. "They don't choose to face it like this. I've been treating terminal patients for over twenty years, and I've only had one other do it this way, so clean and so direct." She dropped her sober eyes to Enrique.

"Really?" Enrique was surprised. Many people he knew swore that they didn't want to linger, that if they were in Margaret's place they would do the same.

"Yes, it's rare, so I have to ask you." She paused for emphasis: "Is this consistent with her character?"

That a hospice doctor felt obliged to ask this question also surprised Enrique. He was ready anyway, because he had asked it of himself over and over since Margaret made the request that he help arrange her farewells, her funeral, and her death. "I'd like to say no because I am not really happy about it. But I've lived with Margaret since I was twenty-one, almost thirty years, and I love her very much, but the fact is she's a control freak. She learned to be that from her mother, who is also very kindhearted and also very, very controlling." Natalie Ko, perhaps thinking of her demanding Chinese mother, smiled ruefully. "In some ways that's been great to live with. In some ways it hasn't, to be honest. It was great in dealing with her illness. She's fought this disease very hard—"

The doctor interrupted, "I know. I looked at her history. She's had a rough time. And she tried everything. More than everything."

Enrique nodded, silent for a moment, to choke off the swell of pity for all that Margaret had endured. "She fought the disease," he said in a television announcer's voice, booming the words as he pushed emotion down into the closeted darkness of his heart, "to control it. To beat it. And now that she knows she's going to lose, that death is certain and imminent, she wants to decide how and when she dies. It's all that's been left to her to control. Yes, it's consistent with her character."

The doctor swallowed and nodded. She cleared her throat. "As I said, it's entirely rational. But I had to ask." She moved to the door, explaining about deliveries of medicine and about hospice care workers who would come daily. She handed him a card with phone numbers to reach her at all hours if something went wrong. Enrique opened the door and, because she had been so gentle and direct with Margaret, and because they had friends in common, he leaned forward to kiss her on the cheek. But she avoided his aim at her cheek, and lifting herself up to reach his tallness, she moved her mouth onto his. She shut her eyes and parted her lips. He felt the wet and warmth of more than mere friendliness. He had the impression that if he leaned in at all, they would be making love.

Enrique withdrew from this kiss abruptly, startled more than anything else. And Natalie Ko looked puzzled, as if someone else had done it. She left quickly. Her somber, formal manner had vanished in a moment. Like Gertie, who had dissolved from demands into heartbroken pliancy. It occurred to Enrique that this was another of fate's jokes on him, the irony that he must be more attractive to women now than he ever had been, or would be again. He had never felt less horny or less tempted. He knew that his apparent sacrifice of everything to Margaret was as much a gift to himself as to her, but to these grown women it must have seemed like their girlhood illusions of love come to life. And it was so much more pleasant, even for a hospice doctor well-acquainted with death, to contemplate his devotion rather than Margaret's suffering.

"Monday works," Gertie blared in his ear with a trill of excitement. "We'll be there at three-thirty. And we can stay until four-thirty, but then we have to go."

Enrique smiled a crooked smile, but no one was there to appreciate it. "Margaret will only have about fifteen minutes. There's a very close old friend, from summer camp days, who's coming at five, and that's going to be a tough good-bye. I don't want to exhaust Margaret. She needs breaks between these visits. They're, you know, kind of tiring."

"Sure." Embarrassed and overwhelmed, Gertie hurried to agree. "Sure. Of course. We'll get there at three-thirty and we'll be gone in fifteen. Can we bring anything? Do you need anything?"

Enrique felt his eyes burn, perhaps with longing to ask her if she could bring a cure. Or perhaps he, too, was leaking toxins. "No, we're fine. See you Monday at three-thirty."

Enrique had conducted nearly twenty such conversations and exchanged another thirty or so e-mails that day and the day before. Most were not irritating, and few brought out this streak of sadism and self-pity in him. The people who loved Margaret and were close to her were easygoing with him. His half brother and mother were more difficult. Leo, having been physically and emotionally absent for the dreary days of Margaret's illness, seemed to be abruptly excited by this dramatic finale and wanted to be there as much as possible, while Enrique's aged mother insisted on showing up with a heartbroken face, pitying looks, and bulletins about her distress. "I can't bear this," she informed Enrique regularly.

But those were old snakes, long ago drained of their venom in therapy. Enrique was too sad and exhausted to fight about the morbid grandiosity of his narcissistic family. He was past complaining, as well, about the shallow emotional support Margaret's parents could offer. Dorothy's and Leonard's terror when they came into her hospital room the first day after their daughter was diagnosed had depleted him of that expectation. They had stood ten feet off, by the door, not offering a hug or a kiss. Enrique accepted that he was the family's emotional resource for this scary and miserable event, the one called on to provide strength and calm when life got too raw, just as he accepted that he had drawn on Margaret's parents for money and stability, and had absorbed from his mother and father and half brother and half sister ambition and inspiration.

He was fifty years old, and no one he knew could claim the heroic nature of characters in so many contemporary books and movies, least of all Enrique. Writers were liars, it seemed to him, when it came to such things, making black villains of those who disappointed or slighted them, and heroes of themselves. Enrique knew that he wanted to feel superior in how he cared for Margaret and his sons, and how he faced her death. He wanted to praise himself and feel scorn for everyone else. Didn't he deserve to believe in this pathetic vanity as a consolation for what he had lost, was losing, and would lose forever? His half brother would fuck tonight the woman he loved, or failed to love, as was more often the case. Margaret's parents had two other children and eight grandchildren, whose births and achievements they had lived to celebrate together. Months and probably years after Margaret's death, Dorothy and Leonard would have each other, a sixty-year marriage still thriving in its routine of bickering and ocean cruises and profound, loving dependency. Enrique was losing the partner of his past and his present and his future just when he most desired her choreography. When Gregory or Max married, he would celebrate alone, or with a stranger to their creation as a partner. When Margaret's grandchildren were born, he would have no one to share the miracle of their baby having a baby. Yes, he resented them all for asking him to make them feel better that a part of their world was ending, when the very center of his was melting in his palms, slipping through his fingers, spilling onto the floor. Soon, very soon, only a puddle of his heart would remain.

But no, he had no desire to complain while Margaret was dying, and no illusion that anyone who had failed him, anyone who had betrayed him, anyone who had willfully misunderstood him would now, out of pity, develop insight about themselves and apologize to Enrique for demanding he put Band-Aids on their scrapes while he was bleeding to death. Bernard would arrive and be celebrated and make Margaret's good-bye an incident in the bestselling memoir that he would someday write, and in his popularizing, sentimental words, Enrique and Margaret would be distorted into the kinds of people who can reassure and flatter readers. So what? Did that really make losing the love of his life any worse? "I am fortune's fool," Enrique quoted silently in the style of his grandiose and melodramatic family. With Bernard and Gertie filling the last free line in his Treo's calendar, his gloomy task as appointment secretary was complete, and it did mean something precious to him that in this he had not failed his wife. The people she wanted to see, she would see. The people she didn't, he had kept away. Could the wildly successful Bernard Weinstein claim that he had done anything so hard and done it so well?

chapter seven

The Competition

E NRIQUE THOUGHT IT lucky that Margaret lived only three blocks away from his apartment for many reasons, but especially after he purchased two bottles of Margaux for the extraordinary sum of twenty-seven dollars and eighty-nine cents. Enrique had never spent more than five bucks on alcohol in any form. He was left with a single faded, tattered dollar bill in his wallet, and a dime and a penny in the pocket of his black jeans. At the end of the evening, he would need the economy of walking home free of charge.

He was relieved to have overspent for a pair of reasons. He liked the sweet pun buying of Margaux for Margaret. And the high price of the bottles alleviated his worry, acquired from his proud, working-class-born father, that he might pick something gauche and inferior. Enrique understood that cost didn't equal quality (as a writer whose books didn't earn much, he had little choice about that conviction), but he also knew that in 1975 an expensive French red, whatever its actual value to a sophisticated wine palate, would display to Margaret and her friend Lily, as well as to the other mystery orphans, that although he might be ignorant, he was not a cheapskate. It seemed unlikely to Enrique that a desirable woman would be interested in a thrifty man.

He had one hundred and sixteen dollars to his name in all the world, but he did not for a moment consider buying something less expensive. He rationalized that in three months he would receive the money owed to him on the publication of his third novel. True, that princely sum of two thousand five hundred dollars was more than half spoken for already, because he had borrowed a thousand dollars from his equally strapped novelist parents six months ago, and would be taking another five hundred from Sal on Monday next. Since he'd left home at sixteen, this had been the rhythm of his finances, borrowing against his publisher's advance so that, by the time a check arrived, he was well on his way to being broke again. At ages seventeen, eighteen, nineteen, twenty, this constant state of indebtedness, impoverishment, and brief states of cash-flush was tolerable, but Enrique knew that, once he married and had children, this pattern of debt to advance to debt while struggling to write masterpieces would shed its romance and be revealed as misery. Worse, he had watched close up at ages ten, eleven, twelve, thirteen, fourteen, and fifteen how not being able to pay the month's rent diminished to silence the booming voice of his Latin father, how, for the proud son of Spanish peasants and Cuban cigar makers, lack of money was a humiliation as intense as the suicidal shame of a ruined aristocrat.

In spite of his extravagance, or perhaps because of it, Enrique considered impoverishment to be his likely future. Certainly more likely for him than for anyone else at the Orphans' Dinner. He suspected that Margaret's other guests, though parentless this Christmas, would be well-provided-for, either through that financial arrangement known as a "trust fund" or because they were college graduates and presumably could become, or had already become, lawyers, doctors, or the like. Enrique, besides having written three slim novels, had no training or experience at anything of true use to the world. Thus his fear of destitution seemed to him real and imminent. He assumed this dread originated in his own breast. He was too young and unanalyzed to have the wit to blame his mother, Rose, as the inspiration for his fear of poverty.

She often spoke of financial disaster. She harped on it no matter how prosperous her current circumstances, presumably because she had been unsettled as a child by her father's multiple grocery store failures, and the family's abrupt moves from the Bronx to Brooklyn and back again as they skipped out on back rent during the Great Depression. Enrique did not recognize that he had been influenced by his mother's evocations of such calamities. Although his freelance parents lived with a modest mortgage in a small, renovated, eighteenth-century Cape on the coast of Maine, and his mother was working on a novel with a one-hundred-thousand-dollar advance, her nightmares of future homelessness—an isolated and personal bankruptcy that no modern FDR would save them from—were always present, anguished visions she often articulated vividly to Enrique, thanks to her expressive and imaginative powers. His mother would have made an excellent saleswoman, provided, of course, that her product was sadness and loss. Without paying attention to the terms of the contract, Enrique had signed up for her entire catalog of defeat and its tragic accessories. Her anxious talk and his father's almost perpetual state of being broke since quitting his day job and becoming a full-time writer had cooked Enrique into an odd soup of a middle-class, young American who had never wanted for very much and yet lived in a state of constant worry that he would end up poor.

He remembered how his mother took him aside when he started seventh grade to explain that she and his father would pay for his first year of college, as they had for his half brother, and would have for his half sister if she had gone to university. Paying for the remaining three years would be up to him. At the age of twelve, Enrique hadn't been aware that college cost anything. He had no notion of how he would both go to school and pay for it. He was alarmed. He went so far as to research how much a university would cost, which increased his distress considerably. He lived for a couple years in a puzzled state—until he began cutting high school and thus no longer cared—as to how he was going to pay for Harvard (where his father wanted him to go) from his one wage-earning activity of delivering the Sunday *New York Times* to neighbors in his parents' apartment building, especially since he made only ten cents a week and hadn't convinced more than five people to sign on. He used to make his mother laugh by coming home Sunday afternoon singing his version of the classic song he had learned from her—"'Ten cents a week, that's what they pay me, Gosh how they weigh me down!'"—and never once told her that he didn't think the whole situation was a laughing matter. He understood the full implication of his mother's college message, quite different from his father's grandiose promises about the fortunes he was going to make and leave to Enrique. His mother was warning him that the life of a writer, namely Guillermo's and Rose's lives, was to cling to driftwood in a sea of indebtedness, half-drowned in hunger and homelessness. She made it clear that he could not expect them to help him survive once he jumped ship—and certainly not if he stayed on their leaking dinghy.

When Enrique announced that he wanted to drop out of out high school to finish his first novel (he had written half), he expected his mother's response to be a simple scream of "No!" Instead, she said, "If you want to be a writer, that's your choice. I would never argue with what a soul wants to do in life. My family did that to me and it was terrible. A terrible thing. Something you never entirely get over. So if you feel you're a writer, then you must try to be one. I would never discourage you. But you'll have to support yourself while you're doing it. That's very important too. Being a writer isn't a hobby. It's a job." Despite her heartfelt statement that she respected his soul's ambition, Enrique suspected that she thought earning a living would prove to be too daunting a requisite.

If so, his mother had miscalculated. Enrique's dread of poverty was irrational in more ways than one. It did not, for example, include a fear about earning money as a writer. The world—at least at first—seemed to agree. His first novel earned him eleven thousand dollars, enough to live on for three years in those happy bankrupt days of New York, when rent on a railroad flat on Broome Street and Sixth Avenue, the location of Sylvie's apartment, was sixty-eight dollars a month.

To Rose's credit, she stuck to her word: that he managed to earn a living as a novelist did seem to satisfy her. She didn't plead with him to apply to universities that had signaled they were prepared to accept him, albeit on academic probation for a term since he hadn't finished high school. She did not worry aloud that a teenager trying to make a living as a writer might be too much pressure, or suggest that more education might prove useful to a novelist. It was 1971, well before the word *yuppie* had been coined, or wide acceptance of the principle that monetary success and value were synonyms. Yet in a perverse way, evolving naturally out of her left-wing cynicism, Rose managed to arrive in one respect at the same standard for an artist's success that Donald Trump would harbor. Making money seemed to be, in some sense, his mother's sole criteria as to whether one could claim to be an artist. To be sure, she sneered at hacks, at novelists whose work seemed calculated to sell books, but that only increased her respect for making money itself, particularly if the writing was, as she liked to say, "serious."

Until this recent loan from his parents against his advance on his novel, they had not helped Enrique financially in any way, not even as creditors. He felt no resentment about this. He would have been surprised at the suggestion that such a feeling was reasonable. Enrique believed himself to be the luckiest person he knew when it came to parents. He relished their entertainment value, their vigorous and firmly held opinions on everything, such as whether any writer without a sense of humor, including one they admired as much as Dreiser, could be considered great, or whether Jerry Lewis was a genius clown or only a dumb clown, or whether an armed uprising against an imperialist American state, although moral, was wise. Most precious of all was their consistent and unstinting praise of Enrique's writing, which seemed to him a treasure beyond any valuation. Enrique could make fun of and tease his parents, and dismiss their extreme opinions so colorfully expressed, but it was the adoring mockery of a fanatic adherent. Money was a great evil in the world, Enrique believed, and thus the natural enemy of his brave and talented parents.

So Enrique was an unstable compound of doubt and arrogance as he once again, sweating in his sweater, was screened by the dyspeptic doorman. At 4D, this time he was greeted by a true shock—an angular, handsome, bearded, and confident male who said, "Who are you?" as he swung wide the door to reveal Margaret and Lily and one other unknown male talking in a loud, self-assured voice. Two peacocks had arrived while he was buying wine. He didn't recognize their colored feathers as displays that he had already faced, but he felt sure that both plumages had the plentiful green of young men with trust funds. The pained spasm he felt inside of an anxious and soon-to-be homeless failed artist was, however, completely concealed by a self-possessed smile and steady gaze as he answered, "I'm Enrique Sabas," a statement of identity that he was also confident would one day require no further explanation as to who he was or what he did for a living.

"Oh yeah, I know who you are," the dark and rude young man admitted as he shut the door behind Enrique, confirming that Enrique was on his way. "You're the prodigy who's up Bernard's ass, right? You published a book when you were twelve or something, right?"

Enrique had been a prodigy for five years. At first he had expected the world to applaud him without reservation. That illusion had died fast and hard. Then he'd flailed at the teasing, resentment, and outright hostility which came his way. Such a combative response hadn't served him better, considering that his goal in life was to be universally admired and unconditionally beloved. In the hopeless quest to achieve said goal, he knew now to raise his shields instantly, unsheathe his sword beneath his cloak, all the while making every attempt to disengage and avoid battle. This was not cowardice but a humanitarian gesture. He did not think that even a handsome peacock, such as this one, with a trim beard and a warrior's voice, was a match for one of his angry displays.

"I'm just an old has-been now," Enrique continued and held out his vinyl bag from University Wine and Spirits to Margaret, white freckled cheeks flushed into two distinct red circles, stirring a large aluminum pot filled to the rim with gently bubbling red sauce in her tiny box of a kitchen. She turned, wielding blue eyes and a wooden spoon, and the most gleeful gap-toothed smile he had ever seen on a grown woman. Exhausted, sweated-through, and wary, Enrique instantly absorbed her delighted energy. The entire troublesome world, including its nettling competitors, seemed to fall away. Enrique found himself talking to her with a confidence that a moment ago was beyond his grasp. "I don't know anything about wine, but I bought these in honor of your name."

He executed this flirtatious parry with ease. Though when Margaret's beam was extinguished by a frown, his épée drooped. "What?" she said in an annoyed tone of confusion. As thirstily as he had drunk in her confidence, he tasted her dismay and lost the nerve to explain his romantic pun.

The neatly trimmed warrior intercepted the package and pulled out one of the Margauxs by its throat. He read the label with the air of an homicide detective. "Ah, Margaux." He glanced at Enrique. "Very funny," he commented. "Get it?" He nodded at Margaret. He didn't offer his hand, both being occupied with Enrique's purchase, but he did say, "I'm Phil." His eyes trailed up to the ceiling with an air of thoughtful consideration, and he announced, "Wait a minute. Does Margaux really mean Margaret in French?" Enrique noticed that this bearded, dark-haired tiger with a skinny face and long jaw had blue eyes. Nothing like the huge violet beams of their hostess Margaux; the warrior's eyes were pale, almost colorless, narrowed into a perpetually skeptical squint. "Hey, Sam," Phil called toward the dining table, where sat another example of this confident male species. Sam was currently engaged in making Lily laugh. Her delighted trill caused Enrique to wince with jealousy, although she was not the object he was pursuing. Dismayed, he watched his bottle of Margaux being waved in the air by Phil like an exhibit in a murder trial. If there were anything stupid or embarrassing about the purchase, it was going to be exposed. "You're fluent in French. Does Margaux mean Margaret in English? Isn't it Marguerite?"

"Marguerite is French for Margaret," answered Sam. He spoke

in a bored, offhand drawl, implying that the question was unworthy of him. He had a bush of kinky hair at the top of his head but no chin. He was tall, perhaps taller than Enrique, although that was impossible to determine because he was tilted back in a gray metal folding chair, which he had pulled away from the glass table and placed against the windowsill so that it commanded a complete view of the studio apartment. He stretched out his very long legs beside the five-foot-tall Lily, seated perpendicular to him, in a chair properly positioned for eating. In this odd arrangement, Sam's extraordinarily large feet encased in work boots, at least size fourteen, were directly in the line of Lily's vision, as if to display their length and width for her to admire or possibly to consume. Even on so long a frame, they looked like clown's feet which, with his bushy head and caved in chin, gave him a generally goofy appearance that, like a clown's, was slightly intimidating.

Phil glanced balefully at Enrique and handed him the bottle with disdain. "Doesn't mean Margaret."

"So what does Margaux mean then?" Lily asked Sam, her eyes fixed on his big feet. "If it doesn't translate as Margaret, what could it possibly mean, I mean translate— Oh my God, I can't speak English!" She raised her wineglass. "Open that bottle whatever the hell it's called."

"Margaux," the goofy Sam said with professorial solemnity, "is Margaux. Doesn't translate into something else. It is the thing itself," Sam concluded with a flourish of a long arm and tapered fingers.

"The thing itself!" cried the pale-eyed warrior. "Sartre," he added, pronouncing the great philosopher's name in perfect French. He gazed at Enrique, still stuck in Army coat, clutching his embarrassingly controversial wine.

Enrique burned with shame and resentment at the ruin this handsome young man had brought to his attempt to please the object of his desire. Enrique offered the bottle to Margaret. She reacted to all this banter as if she had just woken up and wasn't sure who, or even what he was. She held on to the bag with the second bottle of Margaux and made no move for the bottle Enrique was offering. "I don't know," he answered more to her than Phil. "I come from a long line of peasants. To me wine is supposed to come in skins, and I pronounce 'Sart,' 'Sat—rah.' "

Margaret fired off one of her truncated laughs, waking up from her reverie with a start. "Like van Gogh," she said, pronouncing it "Van Go." "I can't stand people calling him 'van Gawk-k-k,' " she said, exaggerating the proper guttural Dutch enunciation. "I know it's right, but it sounds disgusting and anyway . . . who cares?"

"Yeah, so what if you're a philistine?" Phil shrugged off his own remark, making it unclear to Enrique if he truly meant to be so slighting. It was, after all, an insult directed at both Margaret and Enrique. He hoped Phil meant to demean Margaret. Along with the conviction that no woman could like a cheap man, he believed a supercilious and insulting male attitude was equally repugnant to Margaret's sex—in short, he was naïve.

"Maybe that's why Van Gawk-k-k committed suicide," Enrique said, and for the third time offered Margaret his much-analyzed gift of wine. "Couldn't stand the sound of his own name."

It was Lily who laughed, harder than she had at the clown's boots, Enrique was pleased to note. Phil, the champion of disdain, nodded an acknowledgment at Enrique that he had scored. Margaret was in one of those pauses that seemed to overcome her, as if somewhere behind those blue eyes she had frozen all the action to conduct a thorough review. "That's funny," she declared at last without the least bit of amusement in her look or tone. It would have been an unsatisfactory acknowledgment of Enrique's wit except that, at long last, she also accepted his gift from his hands. She glanced at the label and returned to her walk-in closet of a kitchen.

Sam called with the answer to the source of his own quote: "'The Thing Itself.' It's a poem by Wallace Stevens."

"It is!" Lily exclaimed as if that were extraordinary. "What's the poem?" she asked.

"Wallace Stevens. That motherfucker," Phil said in a tone of disgust. He resumed the tirade that had been interrupted by Enrique's appearance, declaiming in a high-volume tenor, suffused with confidence: "Anyway, this fine vintage wine is more evidence of my point. We're all on the road to being good little suburbanites. Just look at that list." Phil gestured at a folded over newsletter with the heading *Cornellians at Three.* "Everyone's either a lawyer or becoming one—or, my God, much worse, a doctor—"

"Wait a minute," Lily protested and launched out of her chair, abandoning the clown and his shoes and joining Enrique, who was relieved to have her deal with Phil.

Phil didn't wait to hear her objection. "We've even got two MBAs in there. My God. What a nightmare. MBAs—"

"What's wrong with being a doctor?" Lily objected. "Don't you want to take your coat off?" she asked Enrique, without a pause for the non sequitur.

Enrique removed the coat and revealed the huge, white, hand-knit sweater. He didn't know that its bulk (not to mention the suggestion of drowned animal odor it released) was the reason Margaret and Lily gave him and its tented enormity a second glance. But he was sufficiently aware that he proceeded to flatten the balloon of the sweater's middle so they wouldn't think it was his stomach.

Fortunately, their attention was yanked back to the charismatic Phil. "Yes, yes, yes, Lily, we all know about your daddy, the small-town doctor," he said, moving into the kitchen and once again taking possession of the Margaux. In those close quarters, he inevitably brushed against Margaret and did so without a trace of the self-consciousness that such contact would have created in Enrique. Phil leaned his hip flush against hers while he pulled open a drawer and poked at the silverware inside. "Where's your corkscrew? I want to open this. I need a drink."

"I already gave you a drink," Margaret said with a sly grin.

"So I'm a drunk. Better than being an acidhead." He bumped her playfully. "Move over. Is it in this drawer?"

"I'll get it!" Margaret snapped, but she laughed with delight. In Enrique's eyes, everything about their behavior was as dismayingly cute as Robert Redford and Jane Fonda in *Barefoot in the Park*, an embarrassingly wrongheaded, sexist romantic comedy by Neil Simon that he had watched with guilty pleasure several times on WPIX's late movie. Only—if such a thing were possible—Phil seemed, as a dark-haired romantic lead, more confident than America's handsomest blond movie star. And a darker suspicion came into Enrique's mind while observing their intimacy—she offered a wine opener and hung on to her end teasingly when Phil attempted to take it—that this confident and disdainful youth had already succeeded in removing the apron on this lively female cook. Worse than that thought of ravishment was a more dismal worry: were they an ongoing couple? Had he misunderstood the entire situation? Was this truly an Orphans' Dinner hosted by a woman with a complete life, this evening merely a bounty born of her pity, a charity event for lost souls like him, men without women to love them? After all, Bernard had never claimed that Margaret was unattached; indeed, he'd made it sound as if all the men at Cornell desired her. He had portrayed her as very picky, but there was no guarantee that she had turned them all away—and certainly none that she was, God forbid, virginal. Enrique had always assumed Bernard's claims of her sexual aloofness were a disguised admission that she had rejected the only Cornell man who mattered to Bernard, namely Bernard.

The gloom of his suspicion was unrelieved by a friendly gesture by Clown Feet. He thumped over and said, "I'm Sam Ackerman," with a chinless grin. "You're Enrique Sabas, I know. Bernard's bragged on you a lot." Enrique didn't show his surprise, only nodded because, despite Sam's air of pleasantness, there was something condescending in his attitude, emphasized by the fact that Sam was literally looking down at Enrique from his greater height of six-six. That was the final blow to Enrique's frail vanity: he wasn't even the tallest peacock in the room.

Enrique fell into a resentful and sullen silence, deepened by Phil's persistent monologue, from which there was no respite, neither during or after the arrival of the three remaining invitees. Two were men—one short, chubby, and pleasant, although warily quiet—and the other self-possessed, as lean as Enrique, although not quite as tall, and dressed à la Bernard, in relentlessly black and smudged clothes. Neither of these male specimens seemed inclined to compete, or up to the task of competing, with the monologuist. The third arrival, Pam, was a very thin, small woman with olive skin and dull brown hair, making the orphans an unbalanced three females to five males; but this meek girl hardly seemed to qualify as a full female participant compared to the bold Margaret and the vivacious Lily. Pam was shy almost to paranoia: she made miserly movements with her lips, never quite opening into what seemed to be intended as a smile, while her small, nervous eyes checked her periphery for a blind-side attack. She appeared overwhelmed by the situation, sitting in a corner of the couch and clutching her glass of wine in both hands as if guarding it from purse snatchers.

Pam's terror did nothing to lure Enrique from hiding. While Margaret passed around Brie on stoned wheat crackers to accompany the bottles of rapidly diminishing Margaux, he scurried into a passivity that felt loathsome. In his eyes, he displayed the least impressive plumage of the assembled males. He stewed in a gray broth of bitterness over his gift to Margaret, which he now felt foolish about. As if his mother had abruptly taken possession of his brain, he calculated that at this rate they would go through eighteen dollars' worth in a matter of ten minutes. The speed and waste seemed disgraceful and insulting all at once.

At last Margaret appeared with a huge white bowl and announced, "Here it is! My traditional Christmas dinner of linguine and shrimp in marinara sauce." If Enrique had assumed that the mass movement to the glass table by the wall of windows would slow down Phil's rant against the bourgeois drift of Cornell's class of '72, he was sadly mistaken. Because Lily seated herself directly opposite Phil, his earlier complaint about doctors was renewed. "Just cause Lily's dad is the last of the good country doctors is no reason to think all these assholes in med school are doing it for anything but the desire to be rich," Phil pronounced as they settled in. "To be rich and to play golf, God help them. That's their punishment. To have to play golf for the rest of their miserable moneygrubbing lives."

Despite Phil's tone of disdain and outrage, it seemed a performance. Half comedy-club, half A-student display of articulate bombast, it flowed effortlessly and left Enrique in particular with nothing to say, since it was the sort of showy left-wing tirade, delivered with just enough wit to redeem it from humorlessness (although substantially less than what Enrique would produce, he liked to believe), that Enrique sometimes orated himself.

Maybe he is better at this I am, Enrique concluded, and that's why I hate him. He withdrew further from the room, these strange young people, and in particular from the velvet-eyed chef, seated at the head of the table, opposite him. In choosing a chair as far away as possible from Margaret, he was conscious only of his moroseness and inclination to give up pursuing her, convinced she belonged to Phil. He was unaware of the symbolism implied by his choice of a seat at the foot of the table opposite Margaret. Phil, however, was not oblivious to his apparent claim of a special role. When Margaret attempted to refute him, he interrupted, "You two are Mom and Dad tonight? Do I ask you for the car keys?" he shot at Enrique.

"Not with only a learner's permit," Enrique answered effortlessly, although he had been silent for half an hour and was embarrassed that his act of self-abnegation had been turned on its head. "When you get your license, we'll talk." Pam seemed to find this very funny. She displayed a hitherto hidden smile and turned to him—she was seated on his left—arching her skinny torso. She spoke in a voice that surprised him with its raspy sexiness. "Don't let him. He's too young to drive."

"Way too young," Enrique agreed. He knew that she was flirting with him. He was so young and fearful of women in general that his typical reaction to interest from a source he wasn't pursuing was to treat the woman as if she had offended him. The truth was that he didn't know what to do with such interest. Once, he had made the mistake of returning the friendliness with like charm and the woman had led him to bed, where he couldn't perform. Shame was thus added to his feeling of stupidity and left him more skittish than ever about behaving like normal young men: that is, if nothing better were on offer, to fuck girls they neither liked nor were attracted to. Even as a long-haired, pot-smoking, teenage Marxist, Enrique had enjoyed watching James Bond undress women he didn't particularly like, and who were sometimes attempting to murder him. It disappointed Enrique that he, on the contrary, needed to feel love, or something very much like it, even to flirt. His lack of a callous heart, a heart that wouldn't interfere with the functioning of his penis, made him feel less than manly. So Pam's interest paradoxically added to his general state of despair about himself.

However he did not want a woman he felt sorry for (and he felt sorry for any woman he thought unattractive) to feel rebuffed. He managed a feeble smile. "Actually, I'm the one who doesn't have a driver's license." His eyes strayed down, surveying the thin boy's body underneath her white peasant blouse. The top three buttons were undone, and rather than the swelling of a pillow he saw the ridge of a breastbone. That further convinced him that if he attempted to plant his flag on that skinny surface it would not fly.

"You can't drive?" Pam's voice, astonished, rose in volume sufficiently to attract a few glances.

"Nope. I can drive," Enrique said. "At least well enough to total a car. But I don't have a license."

"That's unbelievable!" Pam exclaimed with delight, as though he had announced an accomplishment, rather than the absence of one.

"Oh, there are many things I don't have. I don't have a high school diploma because I dropped out in the tenth grade. I don't have a college degree—obviously. I don't have a credit card. I could go on and on about what I don't have. It's what I do have that's a short list."

Of course he had cast a lure, the reliable one, and soon Pam was bobbing her head and saying, "Oh wow. That's incredible. That's great." Between swallows of pasta and shrimp, he told his story of bitter rebellion against his high school and his parents, the publication of his first novel, and his three-plus-year relationship with Sylvie, which he knew meant two things to women: one, he was experienced, in spite of his age; and two, he wasn't afraid of commitment. After his debriefing, he performed a background check on Pam and heard nothing that interested him. Not that he revealed his boredom at her suburban upbringing, her controlling father, her pro-Vietnam war brother, her meek mother, and her longing to be a modern dancer rather than a first-grade teacher— the job she took after graduating from Columbia Ed.

Their conversation became a tête-à-tête, removed from Phil's relentless assault on bourgeois values—which had evolved into an argument between him and Margaret and Lily. Pam's life story was sufficiently banal to allowed Enrique to eavesdrop on the main conversation without losing track of her narrative. He heard Margaret challenge Phil. "Of course most doctors, maybe all of them, want to make money. That's not so terrible. But some, like Brad Corwin, really care. He's doing that program in rural Virginia, right, Lily?"

Enrique's attentiveness to Pam did fail when Lily insisted that there were even lawyers who do good. "Like you, Phil. *J'accuse!*" Lily said with a flourish, raising her hand in the sweeping gesture that was becoming familiar to Enrique. "You're a legal aid lawyer. You defend the poor for way less than you could get for defending the rich."

Amazed, Enrique interrupted Pam to ask her, "He's a legal aid lawyer?"

"What?" Pam said. She had been explaining that the main problem in teaching wasn't unruly students, poor supplies, or overcrowding but all the time she spent herding the kids.

"Phil works for legal aid?" Enrique whispered past her to the skinny man dressed in black who was not Bernard. He nodded. Enrique said to Pam, "I'm sorry. Herding—that's funny. You're right, that's all I remember from first grade. Lining up. And I was always last." Until that moment, a corner of Enrique's mind had been comforting him with the thought that, although Phil might have the inside track, or all of Margaret's tracks, Enrique could contend with this half-assed lefty. Yes, Phil was more handsome than Enrique, more self-confident. He had probably conquered Margaret already, but Enrique had felt sure that he was the person engaged in the more noble endeavor. Now he knew that was not so. Phil wasn't a poseur, he provided actual help to the oppressed. Indeed, Phil was someone Enrique felt compelled to admire as much as his own half brother, Leo, once the Students for a Democratic Society steering committee leader of the Columbia University strike and now dedicated to supporting the Panthers in their various trials. More than Phil's easy familiarity with Margaret's hips in the kitchen, the weight of this revelation crushed Enrique. Phil was simply the better man.

Yet defeat, certain and absolute defeat in a triviality like love, didn't feel like disaster to young Enrique. It was nothing compared to the shame of a second novel that received fewer reviews and achieved half the sales of his first. Yes, the cheerful girl with perfect thighs and laughing eyes was a prize. But not the important one.

It had all become clear. The comforting omniscience of a third-person narrator was restored to his anxious head. The true objective of Margaret's Orphans' Dinner appeared out of the fog and loomed like a forlorn lighthouse: she wanted to fix him up with the pleasant and dull Pam. He ceased perspiring underneath his wool sweater tent. The cotton cloth of his Brooks Brothers white shirt came unstuck from his skin and began to dry. His breathing deepened and eased. His legs and back relaxed from their alert crouch in the male jungle, fearing an attack while planning one. He could see his place and his path. He gave his attention to the chatty Pam, shifting his shoulders to face her as squarely as he could, bearing down with his brown eyes—what Sylvie, in an ardent moment, had called doe eyes—deaf and blind to Margaret and her warriors. He glanced away only once, reaching for his wineglass to drain the last drop of Margaux, and caught Margaret peering at him and Pam with satisfaction—he presumed—that her plan had succeeded.

He returned his attention to Pam with the dismal thought that his hostess was correct. This was the sort of lackluster and harmless girl he deserved. Real men of action and good deeds, such as Phil, merited what was so far away at the end of the table, so much farther than the six feet itself: that gleaming white skin and its adorable sprinkling of freckles, the laughing mouth and bold voice, those dancing blue eyes and the blue jeans their owner filled so nicely. And it was not so bad, really. It would make very little difference to his life, to his real life—the conquering of literature—that this was the last evening he would spend with Margaret.

chapter eight

The Good-bye Land

MARGARET WAS NOT the first to ask where she would be buried, or to raise the subject of what arrangements would be made for her funeral. Her parents did that, shortly after they gave up protesting against her decision to stop all treatments.

They came to Sloan-Kettering to make their case the morning after Margaret announced she wanted to die. Because her release had been delayed overnight to set up her home hospice care, they hoped to convince her to stay and resume her desperate measures. Their arguments were washed away by Margaret's flash flood of tears and pleas that they not fight her. She recited the medical procedures that she had endured in an attempt to extend her life, and illustrated the misery of her current enfeebled and joyless existence by lifting her white and powder blue hospital gown to reveal the hole in her belly where a thick, clear tube emerged, about an inch and a half in diameter, and a second wound for the insertion of another tube into her small bowel. This was an act of cruel immodesty that she had previously spared her parents. Dorothy and Leonard had not cared for her physically during her long illness. Because Margaret had insisted they stay at their winter home in Florida during her surgical recovery and for the harshest of her chemotherapies, they didn't know her struggle as a visual. Enrique—not to be sadistic but to prepare them for the shock of seeing her—had been e-mailing descriptions of her procedures for nine months. Nevertheless, the sight of the bare, battered flesh of one's child, albeit a fifty-three-year-old woman, had an effect.

Although Margaret covered herself up quickly, Enrique felt sorry about the pain in her father's collapsed cheeks and the horror on her mother's frozen face, her head held high and still. Tears appeared in their blue eyes. Both had contributed to their daughter's brilliant sum: Dorothy shared Margaret's round shape, yet her color was paler; the deeper violet hues of Margaret's eyes loomed beneath Leonard's soulful lids. Because she couldn't eat at all, Margaret had finally managed to sustain a thinner figure than the lean racing form of her mother. Cancer had also narrowed Margaret's version of her father's round face, and she had lost his still thick, curly hair. As always they were well-dressed, with a touch of formality compared to most hospital visitors. Dorothy stood in her gray wool skirt and taut black cashmere top beside Leonard in his beige trousers, white button-down oxford, and blue blazer—neat and as attentive as scolded schoolchildren. While their daughter continued her lament, they listened in mute anguish with quivering chins, moist eyes, and paralyzed chests, as if they weren't drawing in any air. They were trying hard not to weep, presumably in the belief their tears would make Margaret feel worse, although they would, in fact, have made her feel loved.

Enrique searched their faces to see if that need had dawned on them. Finding only despair and dread, he wondered if, for the first time in his thirty-year relationship with Dorothy and Leonard, he dared speak with utter honesty about how they should treat her. Margaret didn't want them to argue about her decision to die, or to maintain this forbearance to show their grief. What she longed to receive from them was acceptance and admiration. When his wife finished her monologue, exhausted, she hid in the crook of Enrique's arm (she had asked him to lie beside her when her parents entered) and peered out from this shelter, a wary animal. It was Enrique who was left to study her parents.

Although Leonard's and Dorothy's emotional responses often seemed somewhat childlike to Enrique's intricate and unsentimental mind, he knew her parents were exceptionally smart. They did not repeat their clichéd and well-intentioned pleas for her to continue "the fight" when confronted with overwhelming evidence that there was no fight to fight. They dabbed their wet eyes—Leonard with a handkerchief fished from his back pocket, Dorothy with a tissue she pulled out of a box on the bedside tray—in a chastened silence. Dorothy walked over stiffly and gave her daughter a hurried and awkward embrace, afraid she'd lose the composure that she seemed to think she ought to display. They were overmatched by the situation and ill-equipped to comfort her, but they loved their daughter and were too intelligent to fuss.

Enrique felt deep sorrow for them, for the first time without a mixture of annoyance at their clumsiness. Of course he had often felt sorry for them during the two years and eight months since, confused and terrified himself, he had phoned with the scalding news. But there was usually an aftertaste of resentment that they couldn't help him soothe Margaret; that other than financially, they were unhelpful. And yet their money had been a powerful tool, more useful in the world of illness than in daily life, and in its way as soothing as love. At least they had not, as had his mother, burdened him with the additional task of comforting them.

Enrique knew that Dorothy and Leonard would never thoroughly understand him. Just as he could not thoroughly understand them, or rather how they had lived so long, learned so much, seen so much, and yet reacted to feelings as if they were brand-new purchases that didn't fit inside the room for which they were bought. Enrique had accepted that he was an odd fellow in general and an even odder fellow to people as reserved, cautious, and practical as Dorothy and Leonard. He could tell that they had been surprised by his devotion to their daughter during her illness. That meant they had underestimated his feelings for her in the first place. Perhaps they had always believed that for Enrique it was a sensible, not a passionate marriage: Margaret raised by a stable, well-to-do family, while he came from a reckless, divorced, impoverished knot of neuroses; Margaret quitting work to raise his sons, painting only occasionally, and allowing Enrique to command the stage as the family "artist." Perhaps they assumed that he would have a hard time putting her first. Perhaps they had not understood that for a long time she had come first with him, that for many years she had been his heart's home and his mind's anchor and that fighting to keep her alive was essential to preserving his own soul. In this hopeless and clumsy silence, they, the adults who loved Margaret more than anyone, had something in common so profound that for the first time Enrique felt in his blood, rather than in the empty phrases of marriage toasts, that these once strangers had become his family.

His new bond lulled him into a gross and unprecedented error with Leonard a few minutes later. When Margaret announced that she had to go to the bathroom, Dorothy uncharacteristically offered to help her out of the bed, which entailed moving the various bags to the IV pole, an unsightly chore. Margaret, in turn, uncharacteristically agreed. Leonard was kicked out into the hallway, presumably to spare him the sight of his daughter in immodest garb. Enrique, at a nod from Margaret, trailed after her father, recognizing that his wife wanted to welcome her mother's exceptional offer to be a nursemaid. Margaret had rejected all offers by her mother to be an attendant for the discomforts of recovery and treatments. She did so to spare her mother the sight and sound of her pain, and to spare herself the exertion of resisting Dorothy's anxious need to control the planning and handing of every situation. "I have Puff. He's all I need," she would say. "And he can take it, poor baby, he's as strong as an ox," and thus at once ennoble and pity him.

Following Leonard's hunched back and tortoise pace out into the carpeted elegance of the nineteenth floor, Enrique was amused by the realization that he had been momentarily transported into the duties of the previous generation of men— allowed to leave and discuss the great matters of the world while urine bags and soiled gowns were emptied and changed by women. Once they were clear of being overheard, Leonard turned toward him with a little stumble, catching Enrique's forearm to right himself. From the firm set of downturned lips and the intent look in his soulful eyes, he signaled that he was about to raise an important matter. Invariably that meant something financial. Enrique instantly feared it would be about their apartment.

Eighteen years ago, at the birth of their second child, Margaret and her parents had insisted (without a strenuous objection from Enrique) that they move from their affordable, rent-stabilized, nine-hundred-dollar-a-month two-bedroom, into a three-bedroom, so they wouldn't add to the insult of their four-and-a-half-year-old losing his only-child status with the injury of sharing his space. A few years before, Leonard had sold the business he'd founded and reaped millions. He and Dorothy offered to buy a condominium Margaret wanted that, at eight hundred and fifty thousand dollars, was out of reach for Enrique. Indeed, when Leonard asked if they could afford eighteen hundred a month to cover the maintenance, and Margaret said yes, Enrique knew her confidence was overstated, given the vicissitudes of his career. Margaret had a steady job that paid well, eighty thousand, but wasn't enough to cover all their expenses as it was, and certainly not if they more than doubled their monthly charges. Enrique thought that it was wrong for them to live in a place her parents owned, that they ought to get a mortgage, albeit with Dorothy's and Leonard's cosignatures, since no bank would approve otherwise. But that was pride, not sense talking; there was no hope he could pay both the expenses and a loan. Margaret dismissed his feint toward self-reliance. "This is my inheritance," she said. "I'm just getting it early."

Her mother discreetly echoed that view of their generosity by saying how wrong she thought it was "for rich people to hang on to their wealth until they die. What for? Do they want their children to be looking forward to their death?" She laughed, as if this were a punch line, rather than a psychological insight worthy of a perverse Balzac. This view of the situation overlooked the fact that the money wasn't being given to Margaret; the use of the property was the gift, but the property itself remained in Dorothy and Leonard's possession, and Enrique knew why they wanted it that way.

He had turned thirty, their marriage was seven years old, and the careful, pragmatic, and cynical Dorothy and Leonard must have been aware that this union, despite its happy issue of two grandsons, could end in divorce. It would be better for the apartment to be kept out of contention in whatever greedy acrimony might result. Enrique approved of their caution, because as a novelist he admired the weight given to such considerations of unromantic materialism by Zola, Dickens, and Balzac. He envied nineteenth-century writers for having lived in a time that permitted literature to be detailed about such concerns. Considering himself from that literary vantage, Margaret's parents shouldn't trust him. A gangly, broke, egomaniacal novelist working in Hollywood could easily get a swelled head and a swelled member at the flattery and fresh skin of an ambitious actress, or a devious development executive, and leave their daughter saddled with two children. He might, if the apartment were in both their names, claim he owed her less alimony. God only knows what maneuvers a divorce lawyer might dream up.

Dorothy and Leonard didn't know that Enrique was incapable of making things so acrimonious for the mother of his inheritors. Pride in his sons and fear of damaging them would stay his hand. That his wife's parents didn't automatically understand this facet of his nature didn't hurt his feelings, although it was a blow to his ego. Even more to the point, they could not know, nor did Margaret, that by thirty Enrique had already survived an emotionally dangerous affair. He had been crazy with desire. He had stared long and hard at ending his marriage because of the liaison. He had made a deliberate choice to reject both passion and action, the most painful decision of his young life. He alone knew, as best as one could know the future, that his marriage would not end that way.

When the boys were eleven and seven and their father thirty-eight, Enrique finally had a financial success. He adapted his seventh novel into a screenplay that was shot by one of the world's most talented directors, and that led to more lucrative deals and four more films being produced. In spite of the steep increase in New York real estate, Enrique could afford to buy the apartment from Dorothy and Leonard for the two million or so it was worth, although the purchase would have emptied his bank accounts, and added a large mortgage. He proposed to Margaret that they offer to buy it. She repeated her logic: "No, this is my inheritance. It doesn't really concern you, Puff. They're giving it to me. This is their way of doing it."

Until Margaret was terminal, none of this mattered much to Enrique, though he was aware of the psychological component of two adults being "infantilized" by living as tenants of their parents, no matter how generous the terms. In the eight months following Margaret's second recurrence, however, it had come into Enrique's mind that he was going to be a widower living in his dead wife's parents' apartment.

He didn't see how he could extricate himself from an arrangement that had anticipated all sorts of unhappy endings to his marriage except the one that was about to occur. He couldn't simply move out. Max, their youngest, would be going to college in the fall, only eight weeks after his mother's death. He would return home for five months each year. He had lived his entire life in the apartment. He was about to lose his mother. Should Enrique move him out of the only home he'd known?

Enrique could offer to use all of his savings to buy the place, but he hadn't worked for most of the previous three years because of Margaret's illness and he had just turned fifty, the age at which most screenwriters begin to see a rapid decline in their incomes. His career as a novelist was shaky in general and held no promise of wealth. Margaret's expected inheritance, whether it was the apartment or some sum of money, would go directly to his sons. Enrique knew, no matter what he might feel or declare to them, that Leonard and Dorothy would expect a fifty-year-old widower to remarry. Their prudent cynicism, not to mention evolutionary imperatives, would dictate that their money circumvent him to their bloodline. Enrique wanted it that way as well. He wanted to be free, should he ever fall in love again, to let his new wife be as greedy as Margaret in her love, and expect him to take care of her. The rights to his books and his parents' books, and the house in Maine that Margaret and he had bought and built together, he would leave to his sons. That such an inheritance was not worth much in dollars would be made up for by their maternal grand-parents' wealth. The idea of putting all his money into a three-bedroom apartment in order to preserve an illusion for Max worried Enrique. This combination of financial pressure and the calamity of Margaret's death felt like a huge stone on his shoulders. Could he carry that weight at all, much less for years? It was a question he didn't contemplate for more than a few bewildered seconds because it was premised on an event that, no matter how imminent, still seemed unreal. Life after these next, last two weeks of Margaret's life had no shape or sound. Rather than con-template being either homeless or broke, Enrique stopped think-ing about the future at all.

Enrique had spent most of his life anticipating what was to come: the past something to outpace, the present needing improve-ment as quickly as possible. Margaret's illness had proved to him what a wasteful state of mind that had been. But he knew Dorothy and Leonard would never learn that lesson—they were anxious creatures who continued to cling to the belief, despite evidence to the contrary, that thorough planning and prudence could prevent any calamity.

Out in the hall, Leonard held on to Enrique's arm for balance. "Listen," he said solemnly. "Now that she's decided to let go—and we accept it—I accept it—listening to her I understand—but now that it's going to happen soon, we have some very difficult things to discuss. But now is the time to discuss them. And about one of them, I'm going to push you. Hard." Hearing this vaguely threatening statement and fearful of his future without his wife, with grown sons both away from home, Enrique assumed that Leonard wanted him to buy the apartment or move out.

Enrique interrupted. "Listen, I know, Leonard. I have to decide about the apartment. I don't want to move out until Max has graduated from college. It's the only home he's known, and I don't want him to lose both his mother and it all at once." He was encouraged to go on by the fact that, although Leonard's thick, wavy eyebrows contracted in confusion, he did nod slowly in what appeared to be comprehension. "I can buy the apartment, but it would mean putting everything I have into it, and that scares me. If I could rent it until Max graduates, then I'll move—"

He didn't continue because Leonard grabbed his arm and shook it with impatience. "What are you talking about? You're not moving. We're not selling the apartment. You're our son. What is the matter with you? Are you crazy?"

For a moment Enrique was too surprised to speak. He had himself, only a moment before, felt a similar intimacy with Leonard, but it hadn't occurred to him that it might be reciprocated. They were different in so many ways, and Leonard was utterly unlike Enrique's father; it seemed impossible that Leonard could feel so close to Enrique that he would override his natural caution and pragmatism. So Enrique stumbled ahead on the same mischosen path: "Well, it is your apartment—and I just can't go on living there—"

"Stop it!" Leonard looked toward the hospital room, as if Dorothy might help him quell Enrique. "I was talking about the funeral. Margaret's funeral," he said, his voice low, conspiratorial, and ashamed, as if he were discussing a sexual taboo. "I wanted to say that we would arrange everything. There's room in our family plot and, unless you object, we wanted to use our temple and Rabbi. He's pretty good at these things, and he does know Margaret—" He stopped abruptly, looking up at Enrique with his daughter's eyes, overwhelmed with confusion. "Why would you think that about the apartment? Are you crazy? I don't understand you," he said and did something so unexpected that Enrique would never have invented such a gesture for a man as discreet with his emotions as Leonard. He tugged on Enrique's arm to bring his face lower, and kissed him on the cheek. "You're our son," he said, and then, having trouble finishing the next sentence, "Don't talk about that nonsense anymore."

Enrique was mortified. He thought he had anticipated Dorothy's and Leonard's understandable financial conservatism and fashioned a compassionate solution for all concerned. Instead he had insulted this wounded old man, his sad eyes drowning in the immense tide of his only daughter's death; a man who remained so foreign to Enrique's sensibilities that the subjects of his concerns—who would preside over his daughter's funeral? where she would be buried?—had never occurred to Enrique as things to deal with at all.

The Sabas and Cohen families couldn't have been more different in that respect. Ritual—religious or otherwise—had never been important to the Sabases. Occasionally, in a spasm of sentimentality, his parents overreached and attempted a mass gathering that invariably ended in quarrels and resentments. So bereft of family tradition were the Sabases that Margaret had arranged his father's funeral. She was a natural for that task. Such events were not only the center but the totality of her family's family life. It was for the calendar-enforced intimacies of Passover, birthdays, Mothers' Day, Fathers' Day, Yom Kippur, Thanksgiving that the Cohens assembled—and at no other time. Whereas the handful of truly happy gatherings of the Sabas family were happenstance (accidents of people being in the same city on the same night and having nothing better to do for dinner), a nonholiday gathering of the Cohens had never occurred in Enrique's twenty-nine years with Margaret. In spite of the proximity of her parents living in Great Neck, an easy half hour away, six months of the year, they had dinner with them twice a year and always with at least a month's notice. Enrique spoke to his father every day once he had children, and his mother at least a few times a week; Margaret could go a month without talking to her mother, and far longer without speaking to Leonard. And those contacts were carefully managed. She released information to her parents in the manner that the White House discloses its intentions to the American people, omitting troubling details and the possibility of failure.

The chasm between the way these families functioned was familiar and well-defined for Enrique. He immediately adjusted, obeying his standing orders from Margaret to hide behind her, since she never approved of him dealing directly with her parents. "I'm sorry," he said. "I'm really sorry I misunderstood." Enrique shut his eyes and, for a moment, his legs swayed and he felt that his feet were sinking through the carpet. He opened his eyes to catch himself from falling and saw Leonard regarding him with a new expression: a childlike wonder and a worrying about the mouth. "Uh, sorry," Enrique said, breathing hard. "I don't know about the funeral. I haven't—" He was about to say "discussed it with Margaret," a caveat which seemed, now that it had come into his head, both natural and appalling.

Leonard took hold of his wrist and again shook his entire arm. "We don't have to talk about this now. Forget it. We'll talk about it later."

Telling Margaret was automatic. That was the rule of law of their marriage. Moments after Dorothy and Leonard left, while he and Margaret waited for the hospice social worker, who would discuss the logistics of her dying at home, she asked, "What did my father talk to you about?" Her tone was soft and sweet, but it retained the assured command of a general expecting a full report from her chief of staff.

Dutifully, he told her of Leonard's suggestion that they use Great Neck Temple and its Rabbi and the family plot in Jersey. But for the first time in their marriage, he deliberately omitted a detail of a conversation with her parents—his gaffe about the apartment. He believed that to reveal that he was thinking about his future without Margaret would hurt her feelings. He had read the opposite in an article about how to talk to a dying loved one, written by a woman of Margaret's age who was dying of breast cancer and insisted that she wanted the comfort of knowing what would happen with her children and spouse and friends after she was gone. She felt in that way she could celebrate and encourage their future achievements. Or perhaps, she speculated, she wanted the comfort of knowing that she would not be harming them by dying. Enrique did not believe his wife would enjoy a discussion of the future she was going to miss. Margaret was a middle child, jealous of the fun activities of others. And she needed control, especially of Enrique and her sons. To oblige Margaret to imagine her babies loose, without her present to stop them from making mistakes, would torment her.

As much as possible Enrique tried to give Margaret the comfort of feeling that her job as a mother was complete and a success. The Cohen tradition of ceasing emotional surveillance of their children when they left for college was a help. Leonard and Dorothy expected that, other than paying for school and hearing reports of triumphs, nothing short of an emergency would require parental involvement once a child was in university. Greg, their older son, was well past the age at which the Cohens had kicked their young out of the nest of feeling, and Max, a high school senior, was nearly there. Although Margaret's intimacy with her children was of an entirely different order, she resorted to her family's tradition of emotional distance toward her older son once she became ill, and more so after her first recurrence. "It hurts too much," she gasped at Enrique one night. "I can't help him, I don't have the energy," she confessed, ashamed that she needed to hand the phone to her husband, so that he could listen to Greg complain about his dissatisfaction with college in general and his vibrant pain at his girlfriend's mistreatments. Margaret's impatience with young Max's indifference to working hard in high school classes that bored him spiked to unbearable frustration once she knew that soon she wouldn't even be able to fail at whipping him into shape. Enrique selected what she would learn of her sons' troubles; he focused on how well they were progressing to maturity.

Enrique was glad of that censorship when he observed Margaret's annoyance at learning that her parents were persisting in the very behavior that had pushed her away from being closer to them. Margaret disliked planning. Enrique had presumed that her distaste was a rebellion against the forward planning Dorothy and Leonard insisted on. He was convinced that Dorothy's ceaseless nagging of Margaret—"What is Greg doing for the summer? Is he getting a job?" asked in November; or "I want you to come down to Florida Christmas week," demanded, not asked, in March—had forced her daughter into an equally extreme counterbehavior. If Enrique wondered in November what they were doing for Christmas break, or suggested something they might do, Margaret would snap, "Don't ask me now," as if his timing were outrageously premature.

He grew bitter and resentful about Dorothy's effect on his wife until the middle years of their marriage, when he realized that she didn't want to avoid planning simply out of rebellion against her mother—she was genuinely made happiest by felicities of accident, novelty, and improvisation. On those occasions when they got "lost" while driving, she was gleeful; when a last-minute reservation at some exciting place became available, and with little notice they went, she expressed no smugness that her late planning had worked out; rather she was delighted that everything was unexpected. She was glad that the destination was not drained of surprise by research, the pleasures anticlimactic because they were anticipated. Dorothy the planner and Margaret the improviser had been tethered by blood into an endless tug-of-war. Dorothy, being the mother, won almost all their battles. But the price of her victories was intimacy with her daughter.

In a less painful context, Enrique would have appreciated the irony that Margaret's parents, shortly after accepting her decision to die, wanted to make arrangements for her funeral and use their Rabbi, their Great Neck temple, and their family plot. It was the perfect final battle between her adventurous and artistic nature and her parents' need for order and security. And he too stuck to his role as an obedient soldier in Margaret's campaign of passive resistance to her parents' colonialism, by telling her of their plans instead of dealing with them himself. As soon as he did, he regretted relying on her. But the sad truth was that he didn't know how to arrange Margaret's funeral without her help. She lay dying, but he remained her acolyte and counted on her to be the Mahatma Gandhi who could peacefully liberate them from the oppression of two eighty-year-old Jews from Great Neck.

When he reported her father's suggestions for the arrangements, she winced. He felt like a fool. "Oh no," she moaned in heartfelt despair. He felt cruel as well as stupid. "Forget it!" He tried to erase the conversation. "We'll figure it out—"

"No, no!" she cried out. "I want to talk about it. I don't want to have that silly man do my funeral. I want to use Rabbi Jeff." She had come to trust an eccentric Buddhist-Reform Rabbi who presided at a temple built in 1885 on the Lower East Side on the

Sabbath and high holidays, while on unholy days he offered Eastern meditation for chemotherapy patients—a solace Margaret had found as soothing as his prayers.

Enrique had guessed that much. But when he asked where the service and burial should be, she said with a frown, "I don't know. I have to think about that. I don't want to be buried way out somewhere in the wilds of Jersey, where you and the boys will never come. But I need to think about where. Okay? I need to think."

Of course she did. It was her careful consideration of any choice, whether it be a style of shoe, if the night was pleasant enough to eat in a garden restaurant, if a dumb American movie would be more satisfying than an alienated French film, if Enrique should wear the blue blazer or a gray cashmere sweater, whether they ought to see the new exhibit at the Met or nap and then shop at Costco. These sorts of agonizing decisions often left them doing nothing at all but reading a book or gossiping. Happily so for Enrique. Their times alone together gave him the most pleasure, Margaret being the party invitation that he was always unambiguously glad to accept. His wife didn't so much hate to plan as she hated to make up her mind. Contemplating alternatives was what she enjoyed. She could gladly postpone all decisions to an ever-receding point on the calendar.

But her funeral wasn't much of a future event. She had asked for time to think and so he let some of the precious days left pass. There had been fourteen days to go after they had met with Dr. Ko and decided on how she would die. Thirteen days after he had begun the intravenous steroids to give her energy for a last week of farewells. Twelve days after he had finishing making all the appointments for her friends and family. Only twelve days, give or take a couple, and still she had not answered the question that he knew her parents would quietly, but insistently, ask again tomorrow. Dorothy and Leonard were scheduled to arrive with

Margaret's two brothers and their wives to say their good-byes, the first mass gathering of the Cohens not on a national or religious holiday. Her mother had twice asked him by phone if they had decided what they were doing about the funeral. He had stalled and then Dorothy had wondered aloud, as if she were talking to a third person, how Enrique could know what to do, he had never had to arrange one—implying that he needed their intervention. Margaret and Enrique were surrounded. In twenty-four hours their position would be untenable, and still she had not told her lieutenant what alternative plan he could present to Dorothy and Leonard.

Margaret's answer came with seventeen hours to spare, while he was climbing the stairs to their bedroom, returning with a cup of coffee bought at Dean & Deluca, a dose of caffeine he craved. "Puff," she called at the sound of his tread, as she had since they moved in after Max's birth. He didn't answer right away, transfixed by the comfort of her welcome. "That you?" Her voice was hoarse from chemo tears and worried by his momentary silence. "I want to ask you something," she said when he appeared. She was naked except for a black pair of panties, pushing her IV pole with hydration and her bag of steroids, her torso punctured and bejeweled with medical accesses and drains, her body emaciated, the skin frail and crinkled from fourteen months of chemo. She was struggling to put on a white T-shirt. Enrique helped her make the maneuvers around her IV chest port, removing the bags of liquids to push them through armholes ahead of her thin arms, until she had her wounds covered. During this dance, she said, "Would you do me a favor, Endy? Could you find out if I can be buried in Green-Wood?" She looked meek and girlish, as if this request were naughty.

"Sure . . . ," Enrique said. "Why wouldn't it be possible?"

"It's landmarked. I told you. Kathy was buried there, remember?"

"Yes, yes, I remember—" Enrique was quick to correct because, throughout their marriage, whenever she thought he had not listened to something she had told him, her feelings were so deeply wounded that a casual observer might assume he never paid attention to anything she said. This sensitivity was another legacy of her relationship with her mother. Dorothy often answered her own questions about Margaret's life before her daughter could and, when finally corrected, equally often remembered her own answer and not Margaret's. Margaret had married the right man to satisfy a worry of not being heard. Enrique had the ability to recall what people said almost word for word, a facility that he had once felt blessed to have. He had learned to his sorrow that his gift was not always welcomed by friends and family, and in his business dealings was not acknowledged to exist at all. "You said they were making spaces between the landmarked graves available. Isn't that what Kathy's—?"

"But that was two years ago. They may not be doing that anymore. They were running out of spaces and would soon close it to the public and that was almost two years ago. I even thought of buying one then, but—" She gestured vaguely at herself and her defeated body, and he understood that she was referring to a time when she was in remission, and when purchasing a plot would have seemed too pessimistic.

"I'll find out." He remembered vividly the bravery and sweetness in Margaret's reaction to the funeral of Kathy, a young mother of two small children whom she had befriended in the advanced cancer support group. Margaret went to the burial with her group and without Enrique. She returned full of pity for Kathy's children and gratitude that she had lived to see Greg and Max reach young adulthood. Tears welled above a serene smile. There was a brightness in her voice even as it broke. She was animated by grief and by love, by affection and by sorrow. She seemed a general indeed, a commander of what terrifies and breaks the human heart. She took genuine pleasure in where Kathy had been buried, in Green-Wood, a nineteenth-century graveyard in Brooklyn whose hillocks, two-hundred-year-old maples, and weather-worn head-stones were far more appealing than the practical sameness of the flat white rows of the Cohen dead in New Jersey. Green-Wood's elegance and proximity to the Manhattan Margaret loved seemed to reconcile her to Kathy's death and to death itself, as if there were a way to leave the earth and yet stay amid grace and beauty. Enrique understood why she wanted to be buried there.

He set her up in bed with the *Times* and a frozen orange bar to soothe her dry mouth, and she made a second decision. Enrique was thrilled to have her back in command of his daily errands. "Could you call Rabbi Jeff and ask him if he'll do my service? And also ask him if we can use the Orensanz?" she said, referring to the nineteenth-century shul on the Lower East Side. "I don't think temples are allowed to have funerals," she added anxiously.

"Really?" Enrique asked. "Why?"

"Some crazy germ-phobic Jews probably thought the bodies would cause disease. And they were right. Maybe we could just have the service there. I'd love to have it in the crazy old temple, not in boring Riverside—and then you could just bury me sepa-rately, although I wish—" Tears appeared, at the thought of not being physically present at her own service, he presumed, a final agony for a middle child. How hard to miss a party, and in her honor to boot. "Puff!" she exclaimed. "Maybe it's crazy, maybe you should just let them do it at their stupid temple," she went on, frustrated at the possibility that the details would not be perfect.

"I'll find out. I'll deal with it," he said in a rush to allay her worry and her struggle to sustain her taste and identity against her parents' wishes right up to the moment of her death. Enrique was not proud of himself, that he hadn't felt up to fighting this battle for her on his own. But he knew Dorothy and Leonard would respect her desires, whereas they might suspect him—an irreligious half-Jew from another family—of having invented them. With Margaret alive to command him, and to verify that these were her orders, he had the authority to put them into action.

He hurried downstairs. He left a message on Rabbi Jeff's voice mail and hunched over his laptop. He Googled Green-Wood and reached for the phone, sweat misting on his brow, bursting along his flanks. He wanted to succeed for her, to accomplish this task more than any she had ever asked of him, and he proceeded without reflecting that the gift he desperately hoped to provide was a grave.

chapter nine

First Date

CONSIDERING HOW HOT with anxiety Enrique burned all day waiting for his date with Margaret, it's a proof of the physical limits of emotion that he didn't burst into flames and fly up, a charred husk, into the snow-threatening gray New York sky. A furnace of fear and desire propelled him back and forth across the shiny polyurethaned floor of his studio while a fashion debate raged. Should he wear his black Levi's, his pale blue Levi's, his dark blue Levi's, or his one expensive item of clothing—beige Italian slacks tight to his boy-size twenty-four waist and flared at the bottoms? The tailoring of the Milan pants was dead-center seventies couture, which made sense since it was 1975. What didn't make sense was to wear a thin cotton-linen blend on December 30. And there was the issue of the taut cut of the imported trousers across his groin, designed to show off a manly bulge. This exhibitionism frightened him at both extremes of insecurity: that he had not enough of a bulge and that showing what he had was vulgar.

He would never have bought such pants if it weren't for the influence of his bossy and sexually confident friend Sal. In most matters, and certainly in clothing, Enrique didn't emulate Sal, but since his friend managed to get laid more frequently than he had in the past calendar year (not, in fact, a difficult achievement, one being a superior number in that regard), he had allowed Sal to cajole him into the purchase. All the gray afternoon in the halogen bright of his apartment, he dithered over the sparse selection of jeans and flamboyantly genital trousers, arriving at no satisfactory conclusion.

Except when it came to matters concerning Margaret— evidently—dithering was not characteristic of Enrique. Usually he made choices quickly and easily, buttressed by a reliable technique of research. Enrique relished knowledge and felt soothed by the security of acting out of the informed wisdom of men and women more brilliant and brave than he. But living with Sylvie for over three years had taught him little about what women looked for on a date with a man of twenty-one, nor had he thought to consult the vast numbers of women's magazines offering insight on female critical faculties. He knew a lot about a woman's sexual needs since Sylvie had insisted that he read the relevant chapter in *Our Bodies, Ourselves* and went on to be demanding, verbal, and specific as to oral clitoral stimulation and other advanced sexual intelligence about her likes and dislikes. Much of that could presumably be adapted to other women, but the question of what pants to wear on a first date that was really a third encounter, not to mention the fashion confusion caused by the fact that the date was taking place in casual Greenwich Village but on a Saturday night—where was the sacred text, the instruction manual, the manifesto to answer that conundrum?

Male advisers were in short supply. Bernard, his enemy as regarded Margaret anyway, always wore black jeans and a blue work shirt. His half brother, Leo, eight years his senior, had never gone more than two days without a girlfriend since the age of fifteen and would likely have laughed at him for worrying over his clothes. "If you're worried about what you're wearing, you've already lost," he guessed Leo would say. That left Sal, fanatically loyal to the Italian pants. He insisted that, despite the winter's chill, their flimsiness would lead, inevitably, to human warmth. "Mr. Ricky, with those long legs, you look so good in the Italians. She'll tear them off you. You look like Mick Jagger in them, man."

"I look like I'm on heroin?"

Sal insisted grimly, "Wear the Milan pants, Mr. Ricky. They'll make her mouth water."

To Enrique it seemed unlikely that Margaret would be impressed by anything a young man might put on, including clothing. He had found the nerve to ask for this date in the first place because she had launched, at the end of her Orphans' Dinner, into a general denunciation of his sex.

Shortly after coffee, dessert, and cigarettes had been consumed, Enrique was about to skulk away for good. He was delayed by trying to think up polite words of farewell to say to Pam, the woman he believed Margaret had picked out for him, when he heard his hostess exclaim, "Men always say they're going to call me and then they don't. Obviously I'm hideously unattractive or terrifying in some way. That's okay." She laughed with delight. "But why bother to say you're going to call if you're not?"

Phil and Sam, confident and bombastic all evening, went mute at this challenge. They gaped at azure-eyed, freckled-cheeked Margaret as if she were a fire-breathing dragon.

"Right?" she asked Lily, who immediately answered in a cheerful, ringing voice, "Nobody even bothers to promise to call me."

Margaret looked down the length of the table to Pam for her agreement, but Pam made no reply and appeared to be alarmed, as if suspecting a trap. Margaret redirected her sarcasm to the nonplussed Phil. "Who is asking you guys to call anyway? Why do you have to lie about it? Maybe I don't want you to call!"

"Maybe that's why we don't call," Phil said, snapping out of his momentary loss of debating finesse and using Margaret's own testimony against her.

"Is that why *you* didn't call?" she demanded.

A profound stillness followed this abrupt shift from the general deficiencies of males to Phil's deficiency. Phil looked at Sam, saw no help there, and stammered, "Me? When?"

"Every time I've run into you since we graduated! At the first reunion, at Mary Wells's party in Brooklyn, at the East Hampton beach party. 'I'll call you,' " Margaret imitated Phil's declamatory style of speech, MacArthur declaring he will return. "Every single time. I never asked you. I never said anything about calling or getting together. You volunteer you're going to call, and then you never call. Can you explain yourself, young man?"

Enrique ought to have felt solidarity with his sex, but he was gleeful at this turn in the conversation. He knew perfectly well why a man might make an insincere promise to call an available woman. He certainly planned to mumble something about hoping to see Pam again. To do less would be to invite a hurt or disappointed look and, especially for a Jewish son, said look from a female has a long string of bad memories attached. This was not hypocrisy. He would mean it at the time. Once free of the always compelling spell of a woman, he would decide not to telephone. But that behavior was typical of dull Pam and timid, not sexually predatory Enrique. With his trimmed beard and orator's basso, Phil was killer enough to pursue women he didn't really care for— and anyway Margaret was prime prey. And hadn't Phil called?

Enrique was confused. They had been bumping hips and playing tug-of-war with the wine opener in Margaret's tiny kitchen. Enrique felt sure Phil must have dialed Margaret's number at least once.

Sam laughed at Phil's discomfort. Margaret wheeled on him. "What about you? You also said you would call every time you ran into me—at Mindy's party, at Joel's—you said you would call and you didn't. What happened? AT&T disconnect your phone?"

"I . . . uh . . . I . . . uh . . . I," Sam stammered and then managed to chuckle at himself when the rest of the table erupted with laughter. He added in a grave tone, "I'll call you and we'll discuss it."

Everyone roared again. Margaret smiled as if that had been her plan all along, to reenliven her dinner just as it seemed to be winding down. "No, no!" she protested and slung her right leg over the arm of her chair, exactly the posture she had adopted in Enrique's apartment. "Don't call! Write me a letter. That's what's wrong with men and women today. There's no letter writing. We need to get back to the way it was in Jane Austen's day."

"But then the letters would cross or get lost and there'd be terrible confusion," Lily protested.

"Well, it's better than not getting phone calls!" Margaret argued. "Maybe it's just Cornell men," she said and looked across the table at Enrique. "Is that the problem?" she asked him. Was she warning him not to promise to call her friend Pam unless he meant to follow through? Hadn't she made that situation more awkward by airing this complaint? He glanced at Pam and discovered that her somber face was lit up with delight at what Margaret had accomplished: embarrassing the young lions. Pam studied Enrique, black eyes glistening in anticipation of what he might say.

Phil declared aloud what Enrique was feeling: "Well, now

you've totally fucked with our heads. Are we supposed to call; or write; or say we're not calling; or say we're writing but not calling?"

Margaret, instead of answering right away, reached for the pack of cigarettes resting on the table. She had to stretch, which she accomplished with the limber seductiveness of a cat. She put the Camel Light between her lips and waited for Phil to strike a match for her, a tableau that reminded Enrique, to his dismay, of the choreography of chic lovers in 1930s films. With the release of a puff of smoke, she said. "You should say you're *not* going to call"—she paused to increase the suspense—"and then you should call!"

That's what Enrique did when he left, abandoning the field ahead of all the other males. He said, "Nice to meet you," to Pam and made no other promise. He walked up to his cruelly generous hostess, who liked him enough for her friend but not enough for herself. She stood by the front door closet, offering Enrique his enormous Army coat while continuing to banter with the handsome Phil, who had trailed after her like a favorite dog on her leash. Enrique did not follow his friend Sal's advice to kiss Margaret on the lips. He offered his hand. She took it with an air of surprise as if this were a ritual she hadn't tried before. "I *won't* call you," he said. "But thank you for dinner. It was delicious."

Lily sang out from behind him, "You still have to write a thank-you note."

"No way," Enrique said, turning to the cheerful Lily and offering his hand. "I'm a professional writer," he said. "I don't put finger to typewriter unless I get paid." Lily ignored his hand, got up on tiptoe, and kissed his cheek while Margaret parried: "We gave you supper," she said. "And you didn't have to sing for it."

Enrique left feeling ungracious and hopeless. But while he walked home in the cold—passing the bare trees of Ninth Street, the sealed garbage bags of the closed shops on University Place, the strewn garbage of Eighth—he decided that, despite all the discouraging signs, he would call Margaret. Her bold complaints about men had given him a fatalistic hope that, although he was likely to fail, it was a failure not to be ashamed of. He had published two autobiographical novels, and exposed many embarrassing truths about himself. He had been derided in newspapers and magazines and by readers face-to-face. And since Margaret had mocked a man she obviously liked—the confident Phil—what further harm could it cause him to be ridiculed?

That doomed courage carried him through dialing the phone and asking her out. Now that the hour of their date approached, his nerves failed again. His fashion decision was decided by his mood over his prospect for success with Margaret. As it darkened, so did his pants. He chose the black Levi's and a black turtleneck. He would have added a black coat, but he was stuck with the combat green of the Army Navy store.

Margaret buzzed his intercom at 7:43 to signal he should come downstairs as arranged and walk to the restaurant. He had been skeptical of this arrangement. She had declined his offer to pick her up as if that were silly. A bad romantic sign, he decided. It smacked of friendship, although geographically her plan made sense since they had agreed to eat at the Buffalo Roadhouse near Sheridan Square and Enrique's building was on the way. She was supposed to have arrived thirteen minutes earlier. Enrique had read many a novel explaining that minor tardiness by a woman was to be expected; nevertheless, he had assumed by 7:35 that she was standing him up and so he experienced the buzzing, when it came, as a dramatic reversal of fortune.

He ran down the five flights. A sheen of sweat appeared on his brow in spite of the winter air. He greeted her awkwardly. He attempted to dodge the issue of whether to kiss her, even chastely on the cheek, by heading toward their destination. "Let's move quickly before Bernard sees us," he said to cover the absence of a proper hello.

"We don't want Bernard to see us?" Margaret asked, stepping lively beside him. Despite her ten-inch deficit in comparison to Enrique's height, her gait more than outstripped his within a few paces. He found himself hurrying up to her bubble of a goose-down jacket, but not before noticing how skin-close her jeans fit over her appealing behind. That did nothing to slow down the pace of his heart, still pounding from his rapid descent. He said something he hadn't planned to, and wouldn't have said if he had thought about it, but the impulse to disclose everything about himself whether or not it might prove embarrassing was charac-teristic of him. "Bernard doesn't approve of me dating you." He glanced over and saw that her round blue eyes were more saucer-shaped than usual, and her lips were parted in amazement. "He refused to give me your phone number." That brought her to a complete halt. They had reached the corner of Eighth and Sixth anyway, but the light was green. She made no move to cross.

"What!" she said with an emphasis that managed to be at once outraged and amused.

"He said you were out of my league." Enrique broke into a grin, "Maybe that's why more men don't call you. Bernard won't let them."

Margaret protested. "You're kidding! That's hysterical." She paused, seemed to review the information, and insisted, "You've got to be kidding."

"Nope. He totally fucking refused. He was adamant. I had to look you up in the phone book. Thank God I knew where you lived or I wouldn't have figured out which of the two dozen M. Cohens you are." He gestured at the now red light. "Should we walk down another block and then over?" While they did, he con-tinued on his reckless course of openness. "Obviously Bernard's got a thing for you and he's scared to make a move. Maybe that's what's going on with all those guys you complain about. You intimidate them."

"Me?" she asked with what sounded like genuine surprise.

"Yeah, you're pretty intimidating."

"You don't seem intimidated at all," she parried.

They had reached Waverly and Sixth. The light was red. He turned to look her full in the face. "Oh, I am. I'm terrified of you. It would be so much easier to pretend I wasn't interested in you at all than to have to act like I'm totally cool with us just hanging out. That's what's going on with Bernard and Phil and Sam. That's why they don't call—they don't want to risk getting rejected. So, in the excitement of being with you, they say they're going to call, realize that would mean finding out whether they have a shot with you, and then chicken out. " Articulating the madness of his sex and acutely aware of his own crazy standards of status (what lunacy had provoked him, even for a second, to consider the Italian pants?), he relaxed. He watched those depthless ocean blues soak up his restless thoughts.

The light turned green. She didn't budge. He waited patiently because he could tell that, unlike almost everyone he knew, Margaret was digesting what he had said without at the same time deciding what she ought to answer. He had thought of her as another verbal jouster, but now he understood her silences during the long night of conversation with Bernard weren't breakdowns of her inability to come up with a witty reply. He imagined he could follow, like a road on a map, the progress of her careful dissection. She was discarding the flattery and possible exaggeration in his words. How could he know if Sam was attracted to her? Perhaps Phil was a flirt and thought her beneath serious pursuit. Stingy Bernard might want to keep Enrique from obtaining a pretty and vivacious girlfriend, whether or not he desired Margaret for himself. By the time the green light had turned to flashing red, she had deconstructed his fragmentation bomb of flattery, confession, seduction, and surrender. "Bernard? Sam? No, there's something else going in the heads of those crazy boys," she insisted. "And you're not terrified of me," she said with a sly smile, his explosive defused, and stepped onto Sixth Avenue, hurrying across.

Her meticulous answer unmanned him all over again. He had momentarily mastered his nerves by confessing his intentions, but the anxious currents of longing and fear returned in full force. He was too insecure and excited to put words to his confusion. If he could have, he would have asked what she could want of him other than admiration and desire. What else could he provide?

He hurried across Sixth Avenue and continued west beside her in silence, or rather in a state of stymied speech. He considered several replies, the first being "I *am* terrified of you," but terror didn't appear to describe his behavior, since, rather than flee, he was doing everything he could to remain in her presence. He could insist that Phil, Bernard, and Sam *did* want her, but why persuade her that better men—well, at least two of them were superior—wanted her? What if she ended up agreeing? On the other hand, to agree with her assertion that his rivals weren't rivals, that they weren't attracted to her, seemed unlikely to be a pleasing turn in the conversation for Margaret.

She did seem pleased to have baffled him into silence. She glanced over to him every few steps, and appeared to allow herself a smug nod of congratulations. He tried to smile back with an air of self-confidence, but he felt his chin wobble. As they arrived at the messy three-way intersection of Waverly, Grove, and Christopher, just east of Seventh Avenue, he thought she made a feint toward Christopher and said, "No, this way is faster," nodding in the direction of Grove.

She frowned. "Really?" she said. "I think that way's more direct."

During their predawn breakfast at Sandolino's, he'd pretended to agree with her about something he knew she was wrong about, the existence of two schools called P.S. 173. This time he did not, although he was still reluctant to offend, and he sensed she was vain about her sense of direction. He shook his head in a gentle but firm no, rather than argue out loud.

She studied the disputed choices. After a shrug, which seemed to concede that he must be right, she stepped anyway in the wrong direction toward Christopher Street. This silent and absolute contradiction, compelling him to go her way, or go his way alone, was so forceful and graceful in its self-assurance that, rather than be angry, he felt all the more that she was too much woman for him. He followed, abashed, and when they reached Seventh and had to turn downtown (making it obvious that Grove was the superior route), he waited for Margaret to admit that she had been mistaken.

When she didn't immediately, he couldn't stop himself from looking up at the street sign and then down at her. She understood because she said with a chuckle, an I-told-you-so laugh, "Grove *was* more direct." That baffled him all the more. Why was she so pleased about being proved wrong?

He grinned back—how could he not?—at her cheerful admission of error. "Yes," he said and added, to be gracious about her mistake, "Not much of a difference, but a little closer."

She said with a musical lilt, "Oh, it was definitely closer. That's the way we should have walked."

Since she wanted to be so harsh on herself, he shrugged and agreed. "I guess in December every shortcut counts."

For some reason that he couldn't fathom, his remark seemed to impress her. She moved closer, her black goose-down shoulder whooshing against his Army green. Despite the bulk of material between their flesh, somehow a pleasurable sensation of touch was conducted to his skin. She returned to her cheerful chattering. "I don't know, it's crazy, but Cornell wrecked me. I hate the cold now. Before I went to college, I don't remember it bothering me so much. But now? Soon as it's below fifty, brrr," she said and pretended to shiver, once again brushing against him. He knew that James Bond would take her mock-discomfort as a cue for action, put his arm around her and pretend to keep her warm. All Enrique could manage was a maneuver whose intent was obscure even to himself. He tilted toward her so their jackets collided more often for the half a block that remained until they reached the Buffalo Roadhouse entrance.

When they walked in, he felt excited and wary, as if they were being announced at a Parisian ball in a Balzac novel, being judged as a couple by a sophisticated and critical elite. He was proud to have Margaret as his date. Indeed he half-expected the hostess, whom he thought much less beautiful than Margaret, to demand what the hell she was doing with a scrawny goofball like him. His self-consciousness didn't abate, although a quick scan of their neighbors told him that the clientele of a moderately priced restaurant in bankrupt New York City during the week between Christmas and New Year's, when all the chic and wealthy were in the Caribbean, could hardly be considered the equal of Balzac's Parisian society at the height of the season. But that didn't puncture his thrill at being with her, his intense relief that this wasn't another dreary night eating with Bernard at a bargain Italian pasta paradise, or grabbing burgers with a group before seeing a movie, or sampling some new East Village vegetarian dump with Sal and his girlfriend. He was especially glad not to be hunched over Chinese take-out watching the Knicks lose another game.

He realized, thanks to the amazing mixture of comfort and

excitement thrumming through body and soul, that he had been living with a terrible ache which wasn't, as he had assumed, merely sexual. His renovated fifth-floor walkup didn't qualify as an unheated garret, his skinny frame was due more to a diet of Camels and coffee than to starvation—and even at his most caffeinated he doubted that the novel he had coming out was going to be ranked alongside *The Red and the Black*—but he did share the acute loneliness of the young, ambitious heroes of *A Sentimental Education, Lost Illusions,* and *L'Oeuvre*. He had the same hungry heart as those soulful protagonists, ravenous for affection, understanding, and love. This lively girl, with her amused lips and bejeweled eyes, eager to listen to what he had to say, was just a pleasure to be with, so much so that he almost wished his obligation as a male to seduce her weren't part of the bargain. Especially because, while he watched her sidle out of her goose-down bubble, freeing her elegant, thin shoulders, and while he heard her tell the waiter that she wanted a dry vermouth—a drink which sounded grown-up and sophisticated—observing her ease and confidence out in the world, he thought: She *is* out of my fucking league.

"I'll have—" he began and realized he had no idea what to have. Vaguely he thought he should order a scotch or maybe a beer, although that seemed too boys-night-out. Was he supposed to order wine? He knew only from books how men were supposed to behave on a date and said behavior existed in a parallel universe which seemed to Enrique to have nothing to do with him and Margaret.

"You don't have to have a drink," she said, reading his mind imprecisely but offering the right help anyway. She laughed. "I don't mind if you stay sober."

He laughed, too; something about the word *sober,* especially as applied to him, seemed absurd. "I'll have a Coke," he said, and the waiter departed with what Enrique decided was a disgusted look.

Having lured him to an honest request, Margaret seemed appalled at the result. "A Coke!" she repeated.

"Okay," Enrique said in good humor, "I'll have a real drink."

"No, no. I'm just jealous you're having a real Coke. I haven't had one since college." She added pensively, "Of course, you're still young enough to be in college."

That seemed to be a worry. He didn't consider the three-and-a-half-year gap between their ages significant at all. Margaret was six years younger than Sylvie. "But remember I left home at sixteen. I've been out in the world as long as you," he said. He knew this meant nothing. The facts were on his side; but Margaret was clearly more grown-up, at ease and adult.

"I can't believe you left home so young," she said with sympathy in her voice, rather than the typical approbation his generation awarded him for his rebellious statistics: high school dropout, leaving home, shacking up with a twenty-five-year-old. "That's cool," most of the males said. "Wow. Good for you," said young women. Margaret went further to show her concern. "Was that okay? I wish I could have. By the time I was sixteen my mother was driving me so crazy I could barely stand the sound of her voice. But it must have also been hard."

This subject could easily have become a conversational land mine. How should he recount the story of his three-plus-year relationship with Sylvie? In his heart of hearts, Enrique believed he had been the underlying cause of its failure. He could make himself out to be entirely the victim with the revelation that Sylvie had ended the relationship by cheating on him, but that hardly seemed a more flattering alternative. Besides, he knew that wasn't the true cause of their breakup. He had been so angry and sullen and unpleasant to be with for the last year and a half they were together, that it would have been understandable if Sylvie had beaten him to death with a frying pan. Seeking love and orgasm in another's arms was a relatively mild reaction. It was hard to say which version he was more embarrassed by, although anything that suggested he was sexually inadequate—at least on a first date—seemed a poor strategic move. "What was hard," he said to evade the whole subject, "was having to earn a living by writing a second novel."

"I bet!" Margaret said, with admiration, as if he were a veteran of a war. Enrique felt ashamed that he had elicited false sympathy with his cover story, but he had inadvertently told her the truth, albeit a truth that he didn't understand until years later. The burden of his situation had been not only the work itself, which was more than enough to overwhelm him, but the additional pressure of money, and the reality that at seventeen he had taken on a career the success of which depended entirely on him, on self-generated work whose value to the world would be created, or not, entirely by his unreliable talent. Margaret seemed to understand much more readily than Enrique how arduous was the path he had taken: "Having to be so self-disciplined as a teenager. And writing novels seems so hard anyway. At any age."

"Yeah, it's hard." Feeling that he was being deceptive, he changed the subject. "So how did you meet Bernard exactly? He talks a lot about you, but he never has any details about anything."

"I know," she said. "Bernard is so weird about his friends. He compartmentalizes all his little worlds." She squared the delicate fingers of each hand into a faux box and then moved them apart to illustrate. Her wrists were barely wider than a matchbook. "You're the first of his non-Cornell friends he's ever introduced me to."

Their drinks arrived, Enrique's Coke accompanied by a straw. He felt all the more like a child. Perhaps that, or fear of returning to the worrisome topic of his previous relationship, provoked a long satire of Bernard. Enrique recounted how he had challenged

Bernard into introducing them by pretending that he believed Margaret didn't exist. The story delighted her. She was pleased to be the subject of so much attention between the two men. She was also—he found this reassuring and touching—genuinely surprised. By the time Enrique had finished the entire tale, from the coffee shop quarrel through Bernard's refusal to give out her number, they had eaten their salads and started on their main courses. "Doesn't make sense," Margaret said, cutting into an unappetizing-looking calf's liver. "Why did he take me to your apartment if he was going to get so crazy about you calling me?"

"I've thought about it. I've had plenty of time to think about it, and there are lots of possibilities, but the one I decided on is: he didn't expect you to like me."

Margaret frowned hard. "No," she said, dismissing his conclusion. Enrique couldn't suppress a smile of self-satisfaction at this tacit admission that she liked him. That wasn't the end of this pleasant surprise. She added, "He introduced me to you because he's proud of you."

"What?" Enrique was startled. He was so accustomed to resenting Bernard, bristling at his literary slights, and seething with frustration at their arguments about the merits of realism that the notion that Bernard admired Enrique enough to want to display him as a friend was a shock. That it was a flattering shock intensified its electricity.

"You're a real novelist. You're published. And your parents are both writers. Bernard's proud he knows you. It proves to all of us skeptics from Cornell that he's in the game. You take him seriously. You're for real. He brought me over to show you off."

Enrique looked away from her big eyes, sparkling in the flickering yellow light of the table's candle, to give himself a rest from their spell. Her words were a balm to his raw and worried ego. If he had been challenged, he would have guessed that out of earshot

Bernard disparaged him. He didn't appreciate how bruised he was by the world's reaction to his precocity, how wary he was of his uncertain future. He was three months away from the publication of his third novel, and he knew its prospects were poor. The first printing was only five thousand copies, there was no ad budget, and his editor no longer took his phone calls because she had handed off the routine tasks of his novel's publication to a young associate editor, a sign that he wasn't a star. Most mornings he woke up with intense stomach pain, as if a steel rod had pierced his abdomen. It often took more than an hour of stretching, rubbing, trying to relax his rigid musculature before the pain subsided. He had told no one of that physical symptom of anxiety. He had told none of his friends that he felt no one was on his side, that every writer, reviewer, editor, bookstore owner, and reader was rooting for him to fail, to restore to the world the presumption it cherished, that being a novelist was much harder than it appeared to have been for Enrique. How could he get them to forgive him for his facility? Explain that almost nothing else came easily, that writing his autobiographical and apparently second-rate novels took all his energy, and all the hours of his days? He felt the world was pushing him out the sole door he had managed to open, evicting him from the only home that could keep him safe on the perilous earth.

"Hello?" Margaret had leaned closer and was beaming at him cheerfully. "Where did you go?"

He reclaimed himself, or rather the self she had spoken of, when his eyes returned to the merry light of hers. He smiled as if he were master of the situation. "Now you're teasing me."

"Teasing? About what?"

"Bernard? Proud of me?"

She shrugged her thin, elegant shoulders. "He should be proud of you. The rest of Bernard's friends are tedious and grungy political bores or they're still college boys living with roommates, not having real jobs, trying to figure out who they are. You're a real grown-up. You have a career. You lived with a woman for three years. You're a man."

Enrique fell back against the hard wood of his chair. Three things were suddenly obvious to him. One, he had a real chance to make this sweet, smart, optimistic, and beautiful young woman his. Two, Margaret's view of him, a self-confident artist and a mature man who had been out in the world, was soothing and delightful and woefully inaccurate. And finally that he longed, yes, more than he longed to be in her arms, to become the phantom man reflected in her velvet eyes.

chapter ten

The Perfect Gift

S TANDING ON THE grave of a wealthy New Yorker, Enrique realized he would have to make this aesthetic choice for Margaret, the most permanent of all, without consulting her. He had learned through bitter experience that it was foolhardy to attempt to figure out what her preference would be all on his own. It would be romantic to say that he had made no decisions in the past twenty-nine years without his wife's counsel, but that would be a silly exaggeration. He usually asked her opinion of his writing and his business dealings but couldn't in the middle of a meeting or under deadline pressure, and sometimes didn't want to. And there had been other situations when to ask his wife what he ought to do would have been cruel. But this selection required the benefit of her taste. He had no clue as to whether she would prefer to be on the western or eastern edge of a nineteenth-century burial lot, where room for new graves had been created by eliminating stone pathways between elaborate headstones that had been fashioned for the wealthy families of Henry James's day. He wanted to ask Margaret whether she would choose to lie in an open patch of ground between two leafy maples or under the boughs of an ancient oak.

There was no time to take photos—although Lily was taking them anyway—return to Margaret's deathbed to show them to her, learn her preference, and then double back to sign the documents that would give Enrique title to the grave of her choice. He was physically there already, prepared to pay for one of two lots left among the old, graceful headstones. Other potential buyers were wandering even now among the dead. Her wish to be in the older burial grounds was more important than the choice between sun and shade. Conserving his own time was even more important. Buying a grave entailed taking deed to a specific narrow and deep section of land. Margaret had roughly eleven days to live. Getting the deed processed without wasting those precious hours by coming and going between Manhattan and Green-Wood Cemetery in Brooklyn meant deciding today which site was more to her liking without her help—a lonely foretaste of his approaching loss.

As he walked back and forth between the two alternatives, he was disgusted by his dithering. He hadn't felt this queasy worry that he would fail to make a pleasing choice for Margaret in many years, and he wasn't happy to feel incompetent once again. When Margaret first fell ill, their roles had changed in this respect. During the early years of their marriage, she had relieved him of most decision making. As a young man, he complained that she had arrogated it with the brutality of a colonial imperialist. Nothing purchased for their home, or the choice of schools for their sons, or whom they saw socially, or where they had dinner, or what movie or play they went to—nothing, including his own wardrobe if he were honest—was decided by him. All negotiations with the world were handled by his cheerfully aggressive, bright-eyed, no-nonsense deal maker of a wife—except for his own contracts as a novelist and screenwriter. And, even on those exalted documents, she was consulted.

Occasionally Margaret would use Enrique to handle the world, such as when the movers tried to quit before getting their possessions into the new apartment in one day. They announced at six o'clock that they would come back tomorrow, leaving the young married couple and their new baby with only a mattress and a crib for their first night. Margaret sent Enrique out to the truck to confront the foreman and strong-arm his tattooed biceps into finishing the job. Enrique was to come home with their carving knife or on it. But that wasn't a surrender of leadership; she was sending in her muscle.

Once she was ill, however, managing the outside world became his exclusive task, and they both discovered that he was more than competent at negotiating the byzantine bureaucracies of hospitals and health insurance. Enrique knew that he had won her trust when her cancer went into remission. During those happy ten months, among the most loving and contented of their marriage, she could have resumed her role as commander in chief, yet she continued to allow him to handle her medical affairs. His victory was not total—Margaret's trust extended only to her health care. Evidently matters of life and death were trivial compared to home decorations, or what Enrique should wear to a dinner party, because she continued her reign over those choices. Still, he had gained ground in all areas. She gradually began to consult him on domestic decisions. In a particularly flattering transfer of control, she asked him to make the final judgment between green and white or brown and white as a combination for a new set of towels. That might have seemed to an outsider like a comically small grant of suffrage, but for Enrique it was a stunning gain of his civil right to aesthetic decision making. Her glasnost gave him the courage to strike out on his own. Fifteen months ago he had vowed to select a birthday present for Margaret all by himself.

For years he had tried to buy her a thrilling and gratifying birthday gift while relying on his own taste, and he had failed miserably each time. The first year they lived together he tried to copy his father's gambit of buying jewelry for Enrique's mother, and also of purchasing gifts well beyond his means. But he did not share his father's self-confidence in his own feeling for jewelry, so he fell back on his faith in costly brand names and went uptown to Tiffany's.

At that landmark he felt profoundly out of place with his long hair, black jeans, and scuffed white sneakers. He had trouble getting the attention of the seemingly friendly young woman his age behind the earring counter. Her wares attracted him, in particular a small star-shaped pair with single diamonds set in their centers that Enrique judged would make a perfect fit on Margaret's delicate ears. The Tiffany employee beamed at suited males and older women, including one so hunched over by osteoporosis that she seemed about to pitch into the glass top. With good cheer and energy, the salesgirl pulled out trays of glittering items for those buyers, and greeted two customers who had arrived after Enrique. She stared past his long hair and pale, anxious face as if he were invisible, until there was no one else in front of her. By then he was dripping sweat into his wrinkled work shirt. She frowned and said, "Can I help you?" in a doomed voice as if that were an obvious impossibility.

She was correct in her snobbish assumption. It turned out the earrings he had fallen in love with were forty-three hundred dollars, more than half the advance for his third novel. When he flinched at the price, her withering sneer propelled him back onto Fifth Avenue without further inquiries.

He wandered into the Diamond District, more at home with an Orthodox Jew for a salesman who recognized that a desperate young man hunting for a gift to please a girl was an ideal buyer on whom to unload something cheap and still overpriced. The fast-talking, devout man persuaded Enrique to buy a pair of earrings after an explanation of the pricing logic of the Four C's of diamond grading, which was far more dazzling than anything in his inventory. He claimed that he could offer Enrique a bargain on the diamond earrings in question because they were graded in color, consistency, carats, and cut—the Four C's—right below where the valuation spikes. He assured Enrique that the difference in this lower grade, one down from where prices triple, was too subtle to be discerned by anyone, including the diamond experts who surrounded them at that very moment. The black arms of his suit went up, exposing the salesman's white sleeves and starched cuffs, as he embraced the whole of the district. "No one!" he promised. "Not a soul can tell the difference! Go! Ask them. Anyone can—I give you your money back."

These bargain earrings were much cheaper than the pair at Tiffany's, but at eight hundred dollars they were still a painful stretch of Enrique's wallet. So when he offered his present with trembling and proud hands to his beloved, he was staggered both by his longing to impress her and by the hefty percentage of his annual income they represented.

Margaret tried. She strained to force her mouth into a smile, and did succeed in producing a sort of grimace of delight. Although a credulous consumer, Enrique was a skeptical lover, and he demanded to know what was wrong. He soon regretted his desire for the truth. He had to stop her from completing her painful recitation of the many deficiencies of the earrings. He did learn a crucial hint for future presents: Margaret did not consider diamonds to be a girl's best friend; in fact, she disliked them.

"Didn't you notice I don't have any?" she asked in an amazed tone, as if making an inventory of your girlfriend's jewelry was an essential act of survival.

She tried to be gentle. She kissed and reassured him and thanked him for the thought, but as time passed he felt her to be sarcastic and unfeeling about his gift. Two months later he overheard her joking about the earrings with Lily, and he burned with shame. His humiliation wasn't improved when he noticed that she never wore them, not a single time. He resented her rejection of his present, an embittered feeling that he stored in a secret box for bruises of his pride where they never healed, turning darker and more hideous. He grew more determined to succeed.

For the next birthday he avoided jewelry. Copying another of his father's ploys in gift giving, he bought her an expensive tool to encourage her as an artist. He admired her photographs, as did others, especially her father the economist. Leonard told Enrique that he had stopped taking photos as soon as he saw Margaret's snapshots of her high school graduation trip to Europe, using Leonard's hand-me-down point-and-shoot. Until then he hadn't considered photography an art, since with automatic cameras and unlimited film, sooner or later a monkey would capture an arresting image. Margaret's first roll of thirty-six pictures immediately refuted his assumption. More than half were beautifully composed and intriguing. Her facility convinced him that photography was indeed an art and that Margaret had "an eye." That her work overcame her practical father's resistance was enough for Enrique to want to encourage her, but there was also her enthusiasm for photography. When they first met, he discovered that she had recently completed a course in developing and printing. Her interest had continued during their first year of living together. Margaret spent her leisure time (she was freelancing as a graphic artist) wandering with a 35-millimeter Olympus in shrinking Little Italy, burgeoning SoHo, the messy meat market, and dilapidated Union Square, capturing New York's bankrupt 1970s streets on the cusp of gentrification.

Enrique once again trusted an Orthodox Jew, this time at B & H camera store, where Margaret bought her supplies. He discussed what to get her at length with a young salesman who looked older because of his full beard. His chubby, pasty cheeks wobbled as he suggested what would be an exciting camera for a serious photographer. The answer appealed to Enrique, a Rolleiflex from the 1950s. The dimpled black metal box had the cool retro look and heft of World War II, a romantic time in Enrique's imagination. The devout salesman explained that "Rolleis" had fine-ground lenses, which could yield the kind of detail an art photographer longs for; and since the camera was no longer being manufactured, a lens with this particular quality could only be obtained by purchasing one secondhand.

It sounded to him like bullshit. Cameras were modern technology. In Enrique's experience, technology always progressed. He almost didn't believe the claims of the black-hatted man, who looked, with his payess, suit, and apron also to be from World War II—albeit, *The Sorrow and the Pity* rather than *The Great Escape.* Right up until Margaret opened the lumpy package Enrique had fashioned with happy-birthday wrapping paper, he worried that she would laugh at him for being gullible.

But no. He had not been fooled. No ridicule this time, no complaint about a failure to know her taste. There was a gratifying, eyes-wide look of pleased astonishment, followed by "Oh my God, a Rollei!" as if it were a treasure that she had coveted with such intensity she had thought it wise to keep her craving secret. "Puff!" she exclaimed, using her recently coined nickname for him. "You shouldn't have!" she cried out, eyes glistening, and hopped to her feet, rising on tiptoe to kiss him with wet, cool lips.

Triumph. A reversal of the previous year's humiliation. For a few days Enrique was suffused with a feeling of manly success, punctured only by the frown he got when he asked Margaret why she was going out to take pictures with her Olympus and not the fabulous Rollei. "Oh, I have to learn how to use it," she said with a harassed air, like a student who has a difficult paper to write. Over the following weeks he kept after her. Had she signed up for the course she said she needed to take to learn how to use the Rollei properly? Did she want Enrique to buy the tripod she had told him people require with such a camera? Had she gotten the lens cleaned, since she claimed B & H had sold it without first doing a proper job of restoration? Could he take it back to the salesman and complain? And so on, all asked with the intent to be encouraging, but she seemed to experience as nagging.

To Enrique's puzzlement and annoyance and eventually keen hurt, Margaret never used the thrilling Rollei, not once. "It's too much of a pain," she said when he pushed too hard, eight months after her birthday. "I have to learn and buy all this stuff—also the lens needs to be cleaned. Ugh," she groaned. "I'd rather just go out with my little point-and-shoot." By then they were married. Presumably no question of her commitment to Enrique existed anymore, but the rejection renewed with an intensity that he kept hidden from her the question of whether his love provided anything besides the loyalty and comfort of a pet. What use was he to her? he wondered. Why should she love him? Was there anything more to her feelings for him than a biological and bourgeois reflex?

He joked to her, not long after the Rollei disappointment, that he was the perfect husband for a nice Jewish girl who wanted to escape her cookie-cutter Queens home—an olive-skinned man with a Spanish name whom she could bring to Passover and announce with delight, "He's Jewish, Ma!" Her nod of acknowl-edgment and the trill of her cynical laugh echoed down to him through the years. He had a novelist's belief in the telling nature of such moments, and for a long time he couldn't hear the music of her feelings for him without a clanging bell of satire.

He tried a different approach once they were an old married couple of one year. He convinced himself that romance and art were a mistake with so practical and hedonistic a girl. He had overheard her several times long for a blender after she had bro-ken the glass container and then lost the motorized base of the one she owned. He bought a shiny new Osterizer for her, confident this time that it was something she liked and used. What seemed cer-tain to succeed was the most disastrous of all his gifts. "A blender?" she blurted. "A b-blender?" she repeated, making her appalled horror comic by pronouncing the *bl* of *blender* as if she were blowing into a tuba. "You gave me a b-blender for my birth-day. Aren't you Mr. Romantic? What am I getting next year? A waffle iron?"

She repeated this witty sally to Lily, who also thought his pres-ent hilarious enough to recount to others at a dinner in front of Enrique. He smiled with sheepish good humor but seethed with shame, and wanted to strangle both girls until they turned as pur-ple as one of the fresh fruit drinks Margaret liked to b-blend in his despised gift.

The following year he made another heroic attempt to give her something she would never buy for herself. She had gone back to painting during their vacation at his parents' house in Maine. She was delighted by how Enrique's father raved over her two land-scapes of the rocky coast. When they returned to the city, she kept up her new energy for painting, renting a space with a woman she'd met in a drawing class. During a visit to their one-room stu-dio high above Union Square, he noticed that she was using two stacked cardboard boxes with one of the flaps up as her easel. How could alleviating this deficit fail to delight? He walked to Utrecht on Fourth Avenue, where Margaret bought her art supplies, and purchased a wood easel—expensive but in no way elaborate, a useful and handsome present.

He had a premonition of failure as he brought in his gift from a hiding place in the fire stairs. He heard the whisper from a more insightful Enrique, ignored in the basement of his unconscious, that utility of any sort wouldn't please her. Lily, and her then probably gay boyfriend, were toasting Margaret with champagne over Canadian caviar. All three looked at the noise of his entrance with effervescent expectation. He had a view of the trio's reactions while he stood there with the folded-up easel cradled against his shoulder like a toy wooden rifle. Lily and her friend cheered and raised their glasses as a salute to his thoughtful magnanimity. Margaret's face fell with a look of rejection, as if he'd walked in with another girl on his arm.

Her reaction remained a mystery for years. Her contemporaneous explanation that the easel was "too practical" was not the truth. When they shared confidences about their marriage on their twentieth anniversary, she finally explained.

Although the riddle had been solved, and although he knew her response had nothing to do with his taste, standing now on what could become her grave, and what he supposed would be his grave as well, he still had little faith that he could pick the spot where she would prefer to rest. Perhaps that didn't matter. The elegant plots, no matter whether he chose the maples or the oak as neighbors, allowed three burials stacked one on top of the other. He was choosing their last stop together. Since he would be visiting for a while before joining her, it might as well reflect his taste more than hers. And if they happened to be the same, well, that was the grace of marriage.

He walked back toward the maples once more. "Can't decide?" the always somewhat anxious and loving Lily asked. "I kind of prefer this view," she offered, standing so that she was facing the tomb of Peter Cooper in the distance, a gleaming white temple among the leafy trees of June. She asked her not-gay husband of twenty years, "What do you think?"

"This is a great view," Paul said and put his arm around her. "And we like Peter Cooper, don't we?" They clung to each other and regarded Enrique with gentleness in their postures: chins rueful, shoulders relaxed, heads tilted quizzically.

"You get that view from both of them, though," Enrique pointed out. "Just depends where you stand."

"Oh," Lily sighed, whacking the side of her head. "Duh . . ." Her usually merry brown eyes were big and worried these days, like a child's on the first day in a new school. Her parents were both alive; no one close to her had yet died, and, in a way that only lifelong women friends can be, Margaret was closer to her than anyone. "I don't know," the always opinionated Lily said. "I can't decide. I can't help you."

"You're here. That's a help," he said and meant it. He walked back to the maple. He tried to clear his head of worry and consider which spot was more lovely.

He had taken his time on Margaret's birthday fifteen months ago to see if he could, at last, select a present she would cherish without her help. It had been only a few weeks before they had learned that her cancer had metastasized, that, although they could try to slow the disease, she was incurable. For years their routine on her birthday had been set, a negotiated settlement of their mutual neuroses. He would accompany Margaret to a shop where she had seen something she desired: a hat, a bracelet, a dress, a pair of shoes, and, once, a coffee table. Enrique would go through the charade of purchasing and wrapping what she had picked out for herself and offer it as if it were his idea. "You have such good taste," she would say with enough conviction that unwitting friends sometimes believed her and commented how lucky she was to have so discerning a husband. Margaret never failed to kiss him in front of the crowd, genuinely delighted and satisfied by her own choice. More dismaying than her self-gratification was that he never found her selections predictable. The lesson he learned was that satisfying his wife wasn't something you could memorize out of a chapter in *Our Bodies, Ourselves.* Nevertheless, no matter how daunting the task, her illness and her brave endurance of suffering made him want to try one last time to find her heart's content.

He decided not to devote only a few hours to hunt for a gift. He gave himself a month. He settled on earrings once again. He loved her small and faultless ears, and when he was allowed to nestle behind them, tasting lightly with the tip of his tongue the crevices there, she would shiver with pleasure. He wanted to adorn them.

He went back several times a week to browse three antique jewelry stores in their neighborhood. Margaret had bought gifts in those shops for herself and for her friends. He had learned that she favored antique silver, nearly pewter in color, over shiny gold, and she preferred a single stone set in a design that was intricate but small in scale. By the second week, the shopkeepers had gotten used to his hour-long visits. One discerning saleswoman noticed the general qualities of his interest and pointed out a pair of antique silver earrings. They dated from the 1880s, she claimed. There was provenance to prove it, but that didn't matter to him since they had all the elements he wanted and one that he feared: surrounding the single ruby at the center of each earring was a circle of little diamonds. More like sparkling stars than diamonds, but diamonds nevertheless. When she said, "What about these? I think they're so delicate and lovely," he answered, "Yes, so do I. But they're diamonds. My wife doesn't like diamonds."

She laughed. "Your wife doesn't like diamonds," she repeated as if he were joking.

"No," Enrique said. "She doesn't." He studied them anyway. He brought them kissing close. But for the diamond halos surrounding the warm red rubies, they were her taste. He didn't buy them. He returned to the store twice the following week, tempted more each time. They were the earrings he wanted to buy for her, but he was afraid it was another mistake, another example of his stubborn inability to see the world through her eyes.

In the same store there were similar earrings with no diamonds, but they had a less appealing design encompassing their single red stones. The pair he wanted to buy didn't need their diamonds as far as he was concerned. They were attractive because of the miniature work, a careful weaving of an ivy pattern of antique silver so finely wrought that they looked organic. He knew Margaret would like the design. But the diamonds? Did that matter anymore? If she didn't care for them, so what? So much had happened in the twenty-nine years since his first disastrous gift. So many illusions dispelled. So much strength revealed. She had said things to him as cruel as anyone would ever say; and he had been crueler to her more than once. They had sworn love; they had endured hate. As children they had made children, one of whom was already a man, the other becoming one too fast. By now she must know that he knew that she didn't like diamonds. If he bought them anyway, because he felt sure the rest of the design was to her taste, he had to believe she would understand that he had meant well. She might not like them, she might never wear them (there wasn't much time left anyway to wear them) but she couldn't be offended if, once again, consistent with their entire marriage, he had failed to pick out the right present on his own. They had different tastes, and sometimes wanted different things from each other, and yet they had lived a happy life together—he had to believe she would understand.

He wrapped them in their velvet box in the plain blue tissue paper she favored, and bought her a funny card, the kind she liked to buy for him. He was more earnest than she, so below the jokey line he wrote a heartfelt note: "For the only jewel in my life."

"Uh-oh," she said when she read the note. She looked up at him, dabbing at her nose to make sure it wasn't running from the new chemo protocol. She smiled wanly. "Puff, you didn't spend a lot? It'd be ridiculous to spend a lot on me now."

"Don't say that," he said.

"Well," she said, opening the small box, ever the thrifty Queens girl, "I can leave it to Gregory or Max to give to their wives . . ." She trailed off when the earrings were revealed. She regarded them for a moment as if she didn't recognize what they were. She looked up at him, lips parting slightly, gazing at him with deep puzzlement.

Here it comes, he braced himself, her outrage that I haven't remembered she hates diamonds.

"Endy . . . ," she whispered. She removed the earrings, holding them in her palms long enough to say, "They're beautiful." She ignored him. No kiss, no protest about money, none of the usual dodges. She walked over to the mirror she had hung in the front hall, which she used for a last look before braving the outdoors. She put them on with an intent air of concentration and then stared at herself, in her wig, her eyebrows painted on, turning this way and that. She repeated quietly, "They're beautiful." Two sets of tiny clear tears rolled down each cheek, but they were probably chemo tears, he told himself. He was suspicious of this apparent success, afraid to accept her congratulations. She loved and needed him with such intensity since her diagnosis that he feared she had become too easy on him.

He walked over to say, "I'm not fishing for a compliment, but I made sure that I could take them back, so if you're not happy just say so." To his surprise, she continued to ignore him. She kept her moist eyes fixed on her image in the mirror, again rotating her head this way and that to view each one. He continued to make it easier for her to reject his gift by adding, "There's another pair of earrings there without diam——"

"These are beautiful!" she snapped, annoyed. She didn't look his way. She stepped back, pressing down on her wig to adjust it. "Puff, I love them," she said ardently, wheeling and sliding into his arms. She rose on her toes and pressed her lips to his, whispering between a pair of kisses, "They're perfect. Just perfect."

"Even though they have diamonds?" he whispered back and waited through two more kisses before she said, "I love them. Thank you."

He didn't believe her until she wore them for an entire week, except for the afternoon they went uptown for her PET scan. She even took the trouble to explain that omission, saying she was afraid they would somehow get lost.

Enrique still wasn't absolutely sure that this was a victory he could have won without the advantage of her illness. But he reminded himself that he had at last succeeded in understanding Margaret's taste, and so had a right to make this decision. He walked across the little hillock of the burial lot over to the oak and stood where her, and someday his, headstone would go. He scanned slowly, in a three-hundred-and-sixty-degree arc, taking in the leafy trees, the sentinel headstones, the distant view of New York Harbor, the pretentious tomb with Ionic columns, and the gray serpentine road dividing the manicured lots that would soon, slung low in a black hearse, carry her lifeless body here.

"This one," he said to Lily and Paul.

"It's beautiful," Lily said, although a moment ago she had suggested he choose the other grave. "It's the right one," she added, knowing the depth of his anxiety.

"Maybe," he answered.

chapter eleven

First Kiss

ENRIQUE KNEW BY the time he paid the check with a firmness he had learned from his father—a dismissive shake of the head, waving Margaret off with an air of gravity that implied he was sparing them both an egregious error—that he was never going to be able to forgive himself if he didn't kiss her that night. He had tried not to show it. He had answered her questions, listened to her life so far, and fixed his eyes on hers, not straying to her amused lips, her smooth white neck, her wool-encased breasts. It was a focus he maintained out of fear rather than good manners; the one time he pictured her naked in his arms, he forgot everything they had ever discussed.

In truth, he couldn't imagine holding her hand, much less fucking her. When she turned this way and that, to slide slim arms into her goose-down jacket, he got another peek at her shapely legs and buttocks. They seemed like an impossible dream, not a goal. How had any man in the history of the world summoned the nerve to kiss a woman? He certainly couldn't remember how he had accomplished the feat. As early as age twelve he had angled his lips at a girl and landed without damaging himself on her formidable grill of orthodontia, but the great grown-up man of twenty-one exiting the restaurant and walking back toward their neighborhood felt as if he had never made love, that he was as ignorant and as sexless as a toddler.

Although he couldn't imagine daring to touch her, his mind raced, calculating how to confront himself with just that opportunity. Should he invite her up to his place? With what excuse? Should he ignore his building when they passed, presuming to walk her home? That way Margaret would have to make the call. "Do you want to come up?" she would ask. Or not.

If not, then what? Should he kiss her in front of her snobby doorman? Impossible. Having himself and her for an audience already felt like having too many people. If he could manage it, he would prefer to kiss her without being present himself. Certainly eliminating her blue eyes would make the fearsome challenge much easier.

"Shall we go back the right way?" she asked as they reached Seventh and Grove.

"Any way you like," he said, feeling queasy. How was he going to bring her to ecstasy if he could barely walk? That Margaret seemed available, that this date wasn't a quixotic adventure, perversely struck him as worse luck than if he had had no chance. The ball was in his court, and he was supposed to hit it hard for a winner when he didn't even feel strong enough to lift the racquet.

"You were very good-natured about being wrong," she said. She could have been speaking in Farsi; Enrique's mind was locked up with dread. "What?" he stalled.

"About going the wrong way. When I pointed it out, you were really cool about it."

"But—you—were—" he began slowly as he struggled to catch up to what she meant. He got it: "The one who thought Christopher was faster."

It took a few exchanges before the predinner misunderstanding became clear. After several "But you saids," they realized they had been in complete agreement about which way was more direct. Margaret had mistaken Enrique's vague nod at Grove as meaning he wanted to try Christopher, and she had decided to defer out of politeness. When she proceeded to walk toward Christopher, Enrique, thinking she was stubbornly taking charge, had decided not to protest, also out of politeness. "Jeez!" Margaret bumped her denim hip against his Army coat. "We'd better stop being so nice to each other or we'll never get anywhere."

Enrique leaned close to her pretty face, tempting himself. "The longer it takes us to get where we're going, the more fun we'll have."

Three evenings of talking with Margaret had convinced Enrique that there was one arena in which she would never be his equal—conversation. She was smart, a lot smarter than he had realized at their first meeting, and certainly better-educated. But her careful way of listening to what was being said meant that she wasn't preparing a clever reply, and her caution about accuracy—twice she had paused to check herself as to whether she had a detail right—caused the rhythm of her speech to be clumsy, and spoiled the wittiness of her observations. She hadn't grasped the secret to entertaining conversation, that how things are said is much more important than what is said. So he was surprised to find himself in any sort of repartee with her and certainly didn't expect to lose an exchange of witticisms, as he now did. Margaret gazed at his lips as they came near. When they halted a good foot away from where they wanted to go, she ran her blade clean through him: "What makes you think we'll ever get where we're going?"

He almost gasped, but she didn't let him suffer for long. She raised her rapier graciously by adding, "Maybe we'll just stay lost together forever."

Here was his cue to act. Her chin was tilted up, parted lips lifted to his. There was no moon above bathing the Village town houses in silver light, but the streetlamp's yellow could have been considered a romantic glow. The air, instead of carrying the usual aroma of urine and rotting garbage, was fragrant with the woody smoke of nearby chimneys. Behind her sparkling face, white Christmas lights were strung on a row of trees. Her eyes were merry, her mouth on offer. What more of a signal could she give him, short of grabbing his head and demanding, "Kiss me!"

He smiled, a feeble smile. She had robbed his voice. His body was frozen with fear. The twelve inches between their lips looked to be an infinite chasm to bridge. He was not the romantic hero of his own life. His disappointment in himself could hardly have been greater if she had told him that he was not worthy of her, that he ought to be locked in an airless basement and never permitted the social company of others. He would have agreed with that assessment. Right then and there he accepted in his heart and mind that he was never going to touch this woman. Like the hapless Bernard, he was never going to be more than her friend. In that spirit he said, "I hate being lost."

Probably any other girl would have taken his answer as a rebuff. Certainly once the words escaped his lips, he wished he could have them back. Margaret didn't appear to be put off. Her eyes drifted up to the sky, and she said with a wistful look, "Really? I love being lost." She turned toward Grove, the right direction, and began walking home. "I love an adventure."

He stepped beside her, relieved that the question of sex had been resolved, albeit unsatisfactorily, and said, "Good for you. I wish I was that way."

"You're not?" she exclaimed. She was moving briskly, in such a hurry that he felt sure she wanted a quick end to this date. "Come on, you dropped out of high school. You left home at sixteen. You cohabited"—she smiled at the word—"with an older woman. You're way more adventurous than I am."

"Not really," he insisted. A heavy silence fell, and the quiet panicked him. He was scared they had nothing left to talk about. They were friends, that was a relaxing thought, no more worry about how and when to leap the chasm. But without that worrying undercurrent, his mind seemed to have lost navigation. Was there any point in continuing the evening? He felt that the whole enterprise, the weeks of maneuvering to get her alone, was a waste. Shameful though it was, given his avowed belief in feminism, he had to admit to himself that apparently his sole interest in her was sexual. He didn't miss the pressure to act, but without it he seemed to be just as interested in going home to watch TV. "What about your brothers?" he heard himself say, although he had no awareness of manufacturing this thought. "Are they adventurous?"

She chuckled, making a rich sound in her throat, a complicated mixture of affection and contempt. This was a musical note no male could ever play: knowing and sarcastic, loving and irritated all at once. "My brothers . . . ," she said. "They are the most buttoned-down young men you'll ever meet. Such obedient boys." She sighed. "My mother trained them but good."

Enrique noted that being obedient wasn't a quality she admired in a man. That was the problem, he decided on the spot. Margaret imagined that Enrique was a bad boy. She didn't know that he longed to be obedient, if only he could find a ruler he could trust. "They're younger than you?"

"No, Rob's older. Four years older and prematurely middle-aged. He acts like he's as old as my father." She laughed, another complicated melody, this one of disappointment and forgiveness. "He was so mean to me when I was little. Teased me terribly." She shook her head, dumbfounded by the memory. "My parents left him to babysit me one night. We ordered a pizza, which I was so excited about. My favorite, with mushrooms. While we were waiting for the delivery, we played Cowboys and Indians, and Rob fooled me into letting him tie me up. And then, when the pizza came, he didn't let me go. He ate the entire pie in front of me, taunting me the whole time." Her anger about it was green, yesterday's hurt.

"How old were you?"

"Six? Wait. Seven? I'm not sure. Let's see, it was—"

He stopped her. He'd learned her fetish for precision wouldn't allow her to be off by even a few months, and he wasn't interested in that exactitude. "So your brother was a kid, too, right? He was just being a mischievous boy himself. He's not like that now? Not still tying up girls?"

She laughed. "I wish! Then I would forgive him. No, he was just being mean, not kinky. He's a tenured professor at Yale. An old fogy at twenty-eight."

"He has tenure at twenty-eight?"

"Probably ready to collect his pension." She turned away and said to a town house's steps, "He's brilliant. He's a genius. But he's a genius at microeconomics. So who cares?" She laughed and twisted back toward Enrique to add, "I'm sorry. I'm being terrible. But it's true. Who cares?"

I'm exotic to her, Enrique thought. That's why she likes me. But I'm not. I'm a nerd like her brother, only much less smart. "What's the difference between a microeconomist and a regular economist?"

"Oh, they're very different. Don't make that mistake in my family. They sneer at macroeconomists."

"I'm sorry, but I'm a high school dropout. What's the difference between macro and micro?"

"A macroeconomist is like, you know, someone who makes pronouncements about whether the stock market will go up or down, or interest rates are headed up or down, someone who makes big—well, my father and Rob would say—*guesses* about the economy. They don't do that at all—"

"Your father's also a microeconomist?"

"My father, Rob—and I guess they're making Larry head that way, too."

"So what do microeconomists figure out?"

"If AT&T or Con Ed has to ask the government for a rate increase, or if you have to figure out what to charge in order to cover your costs and other possible disasters and still make a profit, you hire a microeconomist, and using *science*"—she paused to smile at Enrique in order to be clear that this emphasis originated with her father and brother— "you come up with the correct number. Anyway, my brother teaches it, my father used to teach it (now he's got a consulting firm), and my baby brother's studying it also—it's the family business."

"I see," Enrique said. He hadn't had any wine with dinner, but if he had knocked back an entire bottle this would have sobered him up. What an astonishing gap between her family's business and his. That her father worked for AT&T and Con Ed was, in his parents' view, tantamount to collaborating with the Vichy government. And what, my God, what would her parents and her brothers make of his insane left-wing, novel-writing, perpetually broke family?

Another silence had fallen. Enrique's door was only a block and a half away. He feared the silence would remind her that they would soon be making a choice about when and where to say good night. "Your brother's got to be sorry about the pizza thing," he said without having thought it through. "He's got to be very sorry he did that to you. I'm sure he's ashamed of it." What he wasn't sure of was why he was arguing on her brother's behalf. To try out disagreeing with her about something? Isn't that what friends do? Amiably disagree?

Margaret fished in her purse for a cigarette when they paused at the corner of Sixth. "Rob likes to tease. He's sarcastic. Very sarcastic about everything. Listen, I love him. And when I was little, I worshiped him. I thought he was the greatest. He was my big brother and he knew everything. But he was mean to me. You can't blame him. He had my mother breathing down his neck all his life. Having to be perfect and do everything perfectly. Tenure at twenty-eight. I mean, my God. So I understand." She lit her cigarette.

"What about your baby brother?" Enrique asked, dutifully following this sexless turn in the conversation—new friends at camp learning about each other's siblings.

"Aw, Lawrence. My baby brother Larry. Little Lollipop Larry. He's sweet. I'm his big sister, six years older, so I got to be the one who was worshiped."

They were crossing Sixth, drawing near to the probable end of this utter failure of an evening. "And you took great care of him, of course," Enrique said.

She released a laugh from her gut that a male could produce. "Actually, I was a much worse babysitter than Rob. I gave little Larry a concussion one time. And I broke his arm another. Twice, after leaving him with me, my parents had to meet us at the hospital." She laughed with infectious delight.

"How did you give him a concussion?" Enrique asked. "You dropped him on his head?"

"No—" she said, gasping out the words between laughs, "I was trying to teach him to ride a bike."

"And his arm?"

"*I* didn't break his arm—"

"Oh come on. 'Fess up. You were dragging him by the arm to buy drugs—and you snapped it—"

"No, no, no, I was trying to teach him to roller-skate . . ."

They were nearing the corner of Eighth and Sixth. To go to Enrique's apartment, they'd turn east. If they proceeded one block farther north to Ninth, they would be heading to her place.

To distract her as they passed Eighth Street, so the choice of going to her apartment house would occur without a discussion, he belabored the joke: "Roller-skate? Admit it: heroin fix. What did you do? Twist his arm to get his lunch money?"

Margaret grew solemn. He worried she was about to protest his sneaky maneuver. "Poor little Larry. I loved babysitting for him," she said with wistful affection. She crossed the street and headed toward Ninth. "He was such a sweet boy."

"Was? Now he's a serial killer?"

"Oh, he's still sweet. Just a little . . ."

She became pensive and settled into a careful think. He enjoyed this pause in their conversation. Ninth, although taxis were rattling by, was much quieter than raucous Eighth. A few of the town house trees had Christmas lights; most didn't in those bankrupt, vandalizing days. He could smell logs burning in the fireplaces and imagine the cozy happiness of the families within. He no longer understood what he wanted out of knowing Margaret. He had no nerve for a conquest, that was clear, but he didn't want to be friends. He didn't really know what he would do with a young woman as a friend. Go to a museum? Learn to crochet together? But this silence among the town houses and brownstones where Henry James and Mark Twain and Eleanor Roosevelt and Emma Lazarus and dozens of shrinks and their miserable analysands had talked themselves blue, this wait for Margaret to tell him some secret of her heart, this calm of walking beside her, this he could do with contentment.

"Larry should be an architect," she said at last.

"He's also an economist?"

Margaret frowned. "Not yet. My parents—my mom mostly— they're nagging him to become an economist. She thinks being an architect is too risky."

"What!" Enrique laughed. To his high school dropout ears, architects were as likely to find work as economists. Besides, his friend Sal, scratching out a living designing offices and loft spaces, claimed it was his lack of an architectural degree that was the obstacle to his making a fortune.

"Well, it is much harder to make a living as an architect. But when Larry was little, he liked to draw. He still does. He said at Thanksgiving his art course was his favorite. And his drawings were good, really good. That makes my mother very nervous. He's got real feeling and talent for it, but that's—" She shook her head and said softly, "Being an artist. That's not okay in my family. Not for the men, anyway."

They reached the elegance of Fifth Avenue, and they took in a sweeping view south of the Washington Square Arch and beyond, the bright boxes of the World Trade towers; to the north, the antenna of the Empire State seemed to yearn for attention, as if unable to accept that it was no longer the tallest building in Manhattan. "But it's okay for you to be an artist?" he asked.

She turned, to regard Enrique with disappointment. "I'm supposed to get married and have children," she said with the lilt of "isn't that obvious?" suffusing every word.

Suddenly Enrique felt as if he were the villain in a novel, the potential bad guy of her story, the destroyer of a young woman's hopes to realize her talent. His melodramatic mind saw the plot: Margaret, thinking she has found an artist who will support her in breaking free of the Buddenbrooks-like oppression of her bourgeois parents, falls in love with the long-haired prodigy; instead of writing her great novel, she becomes little more than a glorified scullery maid of a wife, harried in a Lower East Side tenement apartment, raising Enrique's brats while he writes failing books and cheats on her with actresses and poetesses. Eventually the selfish flop abandons a middle-aged Margaret without a dime, for a young Upper East Side heiress who thinks the ageless Enrique to be an undiscovered genius, upon which calamity Margaret finally writes a searing play about the plight of obedient Jewish girls that wins the Pulitzer, the Tony, and the Nobel. He would have further elaborated this soap opera, only he had to answer her to avoid the impression that he was an idiot. "Of course," he said. "You're supposed to marry a nice Jewish boy and have three kids."

"Two kids!" Margaret cried out. "Give me a break. I think even my mom would be satisfied with two." The light changed, and she strode across the street, definitely en route to her apartment. He had wondered if she would notice that they had over shot his building, and inform him that he didn't have to walk her home, but no. She moved toward University Place with her rapid walk, so full of energy that it was difficult, despite his long legs, to keep up without exerting himself. He hustled, grateful that he wouldn't have to make the decision to extend the evening. She would either invite him up or not. "And? Have you decided to have them?"

"Decided to have what?" she asked, as if they hadn't been discussing anything in particular. "Kids?" she added abruptly with astonishment. "Oh, I don't think about that. I don't think about that at all."

"You don't care—you're not worried about fulfilling your mom's expectations?"

"Well, I care. A little. I guess. I don't know. I don't think about it. I know I'm going to disappoint and worry my mother no matter what I do."

That seemed to him a very sad remark. Enrique felt that, along with his parents' resentment at not being more successful, along with their never being satisfied by the praise critics granted Enrique's work, along with their claims that his publisher was incompetent and that was why he failed to sell more copies of his novels, the one constant was their admiration for the quality of his work and their unflinching insistence that he must continue to write no matter how discouraging the world's reaction to his books. Not to have that bolstering from parents, he felt, would make everything about being an artist too difficult. Yet he knew otherwise. And he said so. "Well, most of the world's great artists had parents who didn't want them to be artists."

"I'm not a great artist," Margaret protested without heat. "I'm not an artist at all. I don't know what I am," she commented. She sounded like a wondering child, seeing a future both mysterious and possible. "Did you always know you wanted to be a writer? I guess you did. You started so young."

"No I didn't. There were a couple other things I wanted to be before I wrote my novel. Until I was eleven, I wanted to be President of the United States." She laughed. He leaned her way to emphasize his sincerity. "No, I really did. I subscribed to the *Congressional Record* and ran for student council, and it wasn't until the father of a friend of mine said, 'You'll never be elected president. Not in a million years. You're half Spanish and half Jewish—you couldn't be elected dogcatcher in this country.' That's when I gave up."

Margaret touched his arm. "That's terrible," she cried out, as if the wound was still bleeding. He stopped walking. They were a half block from the dreaded farewell in the sight lines of her censorious doorman. He faced her, enjoying the feather weight of her hand on his arm. It lingered before sliding off while she commented, "What a mean thing to say. Why was he so mean to a little boy?"

"He was right," Enrique answered. "Maybe I could be a senator from New York—at best. Not even that, with my parents' politics. Cuban exiles would sooner kill me than elect me."

He was about to make fun of his fantasy life of political success when Margaret, empathetic a moment ago, did the job: "You'd have to finish high school before they'd bother to assassinate you."

"That's why I dropped out. Why finish high school if you can't be president?"

Her lips formed a crooked, close-lipped smile that he had noticed twice before when he said something she enjoyed. It was more pronounced this time: sly smirk, gleeful eyes, an evaluating tilt of her head, full of amused affection; and there was a delicious trace of the pride of ownership in her attitude, as if Enrique was her very own private source of pleasure, available to no one else. Once again he knew that he ought to kiss her, but he remained frozen until she said, emphasizing each word: "You really wanted to be president?"

"I thought I could change the world," he answered.

She released a single report of delighted laughter. "I can see that. I can see the little boy who thought that." She turned to walk the last half block, which would decide all, he believed.

He asked another question, what exactly her father was doing for AT&T, hoping talk would distract both of them from the good-bye decision. While explaining that her father often testified in court and before Congress on their behalf, which sounded very corrupt to the left-wing Enrique, she threw in, "You want to come up and have some coffee? Or some wine or something?"

"Sure," he grabbed at the offer. Immediately, in his mind, this was a date again, and his stomach churned.

She kept talking while they rode up in the elevator, entered her apartment, and shed their coats. She asked if he wanted coffee, and he said yes. She vanished into her closet of a kitchen.

Her living room, or rather the sitting area of her L-shaped studio, was defined by three objects of furniture: a small black and white striped couch, a black leather Eames lounge chair, and a low, plain pine coffee table. The couch was more of a love seat in length, and, if he sat there and she chose to sit beside him, they would be practically kissing every time they looked at each other. The Eames chair was a tempting cowardly alternative, but he made the brave move and settled on the couch. He found it to be very uncomfortable, too low for his long, skinny legs. Nor did he have room for his feet, because the coffee table's base had a shallow shelf that prevented him from stretching out. As a consequence, his knees rose higher. He felt like a praying mantis, or an abandoned puppet collapsed into an awkward jumble of confused limbs. He wanted to turn sideways, put one knee up on the couch to have more room to extend his legs, but that would force Margaret to sit all the way over on the Eames chair, which, for kissing purposes, might as well be across the Atlantic Ocean.

Then it occurred to him that his selection of the couch wasn't the end of the issue: What if she sat in the Eames chair? At that moment she appeared to say, "The water will only be a couple minutes. Do you take milk?" She made a worried face. "I don't think I have any."

"No milk?" Enrique was surprised. Milk was about the only thing he had in his refrigerator.

"You take milk with your coffee," she deduced and ducked

back into the kitchen. He heard the *whoosh* of the refrigerator unsealing its vacuum. "Shit. Sorry. I have some vanilla ice cream. Should I put it in your coffee?" Her top half reappeared, leaning out with a pint of Breyers in her hand, a blue-eyed, freckle-faced girl eager to please.

"You drink your coffee black," Enrique told her. She nodded warily. "You *are* macho. You are one macho girl." He laughed at his own line, pleased in general and with himself. He could hear in her tone and see in every gesture how easy she felt about being alone with him. He relaxed and enjoyed a leisurely survey of her cheerful and puzzled face. He didn't think he had the nerve to test whether she would recoil in horror at the touch of his lips, but he calmed down anyway.

"That doesn't really make sense," she said. "Macho girl?" She shook the pint. "My fingers are freezing. You want the ice cream?"

"I'll take mine black. I can be just as tough as you."

She disappeared again, returning without the ice cream, and ended the suspense of where she would sit. She didn't choose the Eames chair or the couch beside him. Instead she perched on the small sofa's free arm, the one nearest to the kitchen, presumably to be ready to finish making the coffee. Or maybe she liked the novelty of looking down at the tall Enrique. Either way, in his new optimistic turn of mind, he laughed out loud at his absurd calculations over something that was supposed to be accomplished with romantic grace. "Did I say something funny?" she asked.

"No." He confessed the simple truth: "I'm having a really good time."

For a long, disquieting moment, she gaped at him, great eyes round and startled. Her silence went on long enough that he wouldn't have been surprised if she announced that actually she wasn't all that entertained. He had forgotten what he'd learned about her; there would be no snappy comebacks. After careful consideration, she said, "Me too. It's really easy talking to you." The kettle whistled. "That's pretty rare," she added as she left.

She emerged with a pot of coffee and cups, and at long last settled exactly where Enrique had hoped and feared, beside him on the couch, available to be kissed. Their talk resumed its steady and easy flow. When she asked him a question about his past, as an autobiographical writer he found it an easy matter for him to repeat set pieces while his mind was occupied with what truly fascinated it—the almost invisible row of freckles under each of her exquisite eyes, the slight pout of her pale pink lips, the quick way her chin could soften from a stern angle with a smile. When she turned to sip her coffee, talking before and after a swallow in her eagerness to tell him something, he could almost feel his hungry lips nestle in the soft hollow of her white neck and climb, kiss by kiss, to those sly lips to quiet their restless language.

On his side, he had a last question to ask her. It wasn't a question he could ask with words. The worry of receiving the wrong answer mounted and mounted until, although it made no sense given what they were talking about—the Black Panther takeover of the Straight at Cornell on her side, Enrique's attendance at Bobby Seale and Erica Huggins's trial in New Haven on his—when there was a pause, he shifted his whole body on the sofa, moving a few inches toward her until their thighs touched and leaned in.

He halted halfway to his goal. Margaret fell silent. A sober darkness came into her bright blue eyes. She gazed down at his lips as if evaluating how they might taste. He had gone too far to retreat. He moved in close, scared to breathe. She didn't encourage him. She offered no clue as to whether she would part her lips in welcome or open them wide to scream.

He touched them tentatively and with exquisite gentleness, as if they might attack. He shut his eyes, overwhelmed to be so close to her depthless oceans, and pressed harder now that no violent resistance had occurred. Her body yielded, lips parting, the liquid of her mouth bathing his in a brief immersion, only to seal up again and press back. He shifted closer, one arm maneuvering around her slim shoulder, his nose brushing against hers as they opened to each other in unison and, in a wonderful illusion, seemed for a split second to no longer have a beginning or ending. Their mouths shut, satisfied by their brief unity, and he moved off, a smile blossoming. She was not smiling. She regarded him with solemn contemplation. He waited for an answer to his question: May I continue?

She reached out with thoughtful idleness, right forearm balancing on his shoulder, a delicate hand brushing past his cheek. Her index finger and thumb took hold of his earlobe, and she squeezed lightly, as if they were old lovers with all the questions answered and all the time in the world. In that pose she resumed her account of the disappointment of black radical separatism on campus, releasing him after a few sentences, content with what they had accomplished, sitting back, clear of more kisses, seeming to want nothing more from him than to continue their endless conversation.

chapter twelve

Family Feeling

For five days and nights a steady flow of people entered
Enrique and Margaret's home and walked up the stairs that
typically only they, their sons, or their cleaning woman climbed.
These final visitors passed through the small study where Enrique
wrote on weekends and on through a pocket doorway into a bedroom almost as large as Margaret's old studio apartment, where
they first kissed. Their bedroom was filled with light from its
sweeping view of southern Manhattan, which used to be dominated by the shimmering, rectangular boxes of the World Trade
towers and whose emptiness was scarred these days by the tops of
a quartet of cranes. Enrique brought up extra chairs for the larger
groups, such as when Margaret's mother and father, her brothers,
and their wives had come for lunch.

The Cohen family's final meal with Margaret was preceded by

a confrontation that, in one aspect, Enrique had feared all of his marriage. Margaret asked Enrique to tell Dorothy and Leonard that she wanted to have her funeral at the nineteenth-century synagogue on the Lower East Side where the atheistic Enrique had been accompanying her since her diagnosis; that she wanted her service to be presided over by their eccentric Buddhist Rabbi; and that she be buried not in the family plot in New Jersey but in the hillocks of Green-Wood Cemetery, Brooklyn, with its view of southern Manhattan, where Margaret had sown her wild oats, tamed Enrique, raised her children, and would die.

Seeing the look of fear in her husband's eyes at the prospect of confronting her parents without her, Margaret was quick to reassure Enrique, "After you break it to them, I'll confirm it's what I want, but I can't bear to fight with them, so you explain it. That'll get them used to the idea, and then you send them up to me." Enrique made no reply. If she'd been healthy, he would have attempted to weasel out of such a request, but how could he now? Anyway, wasn't this the beginning of a necessary new skill? The Cohens were his sons' grandparents; he had to learn to deal with them by himself. "You can do it," she said into his silence. "They'll fuss, but they'll do what I want. I just don't want to listen to their nonsense about it."

Something was wrong in her construct of the situation, he couldn't pinpoint what, but he had little time to reflect on it, not even half the morning. Her parents arrived for lunch at ten am. Max, having graduated high school a week before, was presumably sleeping off a worrisome quantity of alcohol. Margaret was still upstairs, occupied by the long process of getting dressed. There was the difficulty of tubes and ports that couldn't be concealed entirely, the application of makeup with tearing eyes and lack of brows, and her postchemo hair, which was brittle and thin, yet thick enough to make adjusting her wig difficult. Her preparations left Enrique alone with Dorothy and Leonard in the living room, an excellent opportunity for him to inform them of the funeral arrangements.

He had little choice; it was Dorothy's second question. "Max is still asleep?" she asked immediately after she and Leonard settled on the couch. She almost ran over Enrique's yes to ask, as was typical of her, not a single question but a paragraph of them, sandwiched between assumptions, advice, and answers to her own questions. "So what about the funeral and everything? What are you going to do? I mean, why should you know anything about all that? About services and burial plots. You've never had to do it before. Except for your father, but you didn't have to arrange that, right? Didn't his sister take care of things in Florida? We understand you want to have a memorial service in New York for your friends. And Margs likes her Rabbi. We know that. So her Rabbi could do it here in Manhattan, that's all right. But what about the temple? Is your temple big enough for all the people? A lot of people will want to come. We have a lot of friends. And you have a lot of friends. Isn't that going to be too many people for that little temple? It's so small. What about this idea? We could do the funeral service at our temple for everyone and then you could have a memorial in the city for your friends. That would work. Many people have both a funeral and a memorial. But what about the plot? You don't have a plot, right? You and Margs never did anything about that. Why would you?" She made an embarrassed face and lowered her voice as if they were discussing something pornographic. "And there's plenty of space in our family plot. When the time comes, which we know won't be for a long time, but if you could also—I don't know where you want to go, whether you want to be with your father's family—but we consider you a part of our family, so—" She shook her head as if all these thoughts were flies buzzing her. She cried out, "It's terrible, it's just terrible . . ." And the carapace of her face cracked with anxiety at how to control this last social arrangement for her daughter. Although Dorothy felt compelled to organize it, Enrique could see that this event was too painful for her to think through.

He said gently, putting as much affection as he could into the word, "Dorothy . . ."

But at the sound of his comforting tone, she revved herself away from sorrow, lines smoothing under the weight of makeup, voice returning to the shrill noise of planning: "It's terrible, but we have to think about these things. What about parking, for example? Is there parking for your temple? And your Rabbi. We would have to meet him. He doesn't know us." She stopped abruptly, her barrage ceasing without a tapering off. Enrique's mind reeled as to how to untangle the thicket of erroneous facts and gross presumptions. Dorothy sat ramrod straight on the couch, panic radiating from her pale blue eyes, while Leonard slumped, his mournful violet eyes swimming in despair.

Enrique cleared his throat of the twenty-nine-year clog of swallowed objections, of resentment that Dorothy's way of doing things always took precedence, and the constricting fear that he would be unable to get Margaret what she wanted without also hurting her mother. And then it struck him, staring at her parents in their confusion and their pain. The difficulty for him in this situation was that to negotiate between Margaret and her mother required extraordinary diplomacy, and Enrique wasn't a diplomat at all. The Cohen children were masters of indirection with their mother, of expressing desires without explicit statements, of refusing demands without saying no, of agreement without harmony, of fighting without blows. Enrique was loud and direct, shouting nos and singing yeses, a creature who loved clear skies but also required the inevitable churning seas, black clouds, and howling winds of a yearly hurricane to create in the atmosphere of affection a deeper blue than before. He had never loosed a Sabas storm on Dorothy, and to do it now, of all the times he had been tempted, would be a catastrophe that no amount of volunteers or charitable aid could repair.

And yet without creating hurricane-force winds, how could he be sure that Dorothy's knotted oak of worry and control would bend to the breeze of Margaret's wishes? How else could he overwhelm Dorothy's powerful need for familiarity? She wanted to sit in the same bland building she'd gone to for thirty-five years, secure that there was ample parking. She wanted to be surrounded by lifelong friends while she sat on the same wood bench where yearly she had atoned for sins that would make an angel laugh, and listen to an old friend of a Rabbi who would repeat platitudes that were comforting precisely because they no longer had meaning. She wanted to drive on the same road that she had taken again and again to honor the graves of her mother and her father, and her husband's mother and father; to feel safe in this heartbreaking new context by saying the same words and staring into the same upturned earth.

How could Enrique explain that, although Margaret would be dead at her funeral, in order for her to go in peace she needed to picture herself departing from the people she loved in places that she loved? To say good-bye in the evocative wood-and-stone temple fashioned by European craftsmen in the squalor of Lower East Side streets that had no parking because they were too crowded by striving immigrants. To picture herself mourned in a symbol of Jewish ancestry that Margaret preferred to think of as hers, rather than her anonymous childhood home in Queens or the Long Island lawns and malls of her parents' later prosperity. To have spoken over her lifeless body confused comfort from a Buddhist Rabbi trying to reconcile the Old Testament's frank tribalism and rage with modern longings for acceptance and harmony. For her last gesture as a woman obliged to leave her husband and children this early to be that she would lie forever as close as possible to where she had nurtured them, and in as elegant and as welcoming a place as she could find; that even in death Margaret longed to seduce, rather than demand; that the life lesson she had learned from her mother was that she wanted ardor, not obedience from her family.

The obstacle, Enrique realized, in his twenty-nine-year history with these two mitochondrial creators of his sons, was that in order for him to win with either Dorothy or Margaret, if he had ever really had won any battle with these women, he had had to insist without discussion, to disobey without debate. Whenever he engaged in negotiation, he lost. After the tumultuous early years of their marriage, he'd made a shouting demand of Margaret only a few times, and never of Dorothy. Not directly, anyway. Once or twice he had done so through Margaret to Dorothy, but on those occasions Margaret was on his side anyway—she used him as the offstage bully. But those contradictions of Dorothy's desires were about trivia such as whether they would spend their family school vacation at the Cohens' home in Florida. This sad circumstance could not be decided by fiat. He needed the irreconcilable to be reconciled.

He began, as he imagined a diplomat would, by moving beside Dorothy on the couch, as close as a lover. He spoke in a calm voice. "Margaret and I have discussed all this. Margaret's very clear about what she wants. I don't know if you remember that we stopped going to the little temple, the Village temple over here where Max and Gregory were Bar Mitzvahed? Instead we go down to a big old synagogue on the Lower East Side." Dorothy began to interrupt. Enrique talked over her. "It's a partially restored nineteenth-century synagogue. In fact, it's the oldest surviving temple in New York—"

"Margaret was telling me about this," Leonard said, sitting up straighter, his natural curiosity about Jewish history rousing him from his sorrow. "It's not functioning now, right?"

"Our congregation rents it every other Friday and on the high holidays. Our Rabbi, who is a Buddhist—"

"He's Buddhist?" Dorothy said, her face widening in what might have been either surprise or horror. In any case, the fact didn't inspire her confidence.

"He claims to be a Buddhist, but he was a traditional Rabbi for many years, and we've been going to his services for almost two years, every other Friday night and on the high holidays. Margaret loves him. He's the first Rabbi, she says, that she likes." Dorothy and Leonard both started to speak, to remind him that they had heard all this, but Enrique knew they had somehow slipped back into thinking that he was proposing to have Margaret's funeral at the small temple on Twelfth Street where Margaret used to take the boys on her own, when she was healthy and Enrique could defy her with the pride of his atheism. He talked over their comments. "It's been deliberately kept to look like a nineteenth-century temple which hasn't been that well-maintained. A kind of hip, sort of ruined look. But the building is completely sound, it's clean, it has plenty of room for all your friends and ours. I don't know about parking. I'm sure there's a lot nearby. But that's where Margaret wants her funeral service. And there's something else she wants. She doesn't want to be buried in New Jersey. She wants to be closer to New York. There's a cemetery in Brooklyn, it's a national landmark, but they allow a few new graves and I've arranged to—"

That was too much for Dorothy. "She doesn't want to be buried with us!" she exclaimed, dropping a bomb of hysteria and guilt into Enrique's calm oration. She had converted Margaret's longing to be in a place she admired into a rejection of her mother. For much of his married life, Enrique had wanted to yell at

Dorothy for this blind spot, that she had no idea how much her daughter honored her wishes. He wanted to shout that Dorothy must try to see the world through her daughter's eyes now. He listened passively for his anger to explode, as if he were a bystander. He was sure that he wouldn't be able to restrain his frustration for his wife's sake, given that his fatigue was so heavy and his need to release so urgent. He waited for the old Enrique, the wild, confused young man whom Margaret had rescued, to throw a temper tantrum and make a forlorn situation even more desolate.

But he had no storm in his heart. He took hold of Dorothy's hands, something he had never done. She was startled and tried to pull them back, but he didn't let go. Her stiff fingers and rigid palms relaxed. He said, "Dorothy," in the gentle tone he imagined he would use with a heartbroken daughter. He squeezed her hands, and she squeezed back, her startled, anxious eyes fastened on him. "Dorothy, Margaret loves you. She wants to be buried in Green-Wood *not* because she doesn't want to be with you but because she loves it in Green-Wood. A friend from her cancer group was buried there, and it made her feel okay about losing her. It's not about anything else. She's letting go of us. It's very hard to let go of us. She needs to know that everything about her death is going to be the way she would like it. She needs that in order to accept what's happening. It's all she asks of us. Green-Wood is nearby, much closer than New Jersey. You can visit her there."

Dorothy's pale eyes flickered into darker hues of blue, as if she were raising a shade to allow him to look deeper into her. It felt to Enrique—he wondered if it felt that way to her as well—as if they were gazing into each other's eyes for the very first time. What he saw was not the demanding matriarch he resented, not the bourgeois who would never view him as a success, not the nagging mother who didn't praise her daughter enough. He saw a lonely little girl who longed for her parents' approval. "Dorothy," he pleaded as gently as he could. "Let's do this for her. It's very hard on us. Very, very hard on you, maybe harder on you than on any of us, but let's make this as easy as we can on Margaret. For her, okay?"

"Of course," she said with ardor, hysteria drained. "Of course I want this to be easy for her. I'm her mother. I love her. My heart is breaking," she said, and tears welled. "Of course we'll do what she wants." Embarrassed by showing her grief, she tried to raise her hands to cover her face, and he let them go. She fished in her purse for a tissue. That activity stopped her tears. She needed the appearance of strength to feel strong, he concluded, and let her be, turning to Leonard. The old man's eyes were awash, but he made no move to dry them. He said in the solemn tone of an oath: "We'll do what Margaret wants. Do you need any help with the arrangements?" Enrique shook his head. "You're sure?" the patriarch demanded.

"I'm sure," Enrique said and sighed, breathing easy. For a moment he felt a surge of excited happiness, until he remembered just how sad was his accomplishment.

Margaret's brothers and their wives appeared en masse about eleven, staying until late afternoon. At Margaret's request, lunch was brought in from the Second Avenue Deli, a landmark kosher restaurant. She had two hot dogs with mustard and sauerkraut, and a square potato knish. They ate at the dining room table, but afterward Margaret, feeling tired, asked Enrique to carry the IV pole upstairs, and she invited them to follow. She hosted them from her bed, the family's usual formality discarded as to location but retained as to clothing. They were all neatly attired, the men in slacks, button-down shirts, and jackets, Dorothy and the sisters-in-law in dresses, as if this were Thanksgiving or Passover. But holiday small talk was unbuttoned in favor of heartfelt reminiscences of childhood, and praise for Margaret as a mother. Dorothy did not compliment Margaret directly. Instead she reported flattering remarks made about Margaret by her friends. Those encomiums were inherently unconvincing. Since contact with Margaret was limited to a quick hello in passing at the country club, the true source was Dorothy.

This indirect way of praising Margaret on her deathbed disappointed and irritated Enrique all over again. He knew Dorothy didn't mean to be stingy. He understood, at long last, that Dorothy and Leonard were emotionally shy, not cold; their reserve didn't mean they loved less. Still, there was a time for bravery in all things. Enrique wanted more from them than their chronic diffidence. His resentment grew as the day of reminiscences wore on. He focused his disappointment on the fact that Dorothy had said nothing about her daughter's artwork. Finally, after hours of sitting in front of the large painting of Greg and Max hanging over Margaret's bed, Dorothy said, "I never saw that one before."

Enrique waited for her to add that it was beautiful, or at least that her grandchildren looked beautiful. Instead, she repeated, "No, I never saw that one."

"You haven't seen a lot of her paintings," Enrique replied churlishly.

"She never invited me!" Dorothy squealed as if he had stuck her with a pin and, in a sense, he had. "You never invited me." She turned to accuse Margaret. "I wanted to come. Remember? I said I wanted to see your work and then we could have lunch. There are so many galleries over there, where your studio is, isn't that right, Margs? Do you remember? I said I wanted to come and see your paintings and have lunch and you could show me these new galleries. But you never invited me," Dorothy repeated, as if she were a neglected little girl and Margaret a withholding parent. Dorothy stood on the balls of her feet, erect and alert as a bird on a perch. One hand rested on the wing chair in which her husband was slumped, gazing mournfully at his frail daughter. Dorothy's male progeny were in folding chairs at the foot of Margaret's bed. Both sons were at the top of their professions, wealthy and eminent middle-aged men. They lowered their chins penitently, as if they too were indicted in Margaret's failure to welcome her mother into her world. Margaret stared back in wonderment at Dorothy, puzzled by her complaint. Her eyes looked bigger in a face starved by her disease, and her body was smaller than ever, pale skin rivaling the translucence of the plastic lines running into the ports on her chest. For a long moment no one spoke.

It was then that the full strangeness of this mother-daughter relationship struck Enrique. Dorothy waited for Margaret's explanation in what everyone knew to be one of the final conversations mother and daughter would have. Dorothy was a private person, and this was a profoundly private matter, and yet she asked in a roomful of people, albeit members of her family. Was she afraid that, without an audience, Margaret would say something wounding? Margaret had certainly kept her mother at arm's length during her illness, but everyone in the family, including Dorothy herself, Enrique suspected, had been grateful for that. Her mother's distress at being helpless to stop what was happening to her child only worsened matters for all concerned. Margaret understood this dominating fact of her mother's nature: she needed to be in control in order to feel secure, and yet no one could control illness.

But why had Margaret kept Dorothy at a distance when she was well? That was the question Enrique believed her mother wanted answered. She had complained bitterly ten years ago that Margaret and she weren't as close as Dorothy's friends were with their daughters, and went so far as to accuse Margaret of having "no family feeling." Margaret, a dutiful daughter compared to her women friends, was hurt and angered by the accusation. "My mother doesn't know how to be my friend," she complained to

Enrique. That seemed accurate to Enrique. But he didn't agree that Dorothy wanted friendship from her daughter. He believed she was hurt because Margaret no longer asked for her advice.

Margaret had welcomed her mother's advice once. During the days of mothering the infants Gregory and Max, she had sought Dorothy's counsel about all sorts of child-rearing topics. And ten years into their marriage, she had asked for her mother's help during its greatest economic crisis, shortly after Margaret quit her job to concentrate on raising the boys. Simultaneously Enrique's career, barely keeping them in the black anyway, had collapsed, his income dropping to nothing for over a year. Dorothy had supplied more than money then. She had helped Margaret find a new nanny when the one they had was injured in a car accident. She had encouraged Margaret not to return to work, contrary to the advice of all of their friends, who thought Margaret should, in order to relieve the pressure on Enrique's career. Dorothy insisted that Enrique, along with their financial help, would survive this "problem" as Dorothy described his inability to make enough money from his novels to support them. "He's a creative person," she had said. "Income goes up and down for creative people. And they don't know about money," she added, which incensed Enrique but was beside the point. Dorothy could see that he was trying to earn a living. She didn't blame him for struggling. Her daughter had chosen to love him, and so the Cohens were along for the ride, for better or for worse. Dorothy, with her time and Leonard's money, shored up all the stress fractures that cracked Margaret and Enrique's hopeless attempt to re-create the traditional nuclear family model of the 1950s until Margaret could have what she desired—the freedom to nurture her children while retaining the luxury of nine-to-five help.

Once the young mother Margaret had admitted they needed help, Dorothy had helped all right, rescuing them from having to double up the boys in a small bedroom, from sending the boys to public school, and from a thousand other calamities for young, well-to-do New Yorkers. But Dorothy didn't stop at those successes. She wanted to change the way Margaret managed everything, from determining how much of their laundry was done by their cleaning woman to insisting that Greg, a remarkably unmusical child, be taken to Suzuki violin lessons—then the rage among the daughters of Dorothy's Great Neck friends. She complained that she didn't understand why they were summering in Maine, where there weren't "people like them." She didn't approve when Margaret decided to work at a small start-up magazine for no money, and then later couldn't understand why she rented a studio to paint without also taking a class in drawing. After all, that was what Dorothy's friend who decided to paint had done.

Dorothy nosed her way into every cranny of every decision her daughter made, in the same affectionate and annoying manner Dorothy did with her own friends. Dorothy didn't know that even Enrique was not permitted to shine a light into the recesses of Margaret's mind where she chose to take up or abandon various interests. As a teenager, Margaret had had to push her mother away to find room to grow. Dorothy didn't understand this dominating fact of her daughter's nature: Margaret needed to be in control, and she couldn't control her mother. Neither when Margaret was a teenager, nor later when she was a maturing wife and mother, did Dorothy comprehend her daughter's need to push her away, nor did she feel any less hurt the second time. Enrique also understood that wasn't how Margaret had experienced those two phases of their relationship. Margaret believed that she had been an obedient and dutiful daughter, and that when she tried to be her mother's chum, their different natures collided with too much force for either of them to feel friendly.

After Margaret's diagnosis, for this third and final phase of their relationship, Dorothy and Margaret vowed to be closer. But they hit a bump during the early months of Margaret's treatment, at a particularly inopportune time. Margaret called Dorothy to tell her that she had scheduled the nine-hour surgery during which, among other extraordinary manipulations, her bladder would be removed and replaced by one rebuilt out of a portion of her small intestine. Enrique overheard his wife's side of what turned into an argument about an inept medical suggestion her mother made based on a friend's remark. Dorothy had, and probably needed to have, a poor understanding of the gravity of Margaret's illness in those days, no matter how clearly things were explained to her. As a result, her friend had misunderstood Dorothy's assessment of Margaret's cancer. Dorothy's friend told her that someone she knew had bladder cancer, presumably superficial bladder cancer, and that she didn't need to have the organ removed so maybe Margaret didn't have to, either. "You don't listen to me, Ma!" He heard a frustrated Margaret raise her voice. "That's why you don't understand what's going on. Because you don't listen to me! I have stage three bladder cancer. That means I have to have my bladder taken out. If I want to live, I have to. There's no choice. I don't want to talk about this anymore! I have to go now." And she hung up on her mother.

Consistent with the handful of other occasions when Margaret expressed anger at Dorothy, Enrique got a call from Leonard a few hours later saying, "I don't know if you know what happened. Margaret really blasted her mother this morning. Dorothy's very very upset. Too upset to talk to Margaret about it. And I'm very upset too. I'm sure you know this is very hard on Dorothy. Of course Margaret isn't herself these days, I understand that, but she has to take it easy on her mother. Her mother loves her and she means well. She wants to help. That's all."

Enrique, furious inside, mounted a timid defense of his wife.

"Margaret's the one who has cancer, Leonard. Don't you think she's the one people should take it easy on?" The awkward phrasing revealed to Enrique how unsure he felt about his role in the very foreign diplomacy of peacekeeping in the Cohen family. This sort of third-party-to-third-party negotiation was unknown among the Sabases. In Margaret's place, Enrique would have shouted at his mother, and she would have wept and fired a thousand verbal pulses of guilt through the fiber-optic wires. If his father got involved, more likely it would have been to chortle over the whole episode, or comment from a lofty vantage point, rather than to plead on behalf of his wife. But Guillermo and Rose's marriage had ended in divorce after forty years. That fact, among others, caused Enrique to pause before concluding that Leonard's loyalty to Dorothy was wrongheaded. He decided to mimic Leonard, to defend his wife just as stoutly. He didn't do as good a job. Leonard asserted the primacy of his wife's feelings as though announcing an emergency that all concerned should concentrate on alleviating; Enrique meekly asked whether his wife's feelings ought to take precedence. The true objective of Leonard's call—and this was what Enrique found so enraging—was to provoke Enrique to put pressure on Margaret to apologize to her mother.

His head filled with resentful argument. His wife was facing death and a surgery so intimidating that the dry medical terms made Enrique dizzy no matter how many times he read them— and yet Margaret was supposed to apologize. For what? For speaking her mind when her mother was being thoughtless? Of course Dorothy meant well. But in the real world, not in the planetarium of Long Island country clubs and Florida gated communities, not in a social class where women could go almost their entire lives without working, not in that pleasant world of privilege, where your grown sons and daughter carefully manage information to keep their most worrisome facts secret, not in this bourgeois paradise the Cohens conspired to sustain for Dorothy, but in the real world where Enrique lived, meaning well simply wasn't enough. One also had to *do* well. If Dorothy was too frightened to learn the details of Margaret's illness, that was understandable, but then she shouldn't contradict her daughter's carefully researched medical decisions.

He told himself that he wanted Margaret to choose whether to call her mother without feeling pressure from her father. The truth was that Enrique wanted Dorothy to apologize to her daughter. As absurd and cruel as it sounded to his own ears, he wanted eighty-year-old Dorothy to grow up and admit that she had been wrong. His head was still deadlocked when Margaret announced, "Oh! And I made up with my mother. I felt bad, so I called her."

"But you didn't do anything wrong."

"Yeah, she's being an idiot and she doesn't listen to me, ever, it's incredible how she doesn't listen to me, but she's also . . . you know. Think how she must feel, Puff. I'm her daughter. Imagine if this were happening to Maxy or Greg. And when I apologized, something really sweet happened. She said something kind of wonderful. Hysterical, but wonderful." Margaret reported that Dorothy announced that from now on it was important to remember to say they loved each other at the end of each conversation, that a new day had dawned in their relationship. They would be open and tell each other how they felt. "She was so sweet," Margaret said and added with a rueful smile, "I hope it's true. We'll see."

From then on they did close with "I love you" every time they spoke, but Margaret could not and did not make her mother her confidante while she fought for her life. Nor did her mother complain about being left out. The illness didn't cure them of their differences, but it did, at least, bring peace to their war.

Perhaps that's why Margaret on her deathbed looked confused by her mother's question as to why she hadn't been invited to the studio; she thought it had all been settled. The whole family waited in a hush for her to answer. When she did, there was a disarming truth to it: "I'm weird about my paintings, Mom. I don't like to show them to people. It's not you. I just don't like to show them." She moved as if to sit up while saying to Enrique, "It's crazy, but I think my stomach tube is clogged from the hot dogs. They're backing up." She pulled the covers off. Her PEG was full of the reddish brown and beige material of the Second Avenue Deli lunch. The Cohens scattered at this frank display.

Enrique and Margaret retired to the bathroom, their first time alone since his conversation with Dorothy and Leonard rejecting their funeral arrangements. They conducted their last postmortem of her parents' feelings. Enrique described their reaction while standing at the sink, helping Margaret suction out pieces of undigested food that were too bulky to clear the narrow end of the PEG. They were old hands at this. There was a time when the grotesque procedure would have nauseated one or both of them. When it seemed that more hot dog and knish were coming out than had gone in, they began to laugh, and they laughed harder when Margaret said, "It's like every hot dog I've ever eaten is coming out." Enrique suctioned and Margaret squeezed, and he told her that Dorothy had exclaimed in pain when she heard that Margaret didn't want to be buried with her family. "You did a good job, Puff," she judged.

"How do you know?"

"Because she hasn't said a word to me about it."

That self-censorship didn't last long. Dorothy brought the subject up immediately after they had cleared all the Jew food and restored the tube and its drainage bag to their hiding places. The Cohens reassembled around the matrimonial bed. They settled in chairs, except for Dorothy, who stood behind her older son, the no longer mean Cowboys and Indians Rob, and announced, "You know what, Margs? I was upset you didn't want to be in the family plot with all of us and I was telling Rob and you know what?" She laughed with delight. "He's bought a plot in New Haven!"

Rob winked at Enrique, as if they were in on a conspiracy. "Who wants to be buried in New Jersey? Everyone wants to be buried near where they live. Except for my parents. They want to be buried in a state they've never lived in and don't like."

Leonard said affectionately, "Don't be a wise guy."

Dorothy protested, "Papa Sam bought the plot because it was big and a bargain. You know he liked a bargain. And I thought it was nice that we would all be together. And so convenient! Just one stop." Dorothy laughed at herself. "But it's not important. We love each other, that's what's important."

"Hey, Ma, you want to be buried with me?" Margaret said with a sly smile. "You can. There's another grave available at Green-Wood." Margaret lifted her arm in mock generosity. "We'll be together forever."

Dorothy came over to the bed at last—she seemed to have been avoiding close contact all day. She sat beside her daughter and took her face in her hands. "I don't think you want me living next door for all eternity." She kissed Margaret hard and fast, her usual briskness, and looked back at her daughters-in-law to inform them, "When Margaret was a teenager, she ordered me not to speak to her before breakfast."

"Also during and after breakfast," Margaret said, causing the room to erupt with laughter. "I don't like to be talked to until noon, right, Enrique?"

"Riiight," he said, elongating the word. Her family laughed knowingly at his mock-fearful tone. But his comedy was a lie. He knew how to get his wife to talk as soon as her first cup of coffee was down. She often preferred to be silent and to be alone. There had been many times during the twenty-nine years they had spent together when he understood that his very presence, and the noise and trouble of his sons, and the boom and bust of his career, and the melodramas of his parents made her long to be elsewhere. But even when she felt that deep exhaustion of marriage, in her greatest despair at whom she had chosen to love, even then he knew how to draw her into conversation. He always had.

chapter thirteen

The Great Seducer

ENRIQUE TOLD MARGARET everything about himself. He had read the metaphor, "He poured his heart out to her" in Stendhal and Dickens and Balzac and Lermontov and probably sarcastically in Philip Roth's novels. What came out of him didn't seem to be his heart, however. He emptied his soul, or his self, or whatever made him think he was unique. He disclosed all of his feelings and life secrets, or believed that he did; and he recounted every anecdote in his twenty-one-year-old life.

During that long night of December 30, 1975, while hours and hours passed into the early morning of a new day, the thick darkness outside the wall of windows behind Margaret's pretty head remained unchanged, punctuated but not revealed by the amber halos of New York's streetlights. Inside, there was no dark thanks to Margaret having, like Enrique, bought one of the new halogen standing lamps. She did not dim it for romance. There were no lit candles or the mellowing intoxication of wine. He was surrounded by a cheerful, searching illumination: intense light bounced off the mostly bare white walls, into her blue eyes and out of her ringing voice. They exchanged life stories like students cramming for a test, emptying a pot of coffee and smoking half a pack of cigarettes each. His body was rigid with tension: alert as a predator and as wary as prey. His anxiety didn't arise from baring his feelings to this attentive young woman with her depthless and astonished eyes; rather, he vibrated with anticipation that when he ran out of things to say, he was going to have to proceed with making love. Nay, not love alone. He would have to sexually sate this creature, who seemed to him more beautiful and clever with every passing moment, a human female perhaps, but of such a higher order that he felt there ought to be another classification for so superb a mutation of the species.

Enrique had had little time to reflect on what he had learned about Margaret. His sole opportunity came during a bathroom break, when he excused himself shortly after four o'clock in the morning. The accommodation was tiny even by New York City's standards. There were two feet of cleared space between the tub-shower, sink, and toilet, all squeezed into an area hardly larger than a closet. On the only free wall—the rest being mirror, tub, door—there was an abstract work of art: four thick, broad strokes of black paint on a small white canvas, in the shape of arches or humps, arranged as if they might be clouds floating free or a quartet of angry cats. He looked at it while his bladder seemed to empty ten persons' worth of urine, a comically long and noisy process, and got nothing from the art, the same nothing he usually got from abstract paintings—he couldn't help but attempt to decode them, although he knew the proper approach was to "feel" the work. He hoped this innocuous painting wasn't by Margaret, although he felt sure it was. Unframed and with two patches of canvas not painted at all, it looked like something by a beginner. He was surprised that she had hung it anywhere.

His ex-girlfriend, Sylvie, was a painter—supposedly. Enrique had his doubts. She seemed to have no vision of what she wanted to accomplish, or desire to develop a vision. She took secretarial jobs hoping to be fired after six months, long enough to qualify for unemployment insurance, which during the recessionary seventies was extended to nearly a year. With all that freedom to do her art, she produced little. During the three and half years they cohabited, Enrique wrote one and a half novels while Sylvie made fewer than ten paintings, most of them not completed. She was, in Enrique's considered opinion, lazy. And based on the few sketches she made of the human form, he suspected that her predilection for the abstract had more to do with her failure to master drawing people in proper proportions than with having transcended the need to be representational. By what insane bad luck could he have found himself attracted to another so-called Abstract Expressionist? Margaret couldn't be serious about painting, he tried to reassure himself; he would have heard something about it by now.

Enrique's understanding of Margaret's ultimate ambition, at four-ten in the morning of their third encounter and first date, was vague. His original impression from Bernard was that Margaret worked freelance for magazines. Enrique mistakenly assumed she did copy editing or fact checking, like Bernard; during that first night of conversation at his apartment, Enrique had learned that she was a graphic designer. When he said, "You're an artist?" she demurred, saying, "I do layout and pick pictures. Can't call that art. Although they do. They call it art direction," she said and winked as if she were sharing a lewd secret.

Over challah French toast, she had talked about taking a photography course. At the Orphans' Dinner, Enrique had briefly noticed two framed black-and-white photographs on the wall above the couch, but he hadn't had a chance to give them a good look. At the Buffalo Roadhouse, Margaret had mentioned she was taking acting classes. But when he asked if she wanted to be an actress, she said she was just fooling around, she didn't have the talent or the nerve. She had also mentioned that she was taking tap dancing classes with her friend Lily and was starting a lithography course soon. During their walk to her apartment, when she had reported that her mother didn't want her younger brother, Larry, to be an artist, and Enrique had asked if her mother would allow her to be one, she'd replied for the second time that she wasn't an artist. While zipping up, he reassured himself that the mediocre painting in the bathroom had been the product of one of her dilettantish explorations.

Uncertainty about ambition in life, although he knew it was a common condition of his age group, puzzled Enrique. He had burned every bridge that led away from writing novels so he couldn't give up, no matter how difficult his career became. He knew that if he had something to fall back on, one day he would collapse on it, and fail in his great mission to write a twenty-book series, like Zola's or Balzac's, with intertwining characters, an alternative version of the great city of New York inhabited by Sabas men and women, a dazzling tapestry crammed with insightful portraits of his people's greatness and follies. He didn't understand how someone as smart, clever, and imaginative as Margaret could live without a passion to achieve something. She was baffling and beautifully strange. That was precisely why the prospect of lying naked with her loomed as both exquisite and terrifying. In truth, although he claimed not to be a sexist, if she were a man, Enrique would have felt nothing but contempt for her lack of a focused ambition.

While Margaret took her turn in the bathroom, he studied the two photographs above the couch. He had assumed they were by her, but on closer examination he decided that was unlikely. The first was of two men, one elderly, the other in his twenties, sitting on a cobblestoned street with a large fishing net, which they were presumably repairing, sprawled across their legs. Oddly, they were in street clothes: both wore leather jackets, and the young man was in dress shoes. The expressions on their faces were intimate and relaxed and connected to the photographer, as if he were an old friend. The other picture was of three small children standing in a row in the middle of a village street. Like the fishermen, they appeared to be European, as did the background of low, crooked buildings and uneven cobblestones. The children were joyful and sober all at once. One smiled, another gazed with earnest longing, and the last was pensive. All displayed their feelings with utter unself-consciousness. Although they were looking into the camera, and obviously knew their picture was being taken, it felt as though they were peering directly into the viewer's soul. Enrique felt informed by the work, that he knew them well: this one was always a little sad, this one mischievous, that one loving.

The photographs were clearly by someone who not only had an eye and control over the equipment but loads of experience. The old world setting and the trust that had been gained over the subjects convinced Enrique a middle-aged man had taken them. He worried that his not recognizing these accomplished photographs betrayed his ignorance, that they must be by someone like Robert Capa or an Italian or French genius. He wasn't sure who was famous for doing what sorts of pictures. He had ignored his parents' and older siblings' discussions of Atget and Cartier-Bresson while growing up. Discussions of photography and of movies annoyed Enrique no end, although he enjoyed both media. As an act of self-gratification, going to a movie in the afternoon midweek ranked nearly as high as masturbation, but how could those mechanical tricks—changing lenses, manipulating light and shadow—compare to what Joyce correctly identified as the highest and most spiritual of all the arts, the novel? Painting, sculpture, theater—they were great art forms—but stuff that comes out of a machine? Enrique loved machines precisely because if you worked at them diligently they would eventually do what you wanted them to do. But his brain? It seemed to him that no matter how many hours he put into writing, he couldn't guarantee that effort would allow his mind to construct a sound sentence, much less to fully express what was in his imagination.

Still, these photographs were excellent. Enrique wished he could impress Margaret by identifying their creator. Obviously she valued them. They were elegantly framed, with proper borders. She might have no directed ambition, but based on where she had placed the painting and where she displayed these photographs, she knew the difference between her amateurish creation and the products of a dedicated pursuit of perfection.

"These are great," he said when she reappeared from the bathroom, partly to say what he had been feeling and partly to forestall any suggestion that after four o'clock in the morning he ought to be going home.

"Oh . . ." She stared at the framed photographs as if she had forgotten all about their existence. "Thanks . . . ," she said and added, "Italy is great."

"Italy?" Enrique repeated. Earlier she had told him that she spent a semester abroad living with an Italian family. He had a moment of uncertainty. They were her pictures? No, more likely they were purchased there. He was too timid to admit his ignorance and probed: "So these were taken in Italy?"

"Yeah . . . ," she said again in a faraway tone, as if dreaming of when she lived there. She resumed her earlier position on the couch, and so did he. "I wish I had taken more."

They *were* hers. He was profoundly surprised: they were so good; she was proud enough to display them prominently; they had been talking for hours and yet she'd never mentioned photography as an ambition, or even a hobby. "I took a course last summer in developing." She laughed, glancing at him warily as she confessed why. "You're going to think I'm a total dilettante, taking all these stupid courses, but they're fun. I like to try things out."

"I don't think you're a dilettante!" Enrique lied. "I love to learn too. I'm envious." That was true. He was envious that she had learned about tap dancing, photography, lithography, French, basic acting technique. He too wanted to know as much as possible about how the world worked. Not, however, for something as pointless as having fun. He wanted information to impress readers and to burrow into a character's inner life. Work was the most invested and complicated expenditure of most people's time; it bothered him to write about characters and not know, in a tactile and intimate way, precisely what they did each day on their jobs. He wished he had her curious, adventurous nature. Although he believed his utilitarian and purposeful approach to his career was superior to her casual explorations, he recognized that she was more likely to learn the details he needed to make his characters breathe and bleed.

Margaret looked pleased by his saying he envied her. She raised her right hand to her hair and fluffed out the black curls that had flattened above her perfectly shaped ear. "Oh, I just get bored and like to try something new," she said. "It's silly. I don't have your self-discipline. Or my brother's. It's amazing to me that you've written three novels. How do you do it?"

"By sitting alone in a room for hours and hours," he said, telling the simple truth. He shifted on the couch and pointed up at the photographs, wanting to make sure. "You took those?" She nodded with a rueful pucker of her chin. "They're fantastic," he said. "I thought they were expensive prints by some incredibly famous photographer, and I was embarrassed I didn't know whose they were. I mean, it's really great work. Totally first-rate." He paused there because he saw that this honest flattery had touched her in some deep location that he hadn't reached before.

"Oh . . ." came out of her and nothing more. For the very first time, she looked flustered. The parrying girl, the cool flirt, the evaluating woman, the teasing conversationalist, the sympathetic listener, the independent explorer, the resigned daughter, the pissed off sister, the motherly sister—he had seen and heard all sorts of colors and notes from her, but not before this had he unwomaned her into the blush and stammer of an overmastering pleasure. The effect was so striking, he found himself thinking: *If I could do that to her with my penis, I would be a happy man.*

He consoled himself by remembering what Sylvie had taught him out of *Our Bodies, Ourselves*—that he could guarantee the same result with his mouth—but even a callow young man like Enrique understood that what he had accomplished with his honest reaction to her photographs was more likely to be an enduring satisfaction to Margaret than his various body appendages, no matter how skillfully he wielded them.

He saw in a flash—the sort of illumination of understanding he needed to arrive at before he could write a character well—that her angry comments about her mother not allowing her brother to be an architect, as well as her resigned joke that she was allowed to do any sort of work provided she married and had two children, were her indirect way of declaring her true desire. Despite her denial, she *did* want to be an artist. She probably wanted to be a very great artist, he felt, espying a deeper ambition precisely because it was buried. She wanted to believe in her talent, to be like Enrique, someone who could stay at it day after day, devote her life to a gradual refinement of her natural gift until she produced a body of work that she could display with pride, not above toilets but in the world's living rooms. For a single exhilarating moment, he saw with Tolstoyan clarity what they offered each other: her self-contentment and pleasure in being alive would prevent him from giving in to gloom and resentment at the world's disappointments, poisoning his work; and his quotidian and stubborn faith in the ability of art to elevate artist and audience above the meanness of society would inspire her to become the secret Margaret, the great artist whom she had to hide from her pragmatic family and even from her timid self. She had the grace he could never win, and he had the will she couldn't assert.

He continued to try to hit her pleasure center with more praise about her pictures, but she deflected additional flattery and turned the subject to his persistence. "You said your second novel did badly and got some really mean reviews. But you started your third book right away. How did you stop from getting discouraged?"

By then his insight into the profound logic of their connection was lost, obscured by a collage of lust and anxiety: wondering if under her wool sweater there were freckles trailing down to her perky breasts; if her nipples would harden; if she would prefer to be encircled by his tongue or teased, or first one method and then the other, and underneath all those tantalizing plans and visions he worried, the way a fearful flyer dreads takeoff, whether his penis was going to work. If it didn't, would he lose everything? Would all they had said, all they had exchanged count for nothing?

So he talked passionately, something he could easily do because, whatever his cock was or wasn't up to, his heart and mind were full of passions. He described the sensation of power and grace writing granted him, the great accomplishment of finally, after days upon days, weeks upon weeks, months upon months, at long last finishing a novel, arriving at the very spot you had planned to reach, a satisfaction that was undiminished even if the book didn't turn out as intended. Nothing could lessen his pride at creating something straight out of his head, from the immaterial to the concrete. There, held in his hands, was his universe, as alive and as vivid to Enrique—at least sometimes—as the real world. He unashamedly confessed to the deep self-gratification there was for him in the process of writing. He didn't resort to the fashionable complaints of novelists: the pain of producing it, the nagging feeling of inadequacy, the frustrating search for meaning and innovation. He admitted that he often felt he was bad at writing, that he had yet to accomplish all he had hoped to in any of his novels, but he emphasized that those failures didn't spoil the pleasure of the attempt. He was so proximate to the prison of dullness from which he had escaped: he still woke up each day and thanked fate with earnest gratitude that he didn't have to go to high school anymore, or to some boring job. When he told her the embarrassing truth that holding the finished typescript of a novel suffused him with a warm sensation of achievement, nearly a sufficient reward unto itself, she beamed with approval.

He worked up the nerve to ask if the painting in the bathroom was hers. "Yeah . . . ," she said with a shrug, hiding from his searching eyes. "I don't know what I'm doing with that." She smiled at him bashfully. "But I wish I did. Photography's fun, but I'd like to paint." She looked pensive in a way that he had not seen before, then returned to him with her big eyes as if checking on what he thought.

He was overcome by the urge to touch her animated lips and encircle those slim arms and proud shoulders. Without warning or any physical segue, he dived at her as if she were a pool, and they kissed for the second time. On this occasion, she opened to him longer and he fell in deeper. While submerged, much to his relief, the one part of his body that until then had had no strength or yearning, crawled to attention in his underpants and pushed up to his belt, as if petitioning for freedom.

Thank God, he thought, I'm not going to be impotent like the last time, when his attempt at a one-night stand had ended as a fifteen-minute collapse. That failure loomed in his memory like the traumatic flashback of a near-fatal car wreck. The whole bottom half of him had been numbed with that girl, but not this time, not with Margaret. I'm going to be all right, he thought.

And with the arrival of that soothing prediction, he inexplicably lost all confidence that it was true. Panic flooded his brain. Nor was it quelled when the warm kiss ended, and she pulled her legs up, squatting on the couch so that she was taller, smiling down at him with utter self-assurance while she draped her arm around his shoulder possessively. Although he felt the head of his cock continue to swell, squeezed by the elastic of his underpants and thoroughly blocked by his belt, he worried about its stamina. His fear made no sense since his condition seemed irreversible. He wished he could reach in and push the demanding thing toward a pocket where there would be room for it to expand, but he didn't have the nerve to acknowledge the existence of his erection to Margaret. Why he should be ashamed of his lust for her he didn't know and he didn't wonder. Instead his mind was preoccupied with a scenario wherein the constriction of his leather belt might cause a permanent impairment and he would become, like the sad hero of *The Sun Also Rises*, unable to consummate with the love of his life; in Enrique's case not because of an emasculation inflicted by a war wound but thanks to a no less devastating necking injury.

Bravely, he risked further damage and slid up the length of her draped arm, as if riding a rail, to kiss what had tempted him for hours—the smooth tenderness of her neck. She allowed him to nestle there, although she shivered when he pressed his coffee-warmed lips in its hollow and tasted the dessert of her skin with a flick of his tongue. She nudged him away with her chin, causing alarm for a moment, but it was to make her assault, swooping down, biting his lower lip before she covered his mouth with hers, skinny arms pulling him up with surprising strength as if to swallow him whole.

Even to the profoundly insecure Enrique, this seemed a clear signal that she wanted him. She was willing right now. Besides, he had to change something, at the very least make an adjustment in his pants. The discomfort had become actually painful, and he truly did fear, unless he conquered or abandoned the field at once, that more than an imagined literary harm might befall his least understood and most demanding body part. He had to proceed and risk losing all that he had painstakingly accomplished with this undiscovered genius of a beautiful girl, this endless source of good cheer, this black-haired, blue-eyed, ice cream white gift that some novelist who was much more generous to Enrique than Enrique was to his characters had plunked down like an oasis in the middle of his desolation.

Margaret hovered near his lips. She regarded him with a characteristic look of expectation that he assumed had to do with the newness of their acquaintance—she must want him to reveal something. Her emotions were unreadable to him and broadcast two distinct and confusing messages: that she desired everything he could give and that she was equally prepared to be horrified or delighted.

He felt overwhelmed. And he heard himself say, without having first reviewed the wisdom or lack thereof: "I'm scared."

She nodded as if she had known all along he was going to say that. "Me too," she said, as if what they were scared of had nothing to do with them, was outside lurking in the unchanging black of New York.

"What are you scared of?" Enrique asked. He couldn't imagine anything frightening about this situation for her. He was completely in love with her and, although he might not jump out the window if she asked him to, he would certainly think about it seriously.

"You know," she said with a frown as if he were teasing her.

What the hell did she mean? Not sex? She couldn't be scared of that: it was all on him; she was delicious and beautiful; all she had to do was lie there while he, sensitive to her cues about how he touched her, proceeded to excite her masterfully to liquid receptivity and swelled into a powerful state himself, yet taking care not to become so thrilled that he ended their union prematurely. He'd done it right plenty of times with Sylvie, but only after several disastrous inaugural attempts. What if Margaret was less patient? What if this fantasy she had constructed about him, that he was passionate and confident and determined, what if she never forgave him when she discovered it was false? Wasn't she going to be disgusted when she learned that he was, despite his three and a half years with another woman, still, at heart, a virgin? "I don't," he said. "I know why I'm scared, but I have no idea why you are."

Wariness and annoyance crept into her tone. "You know . . . I'm scared of what everyone's scared of."

He laughed. He was being stupid beyond belief, and that struck him as funny. "What the hell is everyone scared of?"

She grimaced as if he'd poked her with a sharp stick. "Well . . ." She hesitated. "What are you scared of?"

He wanted to say "That my penis won't work or that it will work too quickly," but he wasn't *that* committed to truth. "Me first, huh?" he stalled.

At that she laughed with delight. "Yeah. You first."

"That you won't like me . . . you know . . ." And, overwhelmed by shame, he nodded toward the foot of the L, almost entirely filled by her queen-size bed.

She blinked in astonishment. Not once. Not twice. But three times, as if her brain were a cash register unable to ring up his words. "You mean"—her face collapsed into doubt at the answer she had discovered—"sex?"

Apparently this possibility was so far from her mind that Enrique had to conclude he had made a ghastly error in placing it there at all, much less so prominently.

"Why?" she demanded with her ability to shift directly from sympathetic delicacy to cool sarcasm. "Is there something disgusting about you?" She seemed to regret the harshness of that. "Your kiss isn't disgusting," she added and, to further soften the blow, kissed him, lingering on his lips and making a soft hum of pleasure before she leaned back to restate her question: "What scares you about going to bed?"

She had covered her shock and dismay, but that glimpse of her true reaction of contempt frightened him. His mind scanned frantically for a plausible lie. What came out, paradoxically, was his real feeling. "I'm so nervous about it being our first time and I'm so in love with you that I'm scared I won't get an erection and you'll kick me out and I'll never get to see you again and that'll be"—his voice wobbled with the sadness of it—"so fucking terrible."

As he feared, she blanched. Something this awful had never occurred to her. The surprise and disappointment could be read clearly on her face. She had praised him only hours ago for being a man among boys, and here he was, in a high, querulous voice, admitting to—well, it was an excellent word for it, precise and resonant—his impotence. He met her eyes, glaring blue amazement, and he saw that he had made a fatal error. "I guess I'd better go," he mumbled and cast his eyes down to the parquet floor, overwhelmed by shame.

She was on him before he could raise them. She was crawling

inside his arms, kissing his neck, his lips, his right eyelid, which he shut in the nick of time to prevent blindness, up to his forehead and around to his left eye, his left cheek, and reprised his lips, where she paused and blew words from her mouth into his, a hot breeze. "You don't have to say that."

Her eyes were so close to him, large and drowning in feeling, that he had no sense of himself anymore and fell inside her, speaking to her as if she and he were one individual and these were thoughts they shared. "But it's true," he said. It would be terrible never to see her again, he thought, and didn't know if he had spoken aloud, so he said: "It would be terrible never to see you again."

"You're going to see me again," she whispered, then kissed him angrily, before she angled below and bit his neck hard enough that he almost yelped. She returned to his field of vision, filling it, and saying, "Just do me a favor. Don't say that again unless you mean it. Really mean it."

Enrique's body was thrilled, but his head was confused. "I don't understand," he blurted out, unable to think while being flooded by the light of her eyes.

"We're going to see each other. Don't worry about that. And don't worry about the sex. Just don't say *that*"—she emphasized the word with the contempt impotence deserved—"unless you mean it."

Enrique, hopelessly lost, asked in his bewilderment, "You don't want me to say I'm going to be impotent unless I'm really going to be impotent?"

All night she hadn't laughed at a single one of his witticisms; with this innocent and honest question, he scored. She threw her head back, gap teeth exposed, her vulnerable neck bared, and trilled through her laughter, "No . . . no . . . no . . ." She sighed with relief, her lips pecking at his in between whispering, "Don't say you love me until you really mean it."

"I do mean it," he complained, hurt. He didn't understand that they had been talking at cross-purposes.

She stated in a firm corrective tone, "You like me."

"Yes!" Enrique affirmed, not understanding her distinction.

"I like you," she said.

"Good," Enrique said, still dense. "I'm glad," he added.

She pressed against him, her mouth nearing his right ear while her left hand covered the bulge in his black jeans. She whispered, "Let's just say that," and the thought seemed to be injected directly into his consciousness. All he truly understood at that moment, while she stroked him, and her odd vow of like, not love rattled in his head, was that the distinction meant something to her. He knew, however, that it was meaningless to him, that progressing from liking Margaret to loving her was seamless.

He didn't have to think for a while, anyway, as they awkwardly necked and probed each other's flesh through their respective wool, cotton, and denim obstructions. He floated away on the undulations of teasing sensations and the fascinating discoveries of where she was strong and where she was soft, of how she opened to, and when she was worried by his touch. Eyes closed and entwined in her arms, he had forgotten his name and where they were when she took his hand and rose.

His eyes must have been shut for a long time, because the opaque darkness of New York had turned a hopeful, deep blue, and toward the east he saw an orange glow of the sun's fire. He saw her block naked: the street cleared of cars and people, trees bare of leaves, windows dark. A garbage truck cleared its throat at the corner, a cock's crow that the city was about to awaken. Fully clothed, Margaret pulled him onto the bed, and they lay for the first time length to length, her feet stopping at his knees, Enrique's running over the bed's edge. His sneakers dangled in the air. He kicked them off while they resumed kissing.

The move to the bed had reawakened his consciousness of what he was about to do. He was anxious for them to be naked and to get it over with. He pulled at her sweater and searched underneath, skimming with his fingertips the soft silk of her belly. She hummed at this touch and opened her denim hips wide enough to capture his leg, pushing her sex against the hard post of his skinny thigh. She rubbed on him with the yearning and independence of a cat, arching and making low sounds, using and wanting him, yet somehow also not needing him. When his hands reached the thin fabric of her bra and moved under it effortlessly so that his palms slid rapidly over her hardened nipples, she grunted as if he'd punched her. She pushed her lips, her groin, her stomach at him as if intending to burst through his skin and into him, and abruptly she was sitting up, pulling off her sweater, and rising to undo her jeans, stepping out of them, and tugging at the blanket and undersheet, pulling them down so that Enrique had little choice but to get up and strip to his underpants. He hurried as if he had to be somewhere else, all the while wishing he could slow down.

Margaret shivered as she got under the covers in her bra and panties, and she curled into Enrique's skinny body, then arched away to place her cold feet on his thighs. "You're so warm," she said, burrowing her head against his chest and climbing up into his neck, biting him again, and farther up to his mouth, while she wrapped her thighs around his right leg to ride it. Through the black fabric of her panties, he could feel that she was wet and completely married to her desire. Enrique, however, was divorced from his body which, to his surprise, remained hard all over, his erection seemingly enormous against the thin membrane of cotton that separated it from her cool skin.

Since she could feel pleasure happily, he lowered his head and began to journey and explore, but he didn't get far. As soon as he arrived at her breasts and tried to unfasten the bra's clasp, she sat up, undid it herself, dropping it onto the parquet floor, and then reached below with both hands, pulling off her panties, and flipping them away from the bed as if tossing a hat. He did the same with his underpants and felt profoundly naked. He couldn't remember if he had ever felt so bare of protection. As she retook him into her arms, pressing, sliding, urging him against her now warm skin, delicate fingers curling around his stretched and aching cock, he felt as bewildered and as tender as a newborn.

Again he lowered his head to make love to her body with his mouth, but she pulled him up as if she were too excited to tolerate more excitement and rolled onto her back, pulling him onto her. He was wood hard, as rigid there as he was everywhere, and so it made sense. But as soon as he was above her, he lost all sensation below; he couldn't feel his sex. He thrust at her because he was supposed to. He bounced off where there was supposed to be an opening, like a weakly thrown ball. Not a deadly ricochet, but a dribbling bounce.

He was overwhelmed by sadness. He felt grief at what he would lose because of this inexplicable failure. Just when it seemed that all the hard work was done, to have found his harbor and yet not be able to dock there, to be so proximate to contentment and to understand, in agony, that he was doomed never to penetrate its mystery. He thrust again. But he knew, even before he was crushed by the wall of her body, that he would fail.

Margaret frowned, puzzled. She reached down, taking hold of his penis. It was softening and getting softer at her evaluating hand. Disgusting to the touch, Enrique was sure.

"I'm sorry," he said, and he was. Sorrier than he had ever felt, a deep regret at the lifelong happiness he had lost.

She rolled to her side, dumping his disappointing body. Enrique flopped off, a gasping fish, losing contact with her altogether. In that rejection, he felt how painful this abandonment was and would be—an orphaning worse than anything in Dickens.

But she didn't let him go. She snaked back into his arms, kissed him lightly, and whispered into his ear, "Let's sleep." Her fingers brushed his clenched back in long, soothing strokes. "Let's just lie here and go to sleep."

"I'm . . . ," he began, in wild pain, to excuse his failure. He managed to pronounce only a single word: the sound he made was like the howl of a lost creature. Margaret was quick to cut him off.

"Shh," she soothed, running the flat of her small hand up and down the hollow of his back. "Close your eyes," she said, and he dropped from cold terror into warm fatigue. His muscles were aching as if he'd run a marathon, and his eyes were burning as if he'd walked through a fire. He shut them, and that was a relief.

His thoughts also subsided. They fell from the fearful land scape of her bed onto a beach. He sank deep into the hot sand and watched an undulating sea stretch into an endless blue horizon. She mumbled, "Let's sleep," and he let go. He let go of expectation, he let go of self. For the first time in all the hours he had spent with Margaret, maybe for the first time in his long life of twenty-one years, he let go of the worrisome and ambitious future.

chapter fourteen

A Mother's Love

T HE DAY AFTER Margaret's parents agreed to honor her funeral and burial desires, the Cohen family appeared again en masse at their apartment. Her brothers and their wives had separate audiences upstairs with Margaret, presumably to say their good-byes. The sisters-in-law left ahead of their husbands, so that each brother had some time alone with her. Dorothy and Leonard also went upstairs by themselves but with no plan, it seemed to Enrique, to have a defined last talk. In fact, they seemed to hint that they were planning to drive in from Great Neck every day until the end. Enrique expressed his concern about this to Margaret during one free moment they had together. She raised her painted-on eyebrows and declared, "No way. Don't worry about that."

But he did. He worried more with each passing hour about how little time he had left to be alone with his wife. Giving up a second day to her family meant that, except for a few whispered exchanges of affection before Margaret took her dose of Ativan to help her sleep, another day and night with her was gone. The evening before, four old friends had come over for a final downing of champagne and caviar with Margaret, and then stayed late. Tonight Lily and Paul would come, another emotional and difficult farewell that Enrique knew would drain Margaret and make her long for a sedated sleep. In effect, today would be another day, one of only eight left to them, when he would be near but essentially separated from his wife.

Instead he found himself alone with her kid brother, Larry, now a balding, middle-aged man. Twice, while Margaret babysat him, he had been damaged: a concussion when she tried to teach six-year-old Larry to ride a bike; and a broken arm from an ill fated roller-skate on the access road to Utopia Parkway. Enrique believed that taking care of Larry, no matter how calamitously, had helped teach Margaret to be a cheerful and energetic mother of young boys. When he noticed the camp counselor spirit that animated her while she tussled with his toddler sons, and how easily she jollied his sometimes dour boys into giggles, Enrique fancied that he was meeting the adolescent girl whose idolatrous kid brother forgave her for all his wounds. He dreaded the sorrow that lay ahead for his sons and feared he would be unable to console them. He soothed himself with the hope that a permanent deposit of those carefree hours playing on the hardwood floors with their mother— not a memory of happiness but an unremembered absorption of her joy at having created them—could provide a lifetime's buoyancy that would eventually lift his sons' hearts above the cruelty of losing her.

Enrique had been raised by an unhappy, anxious, and fearful woman. He wondered if providing for his sons a more nurturing mother than his own had been part of the motive for his falling in love with Margaret. It appealed to his literary imagination, the notion that he had selected her not only for her white freckled skin and brilliant blue eyes—signals that she would have different immunities than those granted by his olive complexion and brown eyes—but also because he had noted her affectionate account and easy acceptance of disaster while babysitting young Larry. At interminable Cohen Seders and Thanksgivings, he had observed Larry's continuing loyalty to and love for Margaret. He wondered if the middle-aged Larry understood that he had inadvertently contributed to Enrique's progeny. And he wondered if Margaret's kid brother could comprehend more easily than Enrique what it must feel like to his boys to lose a mother so vigorous, gregarious, and brave.

Enrique searched for a question that Larry could answer without too much effort, and that would also acknowledge his special role in his sister's life. "So—have you forgiven Margaret for breaking your arm and giving you a concussion?" he asked, and thought it a feeble solution.

For a moment, Larry didn't seem able to answer. Then he did with an open heart. "She was a great big sister to me. She was so much fun." Tears appeared and dripped down his face as if he were still a little boy, access to his feelings a routine accomplishment. "I know we joke about those accidents, but they weren't her fault. The truth is, I always felt safe when I was with her. No matter what. I just loved being with her," he said, his face collapsing in pain. Enrique hugged him hard, patting his back until Larry was calm enough to draw easy breaths.

Another flood of emotion came from her father half an hour later. Leonard, his shoulders bowed, moved with pained slowness across the length of the living room to corner Enrique in the kitchen, easy to accomplish in that small, windowless space. Enrique, fighting both fatigue and a headache, was brewing his sixth cup of coffee at one-thirty in the afternoon. Leonard appeared beside him at the stove and laid his hand on Enrique's forearm, a cue that this would be an important matter. "I don't want to intrude, but how much is the plot at Green-Wood?"

"At Green-Wood?" Enrique stalled, to prepare for what was coming. A protest that it was too much? An offer to pay? He had to say no to both, but without delivering another cut to this wounded man. Leonard was the patriarch, unquestioned even by his older son, who had surpassed his father in eminence. But the approaching death of his beautiful daughter had run Leonard through; he looked paler and weaker by the hour, as if he were bleeding out grief.

At times, studying his father-in-law's forsaken face, Enrique worried that Leonard wouldn't survive Margaret by more than a few weeks. In these two days, the acuteness of her parents' suffering was made more tactile and vivid to him than at any time during the two years and eight months of Margaret's illness, and not simply because she was near the end. Until now their visits had been carefully confined on both Margaret's and her parents' side to lengths they could all tolerate. He had sometimes resented and scorned Leonard and Dorothy for their brief comfort, an unreasonable complaint since Margaret wanted them to keep away. But Enrique had to admit that now he was grateful Dorothy and Leonard had spared him from watching up close their agony at this hollowing of their hearts.

Enrique's mother had not. She demanded attention for her pain. Each Saturday morning, when he visited Rose in Riverdale at her assisted-living home, he was obliged to hold her hand while she wept over Margaret's illness, and to reassure her that he and the boys were all right. "How could you be?" she would comment, stubborn in her gloom. Comforting the inconsolable Rose was routine, the role he had played with his depressive mother all his life. During this crisis, though, the effort left him screaming in the isolation of the glass enclosure of his car ride home, and desperate to find time for a nap before returning gratefully to the success of being good-humored with his dying wife. The contrast of these parental reactions allowed Enrique to appreciate that his wife's family had helped him, in their roundabout way, to provide the kind of solace for Margaret that they could not. Dorothy and Leonard—like his parents for him—were not all Margaret wished they could be, but they had found a way to send the aid she required across the embargoed borders of their hearts.

"It's not much money," he said to Leonard, hoping to avoid whatever the broken man wanted to fix. Leonard had taken care of problems for his wife and children and grandchildren all his life. There was nothing he could repair now.

"How much?" Leonard said in a stern tone.

"Ten thousand," Enrique reported.

"Really? That's all?" the microeconomist wondered aloud. "Even though there are so few graves available?"

Enrique, although usually of a satirical cast of mind, didn't find it funny that Leonard bothered to think about supply and demand. It was his way of negotiating the world. If he couldn't soothe himself with such considerations at this time, when could he? "Well, I guess people want to be able to buy large plots, not just a single grave here and there," Enrique offered, thinking of Dorothy, who would never dream of choosing a solitary grave with only nineteenth-century goyim for company.

Leonard looked thoughtful, studying the pricing issues, Enrique assumed. Under normal circumstances, his father-in-law might ask to see the brochure or the website, and muse on the relative cost of the mausoleum spaces in the new area of Green-Wood, as opposed to spare plots squeezed between landmarked graves in the old section; and then he might speculate about the inconvenience of Brooklyn for buyers from well-to-do places such as Long Island, and sundry other factors. Enrique could imagine Leonard concluding that Green-Wood's managers ought to charge more. Certainly he would announce with pride that his daughter had found a bargain. But Enrique had misunderstood the way his father-in-law's mind worked. "I don't mean to pry," Leonard declared at last, "but is ten thousand a lot for you?"

Dorothy appeared without warning, talking as she entered the crowded kitchen. "Are you having more coffee? Isn't that too much? I guess you need it." Uncharacteristically, she kissed Enrique on the cheek. "Are you getting any sleep?"

"Dorothy!" Leonard said sharply.

"What?" she said, knowing from over fifty years of marriage his tone meant she had interrupted. She pretended she hadn't. "I just wanted to know what you're talking about. Not that I'm nosy," she added with a delighted, self-knowing laugh.

"I was asking Enrique about the cost of the plot. He said it's ten thousand—"

"Ten thousand?" she said with the same ambiguous shock she had expressed on hearing that Margaret's Rabbi was a Buddhist. Did she agree that ten thousand seemed low or, given that she would never select so lonely a grave, too high?

"I was asking Enrique if that's a lot for him."

"We don't mean to pry!" she exclaimed, as if she'd been accused of doing just that. "We just don't want you to spend too much. We want to help."

"No, it's not too much," Enrique said. There had been many times after his first movie was made, and he was finally solvent, when he had wanted to inform Leonard and Dorothy that he was no longer a broke writer. But Margaret had forbidden him to discuss money with her parents. When he asked why not, she'd say, "They won't understand," which seemed preposterous given that Leonard understood more about money than almost anybody on the face of the earth and that Dorothy also seemed to have an exceptionally good grasp of the consequences of monetary policy on the stock market. But Margaret insisted, "They won't understand that it's feast or famine for you and that what just happened to something you wrote has nothing to do with what's going to happen next. They're like everybody, Enrique, they don't understand the craziness you're dealing with, they won't understand that it has nothing to do with how well you write." She sighed, as if exhausted by having lived in such close proximity to his career. "Anyway, it's not their business!" she concluded in an exasperated tone that he knew not to disobey. They were her parents, and she was in charge of his relationship with them.

However, her injunction had been made when she was well and alive; now that she was dying, he couldn't, in good conscience, allow her parents to think ten thousand dollars was more than he could afford. "Listen," he announced, "let me explain about my situation with money—"

Dorothy cried out in a panic, "No details! Don't tell us any details! We don't want to pry—"

"I don't mind," Enrique said, not believing her. Indeed, she immediately fell into a deep and attentive silence, and that was rare. "We have a little over two million dollars in stocks and bonds. The house in Maine is worth around a million, and we don't have a mortgage. Now I haven't worked for a while, and I probably will have trouble making a lot of money from here on because most writers, once they pass fifty, earn much less unless they're world famous, and sadly I'm not. But at sixty-six I'll get a pension from the Writers Guild—" He paused here to check on their silent faces. Their lips were sealed, eyes attentive, bodies still, as if he had cast a spell. "I'll have a pension of about one hundred thousand a year, so with what we've saved, even if I don't make any more money, I should be able to live comfortably. Especially if I stop living like a king."

There was a long pause. Leonard blinked and sighed. Dorothy finally broke the silence: "Two million."

"A little over two million in stocks and—"

She cut him off, "Two million's not a lot of money. That's not a lot of money anymore. And you have no idea what your income's going to be. Hollywood is unreliable," she declared and kissed him on the cheek again, a remarkable act of random affection. She added in her brisk, have-to-catch-a-train tone: "Don't worry. Margaret asked us to promise to take care of you, and I told her we think of you as our son. Of course we'll take care of you." She turned away abruptly and called out, "Rob? Are you still upstairs?" She disappeared from the tiny kitchen, calling, "When you're done I want to ask Margs something. Rob, are you still up there?"

Nonplussed, Enrique looked at Leonard who, it turned out, was studying him. His wan eyes seemed to be waiting for Enrique to speak. Enrique had more in common with his mother-in-law than he would care to admit, granting great power to the subject of money, especially regarding others; convinced, for example, that the price of the plot was more important to Leonard than it was to Enrique, although there was no proof of that. He assumed Leonard still required reassurance about the cost of the grave and stated the obvious, "Anyway, the ten thousand isn't a lot to me. Margaret asked me to get the plot for her, and it means a lot to me—maybe it's a meaningless distinction—but I'd like pay for it."

Leonard nodded with so ponderous an air of gravity that Enrique thought he was reluctant to agree. "You know," Leonard began, but he had trouble getting the words out. He paused to clear his throat. "One of our friends asked me, 'Are you reconciled to this?' " He stopped and met Enrique's eyes. There was an emotion revealed in them that Enrique had rarely seen in his father-in-law: anger.

"Reconciled?" Enrique said, taking a moment to adjust to this shift in the conversation. "Reconciled?" he repeated in a puzzled tone, although he knew what was meant. "Reconciled to what? Margaret dying?" he added with contempt.

Leonard nodded with an embittered smile. " 'Are you reconciled to this?' my friend asked. 'Have you accepted it?' he asked me." Leonard's eyes filled as he frowned with disgust. "I said, 'I don't have a choice. I have to accept it. But am I reconciled to it?' " He shook his head like a bull trying to rid himself of the matador's sword. "No," he declared as if swearing an oath in court. " 'No,' I told my friend." He pronounced *friend* as if the word meant "enemy." " 'I am not reconciled.' " He staggered back against the stove, quaking as he stammered out his hopeless defiance: "I am not reconciled to my daughter dying." Enrique embraced him, almost as much to keep him safely on his feet as to comfort him. He felt intrusive about the physical gesture, half-convinced Leonard might pull away, but the old man let Enrique hold him, and his chest heaved twice with heavy sobs, releases of utter despair. When they were expelled, Leonard pulled away, searching for and finding his handkerchief. "That's enough," he declared. He discreetly wiped his tears and blew his nose. "That's enough of that," he decided. "I got it out. I'm sorry," he said.

"Nothing to be sorry for," Enrique assured him.

Margaret's father nodded. "I don't know how you've handled all this. I couldn't have done it." And for the thousandth time, when paid this compliment by friends or family, Enrique wondered if there was some hidden criticism in it.

Should he have fallen apart? He'd wanted to, often enough, and had in secret, in his office, in the car, and twice in a crowd of strangers on a New York street. But he had sons. Like Dorothy and Leonard, he had children to see through to the end. He had always assumed that Margaret would do that job, outlive Enrique, and harass the boys through adulthood. That task lay ahead. To his surprise, comforting his sons so far had been straightforward, a matter of managing information honestly and letting them feel free to be sad and scared. Their emotions, although keenly painful to see bearing down on young shoulders, were pure, untainted by the narcissism of people closer in age to Margaret, who felt themselves nearer to the bullet that had mortally wounded her. Max and Gregory were in shock, bewildered by their mother's illness and dreading her approaching death. Enrique was sure that the acute loss was yet to come: when she no longer answered the phone if they lost their wallet; or their e-mail failed to ping with advice about the big job interview; or when no one warned them to have a jacket ready when they visited their grandparents at the golf club; or when they couldn't call to hear her say they were handsome and charming after a heartless girl rejected them, or listen to her squeal with delight at a career triumph; when they walked down the aisle to wed their beloved and didn't see her in the front row; when they held Margaret's grandchildren in their arms and couldn't hand the future to her—that's when they would need Enrique. If he had fallen apart during her illness, he would have failed Margaret and frightened the boys, and after such a disaster, how could he stitch his sons back together? And how could Dorothy and Leonard feel reassured that there was someone relatively sane and loving to care for their grandsons? At last, after years of confusion, he could see that what he had assumed was his strength in life, his writing, wasn't what he could contribute to the people he loved. That he could accept what they felt, no matter how different from his own nature, this was his real talent.

He carried his coffee to the couch, mentally reviewing Margaret's schedule. Tomorrow was Greg's day with his mother and ought also to be Max's last private talk with her. Greg was arriving tonight from D.C., where he had been working since graduating college two years ago. The plan was that he would spend the day alone with his mother. Max, who had been obliged to witness day by day his mother's illness during his sophomore, junior, and senior years of high school, had yet to declare when he wanted his final hours with her, or if he wanted them at all. At noon, Max had appeared from sleeping off last night's attempt to blind himself to what was happening. He took one look at the long faces of grandparents and aunts and uncles and headed out, to meet someone, he said. Enrique stopped him at the elevator to remind him that if he wanted some time alone with his mother it should be pretty soon, given that she would stop the steroids tomorrow and then might get very sleepy or fall into unconsciousness. "I'll tell you later," Max said.

"Don't you want to have some time alone with her?" Enrique nagged and wished he hadn't even before Max's bloodshot eyes winced.

"I don't know," he said, "stop asking me about it," and rushed into the elevator.

Enrique had to conclude that Max was seriously weighing the possibility of not saying good-bye to his beloved mother. That seemed preposterous. He was devoted to her. During the worst of her illness, Max would climb under IV lines and nestle up to her wounded body, to lie his head on her shoulder. When she got frailer, he placed her head on his growing shoulder and stroked her cheek. Enrique believed this reluctance to say good-bye was anger at death. Max was furious that every effort to stop the disease had failed, and in a deeper rage that all his mother seemed to care about was what college he got into, and what job he would have the summer she died.

Enrique tried to save Max from Margaret's last attempt to control her baby boy's life. "I don't want him sitting around after I'm dead, getting morose and drinking too much," she declared. She noticed Enrique's look of disapproval and pleaded breathlessly, "I have to keep nagging him, Puff. I can let go of everything else, but I can't let go of nagging my boys." That aborted his attempt at shielding Max. All their marriage Margaret had wielded this sort of emotional imperative to get her way. Enrique would fight back with declarations that she was unreasonable, rattle verbal swords of defiance, and sometimes berate and bully or whine and plead. No matter. All tactics failed. Perhaps once or twice in twenty-nine years after announcing, "I can't," she had given way, but he could hardly expect to win this one. He felt equally helpless against Max's refusal to schedule a time with his mother. And he was afraid of the consequences. Enrique felt pity for Max's raw and irritated feelings, but an intemperate "No" to saying good-bye to his mother would become a lifelong regret.

And when would Enrique's turn come to say good-bye? She had only one more day of steroids. Greg would use that up, and then the last group of her friends would take another day, and Enrique hoped Max would take some time. He worried that she would decline more rapidly than predicted and he would lose his precious opportunity. He had to let the others go first, because he was the host of this gloomy party and Margaret had insisted he help her through it. Okay. But they had so much to say to each other. Was there going to be enough time?

Rob, Margaret's brilliant, distinguished older brother, came downstairs from his audience and strode purposefully across the living room to sit next to Enrique, dosing with caffeine on the couch. "Margaret and I talked," he said with a kind air and an amused smile. "She asked me to help give her a break from our parents. I'll get them to stay away for a couple days. It isn't good for them, anyway. They should be with their friends. That's who can comfort them."

"Are you sure?" Enrique asked, wondering about Leonard's "reconciled" friend.

Rob was certain. "Yes. Janice and I will stay in Great Neck with them. We'll keep them busy. That'll give you, Margaret, and the boys time alone together."

Enrique, said, "Thank you," in as slow and heartfelt a voice as he could muster.

Rob nodded. "I promised Margaret that you and I will stay in touch. I know you'll move on, of course, you should move on, we all know that, and we want you to. But if you need help with anything, Max or Gregory, I told her I'm here for you. She doesn't want you to hesitate to call me. So you won't, right?"

Enrique was confused for a moment. He wasn't a widower yet and didn't immediately understand that "move on" referred to falling in love with another woman. He also assumed that he would eventually live with or marry another woman, given that he liked both women and relationships. Yet it felt bizarre, like being told that all objects, no matter what their weight, fall at the same rate of speed. That was demonstrably true but seemed impossible. After a second's hesitation, he got what "move on" meant. He had thought about the question of another relationship long enough to have decided that, for his sons' sake, he would be sure to let at least four years go by before appearing with a replacement, no matter how unthreatening, to their mother. Four years of Max in college seemed the right hiatus. He was about to tell Rob this notion when he realized such a conversation with Margaret's older brother was preposterous and tasteless. Instead he answered the real question, or the one he thought was being asked. "Of course, I'll stay in touch. The boys and I will see you at Passover, Thanksgiving. We'll be at all the family gatherings."

It was Rob's turn to look confused. He frowned, head cocked as if trying to puzzle out what had been said. "Sure, but I mean if something comes up I can help with. Margaret wants to be sure that we stay in touch. In case you need anything."

Only then did the self-absorbed Enrique realize what truly must have been going on upstairs. He had assumed Margaret's final words to her family were about them. Instead, Margaret was pleading for Enrique and her sons, making sure that whatever she couldn't take care of herself would be handled by her proxies. She was busy talking about him, for God's sakes.

Enrique reassured Rob in a hurry, promising that he would call on him if he needed anything, and fiddled with various insurance and other papers from Green-Wood at the base of the stairs. He waited until all of the Cohens, except for Dorothy, had gathered in the living room. He climbed the steps to sit in his home office outside the bedroom, queued up to be next in line after her mother. As he neared the landing, he heard them talking. He softened his tread, hoping to eavesdrop on this postdeath supervision his wife was attempting. What was Margaret charging her people to do for him? See him happily remarried? Supervise his care of the boys? What didn't she think he could manage for himself?

The pocket door between the alcove of his office and the bedroom was open all the way, but a wall shielded him from a view of the marital bed around a corner. As he neared the door, he wondered whether he should enter and interrupt if Dorothy was saying something bothersome to Margaret. Listening in proved easy. They hadn't heard his footfall, probably because their voices were only loud but ecstatic. Dorothy's was full of warmth instead of her typical brittleness, and a kind of delight as she sang a fugue of praise. "I tell all my friends what a great mother you are, so much better than I was. Max and Gregory are such brilliant young men, so loving and so smart and confident and that's because you are such a good friend to them, such a good mother to them. They trust you and they love you and they're such serious and good young men, they're going to do good work in the world. I'm so proud of you, Margs, so proud—"

And Margaret, in a voice liquid with love, was talking too, not over her mother, rather in harmony. "That's because of you, Ma. I learned how to be a mother from you—"

"No, no," Dorothy was saying. "You raised them your own way. I thought you were crazy to stay in Manhattan and to send them to those schools, that crazy Christian church school frightened me, but you were—"

"Ma, Ma, Ma," Margaret called out, as if Dorothy had her back turned to her and she needed her attention. "Ma, please listen. Listen. Listen."

"What, darling?" Dorothy seemed to have made her voice even more gentle, all of her anxious shrillness gone, replaced with breathless ardor. "I am listening," she said, not in defense but as a promise.

There was a pause. He heard sheets rustling and was curious enough to lean out and peer around the doorway. From there he could see a reflection of mother and daughter in the glass of a framed photograph of Max and Greg as toddlers, hanging on the wall opposite the bed. Margaret had maneuvered to rise to a sitting position and was hugging her mother, not one of their efficient and rigid hugs of alienation but holding and keeping her against her chest, as if Dorothy were her child. She was whispering down past the stiff curve of her mother's lacquered hairdo, into an ear that was as small and as perfectly shaped as Margaret's: "I learned from you. Everything I know about being a mother I learned from you. You were my hero, Ma. You were always my hero."

Dorothy, her head held against her daughter's heart, sobbed

out her answer like a grateful child. "You're mine, you're mine, you're mine." Overcome, she couldn't say more, and Enrique, ashamed, head pounding with tears that were stuck somewhere in his skull, backed away into the windowless desk area to give them privacy. Standing in the shadows, he thought about the withholding wife he had resented so often, the scolding woman he had sometimes desperately longed to be free of, head thumping with words that beat like drums on his soul, as if God were hammering him into the ground: *She is good. She is so good and so kind and I am so mean and so bitter. She is full of love and I am empty without her.*

chapter fifteen

Lost Love

ENRIQUE WAS IN love. He couldn't stop thinking about her. While he typed, while ordering coffee at the deli, while standing under the shower, when lighting a cigarette, when pushing his nearly two-year-old son in a stroller, he thought of tasting her, of how her lithe body bent in his eager hands as if lust had melted her spine, how her taut skin surrendered to his tongue, how all the parts of her, the bright and the dark, tasted sweet and rich as if she were the very soil of mother earth. Her warm and fragrant smell lingered in his nostrils wherever he went, a breeze of perpetual springtime in the raw February slush of Manhattan, and he grinned while changing diapers or unloading the dishwasher at the flashes of tactile memory: how her curved, moist lips opened like the petals of a flower; how her hips rose and her belly arched as she climaxed. He was eager to hear her amusing, scatterbrained woes, told with delightful wit and self-deprecation, and he was thrilled by her frank longing for sex. He felt encouraged by her vehement partisanship of him against all those with whom he felt powerless: his useless partner of a half brother, his chatty and ineffectual agent, his craven and indecisive producer, and most of all, his demanding and unsatisfying wife.

Enrique was in love with Sally Winthrop. He was brimming with love, a deep, passionate, mature love that also happened to be illicit. This was nothing like that mirage of love he had felt for Margaret, which had soon enough turned into the bourgeois drudgery of a marriage, a humorless schoolgirl's notion of life: a brutal routine of dawn risings to the stale smell of bottle formula, the slow spooning of pureed vegetables, and then early to bed reeking of the alcohol of baby wipes, relieved only by long hours midday on the phone with his lazy, meandering half brother while they worked on stories so empty of real feeling and difficult conflict, so chock-full of plot clichés and false characters that he sometimes wondered if the impossible dream did happen, and one of these seven screenplays for which he was paid ten times the amount he had received for his three out-of-print novels (and that was only half the total money paid, since he split it, appropriately enough, with his half brother) were miraculously made, he wondered whether he could bear to watch it on the big screen, much less expect strangers to enjoy themselves.

And then there was the painful, stultifying routine of socializing. Dinner once a week with Margaret's old camp friend, Wendy, and her left-wing husband, who subtly tried to convince you that his toddler was superior to baby Gregory because his genius was already pooping in the toilet, a veritable Einstein of the bowels. And there were long, painful weekends of gazing through bleary eyes at sandboxes, slumped shoulder to slumped shoulder with bragging fathers while Margaret huddled with the mothers. Sitting with the daddies, he could overhear Margaret echoing the strident pulse of her mother's voice at Passover and Thanksgiving, orating at length and in extraordinary detail about matters so dull he sometimes suspected his wife of a new performance art, twenty-four-hour self-satire: "Does Maclaren really expect those cheesy aluminum legs on its fold-up stroller to take the beating of New York's streets? Or even the suburban thing of being taken in and out of the car trunk? Especially the way Enrique kicks it closed! Soon as he touches them they break. You know what Manhattan really needs? A big box store. Paying Gristedes' prices for Pampers is just, I don't know, obscene. And, ugh, God, do I really have to start applying for kindergarten before Greggy is two?"

And following those acute social observations, after Enrique fetched a second cup of take-out coffee, came her diatribes about work, especially the complaints about her bosses, the top editors of *Newsweek,* where she was employed as an associate art director, with their heavy drinking and groping and hideous taste in ties and composition-blind choices in photos, and jarring color schemes for graphs, and their indecisive and constant tearing up of the cover in a hopeless attempt to figure out on Friday what story would still be big by Monday's release of the magazine, when, my God, wasn't it obvious that trying to be relevant was pointless, given the new twenty-four-hour TV cable news and the daily newspapers, which would have the latest anyway? All news-magazines could hope especially to provide their readers was an in-depth look at last week's headlines, but no, they said those covers didn't sell. The truth, she announced for the ten thousandth time, is that what sells is movie stars. They should just give up and publish only clones of *People* magazine, Margaret declaimed weekend after weekend, winter, spring, summer, and fall.

That she was boring was bad, yet he could tolerate the tedium, he swore to himself, except that she wouldn't, at the end of six-

teen hours of physical and mental drudgery, fuck him. Not even
the quick pleasure of a ten-minute screw. No hope for relief from
this eunuch's life of domesticity. No expectation of reward. Except
for one begrudged, clinical act of sexual intercourse a month at the
very best—and just as often only one night out of every two
months. And those rare successes were achieved only after hours
of coaxes and pleas. Nearly every night, at the end of all his obei-
sance to creating a young, vibrant family together, they went to
bed like a sexless couple in their eighties. That was the quiet horror he felt as they huddled in neutered bedclothes on the far borders of their marriage bed: this prune of lust she offered to him at
the age of twenty-eight as his now and future diet—that was the
soul-destroying thing.

And surrounding the pulp of his simmering resentment, like
the thick skin of a tropical fruit, was shame at his complaint. He
joked with other young fathers about their mutual frustration.
Sometimes at dinners of parenting couples, there were coed jokes
about their sex-deprived lives. They were a liberated generation,
after all, who had fucked themselves silly, and that was exactly
what embarrassed Enrique. He hadn't. He had only fucked himself into seriousness, into the grave work of family life, after
entirely missing the psychedelic joys of college. But there was a
deeper sense of moral failure in his feelings of woe and anger at his
wife's neglect: he was betraying the political imperatives of his
feminist mother and the feminist realm in which he lived. Margaret was a paradigm of the New Mother of the 1980s, a brave
example of having and doing it all, working at a high-pressure
job, earning nearly as much as Enrique in his new guise as an over-
paid, underproduced screenwriter, and she was, relative to most of
her friends, a success at getting her husband to share the home-
making duties. Enrique never cooked, but he genuinely cleaned
up, not only after himself and the baby but after his wife too, and

he took sole care of Gregory on Wednesday, Thursday, and Friday evenings, and all day Saturday, so that Margaret could recover from the magazine's late closing schedule on Friday, which usually kept her at the office until two am and sometimes until dawn. When his affair blossomed into love, he tried to convince himself that Margaret must be cheating on him, given her lack of interest in sex with him and her late-night hours. Indeed, his paramour, Sally, also wondered aloud about whether Margaret was having an office romance, no doubt to spur him to end his marriage. But even a cursory investigation persuaded him that, although she might have time for a quickie now and then, Margaret's schedule was too jammed, packed with work and motherhood, to allow for anything like what Enrique was enjoying with Sally. Blond, luscious, randy, Waspy Sally, with her lovely, full white breasts and thick brown nipples, her delighted laugh at his wit, her admiring green-eyed gaze at his brilliant insights into the absurdities of the movie business, and the willing shudders of her orgasms, so different from the reluctant groans of the young mother Margaret, whose grudging release seemed more bullied than seduced.

Enrique, on the other hand, had the luxury of enjoying Sally every night and every morning for as much as a week at a time, their passion comfortably hidden in a four-star L.A. hotel paid for by Warner Bros. or Columbia or Universal, because almost every other month he and his brother were flown out first-class and taken to dinners at chic Spago or old-time Musso & Frank, presumably to soften them up for the bombardment of movie studio notes during the day. Sally had moved out there, abandoning her disastrous early career as an assistant in publishing—more hit upon than discovering a hit—to try her own hand at the crack cocaine of writing: the Hollywood development deal.

Enrique knew Sally well from New York, and it was natural, and presumed by all to be innocent, that they look each other up while they both happened to be in Los Angeles. Margaret and Lily, and all of Enrique's friends in New York or acquaintances in L.A., didn't think it odd because, after all, Sally had gone to college with Margaret and Lily. Indeed, Sally was one of Margaret's closest friends, the third member of a Cornell trio of young women who had formed a perfumed phalanx to conquer Manhattan. The only reason Sally hadn't been at the Orphans' Dinner was that she had gone home for the Christmas holidays. With their profound physical union throbbing in his veins, Enrique sometimes wondered—a thought that seemed to him almost worse than the affair itself, if for no other reason than that it collaterally wished his beloved son Gregory into nonexistence—whether, if Sally had been seated beside him at Margaret's glass table instead of the dull Pam, he would be married to the lusty Miss Winthrop now, and the whole sad mistake of his marriage to Margaret would never have happened.

This dark pulp of emotional betrayal of his wife, added to the thick skin of ideological shame, made Enrique, in his own eyes, as greedy, as manipulative, and as devious as Iago. It also made sex with Sally—after dinners in Beverly Hills with mutual friends and his clueless half brother (too busy with his own consistent adulteries to notice Enrique's passionate affair) and after well-acted good-byes at the valet park, and after Sally drove in circles for fifteen minutes before heading to the Chateau Marmont Hotel to knock softly on the door to his suite—it made the taste of every kiss, the bath of each liquid embrace a succulent forbidden fruit. And during the two trips Sally made to New York, she met Enrique each day in his one-room office, a block from where he and Margaret were raising their son. There they covered each other's mouths as they climaxed awkwardly on his sofa or roughly on the rug, so that the shrinks and their patients in the rooms next door wouldn't be tempted to investigate libidos other than their own.

For nearly a year, Enrique had all the lovemaking that he had ever dreamed of. More than he had ever dreamed of because that abandon and recklessness included one unforgivable and shameful night (that he gleefully relished) when Margaret initiated sex— an unprecedented postchildbirth event, no doubt unconsciously cued by the dangerous pheromones emitting from her husband— the evening after he had screwed her friend Sally in the afternoon. And the weird thing, an invitation to becoming even more evil, was that he was relaxed, almost bored, while inside his wife that night—no doubt because he hadn't had to wait two months for this opportunity and thus didn't care that after Margaret finished executing her perfunctory marital duty, another two months loomed before he would again enjoy with her the intense and calming welcome only a woman could grant. As an act of physical intimacy, that night's grotesque betrayal didn't feel wrong at all: they were lovers fucking, instead of business partners doing the books. And apparently Margaret also preferred his lust to be less eager, certainly less desperate. Perhaps because he wasn't pent up and holding back, because he wasn't anxious about prolonging the pleasure, Margaret, a rarity since the first year of their relationship, eased into the fucking. She softened and moaned as she used to when they first met, when she loved him, when she wanted *him*—not as the errand-running daddy to her son, not as the trophy husband to unload the stroller at her parents' house in Great Neck, not as a matching accessory to her cutting-edge life—but as a man.

And yes, thank God, hallelujah, that was why he didn't hate himself sufficiently to stop his betrayal, his twofold betrayal, because for the first time in the interminable twenty-eight years of his frustrating and ineffective life, at long last he was a real man with a real cock that had found its way into not one but two beautiful women and on the same glorious fucking day. He had failed as a novelist, he had given up his dream of being a modern Balzac after his fourth book couldn't find a publisher willing to pay more than five lousy thousand dollars, and that only if he would change the ending to a happy one. What kind of happy ending was five thousand dollars for two years' work? "If they want me to be a hack," he declared bitterly, "they should at least pay me well." He had found that bargain in Hollywood.

And he had found a greater prize there too, this expansive freedom with Sally, both sexual and emotional. She was funnier than Margaret about his script woes, and yet she had no sarcasm in her about his Hollywood jobs, no mockery of the pandering story ideas, no impatience at the idiots he was dealing with, no world-weary looks of skepticism about Enrique becoming a producer or a director, and certainly no opposition to his wondering aloud whether, for the sake of advancing his career in the movie business, he ought to live in Los Angeles. Margaret seemed to be satisfied by the drudgery of their striving family life, despite her playground complaints to her fellow mothers, whereas Enrique, except for the parole of Sally's arms, was in a prison.

Enrique did not propose that he escape from his internment. Sally did. Approaching the one-year anniversary of their affair, she settled in L.A. for good, having gotten a job on a TV series, a position that came with the promise of writing an episode and, if that went well, being promoted to staff writer. She told Enrique that someone with his experience and skills could have any number of jobs in TV, and that he would start nearly at the top to boot, perhaps not as an executive producing writer but certainly as a head writer and co–executive producer, and soon, with his fabulous ideas, he would be making millions. He had been told the same by less self-interested and more knowledgeable sources: his agent, producers in general, and all the writers he had met out there. It was aphoristic in Hollywood that the screenwriters had the glamour and rubbed elbows with movie stars, but it was the television writers who had the money and power. Sally's plan was that he divorce Margaret, end his frustrating partnership with his half brother, move in with her in L.A., and become wealthy as the creator of a television series. As bold, selfish, and meretricious as that course sounded to his soul, it also seemed more likely to make him rich and famous and happy than sulking as a failed novelist in Manhattan. If he stayed put, his only hope of success would be to hit the lottery of getting a script made into a big-time movie in between changing diapers and waiting for his sexless wife to catch up on her sleep.

And yes, of course, without question, he would be turning his back on everything that he had been raised to believe in: his parents' obsolescent faith in the literary novel, their ethical disapproval of Hollywood's imperative of pandering to the audience, and, from the way they spoke of their divorced friends, the moral disapproval he could easily imagine Guillermo and Rose would feel for a son who valued sex above all else in a relationship, and who would abandon their grandson to be raised by his maternal grandparents in the easy material comforts but timorous values of that least adventurous and most cynical of bourgeois cultures— Long Island Jews.

His parents' disdain for the world of the Cohens long predated his meeting Margaret. Guillermo and Rose had rejected the middle-class ideal of the upwardly striving, conventionally religious, culturally dutiful, intellectually tame, and politically cautious well before Enrique was born. In their youth they had worked for and put their lives at risk in support of their belief in a workers' revolution, which would have destroyed that comfortable world. The revelations of the horrors of the Soviet Union in the late 1940s didn't convince them that they had been mistaken, only that Stalin was evil. In the post-Vietnam, Reagan era of unselfconscious pursuit of money and the idealization of America into the Good and the rest of the world into the Bad and the Weak, his parents had modified their extreme talk, but not their basic disapproval of a life lived for selfish material gain, and especially their contempt for artists who cared more for public approval than for revealing their world as honestly as possible.

Twenty-eight-year-old Enrique believed that his parents approved of him making a living for the sake of raising their grandchild. Although they claimed they wanted him to return to writing his serious novels, they also recognized that he drew a bright line between cheapening his writing of books and pandering in the screenplays he wrote with his half brother. They regretted, but applauded, that he had refused to tailor the ending of his fourth novel for a publisher, preferring to write dumb scripts. And they seemed to understand that in choosing Margaret he had chosen a good mate, despite her conventional idea of how they ought to live: in a doorman building, intending to send their child to private school, expecting Enrique to find a way to write his novels only after he had managed to make enough to pay for their Manhattan expenses.

In no way—that he was conscious of—did they make him feel ashamed of marrying her. On the contrary, his father adored Margaret, with her laughing blue eyes, her teasing mockery of Enrique, and her close attention to Guillermo's anecdotes. In turn, Guillermo performed his trick of flattery on Margaret, his standard exaggerated praise of anyone who showed the slightest inclination to be creative, proclaiming her photographs and her paintings to reveal extraordinary talent, and insisting that she ought to devote more time to her art, that working at it was all that stood between her and worldwide acclamation. He conveniently ignored that Margaret had no spare hours to become Mary Cassatt; she had barely half an hour to get her hair done, much more crucial than aesthetic fulfillment for a New York career woman.

Rose also liked Margaret, or at least as well as she could like any woman who took primacy in the heart of her son. And his parents were pleasant, although insistently condescending, about the Cohens. "They're really smart, much smarter than they allow themselves to be," his father would say, and Enrique knew he might as well be speaking of educating the working classes to revolt. "And like all Jews," his backhanded anti-Semitic father added, "they're very good about culture. Go to all the museums, see all the serious plays, buy all the important books. Don't know if they read them, but they buy them. God knows what they get out of all of it, but they support the arts and God bless them for that," he said with the approval and affection one might express for a faithful family servant. "They're really generous to Margaret," his mother would comment with a wan smile, as if it had been an exhausting search to come up with this compliment. "That's a wonderful quality. Lots of people with their kind of money are stingy with their children." And then she couldn't resist adding, "Her mother is one of those women who likes to remain young, you know? Pretend that she's still a girl? I don't really care for . . ." Another wan smile as she failed to finish that characterization. "I think it's important to accept your age," she added instead and smiled with rueful beneficence, as if this insight, although painful, was a gift to be treasured and not an expression of her envy that Dorothy hadn't been obliged to put her dress size in a time capsule.

Enrique did not see through his parents' condescension to its origins in their insecurities. He absorbed their view of the Cohens with the unthinking fidelity of a Communist Party member. But whatever he thought in his head, in his heart he felt that there was a struggle going on between the in-laws for the soul of his marriage. For him to succeed as the perfect son, although it was for-givable that his wife worked at *Newsweek* and he was writing screenplays, they were supposed to evolve into a brilliant novelist and an exquisite painter, a marriage of artists, like Guillermo and Rose. And he knew as well that for Margaret to succeed as the per-fect daughter, Enrique would have to earn the kind of money that would impress Dorothy and Leonard's friends at their golf club, not the eighty thousand dollars a year he was wowing his fellow freelance writers with, but the millions that caused heads to turn at Temple Beth-El. He was at least supposed to earn enough money for Margaret to stop working if she wished, although he suspected that the socially conventional Dorothy would top all the mothers in Great Neck, feminist or not, if her daughter managed to have a second child *and* get promoted to art director of *Newsweek.*

It was Sally—wacky, laughing, big-lipped Sally Winthrop, whose family had come over on the *Mayflower* and down the gen-erations had not once dreamed of changing American society—it was she alone who seemed to have a vision for Enrique's future that would slake his parched longings. She offered sex, money, fast cars, and a life free of diapers, free of Communist and Capitalist cant. It was, however, free of something else, namely his son, Gre-gory. He wasn't much in size, Enrique's twenty-month-old son. A heated bundle of soft flesh, a Michelin baby chewing on a pacifier, a tiny sumo wrestler stamping on his turf in the Washington Square sandbox, a round-faced innocent with huge blue eyes, a baby who had begun talking at an early age and who seemed, incredibly, already to have started to recognize letters. It was all Enrique could do not to bellow the bragging fathers into the mon-key bars with accounts of his son's nascent genius. But that was merely the Sabas grandiosity and family pride. He wrote that off. He wrote off, as well, that he felt deeply comforted whenever his son was in his arms, or pressed against his chest in the Snugli, or curled into his shoulder for a nap. Lately Gregory had taken to sitting beside Enrique on the living room rug and playing patiently with his wooden blocks while his father raged and cheered at the annoying Knicks. Gregory would look up curiously at the television and, based on whether Enrique screamed or clapped, comment, "No good" or "Is good!"

That was funny and charming, but the deeper pleasure for Enrique, something he had not expressed to anyone, including Margaret, was coming back from another desperately stupid day of writing down, down, down in order to meet the subterranean simplicities of the motion picture business, entering in despair covered in the muck of clichés to a home of sexless drudgery, and there, for his labors, he would be handed a tired Gregory, who'd lay his sweaty head on Enrique's chest and sigh with relief and gratitude. Or he would enter and hear from the bedroom his son's high voice ring out with gladness, "Daddy!" followed by the thump of his sumo strides as he rushed to be picked up. It did not occur to Enrique that this was a manly feeling. It embarrassed him, seemed more maternal than James Bond. What he understood was that Gregory loved him in a way no else did, or ever could—or, for that matter, ever would.

He said to Sally, "I don't know if I can leave my son." But that noble sentiment wasn't what he felt. There was something physical about the connection, this umbilical bond with his still stumbling, fussy, sweet, diapered, and brilliant heir. Those hours he spent alone taking care of Gregory, including the drudgery that he liked to believe excused his gross betrayal of Margaret, had stored up a faith in something he couldn't name or account for, and also didn't trust. Did he propose to become the living embodiment of the Jewish joke about the ninety-year-old couple seeking a divorce after seventy years together hating each other? When asked why it had taken them so long, they explained they wanted to wait until the children were dead. Could he really tolerate a life without love or lust solely to preserve his son from the trauma of parental separation? Could he really live a lifetime with a woman whom he would leave now without a second's thought but for the miraculous child she had created?

He could make a new family in L.A. with Sally and, like millions of other divorced parents, they would share custody of Gregory and it would be better for all concerned, including Margaret, who obviously didn't love Enrique and certainly wasn't being made happy by him.

But. But. But, he worried, would it all come to the same in L.A., behind his sunglasses and his tinted Beemer's windshield, beyond his parking space on the Warners lot, and behind the shaded windows of his bungalow office? Would Sally blow up and expel a child and get bored with his career ups and downs and become obsessed with the metal fatigue of strollers and which Beverly Hills nursery school would be the fastest route to Harvard? Was there an escape from the internment of marriage other than staying single? Had any great artist ever been happily married? Had any second-rate artist, for that matter? Was the hidden, simpler truth that he was attempting to live a life he didn't want on any coast? Where was the reckless high school dropout who cared for nothing but his art? Was he—the prodigy novelist long orphaned—was he the prisoner who now rattled Enrique's cage?

Sally made him face these questions. She was, as always, funny and blunt and honest and sympathetic and greedy and somehow, like her body, soft and hard, giving and taking all at once. "It's great for you. I wouldn't want to give anything up, either. You've got two great women in love with you, you've got your mistress out here in L.A. when Warner Bros. flies you in first-class to call you a genius, and you've got your successful, beautiful wife in

N.Y. raising your beautiful boy. I wouldn't give it up if I were you. But lookit: I don't have any self-esteem, but I'm in love with you and I want you, I want all of you or I'm going to have to find some other good Jewish husband, or at least a half-Jewish husband—'cause I'm through with WASP men, they're all alcoholics and they don't make sure you have an orgasm before they come. They're so polite about everything except sex! So you have to choose. I want you to marry me and worship me the way you worship Margaret, and I want you to make me rich and fuck me and give me children and be a great father to them the way you are to Greggy, and if you won't, okay. I understand. You shouldn't. You probably shouldn't. I mean, lookit: it's horrible what I'm doing! I love Margaret. She's one of my best friends and she's always been good to me—well, actually, she's kind of a bitch to me sometimes, but that's because she thinks I'm self-destructive and she's right, I am! Anyway, that's no reason for me to be sitting around wishing she was dead. That's horrible. Am I a monster? I can't go on feeling this way about her. I can't go on feeling this way about you. I can't go on feeling this way about me. You have to leave her. I can't believe I have no scruples at all, I always thought I was a good girl, but I'm not. And it doesn't matter, none of that matters, because the truth is you're miserable with Margaret and you're ecstatic with me. Isn't that right? Tell me. Isn't that right?"

This was a phone call. Sally was in a new sublet in Santa Monica and he was in his office in Manhattan staring at a page of dialogue about nothing. Maybe it would divert someone. A moron, no doubt. "Yes," he answered her admirably direct question. He had to admit the simple and human truth of the situation: he was always happy when he was with Sally. She could irritate, but she never made him feel inadequate.

And so he took the first step toward divorce, the stride of a coward, but a forward movement nevertheless. He waited until he had put Gregory down for the night after a long Saturday of caring for him so that Margaret could recover from her late hours at work, walked into their bedroom, where his wife was lying fully dressed on top of the bed reading a murder mystery, sat down close enough to brush against her legs, and stared at her. When she looked up at him with those great blue eyes and asked, "Everything okay?" he sighed. A long, heavy sigh. Some part of her must have been worried all along underneath her chatty, demanding surface, because she put the book down, straightened to a seated position, and asked, "What's wrong?"

He attempted to make a speech, a heavy, awkward speech. He felt he could easily cry, as if he were the one whose heart was breaking, which made little sense to him because he believed that he was the bad guy here, a mean and weak man. Perhaps he was scared of her reaction. He had pushed Margaret only a few times when she didn't want to be moved, and the effect was daunting. Her arms flailed, and she screeched hyperbolic proclamations of emotional distress. They were perfect demonstrations of hysteria. His immediate reflex was to redact everything in order to restore her core. It appeared, otherwise, that she might fly apart, never to be reconstituted, that he was—in actual fact—destroying her by refusing to go to Yom Kippur services with her parents the first year they lived together; or by staying out late gambling at the local backgammon club; or by sleeping until noon day after day when his fourth book was rejected again and again. "I can't take this!" she would exclaim. What struck him as especially infuriating was that in every case Enrique thought the opposite was true. He was the one who couldn't bear it. How could she expect him to pretend to believe in a religion he didn't? How could she expect him to give up something he enjoyed because it didn't interest her? But most of all, how in God's name did she expect him to be cheerful while his life's dream of being a novelist was destroyed?

Because they were meaningless concessions, she claimed. All she asked was that he behave like a responsible grown-up and, besides, she knew that he would be happier if he did things her way. She was selfish in the only effective way people can be selfish, by acting out of an earnest conviction that their way of life is superior. Every attempt he had made to modify her rules she transformed into a whirling dervish of fragile and frantic feelings that allowed no discussion, much less compromise. And whether he raged, or sulked, or consoled, or hid under the bed like a frightened dog, after the storm passed, his buildings were leveled and hers stood tall. He was frightened she would react the same way now, only now he would not be able to contain his rage, because he knew for sure that she was wrong: he was not happier living her way.

And that's what he said, sitting beside her on the bed in a choked, hardly audible, hoarse voice. He told a lie of omission. He said nothing about Sally or their affair, but he did state the truth of his feelings: "I'm not happy. I can't"—the words were so laden he had to stop and inhale to push them out—"I can't go on living like this."

"Can't go on living like what? What are you talking about? Sex? Is this about sex?" she said, as if the word itself were contemptible. "I'm tired, for Christ's sakes. We have a baby, I have a job. I can't just turn it on and off like you. I'm not a light switch—" He could hear the exasperation that would soon swirl and become a tornado of "I can't"s, laying waste to his needs and desires.

"That's bullshit," he said, not frightened anymore by her darkening skies and the threat of eighty-mile-an-hour emotions.

"What?" she said, startled.

He repeated quietly, "That's bullshit. We don't have sex because there's something really wrong with our marriage. And either we deal with it or it's going . . ." He sighed again, feeling so sad and scared that he was light-headed and wondered if he might faint. "It's going to end," he said with firm regret.

"It's going to"—she hesitated—"end?" she repeated, more in disbelief than in anguish.

He met her big eyes. They often looked startled. Only now, when he had finally made a truly startling statement, she didn't look surprised. Instead, they went dark with anger. He didn't flinch. He said, slow and steady, "It's going to end. I can't do this anymore. I really can't." He had resolved that much: at least he would be honest about the stakes.

He had frightened her, all right. Frightened her to the depths, so that sobriety replaced hysteria as her response. She reached for her pack of Camel Lights—she had stopped smoking for a while when pregnant but returned to it after only a few months—took one out, lit it, and sat up, retracting her legs so that they were no longer close to Enrique. She glared at him, mouth set, chin thrust forward, cold with rage. "What is it? What the fuck do you expect me to do?"

Sally—Enrique's mistress, Margaret's friend, his love, her rival—had suggested the solution, the cowardly compromise that she wisely estimated Enrique would have the nerve to propose: marriage counseling. He had seized on the idea because it would stall for at least a couple of weeks his having to make this terrifying choice that Sally was forcing on him. Enrique had no illusions about why Sally suggested this temporizing move. He knew the statistics: most people who went into marriage counseling ended up divorced. It was a halfway house for the emotionally retarded: people like Enrique, too timid to tell the truth without a referee. He understood that Sally was calculating that, though it would delay his decision, it would mean his choice would be more likely to come out in her favor.

Margaret had never been in therapy, but she was, after all, Jewish and could hardly refuse to see a doctor for help with a problem. She did say, "What are we going to talk about? Changing diapers?"

"That's the problem," Enrique said. "That's all we talk about."

"You think that's my fault?"

"Let's talk about that with the therapist," he said and stood up, ending further conversation, a first in their marriage.

True to form, however, Enrique let Margaret find and choose the therapist, a Dr. Goldfarb. He was recommended by a friend of Lily's who reported that Goldfarb had saved their marriage. Margaret must have been impressed by Enrique's demanding speech and subsequent silence. She made the appointment for that very week, Tuesday, when she was obliged to go into the magazine for only a few hours.

They arrived separately, which seemed appropriate to the situation, meeting in Goldfarb's hushed waiting room with its ubiquitous Metropolitan Museum of Art exhibition poster and obligatory wicker magazine holder jammed with issues of *New York* magazine and *The New Yorker.* Margaret picked one up and flipped through it violently, as though its editor had personally offended her. She did everything, and had done everything since their bedside chat, in stiff, angry motions, her mouth thin-lipped, her blue eyes glacial. Everything about her scolding and cold manner confirmed that not only didn't she love him but she didn't approve of him. Despite all her condescending talk about her brothers, and complaint that her father was too timid to contradict Dorothy's arrangements and rules, Margaret expected the same obedience from Enrique. He was allowed to be the free-range artist that she had adventurously married—except with her; *she* wanted him trussed up like a roast.

Soon they were called into Goldfarb's office. They sat uncomfortably in its pair of nude hardwood captain's chairs on the patients' side of the desk; Goldfarb was behind it, in a leather-upholstered, high-backed swivel chair, which looked considerably more cozy. The heavy bags under the psychiatrist's bulging eyes and their dull, flat gray color made him appear to be on the verge of sleep. Dr. Goldfarb explained that, although he was a traditional Freudian, obviously couples' therapy didn't permit him to be silent, and so he conducted these sessions somewhat differently. He added, however, that he still preferred to listen to what they had to say rather than hear himself talk.

He took down their vital information, including insurance, and then looked balefully, first at Enrique, saying, "So what brings you here?" He turned to Margaret before an answer could be made, to add, "What's going on in your marriage?" leaving it up to them to decide who should respond.

Margaret smiled broadly and artificially at Goldfarb, a cocktail party smile, and said nothing. Goldfarb returned his gaze to Enrique. "What are you feeling, Ricky?" Margaret corrected him before Enrique could. "Enrique," she said. Goldfarb appeared to be deeply bored by this. "I'm sorry. En-ricky," he said, continuing to Americanize the second syllable. "What's going on that brings you here?" he asked.

I'm not in love with her, Enrique wanted to say. In fact, I don't even like her. How do you fix that? Unable to express those feelings out loud, he looked away from the psychiatrist's fish eyes at the profile of his pretty and cold wife. She was beaming with her newly bonded teeth, perfect in proportion and brilliantly white, hiding her disapproval and rejection of him behind her cheerful and thoroughly superficial party manners.

There was a long silence. Enrique looking at her, Margaret looking at the doctor, the psychiatrist studying them both. "He seems to want you to start, Margaret," Goldfarb said, speaking slowly in a droll tone. "Are you willing?"

With a shock, Enrique realized he didn't know what she was going to say. He assumed she was unhappy, but had she said so? He assumed she would complain about him, but he didn't know for sure. He knew what she thought about the plays and movies they had seen. He knew what she thought about their friends, their families, and Gregory. He knew what she thought about Ronald Reagan and the pooper-scooper law. He did not know what she was going to say about their marriage. He was eager now to hear, afraid now to hear, and afraid now to make any motion or noise lest it startle her real feelings away.

But she didn't speak. Margaret stared at nothing, like a cautious New Yorker on a subway pretending her fellow passengers didn't exist. Enrique felt panic at her statuary silence. Goldfarb, however, wasn't impatient. He settled deeper into his soft chair, apparently prepared to hear a long story, and made a request that the young Enrique never had: "Tell me, Margaret. Tell me how you feel about your marriage."

chapter sixteen

Last Words

A T FIVE O'CLOCK in the afternoon of the third day after Margaret stopped taking steroids and intravenous hydration, Enrique showed the last of her friends upstairs. Diane, a member of Margaret's advanced cancer support group, wasn't strictly speaking a friend, but Margaret felt she couldn't deny a fellow combatant the chance to stare down what she might soon confront. Enrique immediately returned to the living room, having resolved, after eavesdropping on Margaret's talk with Dorothy, to thoroughly respect the privacy of her farewells. At most she had five days left to live. Her family, her closest friends, and her sons had all said good-bye. That evening would be their first alone since she had announced to Enrique that she wanted to die as quickly as possible within the strictures of the law. She was noticeably weaker and sleepier than the day before; soon she would lapse into a coma. He settled on the couch to wait for Diane to depart in half an hour, when his turn would at last arrive.

During the past week, he had done what she had asked of him, helping her manage the painful good-byes of family and friends. He had not, except for one brief outburst, obliged Margaret to comfort him. And he hoped to avoid exposing her to the dread he felt at living without her. He certainly hoped to say nothing that would hurt her, although he wondered if they could have a satisfying good-bye without both of them taking that risk. Whatever they did say to each other, it would be the end of the conversations they had begun when he was twenty-one and had continued, for good or ill, until he was fifty. He longed to penetrate the mystery of how they had managed to live a life together while they were so different in their natures and in their expectations of one another. And if there was no answer to be found in a last talk with his wife, at least he wanted to tell her what she had meant to him, and to hear what he had meant to her, because soon there would be only the loneliness of monologue.

A lot that had worried him about these final days had been accomplished. Gregory and Max had said good-bye to their mother. Both farewells had been characteristic of her different relationships with them and their different experiences of her illness. When Margaret was diagnosed, Gregory was twenty and in college. On graduation a year later, while his mother was in remission, he took a job at a liberal magazine in Washington, D.C. Within months he established himself as a young star in political journalism, particularly as a blogger, which also led to appearances on radio and TV, so that his proud parents were able to enjoy his precocious success from his mother's hospital bed. Because he had to travel to see Margaret, nearly all of Gregory's audiences with her were scheduled ahead of time. She could prepare herself, disguise as much as possible the ravages of her illness and the strenuous treatments that she had endured to stay alive. Twice, a crisis serious enough to bring Gregory to New York had exposed him to the unadorned patient: wigless, insufficiently covered by a hospital gown, too feverish or weak to summon her usual conversational energy, too saddened by the knowledge that she wouldn't live to see her firstborn grow fat and bald and eminent. Gregory looked bewildered when his mother sometimes cut their conversations short, but Enrique understood why. As hope for a cure waned, it had become impossible to gaze at her sons for long without tears darkening her bright eyes; she wanted to spare them the only thing she could of her death—her grief at leaving them.

Greg had been brave when he glimpsed his mother at her lowest in those two medical emergencies. So had his brother, Max. But because Max lived with his parents throughout the entire course of her illness, he had been obliged to be stoic about such sights, and worse spectacles, far more often. Margaret's bouts with severe infections and the growing crises of her digestive blockages had forced Enrique to take her to Urgent Care at Sloan-Kettering in the middle of the night at least a dozen times, abandoning their teenage son with little or no warning. Each time Enrique left a note to be found in case Max woke up, or he whispered a quick explanation at his son's bedside if his light was still on, or gambled that he would get back before Max's alarm clock blared at seven am. Gregory had had a healthy mother for his miserable years of high school. For better and certainly sometimes for worse, he had had the complete attention of both Enrique and Margaret during the weird stress and excitement of applying to college and leaving home. Max had lost his mother's attention for those years, and the lion's share of his father's as well.

Neither boy complained to Enrique about their mother's decay. Their statements were brief and inarguable: "It sucks. I hope she feels better soon." They asked simple and direct questions about her medical care: "Can't her doctors do anything about her not being able to eat or drink?" And the hardest one to answer accurately: "Is she going to be okay?" until last September, when Enrique had explained that, as far as science was concerned, she could never be cured.

In style and content, the two sons had always reacted differently to their mother. Gregory had been an obedient boy, so intimidated by Margaret that if she said his namely sharply, he would jump an inch in the air. When he disobeyed her, he did it in the way that Margaret disobeyed her own mother. "I don't know if that's a good idea," he would say and sulk, refusing to engage in further discussion. He resorted, if possible, to an invisible act of defiance or passive inaction, in order to keep confrontations to a minimum while also refusing to surrender. When he chose to collapse his will and do her bidding, he did so with the same begrudging expression that shuttered Margaret's face when she felt bullied by her mother. Gregory wanted, as did Margaret with her mother, for their relations to be pacific and loving.

It seemed fitting then that yesterday, after Gregory had spent five and a half hours upstairs alone with his mother, he trudged down the steps and appeared with a peaceful look on his face. He stood in the dining room area, a good distance from his father's position on the couch, regarding him with what appeared to be patient contemplation through his hip rectangular glasses. Relieved to see him so calm, Enrique walked over to embrace him. Close up, he saw that he had been mistaken. His son's blue eyes, although dry, were swimming in pain.

Greg averted them to the floor and released a sigh of utter despair. Wanting to send grief packing, Enrique attempted to hug his son. Greg had grown nearly as tall as his father, and thicker in the chest and shoulders than Enrique had ever been. Margaret had liked to call him Little Bear when he was only a warm muffin of a baby, but these days there was something bear-like about his appearance: big, gentle, and thoughtful. He could roar too, he'd proved that as a writer. But now Gregory pressed the top of his skull awkwardly against his father's chest, as if he wished he could burrow inside. His strong arms came around and locked across Enrique's back, not so much embracing his father as attaching himself.

In this half hug, Enrique couldn't see his son's face or pat his back. He could kiss the top of his head, the way he used to when carrying baby Gregory in his seersucker Snugli. He kissed him twice and whispered, "You okay?" although it was obvious that nothing about this was okay or ever would be. He had made this hopeless inquiry so many times that one sleepless night he thought about why he kept asking so impossible a thing of his children. He decided it was because, despite all the evidence to the contrary, he thought there must be a way for him to make it okay. Enrique felt contempt for himself that he was indulging in such grandiosity. What desperate vanity made him think he could transform their mother's death into something good—or bad? He was astonishingly irrelevant. He was stumbling around outside, unable to find the key that would let him enter the room of his sons' loss. Their father ought to be the person who could best console them, but Enrique felt that he was considerably less helpful than their friends, and Lord knows what else they sought as balm, certainly alcohol and—Enrique hoped and prayed—comfort in the arms of loving young women. Whenever he tried to soothe them, they seemed to feel worse. He repeatedly tried to reassure them that they were being great about their mother's illness, that Margaret and he were very proud of them. Although never truer, every word sounded hollow and false. Many times in life Enrique had felt stupid, foolish, inept, clumsy, but never so thoroughly useless.

Gregory mumbled something in a teary voice.

"What?" Enrique whispered into his son's ear. Greg brought his head straight up and whacked his father's chin hard enough to send him back a step.

"Sorry," he said, reaching for Enrique, massaging his father's shoulder.

"I'm okay." Enrique laughed at their clumsiness before he asked again, "What did you say? I couldn't hear you."

Greg shook his head, chin wobbling. Enrique put an arm around his boy and maneuvered so they were shoulder to shoulder, bearing each other up. "Tell me," he pleaded.

"It's so sad," Greg whispered before his throat closed and he had to shut his blue, bespectacled eyes against the tears. Enrique mumbled, "Yes," and had nothing more to say. Gregory could not fight this loss; it overwhelmed him. Enrique pulled his child into his arms and fully embraced his great sorrow. He wanted to soak up every drop of his son's grief. He realized that this was what a father should be able to accomplish: to physically eradicate his son's unhappiness. After all, he and Margaret had created the tragedy of Gregory's pain in the first place. His suffering belonged to them. It felt to Enrique, while Greg quaked in his arms, that his boy's agony ought to be something that he could erase with inarticulate love.

When Gregory left for a walk, Enrique climbed the stairs, expecting to find his wife sobbing. Margaret was sitting up, her wig discarded beside her on the bed. It resembled a furry animal with a broken back. She gazed out the wall of windows at the June blue sky of southern Manhattan with a contented look. Tears shimmered, but that was a constant these days, most likely from chemo. "How was that?" he asked.

She turned to Enrique, a wistful sadness mixed with satisfaction on her face. "He let me baby him," she confessed, as if to a guilty pleasure. "He let me sew his button on his shirt, and tell him to get his hair cut, and just act like a dumb mom, and he didn't fuss at all. He was so sweet." Drops of water rolled down her cheeks, but there was no distress in her voice.

He got into bed beside her, careful to snake around the various medical attachments, and cradled her in his arms. She had always been physically much smaller than he, although in every other way she seemed bigger, especially in spirit. She was smaller than ever, less than a hundred pounds, the fine bones of her face outlined like tent poles against her almost translucent skin. She was fading away. Not elegantly, like a dissolve in a Hollywood film; elegance was spoiled by the tube draining the contents of her stunned stomach and the catheters above her right breast. But there was great beauty in the deep sea-blue of her eyes, made larger by a narrowing, delicate face. She looked quite different but was easily recognizable as the same beauty when young and healthy—ghosts lingered of the vigorous good cheer of her high cheeks and the sparkle of her laughing, azure eyes in a setting of white skin and black hair. "You're so warm," she whispered, kneading her head, with its thin layer of postchemo fuzz, into the crook of his shoulder. She shut her watering eyes. Strength, he realized, as he felt her frailty all along the length of his body, strength was what he had always obtained from this small woman. Illness had taken that from him, reversing the polarity of their marriage.

In his presence five weeks ago, Margaret had said to Lily, "Enrique is strong. He can carry any weight," after recounting how she had instructed him to fight with her doctors to agree to a desperate operation, and had asked him to explain why to her agitated and confused parents. "Those are tall orders," the sympathetic Lily had commented to Margaret, that being her gentle way of making a plea on his behalf that perhaps her best friend was asking too much of Enrique. "He bears every load I put on him,"

Margaret answered, and both women gazed at him as if he were a familiar and pleasing landmark. He suspected Margaret hadn't felt that confidence in his strength before her illness. He certainly hadn't.

After a silence in each other's arms, Margaret exclaimed, "I love being with you and the boys," as if she were confessing to an affair. "That's what I'm going to miss," she said. "I'm not scared of dying." She lifted her head up to look at him. Tears were flowing, but she smiled through them, impossibly free of bitterness or regret. "I know that sounds crazy, but I'm really not. What's so hard, what I'm going to miss is hanging out with you and Greggy and Maxy. I have so much fun with all of you. I'm going to miss you so much," she whispered, making no philosophical sense of life and death but all the sense in the world about her feelings. "That's what makes me sad. Giving up you and the boys," she said in sweet notes of utter love.

He was dumbfounded, comforted to his core to hear that being with him and his sons was her great joy in life. If a stranger had asked him, at any point in his marriage including that day, what he had given Margaret as a husband, the pleasure of his company would not have been his guess. He supposed that it made sense, since she had chosen to live her life with him, but it had never occurred to him because he so often was irritated and unhappy with his career, worried over the simplest social plan, asked if he looked good in this sweater or those trousers, picked his teeth after meals, never forgot the slightest slight from the slightest of friends, and sometimes raged in political arguments at people he loved as though they were members of the Nazi Party. He felt he was quite unpleasant to be with, and he ought to know since he was stuck with himself twenty-four hours a day. How had Margaret, living with him for almost three decades, missed the obvious fact that he was a drag?

Perhaps she'd forgotten what a misery he used to be. Her illness had changed something basic in the mechanism of Enrique's head and heart. After the shock of her diagnosis, when she was well enough to go to a movie or a play, he no longer cared whether it was any good, or if some hack who was making ten times what Enrique could command had gotten away with inept dialogue, sloppy plotting, rickety characters, and a dishonest story. He no longer cherished his resentment of friends who had begged for a copy of one of his novels and then never made a comment. Nearly all of them had been kind and loving to Margaret in her sickness, and he wouldn't trade that compassion for fulsome praise of an out-of-print novel.

At long last, after decades of fussing, having watched his father die slowly, and now the mother of his children waste away, he was convinced that death was more than the neatest way to resolve a character's story, that death was, in fact, real. He understood, right into the nucleus of every one of his brain cells, that he and everyone on the earth would soon be gone. With that knowledge beside him all day and every night, it rang false to stay angry about anything, including death, since death was, after all, the most even-handed consequence of being alive.

He lay beside Margaret, basking in the glow of her praise, happy to have his frail wife warming herself on him as though he were a comforting fire, and felt ready to begin to say good-bye himself. It wasn't time for their last conversation, but he had a preliminary speech. First, he wanted to thank her for saying that what she would miss of life above all was being with him and his sons. And then he wanted to say something that might sound cruel at first. He wanted to tell her that, until the week she was diagnosed, he didn't know for sure if he was in love with her. He had met her so young, they had had children so young, he had been so unhappy with himself when they were young, and he'd had no way of knowing how much was love and how much was the lazy drift of daily life. He had assumed he loved her, but he hadn't known to a certainty until he was faced with the terror, the fact, and the drudgery of her illness. Only then did he know, by being presented with the immediate, tactile reality, that he would do whatever was necessary to keep her alive, including giving up his precious writing, and sex, and money, and what was left of his vanity. He would have surrendered all, except their sons, to keep her with him. "Mugs," he whispered and drew a deep breath, prepared to be honest and risk frightening her for a minute about the ignorance in which he had lived. Then he heard his half sister, Rebecca, call from downstairs: "Enrique? I'm sorry, Enrique? Are you up there?"

"I'm here," he said. "What's the matter?" Rebecca had taken excellent care of them during the illness and especially during these last weeks. She had stayed in the spare bedroom, spelled Enrique, comforted Margaret, provided soothing company for Max and for Margaret's family. Her consideration for their feelings was precise and thoughtful. She wouldn't interrupt them unless something was wrong.

It was his brother, she explained from the base of the stairs, or rather her brother, his half brother. Leo had called to say he was coming by in fifteen minutes with his son, Jonah, Max and Greg's seventeen-year-old cousin, so that he could say good-bye to Margaret. "Oh my God," Margaret mumbled in despair.

Enrique gently untangled from his wife so as not to tug on her stomach PEG. He walked to the head of the stairs. "What?" he asked, looking down at his sister. "Why the hell is he coming?"

Rebecca, abashed, stammered, "I'm sorry. I couldn't stop him. He wouldn't take no for an answer. I even lied and said it was Max's time to be with Margaret today, but he said it'll only take ten minutes."

"Leo's already said good-bye," Enrique complained. "Everybody else gets one good-bye, he gets two? What is this, some kind of competition? Most deathbed visits—and the winner is Leo Rosen."

Rebecca laughed at Enrique's mockery of their brother's self-importance. From the bed he heard Margaret release a staccato burst. In their entire marriage he had rarely succeeded at getting her even to smile thinly at one of his witticisms. The few belly laughs he'd won were in reaction to genuine pratfalls. Once he'd slipped on the recently waxed living room floor while carrying a glass of Diet Coke. The glass flew out of his hand and he landed flat on his back. From his prone position, he managed to catch the glass, an impressive save but for the fact that he had snagged it upside down. The fizzing contents emptied on his face. She laughed like that now.

Rebecca tried, as always, to make the best out of a bad situation, "I guess Leo thinks it's important for Jonah to say good-bye. I mean, I know it's sentimental, but that's who he is, he's very sentimental—"

"Jonah barely knows us," Enrique complained. "He sees us once a year. Tops."

"It's okay," Margaret called out.

"Do you not want me to let him up?" Rebecca offered. "I can tell him she's asleep or Max is with her."

"Yes, tell him to go away! Tell him Margaret's with Max," Enrique said. He wanted to return to his wife's side and tell her how much she had ameliorated his life's disappointments, how much of its daily pleasures she had granted him, and how much of what she had done for him he had taken unacknowledged; and that in the last decade, especially during these years while she was in remission and while she was ill, he had come to love her more deeply than ever; that along with their children she was what he most valued in life.

The intercom buzzed. "He's here already?" Enrique asked, close to tears of frustration.

"He said he was fifteen minutes away." Rebecca stamped her foot. "But you know Leo. He's always half an hour late! I can't believe this time he isn't exaggerating." She stood at attention. "I'll tell him whatever you want."

"For Chrissakes," Enrique whined like a child, "he visited us in the hospital twice in three years." He announced this complaint as if it were shocking news, although both Rebecca and Margaret knew it very well. "Now he's come twice in two days to say good-bye?"

Margaret appeared in the doorway. Traveling the ten feet from the bed had exhausted her. She propped herself on the doorframe and gasped for breath: "Puff," she pleaded. "Let him up." The intercom buzzed again. He wanted to fight with her about this. His brother had deserted them at a time of their greatest need, as he had during other, albeit less painful stretches of Enrique's life; and now he was stealing precious minutes of the time Enrique had left with her. His wife's way of dealing with Leo's narcissism—she would be chilly and excessively polite—was ineffective. The truly self-absorbed, like his brother, didn't notice subtle cues of rejection; they required a punch in the nose.

Besides, with death only a few days away, why was she bothering to be civil at all? Enrique wanted to ask. He looked at her— eyebrows gone, hair a scouring pad, the bones of her elbows poking the skin, her left hand carrying a bag with the contents of her stomach, her right hand leaning on the wall as if she could hardly stand up—and he felt, as he had so often, that he was powerless to defy her. "I'll get rid of him fast, Puff," she tried to reassure him. "This time I won't hide. I'll stand up so he can see all of me. He won't stay long, I promise you. Okay?" She sighed, exhausted, while the intercom buzzed a third time.

Enrique instructed Rebecca to let them up. He stood aside, a sentry in the corner. From the shock on Leo's face, it was clear that Margaret had fooled him thoroughly when she'd prettified herself for his first good-bye. Leo averted his eyes from Margaret's punctured torso while he delivered the sentimental speech that he had obviously prepared hours ago, and equally obviously felt vain about delivering. Enrique could tell, in the way Leo puffed up as he made his declaration, that he was looking forward to recounting to others the moving remarks he had made to his dying sister-in-law, and how loving and thoughtful Jonah had been in accompanying him. Leo told Margaret that he had been saying to Jonah how much he admired the way Margaret had raised Jonah's cousins; that of all the mothers he knew, she had the most consistent and encouraging style, allowing Greg and Max to be independent and bold thinkers. It didn't worry Leo that, by testifying to Margaret's superiority, he might undermine his own son's confidence in how well he had been raised by *his* mother. On the contrary, that was his gambit: he would get credit for praising a dying woman while launching a covert attack on his ex-wife.

Leo's convoluted spitefulness would have been amusing to contemplate if Enrique weren't so tired—in his flesh, in his bones, in his head and heart and soul. So tired that he forgot exactly what he had intended to say to Margaret other than how much he loved her, and that he hadn't realize how much he loved her until he was about to lose her. Was that really what he wanted to say? It suddenly sounded stupid and cruel.

Margaret listened politely to her brother-in-law, gently lifting and tugging on the bag of green and orange stomach fluid to speed up the draining process, thereby calling attention to the repulsive liquid. The mixture was green from bile, orange from a frozen fruit bar and looked like radioactive waste. The way Leo's eyes fled from the sight was laugh-out-loud funny, but all

Enrique could think about—instead of reconstructing the beautiful and truthful feeling that he had earlier wanted to proclaim to Margaret—was that this was what he had to look forward to: a world missing his controlled and controlling, beautiful and brave, fun and demanding, loving and reserved wife; but chockfull of needy narcissists like his brother, who, even at Margaret's imminent death, was too busy settling scores to say a simple and loving endearment.

Was that the flaw in what he wanted to tell Margaret? he wondered as he accepted an awkward hug from his brother and nephew, escorted them downstairs, and held the front door open to make sure they left. Was he mired in the convoluted, self-referential posturing of his clever but useless family? Why not just say, I love you, I will miss you more than anything in life, and thank you for managing to love me, the difficult, childish, malformed me, thank you, thank you, thank you . . .

He didn't get to say that either. The phone rang. Rebecca tried to handle it, and then Max appeared from his bedroom. Enrique had thought he was out, and was doubly surprised to see that a young woman was with him. She was introduced as Lisa. Max had referred to her a lot lately, although always as part of a group he was going out with. Enrique had never asked if they were a couple. He didn't have to after this hello. Lisa looked up at Enrique with very large blue eyes in the center of a cheerful and kind face. He wanted to say "Congratulations," to his son. Instead, like the dreary nag he had become, he asked, "I've reserved time for you with your mom tomorrow at noon. Are you on for that?"

Max nodded. He had raccoon eyes from lack of sleep, and his shoulders were always hunched these days, as if a perpetual cold wind were blowing on his back. "We have to go now," he mumbled and tugged Lisa's hand. She twirled happily, pleased to be his dance partner. She followed him out. "Nice to meet you," she called to Enrique with a smile that seemed to be apologizing for the brusqueness of Max's pain.

In his heart, Max was still fighting his mother's illness, but he had agreed to say good-bye at last. Enrique could tell that it remained a defeat his younger son would never fully accept.

Enrique had done his best to keep Margaret in the dark about Max's reluctance, but she had sensed it anyway. He knew from the way she'd remarked with relief, "Good." She'd whispered, "I hope I can keep it together with Maxy It's so hard with him, because I couldn't finish"—her voice had broken—"because I couldn't help him get into college, I couldn't do anything for him. It was too hard."

"You did more than enough for him," Enrique had said, kissing her forehead.

"You did, Puff. You took great care of him."

"I didn't do shit," Enrique'd said. "He did it. He did it all on his own." Father and son had had a frank talk about a month into his mother's illness, a conversation that he had never relayed to Margaret. Max was not an obedient boy like his older brother: he argued and teased his mother into keen irritation when she nagged him; and he didn't have the slightest fear of her temper. In ninth grade he'd seemed to be preparing to give her hell through all of high school. The battle lines had already formed. She knew Max was every bit as smart as his older, straight-A brother, and Max knew that Margaret possessed the faith of all Jewish mothers that getting top grades was the best measure of a successful education. Max struck a series of ghastly blows at his mother during that spring term: he received two B pluses, putting his Ivy League future at risk. Then, a month into tenth grade, they were given early warning that his work in two courses was lax: he failed to hand in a paper in English and was unprepared for a test in math. Margaret was diagnosed a week later.

During the second week of his mother's first course of chemo, Max took his father aside and asked how he could help. "Okay. I'll be honest," Enrique said. "I love your mother, you love your mother, but we both know she is insane about grades. She believes if you're getting straight A's, you're okay. You could be mainlining heroin and burying bodies in your bathroom wall, but while she's fighting to stay alive, if you get A's she will believe that you're okay. If you want to help me take care of her, you'll do your schoolwork as well as you can." That was the end of Max's B pluses. Enrique believed that part of the reason Margaret could bear to face her death with grace and calm was that Max had gotten into Yale.

Lisa's existence was the other news of Max that Enrique brought Margaret after he dealt with the phone call, which was from the hospice nurse, who wanted to move up his visit to check on Margaret and their supplies. Enrique didn't say any of those grand things he was fussing about in his head. He informed his wife about Max's girlfriend. For a little while they talked as if life was normal, Margaret grinning when Enrique reported that Lisa had big blue eyes. He managed to coax a second laugh out of her that day by adding, "They're not as beautiful as yours."

"But she's nice? She's sweet to him?"

"Yes," Enrique said, although he knew nothing about her, and wasn't even sure she was Max's girlfriend. The hospice nurse arrived. And then Rebecca had to go home for a night and wanted to say good-bye just in case. And then Greg returned. And then Enrique gave his wife an intravenous dose of Ativan and prepared her for sleep. Greg woke him after he'd nodded off in front of another Mets loss on TV and said, "You'd better go to bed, Dad." He got in beside his heavily asleep wife, kissing her head gently so as not to rouse her. And soon he woke up, as always, at five in the morning, feeling as though he hadn't slept at all. He showered and shaved and ate a bowl of cereal and let Lily in for her morning visit. During this last week, Lily had dropped by on her way back and forth to work. Enrique went out for coffee and a stroll.

While he was gone, Margaret picked out the clothes she wanted to be buried in. It hadn't occurred to Enrique that Margaret would want to choose the outfit for her last social event, but it should have. She had chosen the cemetery, the temple, the Rabbi, and the music. Lily, consistent with their long history, helped her. They had shopped together as young women, they had advised each other about wedding dresses, and Margaret had handed down her children's clothing to Lily's daughter and son. They had conferred before any significant social event about what to wear. They had even discussed what their husbands should wear. It was a logical final collaboration for the two best friends.

Lily was gone when Enrique returned to find his wife sitting in a chair, still in her nightgown, gazing at a large box on her bed.

"My last chore," Margaret said. She pointed to the box, its cover off, that had once contained a favorite pair of black boots she had bought while she was in remission, embarrassed by their price and in love with their luxurious leather. The boots were standing on the floor. In the box was a white silk blouse, a long black skirt that used to cling to her slim hips and elegant legs, and a favorite textured gray wool jacket with flecks of yellow and black. "I'd like to be buried in those. Okay, Puff?" She smiled. "And the boots." Enrique nodded. She looked shy. "And one more thing, I hope you don't mind. I know it's a terrible waste, I know you spent a lot of money, but would it be okay if you buried me with the earrings you gave me?" She opened her hand to reveal the small velvet box that contained the first gift he had selected for her that she liked. "I love them so much. I know it's crazy, just a crazy waste of money, but will you make sure I'm wearing them?"

"Of course it's all right," he blurted out before a river of water in his head could flow. "I'll make sure. Don't worry."

"Thank you," she said. "Okay. That's it." She offered him the box. He moved to the chair, kneeling to be on her level as if he were proposing to her, and took the velvet box. "I got it done," she commented with a little girl's shrug and a demure smile, as if she were seeking his approval. "I've done my last errand." She rested her head on his shoulder, and they stayed in the embrace for a long time. Enrique wanted to speak but was unable to manufacture a word. Holding her frail body in his heavy arms, he couldn't stop himself from doing what he had promised he wouldn't. He allowed himself to feel what he was losing, and sobbed in his wife's arms.

"I'm sorry, I'm sorry," he mumbled.

She caressed his right cheek with her hand, and that made him weep more. He covered his eyes until Margaret said something sweet and silly. "Thank you, Enrique. Thank you for making my life fun. I would have lived such a stupid life in Queens, or somewhere boring. Some dumb life, just a stupid boring life without you."

"That's not true," he said, because it was untrue.

"Yes, it is. You made it so much fun."

He stopped arguing with her. He knew she was trying to make him feel better, forgiving him for what he couldn't forgive himself for, all the times that he had not made life fun for her. "Would you help me get dressed and fixed up for Maxy?" she asked.

He helped her shower, bagging the tubes to protect them from the water, adjusting her wig, bringing her a bra and a white T-shirt, helping her step into jeans that were swimming on her and a belt for her to cinch them tight.

Enrique sat downstairs during the three hours his younger son spent with his mother and realized a very sad thing, so sad and so unacknowledged by him that he almost raced upstairs to interrupt before his tired brain forgot. Margaret had just said good-bye to him. Asking to wear the earrings forever was her farewell, her way of telling him that he had satisfied her as a husband. Instead of bawling, that was when he ought to have said his piece. Well, it's all right, he told himself. I have tomorrow. I have all day tomorrow.

Max appeared, storming down the steps and rushing to the front door, calling to Enrique, "I have to go."

Enrique raced over before he could leave. "How was it?"

"How was it!" Max answered as if the question were worthy of a lunatic. There was still the reflex of fight, the loathing to let her go.

"Sorry." Enrique realized that he was coaxing pain from his child.

"I guess it went okay," he said. "I don't know," He gasped with a sob, "What am I supposed to say?" Enrique tried to hug him. "Okay, okay," Max said, pushing his father away, although his chest was shaking and tears flowed out of his blue eyes. "I have to go. I have to meet Lisa. This was good, talking to Mom was good, but I have to go."

Enrique released him. There was a brief opportunity to ask Margaret how it went for her. She reported that Max had been loving with her physically, as always, snuggling and showing no fear of her ill body. But he couldn't say much, his pain made him mute. "He told me about Lisa, though," she said. "I was glad he was willing to tell me about her. And I got to hold him for a long time," she whispered, grateful.

And then Diane arrived, the last person to say good-bye. Enrique banished himself to the living room, to wait through this final interruption. He watched the clock on the cable TV box turn to 5:26 and thought, Four more minutes and she's mine.

That was when Diane called out, "Enrique? Can you come upstairs? She's not feeling well."

Panicked, he took the stairs two at a time. When he entered the bedroom, he couldn't see Margaret. Diane was inclined over the bed but turned at his approach. "I'd better go," she said and disappeared out of view. Margaret was huddled in a fetal position, buried from head to toe under a quilt that he had folded at the foot of the bed now that it was June. She must have asked Diane to cover her with it.

Before he pulled the quilt down enough to see her face, he knew. He knew from four other bouts of severe infection and high fevers, he knew from the trembling of the covers, and he knew from her desperate cries when he tried to pull them away.

"No, no, no," she said through chattering teeth. "Don't take it off. I'm freezing," she pleaded. He disobeyed, lowering the blanket to climb in with his long body that she liked to praise for its warmth. As fast as he could, he pulled the covers up to his chin, leaving only the top of her head exposed. He put his arms around her and pressed against her quaking body and prayed the shaking would stop. If not, he would be forced to call the hospice doctor and ask what drugs he should administer. But he hoped it would not come to that. Margaret had forbidden all measures to extend her life. If he called, Dr. Ko would instruct him to eliminate Margaret's awareness of what was happening—put her into a coma if necessary. The drugs would make her comfortable, which of course he wanted, but that meant there would be no more conversation, no last words from Enrique to thank her.

She cried out, "The blanket, the blanket!" Enrique pulled it over both their heads, sealing them in a hot cave. In the dark, she said through chattering teeth, "I feel so bad. I feel so bad."

"I'm sorry," he whispered and clutched her tight. "I love you." And he prayed, although he was a Godless man, that those weren't the last words she would hear him speak.

chapter seventeen

A Happy Marriage

ENRIQUE WOKE UP beside his wife, a gradual and easy awakening. He rolled onto his back and stretched, as drowsy as a sunbather, gazing at the blue predawn light glowing from the open window. He listened to water slap softly at the piles of the Hotel Danieli. Venice really *is* a drowning city, he thought. The October air wafting in was mild, and Enrique wasn't troubled that it came through the most expensive window he had ever paid for. He felt thoroughly becalmed. This contented absence of expectation or worry was rare, almost unique in his life, and for a month he had been feeling only its opposite.

During the weeks before Margaret flew from New York to meet him at the Frankfurt Airport so they could travel together to Italy, he had slept in a clenched fetal bundle, as if he were enduring bombardment in a trench. Each morning he had woken up with his jaw and gums hurting, which he knew from his dentist's grim warnings meant he was grinding his teeth, and there was the familiar stomach pain of career anxiety—but not last night, his first in Venice, not this dawn in the Danieli.

He had spent three days at the Frankfurt Book Fair to promote the German publication of his eighth novel, which had been published unsuccessfully in the United States a year and a half before. The source of all those agonized nights of sleep was the old discouragement at the world's reception of his writing, the profound reverberation of failure. Thinking in this vein about his career, he could hear his good friend and fellow novelist Porter complain, "You're not a failure, Enrique. You're confusing money with quality."

Porter Beekman, a bastion of New England piousness and cynicism about literature, was no doubt correct in drawing that distinction, but it failed to comfort. True, years ago Enrique had felt like a complete bust when the commercial disappointment of his novels forced him to confront his buried belief that they weren't good. But the poor sales of his last book had not shaken his own satisfaction with the work. No, its failure to capture a large audience left him in despair precisely because he believed he had done his best. Not the melodramatic, grand emotion—I'm going to kill myself—of his youthful disappointments. This was like hearing the sentence of a court of last appeal, a submissive acceptance of aging and death.

He had aged; he was forty-three. He'd lived through the death of someone he loved, who represented all that was vigorous in life to him, his father. He had seen that handsome and vibrant face immobile and bloodless. He had heard the resonant voice, angry or ecstatic, stilled forever. And eight months after the loss of his progenitor, Enrique had passed through the death of his ambition as his most ambitious novel came and went with little notice. He knew that whatever he might achieve in the future, it would never come near to the dreams of his youth.

For well over a year he'd told himself that his general despair was temporary, the natural process of grieving for his father and for a book that had demanded so much of him. The novel had taken two years to research and almost as much time to write, and there was another year of necessary interruptions to do movie scripts, which paid for the literary enterprise. Even more significant than the investment of five years in the book was how spent he felt—the nine hundred pages were closer to three novels than to one and seemed to have exhausted all of his knowledge of people and the world. Be patient, he told himself, and you'll get over both loss and defeat.

However, they were not temporary feelings of abandonment and discouragement. Well before he flew to Frankfurt he knew why. The loss of his father, the engine of his career, was a permanent and irreplaceable loss. If anything, Guillermo had been too devoted a fan. When Enrique, in an effort to spare his dying father such trivia, stopped relating accounts of his script conferences, Guillermo immediately complained. "You think it's your business. But I think you and I are the same person," he said with a knowing wink at his narcissism. "By not telling me what's happening in your meetings, you're cutting me off from my career." And, although he was proud of his long novel, Enrique believed that it was his crowning failure. That when so ambitious a book falls short of establishing its author as central to his generation, it becomes a final assessment of the limits of a writer's talent, especially to himself.

He wondered how he could live the remainder of his life and manage to feel inspired, engaged, and hopeful. He could, of course, live through his children, and presumably destroy them, since, he had concluded based on his own experience, there is no greater likelihood of disappointment than being colonized by a parent's ambition. Perhaps that was blaming his father for his own deficits. After all, Freud had observed that "the man who is the undisputed favorite of his mother carries within him always the feeling that he can conquer the world." Evidently Enrique had had the wrong parent rooting for him.

On the surface, he ought not to have felt anxiety about the book fair. His German publisher was simply being gracious in flying him over to do press for their edition; little was expected of him or his novel. Unfortunately for Enrique, the trip caused him to relive the disappointment of the U.S. publication like a shattered war veteran flashing back to his most traumatic memory, and to feel keenly the absence of his father's partisanship in body and soul, particularly when he tried to sleep. Worse, whatever suppressed hope Enrique might have had that Germany would see his book differently than his own country had been deflated by a prominent and dismissive review on the day of his arrival. He sat in the wreckage for three days, droning on through meaningless interviews to small outlets, and waited to join Margaret for a celebration of their twentieth wedding anniversary in Venice.

They arrived on the morning of the actual day, October 15. He had no expectation that he was going to be good company or much fun and less expectation that he was going to enjoy himself. He was wrong.

They took a nap after checking into a rambling, high-ceilinged suite: a grand and foolishly elegant sitting room, sofa and wing chair gilt-edged and swathed in yards of maroon velvet; a sedate, gray-carpeted bedroom, dominated by a large lead-glass mirror hanging over a modest fireplace and a romantic and classic view of the Gulf of Venice. When they woke up, she surprised him by escalating from snuggling into full-blown lovemaking. Years ago they had thoroughly talked out that his constant sexual eagerness only pushed her deeper into reluctance. He knew it was unwise to propose sex when it was already in the air, and especially on their anniversary. He had assumed she would wait until after dinner, because naps blanketed her in a grouchy fog until she had coffee and was left alone for an hour. Her lustful awakening was a gift.

And it wasn't typical of their lovemaking. She languished, stretched and arched like a cat, whereas usually she had a tighter, athletic feel to her movements, a resistance to surrender to pleasure. Her body felt liquid and welcoming until her climax, which didn't build slowly but this time arrived without warning. She grabbed him as if to hold him in place, dug her fingernails into his back, and bit his shoulder right before her orgasm, and yet she also found room in the middle of ecstasy to shoot her husband a sideways smile and comment as if they were taking a stroll, "Guess I'm hungry," instead of remaining solemn and silent during intercourse. And it was different for him. His release wasn't as spasmodic, more like a tap opening and flowing. While Margaret and Enrique took their daytime swim on the Danieli bed, they were oddly calm in the midst of their excitement.

And then they had espresso, as tourists are supposed to, in the Piazza San Marco, and made sure, along with dozens of other couples, to watch the clock tower strike, and walked through the old, narrow, and comforting streets to the restaurant where his L.A. agent, Rick, had arranged for them to celebrate their anniversary. Margaret had warned Enrique that Venice was notorious for poor food. Rick had volunteered that he knew the chef and proprietor of a great restaurant in Venice and would organize a special meal for them.

When they arrived, the allegedly fine restaurant looked too modest to Enrique. It was hardly more than an empty storefront— ten small tables and without so much as a pull-down shade to conceal its patrons from prying eyes. The bare wood floor and painted white walls suited Margaret's taste perfectly, precisely because the room was casual and blended with the narrow cobblestoned street they had reached by following the route their concierge had drawn for them on the hotel map. The restaurant was full of customers, and there was a line of people waiting outside, which quickly transformed Enrique's skepticism into anxiety about their reservation.

He needn't have worried. They were seated ahead of the others at the one free table, in the quietest corner of the lively restaurant. The round-faced, red-cheeked chef came to shake his hand and kiss Margaret's and to announce, in stumbling English, that they didn't have to decide anything, all was arranged. Could you select the wine? Enrique asked, and the owner nodded as if anything else would be absurd.

That food and wine appeared and plates were cleared in rhythm with their appetites and the flow of conversation, that the close quarters were absent formality, made it seem as though they had been welcomed into a friend's home. There was no sense of being strangers here. And that they were the only diners speaking English lent the evening a feeling of privacy as well as family, a magical and impossible combination.

Their waitress, the owner's wife, beamed at them between courses and managed to convince Enrique that the spectacle of a middle-aged couple being romantic wasn't laughable. They held hands walking back, arms swinging in a childlike rhythm, until they reached the Piazza San Marco, where a breeze chilled Margaret. He gathered her to him, and they walked as one across the square, listening to the echoes of a group of young people shouting and singing, chamber music drifting from a window, wind whispering through the tunnels of narrower side streets, and water lapping over the seawall. It was the season of *acqua alta,* high water. Wood planks, elevated two feet, had been put over the cobblestones leading to the Hotel Danieli, and their shoes clattered as if they were on horseback.

There was a fax waiting for him at the hotel. It was from Rick, relaying an offer from a studio to rewrite an adaptation of what in Enrique's childhood had been called a comic book but had been promoted to graphic novel as they neared the millennium. Margaret didn't frown as she normally would have at the lack of boundaries in the movie business. It was 1997, and Enrique didn't yet have a cell phone that could be used in Europe; if he had, Rick would have interrupted their anniversary dinner. Of course, Enrique was a grown-up and could ignore the call, or for that matter throw this fax into the garbage, but Margaret and Enrique both understood that he was addicted to writing and this, adapting a comic book for a movie that might or might not ever be made, was what was left to feed his addiction.

"Sorry," he said as he took the fax, and the brass skeleton key to their room, from a courtly man at the front desk.

"It's okay," Margaret conceded. "Dinner was great. Rick's got credit with me."

Enrique opened the fax while they climbed the carpeted golden staircase, passing under Gothic arches up to the third floor, ascending almost to the glass ceiling of this part of the hotel, its oldest, a fourteenth-century converted palace. He had read in the hotel brochure that the French novelist George Sand had stayed there with her lover Alfred de Musset. These four days in Venice were going to cost well north of ten thousand dollars, booked over Margaret's thrifty Queens girl objections. "We can be funky and cheap while we're there," Enrique said, "but I didn't write all this crap for all these years to fly coach and stay in a Days Inn." She laughed and said, "Venice Days Inn," as if the idea were delightful. She agreed to all his travel extravagances and initiated her own, including tomorrow's Locanda Cipriani lunch on Torcello Island, where

Princess Di and Hemingway—and some other person who seemed unlikely to be linked with Papa and royalty, Madonna or Stephen Hawking, he couldn't remember which—used to go.

When they got to their room, he read the fax carefully. The studio had agreed to pay him his last fee, his "quote" as the business liked to call it, with the condition that he say yes or no on Monday so that he could fly to L.A. by the end of the week to get started with the director and the studio's notes. Notes prior to his writing. That was one of Hollywood's brilliant innovations, criticizing a writer before he starts. They needed a script fast, they claimed, in order to begin shooting after New Year's. He wasn't impressed. Studios always demanded that the writer hurry because shooting was imminent, and then, after receiving the script, progress slowed to a crawl.

"They've agreed to my price," Enrique said lugubriously.

"Good," Margaret said, compressing the word into little more than a chirp, a signal that she didn't want to discuss it.

"They want me to fly to L.A. next weekend for a Monday meeting."

"We'll be back Wednesday." She shrugged. "You'll have plenty of time to pack."

"You think I should do it?" he asked.

"Do what you want."

"Come on," he pleaded. "Tell me. What do you think?"

She ignored him, standing in the center of the maroon sitting room, looking back and forth between an uncomfortably small divan and a sumptuous wing chair, as if the choice between them was not obvious. "It's crazy, but I'm going to take another bath," she announced, making it clear that bugging her about his career was unromantic. But he hated making these decisions without her. "Should I take a bath with you?" he asked, not sincerely.

"You won't fit, Puff," she said, laughing. "Didn't you see what a tiny tub it is! I barely fit." She walked up and caressed his cheek. "Poor baby," she teased. "You're too big for this world."

He undressed, put on the Danieli's thick robe, and settled in the wing chair. He listened to the water slap softly around his wife and reread the fax. It was quite a small piece of driftwood the current of his career had deposited at his bare feet. He didn't feel sorry for himself; he felt embarrassed. He had been given so long a lead, publishing a novel at seventeen, and despite the consoling speeches of Porter, Margaret, other family and friends, what nagged him, truly bothered him, was that he suspected he had earned his fate.

He stowed the fax with his passport, to put it out of sight but safe until Monday. I must enjoy this weekend, he ordered himself, and walked to the bathroom to take a good, long look at his wife naked in the tub.

She was forty-seven. Her white skin was freckled below her collarbone. There was an irregular line he liked to trace across her breasts, and on the outside of her smooth, hairless arms, fading away to the tender hollows of her elbows and the cream of her forearms. She was dotted here and there on the inside of her soft and lean thighs. Enrique remembered her surprise when he first confessed his love for her freckles; they had always embarrassed her. She was vainer than most of the women he knew who weren't actresses. She often came away from a session in the bathroom threatening to get an eye lift because she was developing her father's bags. She sounded sincere and scared Enrique that she would one day indulge, and surgery by surgery turn into one of those women with startled, frozen faces and bodies so emaciated that their heads looked wider than their shoulders. So far she worked out nearly every day and had maintained her figure without silicone or a scalpel. Yet even so, he knew she was unhappy about her body. And her body was not what it was, of course, twenty-two years ago, when he first saw her without clothes. Her breasts, that had suckled his sons, were smaller, the nipples browner and no longer resistant to gravity; her stomach, although still flat, was broader and softer; and there was a thin white scar from the cesarean drawn above the ridge of her still black pubic hair. When he'd grabbed her buttocks that afternoon to push into her deeper, her cheeks had filled his hands without spillage, but they were pillows, not firm fruit. Enrique would not admit it to a male friend, but Margaret's middle-aged body excited him precisely because it was not the same flesh that he had lusted after as a young and stupid man. He wanted her today because what he had once desired was now landscaped by the history of their life together; and, although he didn't know this and couldn't know it as long as she was alive, he wanted her because, while in her arms, he felt safe.

"Are you looking at me?" Margaret asked. Her head faced away from the door, toward a window in red velvet.

"You're beautiful," he said.

"Stop looking at me," she answered.

"Why?" he demanded, so he could tell her, when she confessed that she was ashamed of her aging body, that she was still beautiful.

"Because I don't know you well enough," she said.

Margaret wasn't often witty. In keeping with the tradition and manners of Ashkenazi women from Poland to Queens, she kept conversation practical. Rarely did she show off the intelligence that she had passed on and encouraged in their sons. He retreated to the bed. Knowing that they had already had their anniversary coupling was very relaxing. Until he'd gotten that fax, the trip had been magical. He was determined not to let his career once again ruin his fun.

He heard her rise from the tub and step out onto the marble floor. He imagined her groin wet and black. He wondered why her joke about him looking at her naked lingered in his mind. When she appeared in her white silk teddy, bought for this sexy vacation, he noted the big freckle above her right knee, that he always enjoyed seeing during the summer months of shorts, and then he knew what had struck him about her comment: *She knows me, that's what's funny. She knows me through and through; I'm the one who doesn't know her.*

They kissed long and deep, and he got hard again, but when she asked, with a slight reluctance, "Do you want to?" he lied and said, "I'm fine." She kissed him good night with obvious gratitude and fell asleep within seconds. He lay on his side, listening to the slapping water, and he thought—*I am in love with Margaret.* He relished this surprising fact with deep satisfaction, and decided that he would bring up the unmentionable subject tomorrow during the fancy lunch on Torcello.

He knew that to bring up ugly memories would be to jeopardize their romantic mood, but he believed that nothing too awful could happen in such a musically named place. Torcello. Torcello. He wanted to know more about the wound Margaret carried with her and never discussed, and to heal it if he could. He resolved that on Torcello he would dare to speak of it.

His sleep was dreamless and relaxed, his first good rest in months. During the expansive, languorous predawn awakening, Margaret sighed and rolled over to him wordlessly, resuming a slow and rhythmic breathing as if heavily asleep. Her arm, fragrant with bath oils, snaked around his shoulder, and small, cool fingers crept down his stomach until she took hold of his cock—something she hadn't done on waking up since their first year together. Another unusual, relaxed, drowsy lovemaking followed, and he forgot all about his resolution to have a frank conversation. Nor did he recall it while they had coffee and bread from a café squeezed into a space no larger than a newspaper kiosk, nor while they hunted for the Peggy Guggenheim museum in another converted Venetian palazzo on the Grand Canal.

As they shuffled along with the flow of tourists past the Cubists and Futurists, he remembered. He paid no attention to the paintings. He watched Margaret study them, a more intriguing show for him. He was fascinated by her knowledgeable and mysterious method of surveying the art, walking right past this Braque and then standing at a Kandinsky for a long two minutes, squinting as if it were out of focus, and moving on with a wistful sigh. "You like that?" he asked, and she said, "It's okay," which made him laugh.

He knew well from her clothing, her decoration of their apartment, her photographs and paintings that she had a discerning and creative eye. She read a lot, much more than he, and was smart about books. But she didn't care whether they were original or profound; she read to be entertained. With images, though, she wanted more than to be soothed or delighted. She had a gift which was mysterious even to her. To Enrique, the proof of her innate ability was that he couldn't reconstruct backward how she had known her choice of color and composition would work. Often what she was attempting seemed doomed. But from the choice of an outfit to the composition of a painting, it always turned out well. For Enrique, that was the telltale difference between craft and talent, between learning what ought to be right and possessing the felicity of impeccable taste.

She was a mystery to him. In truth, she was a mystery to their friends. Certainly she was underestimated. Few of the people they knew thought her the talented one in their marriage. Most knew that, although she was gregarious and pleasant, he was the one who would say something that would provoke either irritation or delight, an exchange they would remember. And when one of their friends had a crisis, they turned to him for sympathy and help; Margaret might scold or insist on her advice as a remedy. In the early years of their marriage, his greater popularity surprised her, and it surprised him, because he knew, as he assumed she did, that she was as smart as, and certainly better educated than he; that her estimations of the people they knew were often less naïve than his, and that her advice was likely to be wiser. The true difference in how their friends felt toward them individually was that, despite Margaret's broad smile and friendly conversation, in contrast to Enrique's self-pitying confessionals and rants at society, she remained opaque to everyone—acquaintances, family, and close friends. She kept a part of herself secluded, in a secret location unknown even to Enrique.

Margaret informed him that the Locanda Cipriani on Torcello could be reached expensively on the restaurant's private boat—presumably the way Papa, Madonna, Princess Di, and Stephen Hawking traveled—but that she wanted to take the vaporetto, the public water bus, because it would be more fun. He glanced enviously at the handsome, wood-paneled cruiser, but she was right about the gaiety of riding the vaporetto. It was cheering to stand shoulder to shoulder with a boatload of merry tourists, who didn't look decorous and miserable in splendid isolation like rich travelers but were babbling and pointing and snacking and complaining and laughing, all full of life, except for one young man who had turned green. And Margaret had the girlish fun of photographing the two strapping, olive-skinned, young Venetians who manned the water bus, dashing in their striped blue and white naval shirts and bell-bottomed blue pants, smart red caps atop handsome heads of thick black hair. "You're in love," Enrique accused her when she convinced the handsomer of the two to pose for her on the prow, pulling in the dock line.

His wife answered the charge with a sly smile. "They look like you, Puff," she whispered and kissed him fast and light on the lips, hers wet, cool, and salty from the Gulf of Venice spray. Enrique made a skeptical face. "That's how you looked when I met you," she amended.

She was being kind. He had been scrawny and gawky, no sailor's lean muscular body. But he did once have a thick, full head of raven hair. "You could sue me for false advertising," he said, pointing to his balding head.

She smiled ruefully. "You think the court will give me my waist back?"

They arrived forty-five minutes before their one o'clock reservation. Margaret was prepared for that and guided Enrique to a recommended walk on a path cut around the island's perimeter. "We're supposed to have champagne," she told him. "It's a very decadent lunch. We probably won't need to eat dinner."

"I always need to eat dinner," Enrique said and stopped at a cleared spot on the path, with a sweeping view. He stretched his right arm wide and beckoned for her to enter. She did, although he could tell she wanted to keep moving. There was a small bush with tiny yellow flowers fluttering between them and the water and the floating city in the distance. The day was hot. Bees buzzed, and blossoms seemed to be everywhere. He wondered how it could be October. Perhaps the island was located in some magical latitude for the very rich, where it was forever springtime. He hugged her hard and then released her. "You want to keep walking?"

"We should head back. I want to get there a little early so we can pick a table in the shade. It's really hot today. Like summer. I love it."

They turned, walking back to the low green building she had identified as the Locanda. He sighed heavily. She asked, "Are you thinking about the deal?"

"Yes," he lied.

"Don't do it if you don't want to. We have enough money if you want to write another novel."

That was a surprise. Pleased, he took her hand and swung their arms the way they used to when bookending a walk with their toddler sons. They reached the finish of the cleared path and stepped onto the graveled drive up to the Locanda. "So you think I should write another novel?" She didn't answer. She kept her profile to him, not meeting his eyes. The silence went on too long. She was reluctant to say, but like him, he thought, she wanted to tell the truth today. "You can tell me," he urged her.

"No, I don't think you should," she answered at that prompt. She met his eyes and pouted regretfully, a sign that she expected him to feel hurt.

He didn't respond while they wandered into the restaurant and down a hall past photographs of Papa and Prince Charles through the interior to the outside garden, where tables were set with thick linen, sparkling crystal, and gleaming silverware.

At Margaret's instruction, Enrique had dressed up, in blue blazer, gray trousers, a striped blue and white shirt. He had balked at wearing a tie. He almost wished he hadn't. He felt naked compared to the black-suited, bow-tied waiters and two florid-faced, elderly men in pin-striped suits at a table nearby, accompanied by a pair of bejeweled women in floral print dresses. On the other hand, although they were seated in a well-shaded table under a canopy of vines, it was hot in the still garden air, and he was glad he had nothing around his neck. He wanted to take his jacket off but was afraid they would toss him out for so shocking a disrobing. Despite this discomfort of formality, when he regarded his smiling wife, pretty and merry as a young woman in her silk black dress, with a red, curving, abstract pattern swirling down one breast and across her waist and disappearing around a hip, he felt at ease and free of all worldly concerns.

He said yes to the waiter's suggestion that they begin with champagne, and Margaret beamed when he popped the cork, pouring the golden bubbles into fluted glasses. First, Enrique toasted her, "I love you," and she answered, "I love you." And then he got back to it. "So you don't want me to write a novel." She looked abashed and worried. "It's okay," Enrique said. "I'm not upset. Don't get scared. Tell me the truth."

"I'm not scared," she insisted. She sighed. "I'm being selfish. Has nothing to do with what you want. If you want to write them you should, but they're no fun for me. I don't think they're much fun for you either, but that's your business."

"Not fun because I get moody?"

"No!" She shook her head with irritation, as she did whenever he didn't automatically understand her meaning. "You don't get moody about writing your books. Not anymore. I don't think you should write books because there's only a tiny audience for serious novels. People love movies. Everybody loves movies. Especially publishing people. Anyway, I'm just being selfish. Your movie projects are fun for me. I get to visit you on the set in Prague, in London, in Paris, and I get to meet stars and directors and go to premieres and have caviar on Air France and"—she raised her flute, just missing colliding with a bee en route from the trellis above, buzzing toward a rosebush softening the main building's edge—"I get to have lunch with my husband on Torcello."

While they selected from the three-course prix fixe and watched the tables fill up with more well-dressed and beautiful, or ancient and wealthy patrons, Enrique prepared to raise the sore topic. After all, she had said her difficult piece, that his great ambition in life was a drag for her and something she'd rather he didn't do. He had a right to say his difficult piece. "Margaret." He sat up straight in the wicker chair and looked at her full-on. "There's something I want to say to you."

"Uh-oh!" she said, making a scared face like a little girl.

Puzzled, he peered into her eyes, saw adult terror, and was

confused. He still wasn't sure how to broach it. "No, nothing terrible. I just want to ask you if I'm the reason, or part of the reason, you've stopped painting."

She blinked, confused. He hadn't framed the question properly. On the boat and during their walk, he had been reviewing what happened three years ago, when she'd finally directed her energy into painting without distraction. She had put in long hours at the studio every day, at night wearing the abstracted gaze of an artist whose work has taken up full-time residence in her head. Unlike during earlier bursts of effort, this time she finished painting after painting. More surprising was that she brought home four of them and hung them for all to see. They were confident works, massive paintings of their sons from photographs she had taken. The paintings were full of her clear-eyed acceptance of the illusion and longing for attention in children, blown up so that you could see that, in their gleeful and poignant narcissism, adulthood—including disappointed adulthood—loomed.

Friends were impressed, and they asked to commission portraits of their children. She smiled but never accepted. Only after Enrique pressed her to the point of irritation did she explain. She didn't want to paint to order, she said. Eventually a friend of a friend, who ran one of New York's premier galleries, came over to see the paintings she had on display in their apartment and then went to her studio to see the rest, and told her the work was excellent and commercial and should get a show. It was too much to expect to start at the top, so she offered to recommend Margaret to a dozen of the hottest smaller galleries in SoHo and the Lower East Side. She advised Margaret to send out a portfolio of slides of her paintings, and she returned to the studio a second time to help her select the best. Margaret followed up immediately, displaying no signs of her usual reluctance and wariness of pushing her work. She mailed the slides to the galleries as soon as possible. The energy and excitement which infused her body during the week that she waited for responses was startling and significant to Enrique. While he listened to her enthusiastic plans for a new and different series, he concluded that all those years of diffidence about being an artist had been self-protection. It was apparent that she wanted, as much as he did, to be recognized.

The rejections arrived slowly at first. By the second week, she had gotten three. They were, as Enrique well knew, the kinds of rejections beginning artists long for. Not form letters but thoughtful explanations as to why her series, although provocative and well-executed, didn't fit into their notions of what their clients were seeking. Some offered to recommend her to other galleries; one suggested she take commissions for portraits and gradually build a following. All asked her, if she moved to another subject, to please show her new work to them first. "Someone will take them," Enrique encouraged her.

On Tuesday of the following week, he came home to have lunch with her. She had already picked up the mail. He found her lying on the chaise under the stairs, where she liked to read murder mysteries in the afternoon. Her face was awash in tears. Tossed on the floor were eight rejections. She answered his question, "What's the matter?" by pointing to them. He read them. Each was encouraging, regretful, making suggestions about other venues, many repeating the advice that she take commissions to do people's children and build a following that way. All requested that when she tried a different series, not portraits, she please come to them first. "Margaret," Enrique said and meant every word, "if I had gotten these rejection letters when I was starting out, I would have been thrilled. They genuinely like your work. They took time to write these letters. If they thought you were wasting your time and theirs, they would send out form letters. They don't think they can sell this, but they want you to keep going, and eventually one of them will take you on. Don't be discouraged. I know it seems like I'm bullshitting when I say this, but these are great rejections."

The tears had stopped. Her eyes were sad and bereft and, oddly, loving. She said nothing for a moment. He feared she was going to lapse into her typical reticence and refuse to reveal her private thoughts. But she did speak. "I've watched you," she said and paused.

"What?" he asked, confused.

"For twenty years I've watched you take this"—she gestured at the rejections—"and keep going, and I don't know how you do it. I can't. I just can't. I'm sorry. I'm not strong enough."

He lifted her from the chaise, her arms limp with defeat, held her, and whispered, "Then just paint. Don't show the work. If you can't take it, just paint."

She agreed. For a while, she did paint, beginning the new series that, to his surprise, was better, more confident, more accomplished, as if the rejections had strengthened her. But they hadn't; or something else sapped her strength. The energy to fight was short-lived. Fewer canvases came home, and soon none did. After six months she stopped going regularly to the studio, and, while they were in Maine during August, she mentioned that she planned to allow the lease to lapse in December.

The anticipatory look of terror at what he might say had left his wife's face. She snagged her champagne glass and smirked. "You? I didn't stop painting because of you. Why would I have stopped because of you? It has nothing to do with you."

This thorniness was why he feared talking to her about this subject or any other that she had quarantined. "Wait. Slow down. You don't understand."

"What?" The thorn bush waggled at him. "What don't I understand?"

"I've had a lot of setbacks in my career. A lot of times I wanted to quit, and you've always encouraged me and kept me going. Even when I got us into debt you backed me up. But when you had that one disappointment because of the galleries passing on your series and you stopped, I didn't—"

She cut him off. "It had nothing to do with that." Their first course arrived, and they fell silent while the dishes were maneuvered in front of them. He had ruined the mood. Her girlish smile, her naughty laugh, her gleaming eyes had fled. This had been a mistake. The hurt was too deep. When the waiter departed, she said, "Let's not talk about this."

"I'm sorry I brought it up, but let's try to finish now that—"

"I don't want to," she snapped, refusing to look at him.

He was beaten. *Do I really love this woman?* he wondered. *I need her. She is my life. But do I love her—her privacy, and her fussy, controlling nature? I hate that she won't give an inch.* He poked at the first course, ravioli stuffed with tuna—enough food for a full meal— and felt glum. He heard a bee buzz past and a low murmur of English accents from the old men nearby. And then he heard his wife speak, in a sweet, conciliating tone:

"I'm not like you. I don't need to do it to be happy." He looked up into her great blue eyes, paler than usual in the bright sunlight of the perpetual springtime of Torcello, gazing at him with an open plea for understanding. "And what bothers me, what I always feel from you, is that I'm not good enough for you unless I'm an artist. Sometimes I think you won't love me unless I'm an artist."

Enrique was astounded. He had no inkling she felt this from him. But he didn't deny it right away.

"In your family there's a kind of craziness about it. They all have to be artists or they're not good enough. I like painting. I like taking photos. But I don't want to make a career of it. Trying to make a career of it made me miserable. I'm not like you. It took me a while to find out. I don't need to paint to be happy. I'm happy. Here. With you. Doing this." She gestured at the garden, at the old English people, at the bees, and the October flowering bushes, at the waiters in their black suits, and at last at Enrique. "I'm happy," she said, merriment spreading her plea into a smile. "If you're happy with me, like this, then I'm happy."

He knew that her accusation had merit. He had spent years in therapy trying to be free of his parents' prejudices, gripes, snobberies, ignorance—she must have suffered during that struggle. But he didn't offer that excuse. He swore to her, until he felt sure that Margaret believed him, that he didn't care if she never touched a brush or picked up a camera, that she was everything he wanted.

And for a moment, in the amnesty of their anniversary, he understood his marriage. That sunny afternoon in Torcello he understood that he lived in awe of her contented place on earth; that she embodied what had endured for him: that his father was gone, his vanity was gone, his belief in art was gone, and that what he had extracted of true value out of life was the life she had given him.

chapter eighteen

Loveless

"WE DON'T HAVE a marriage. We're just people doing errands who share an apartment. We hand off Greg to each other. That's the most contact we have. I come home, he hands me the baby—"

"I don't hand you the baby when you come home." Enrique couldn't stop himself from interrupting, although he assumed Dr. Goldfarb would object now that, as requested, Margaret was expressing her feelings about their marriage. "You come home at two o'clock in the morning! I don't hand you—"

"I mean on Wednesday." She didn't glance his way. Her sunny face was shining on the marriage counselor, on the marriage counselor alone. "And on the rare Thursday Enrique doesn't go to a screening with Porter." She added, "He'd much rather spend time with Porter than me."

The psychiatrist shot him a look. What does that sourpuss mean? Enrique wondered. Does he think I'm gay? Porter doesn't fuck me either, but at least he talks about something other than the durability of strollers. "Who is . . . Paula?" the shrink asked in a lugubrious basso.

"Porter," Enrique corrected.

"Porter Beekman. The critic," she announced, as if introducing him at a dinner party. She was sitting ramrod straight, her teeth—newly bonded to a gleaming white and correct proportionate size—were on display thanks to a beauty-queen-wide smile. "The *New York Times* movie critic—"

"Second-string movie critic," Enrique corrected. "And he's a novelist also."

"Second-string?" Goldfarb said. "I know his name. But I don't know what that means . . . second-string?"

Enrique gave a rough explanation that the first-string critic took his pick of what to review and the second-string got the leavings, all the while wondering what the hell they were doing paying one hundred and twenty dollars an hour to explain the intricacies of journalism's hierarchy.

Meanwhile Margaret continued to sit smartly and beam at the gloomy psychiatrist as if he were the head of a co-op board and she needed his approval to move into the apartment of her dreams. The cheer flowing out of her and disappearing into the black hole of his Freudian silence seemed heroic, and crazy too, like the charge of the Light Brigade. When he asked her, "Why do you feel En-Ricky would rather spent time with Porter than you?" she answered in a hearty voice, as if announcing that she had won the lottery, "He'd rather spend time with anyone other than me."

Enrique shook his head at Dr. Goldfarb. He didn't want to interrupt again but couldn't bear to let that pass. She was the one who didn't want to be with him, his evidence being that she never wanted to have sex. On reflection, he was glad that he didn't pipe up with that proof, since no doubt Margaret didn't think having sex and spending time together were equivalent. It might fail to persuade the fish-eyed shrink as well, since many people seemed to believe fucking was somehow less intimate than dinner at a three-star restaurant. How he loathed the bourgeois jail he had sentenced himself to. How he loathed what he was doing at that very moment, sitting in a Park Avenue psychiatrist's office waiting for the right moment to say, "Look, I'm not even asking for a blow job. This marriage would be fine if she would only spread her legs more than once every two months!" But his vanity would never allow him to be that crude and that honest. Besides, he was sure he'd get a scolding, either feminist from Margaret or Freudian from the psychiatrist. Considering how crucial intercourse is to the continuation of the species, it seemed remarkable how little public support there was for the sexual act.

"Are you jealous of this . . . Porter?" the analyst asked, hesitating over the WASP name as much as he did over the Latino Enrique. I guess he can only pronounce Jewish names, Enrique thought bitterly, convinced the old fart was a waste of time. But that was a perverse complaint: Enrique had asked for counseling as a passive and hypocritical way of getting out of his marriage; incompetence could prove useful.

For a moment Margaret hesitated. Jealous of Porter? Does *she* think I'm gay? Enrique wondered, outrage beginning to well at the idea. First, she stops fucking me. Second, she decides I'm a fag. One of your best friends definitely doesn't think I'm gay, he sniped back in his head.

"No. It's not that. I don't care who his friends are. I just don't feel that Enrique wants to spend any time with me. He'd rather go out with our friend Lily and listen to her dating disasters—"

What is she talking about? Enrique wondered. Lily is practically engaged; she's not having dating disasters anymore.

"He spent a whole year, right after we moved in together, gambling until all hours at a backgammon club and sleeping all day so I never saw him."

"I stopped!" Enrique squealed, voice in a prepubescent climb. "That was six years ago. Before we even got married."

"He only stopped because I threatened to leave." Although she didn't look Enrique's way, she paused long enough to establish that he couldn't contradict her. "There's always something he'd rather do than spend time with me," she resumed her indictment. "When we're home alone, he stays up late watching television. He never goes to bed with me—"

"I'm not tired, and you never want to make love. What am I supposed to do? Lie there in the dark?"

Margaret smiled broadly, but her voice got louder and more strident. She sounded like her mother, trying to dominate conversation at the long, crowded Passover table. "That's all I feel Enrique is interested in from me. Having sex. If he wants to talk, he calls Porter or his brother or his father. He'd rather talk to Lily than to me." Goldfarb raised his eyebrows at this second mention of Lily. Margaret explained: "She's my best friend. Enrique loves to call her to get advice about his career—"

"Lily's an editor, I'm a writer—" Enrique began to object, but Margaret talked right over him.

"I can't think of anything he likes to do with me. He never wants to go anywhere, just the two of us. And when we finally go to a party—and he never wants, never ever wants to go anywhere—Enrique leaves my side immediately and talks to other people. He has lunches every day with his friends and tells them everything. His parents come over all the time, and he's always happy to talk to them. They're great babysitters, and I don't mind when they're around, but I feel like he's closer to his parents than to me. I don't think he wants to spend time with me, or talk to me, or that he cares about how I feel about anything. He's only interested in fucking me."

Enrique was tongue-tied by anger and shame. He was outraged by her presentation of the facts. Whether he could dispute that they were accurate, however, was another matter. Of course, after seven years of living together, he didn't want to spend all his time with her. Of course, he liked to be with friends and family and to talk to them about his feelings. Of course, he wanted to have sex with his wife rather than with his father. He was profoundly loyal to Margaret, it seemed to him, forgetting, for the moment, that he was having an affair with one of her closest friends. He wanted to refute her. He wanted to point out that their not having enough sex had been going on for years, and that he had accepted this deprivation with hardly a whimper. He had been much more patient than, say, his unfaithful half brother, who screwed around every week, not once in seven years. But that distinction would entail confessing to the affair. Instead, he stared at the psychiatrist and hoped he would set her straight.

"Margaret," the dour analyst began. She nodded eagerly, on the edge of her chair, an attentive student. "You're very clear about what you feel. And you've expressed it very clearly. But here's what puzzles me"—ah, Enrique thought with some satisfaction, he's going to hit her with how unreasonable she's being—"you're saying all these things about how unhappy you feel with a big smile on your face and in an excited way, like it's all good news. Why is that? These are sad feelings. Don't you feel sad about them?"

Enrique turned to look at her. He agreed. Her party manners while unburdening herself were odd. It pissed him off that she was so loud and boastful about her complaints. Her smile was gone.

The shrink had dumbfounded her. Enrique was gleeful. He lost arguments with his wife because of this trick she had mastered: she flipped his criticisms of her into what she didn't like about him. Look at the jujitsu she had just pulled off: the problem in their marriage is that Enrique wants to have sex with his wife. Disgusting! Maybe, just maybe, this sluggish fish of a marriage counselor will show her how bizarre her thinking is.

Margaret faced the windows. A block away, the sun slanted over Central Park and crossed the Fifth Avenue rooftops, filling her sea blue eyes. The beams pooled, overflowed, and began to fall—blue and yellow skating down her cheek. It took Enrique a moment to realize those were tears, not sunbeams. "I am sad," she said, the harsh, anxious voice gone. This was the tender tone she used with baby Gregory to soothe him, or to whisper endearments when she was pleased with Enrique. "I'm very sad," she repeated, teardrops clinging to her chin before they fell into her lap. "I love Enrique and I don't think he loves me anymore. We're strangers. He doesn't want me, he doesn't want to know me, he doesn't care about me, I'm just a drag for him." Her face shimmered with sorrow, and she sobbed. As if anteing up poker chips, Dr. Goldfarb used two fingers to move a box of Kleenex from his side of the desk to hers. She blotted her face, said, "Thank you," and blew her nose.

Enrique wanted to hug her. He wanted to assure her that he loved her. But he didn't move or speak. Wasn't this why he had come? Hadn't he hoped that through these sessions she would accept that he no longer loved her? Then he would be free to leave the marriage and live happily with Sally, who opened her full lips every day to kiss him and volunteer that she loved him without prompting from a psychiatrist. Sally was funny and demanding and giving and told him every single thought that came into her head. Sally, in some fundamental way, was much easier to love than Margaret. Although he felt miserable and unworthy—a villain who should be hissed in a movie, a coldhearted guard in a concentration camp, the shallow, materialistic boy whom the heroine is supposed to fall out of love with so she can find the right, warmhearted, nurturing man—although he knew he was bad and unworthy and that he ought to apologize, he said nothing.

Margaret was silent too. She wept steadily, small and still in her chair, a heartbroken little girl. That he continued to say nothing, not a word of reassurance, appalled even him. He assumed she must also be shocked and deeply hurt that he hadn't declared his love for her. Dr. Goldfarb, like a rhinoceros, maneuvered his great bald head and fixed his dead eyes on Enrique. Not with challenge. Or disgust. With faint curiosity. "How do you feel about that, En-Ricky?" he asked. "How does what Margaret is saying make you feel?"

"Well, of course I love Margaret," he said in an aggrieved tone. "I married her." Another sob burst out of his wife. She grabbed more tissues and brought them like reinforcements to her mouth, damming up the hurt feelings. She glanced at him, and he caught her eye, the first direct look they had exchanged since meeting in the waiting room. Her normally bold gaze was in a chaos of acute pain. The wince and wound of this contact was startling. She couldn't look at him that nakedly for long. She shifted away from him, staring into a corner, at empty carpet and a wicker wastebasket. She cleared her throat and got herself under control. Observing this struggle, he realized, for the first time in the seven years he had known her, that her cool manner—the clipped and strident voice, the alert girlish posture—was a shield and a disguise. "I didn't know she felt this way," Enrique told the doctor. He turned on the hard wood chair to address Margaret's dignified profile. "I didn't know you cared about me that much."

"What!" Margaret snapped, the scolding second-grade teacher restored to her tone, ice freezing her eyes. "That's ridiculous."

"I didn't," Enrique said to her. She kept her face averted from him. He pleaded to Goldfarb, "I didn't. I feel like she doesn't want to be with me. Part of that's sex, yes. But I think she's bored hearing me whine about my career and bored by . . ." He recounted a litany of facts—that she didn't seem to like Porter; that his closeness to his mother and father, so different from her alienation from her parents, seemed to irritate her; that she was bored with his unhappiness collaborating on screenplays with his half brother; that she hadn't wanted to make love for years, not simply since Greg was born.

From the very beginning of their relationship, Enrique told the doctor, she had tried to control every aspect of his behavior. "Every single thing we do, from the friends we see, to the parties we go to, to whether we have sex, she decides." Margaret had changed his quotidian behavior in the years before their son was born, insisting that Enrique stop behaving like a child, playing games late into the night, sleeping half the day, dropping his clothes on the floor, leaving dishes in the sink, sulking at home, watching baseball rather than going out and enjoying the world. She had mothered him out of adolescence into adulthood, and in the process she had controlled him. An investigation by a crack detective couldn't have disproved his statement. Nevertheless, Enrique felt his testimony amounted to a monumental lie. In fact, he was glad she had nagged him to grow up. If she hadn't, how would he ever have persuaded Sally to fall in love with him?

Apparently it was a convincing lie. Margaret seemed to want to believe how unhappy he was about his work and that he thought she was bored with his despair. The shrink too, when Enrique complained about Margaret's controlling behavior. But Enrique hadn't fooled himself. The truth was that he didn't love her anymore. She wasn't the problem in the marriage. He was. She wasn't the cause of his feeling oppressed by his parents' expectations, by his half brother's lack of talent and irresponsibility. She wasn't responsible for the fact that he was too passive about his career, unlike Porter and the other writers he knew. She wasn't the sole cause that in every area of his life—family and work—his days were unsatisfying. It wasn't her fault that only in Sally's arms did he feel alive. If he could escape from the cell of his New York existence, from his family, from his career, from his own expectations, he could be happy. Walking out on Margaret, and on all of his past, and fleeing to the sun and pleasures of L.A. would solve everything. It would all be so simple, really, if it weren't for Greg.

Dr. Goldfarb returned his focus to Margaret. "Why don't you want to have sex with your husband?" he asked.

"I do want to," she protested. "I'm just not turned on all the time like he is. And I can't make the switch from diapers to blow jobs like that—"

"Why not? It's the same general area," Enrique said and laughed—alone. She no longer deigned to provide oral sex, he wanted to say. She was stingy in her affection. That had to mean she didn't like him. She was hiding that from the shrink. Maybe she loved him, but she didn't like him. And he neither liked nor loved her. That was the truth. This marriage was a mistake.

"I can't just flip it on like a switch," she insisted. "There has to be some romance, some intimacy."

"That's ridiculous. We're totally intimate," he said and, while he said it, believed it.

"What about as parents?" Goldfarb asked, a bizarre question Enrique thought, from out of nowhere. "How is Enrique as a father?" he asked Margaret.

"Oh, he's a good father." She dismissed the compliment, an achievement beneath contempt.

"Margaret's a really good, really loving mother," Enrique conceded in a tone that suggested her maternal skills were some sort of facile trick.

That was all the ground they could cover in a first session. Enrique looked at the psychiatrist for an answer. Margaret did too. They wanted a verdict. The judgment was that they would benefit from further therapy at one hundred twenty dollars an hour and that if they had insurance, they should bring the forms next time.

They caught a cab on Fifth and rode home in silence. When they stopped at a red light on Fifty-ninth, he looked away from the Plaza hotel and saw tears were rolling down her cheeks. Feeling his eyes on her, she wiped them away with the flat of her hand. When her delicate fingers came to rest on the taxi's vinyl, he put his hand over hers. She didn't object or move it away, but she didn't react. She stared ahead, and her hand lay beneath his lifelessly.

They arrived at the apartment and listened to their nanny's report on Gregory's day. He'd had a tough one. Took a fall running in the park and scraped his knee, a striation of at least a dozen cuts across the joint that still looked raw. He'd also gotten sand in his right eye, which was bloodshot and puffy. Nor had Greg taken his afternoon nap, so he was overtired and generally uncomfortable. And to top off the day's derangements, once he felt water touch his wounded knee, he had refused to bathe. His hair was matted and his neck dirty. "You're a wreck," Margaret said with sad affection, taking his plump torso into her arms. Greg embraced her, throwing his chubby arms around her neck, shutting his eyes with relief. "No bath, baby. You don't want to have a bath, that's okay," she mumbled, kissing him on his sweaty brow.

The nanny left. Margaret and Greg settled on the couch with his comforting yellow blanket, the satin edge worn away. The frayed ends promised a disastrous erosion over the next few months. That had already prompted Margaret to get a second yellow blanket and gradually introduce it as an acceptable substitute. Greg would agree to clutch the new one only if the original blankey was there. With the two fetishes entwined, all but the top of him disappeared under a yellow tent, fragrant and warm from the bakery of his twenty-month-old skin.

Enrique settled in the Eames chair nearby and watched them, thinking hard about when to tell her that he wanted a divorce. Their next session with Goldfarb was a week away. The harshness of today's session didn't make him look forward to more. He still hadn't apologized to her, or told her that he loved her with the earnestness and reassurance she deserved. "Of course I love Margaret," he had whined to Goldfarb. "I married her," he had offered as proof. Replaying that highlight of the session in his head while watching Margaret soothe his son, he winced at his ungenerous words. Okay, he thought, gazing at mother and child, can I do this? Can I really do this to them?

It was a cliché of his social class and time, New York 1983, that a bad marriage was worse for a child than a divorce. Most of his friends, as well as his half siblings, Leo and Rebecca, were children of divorce. Although they were all neurotic and unhappy, many were less so than Enrique, the product of a fractious but as yet unbroken home. Unquestionably, a divorce would be better for Enrique. Listening to the rejected Margaret, he had to conclude that it would be better for her. The truth is always better was the mantra of the generation that had endured the Nixon administration. What he felt—that she didn't like him—and what she felt— that he didn't love her—amounted, no matter how you judged those claims, to the same sum: they shouldn't be together. If I'm right and she's too controlling, then she needs a man who doesn't mind. And if she's right, that I don't know how to be happy with her, then she needs a man who does. Ultimately who was right and who was wrong about the summation of the evidence was irrelevant to the verdict.

"He's asleep," Enrique said, noticing that Greg's heavy lids had shut and the rise and fall of his yellow-covered chest had become slow and deep.

"I know," she said.

"Isn't it too close to bedtime to be napping?"

She shrugged and frowned as if to say, Who cares? The world is coming to an end. "I have to pee," she announced.

"Give him to me."

She glared. "Don't wake him," she warned.

"Of course I won't wake him," he said in a disgusted voice. She rose gingerly. Greg briefly opened his eyes, made a soft peep of complaint. She cooed at him, kissed his brow, and lowered him into Enrique's lap. Greg nestled his hot head into the crook of his father's shoulder and fell back into a comforted sleep.

Margaret paused before leaving. She looked at her child's calm head on his father and smiled with approval at that conjoining, and only at that.

"We're ordering in?" Enrique asked.

"Chinese," she said and walked away.

Enrique looked out the living room window. Although they lived on Tenth Street, a block north of Margaret's old studio apartment, this view was eleven stories above a courtyard facing south. The yard wasn't fully enclosed; an opening provided a view of Ninth Street. He didn't remember that he had once anxiously paced between those trees killing time before Margaret's Orphans' Dinner. He watched without memory the same branches swaying in a gentle breeze and smelled the muffin fragrance of his son, and saw himself in a burgundy convertible Beemer, driving on Sunset Boulevard with Sally's blond hair flowing beside him, and he thought: *Who the fuck am I kidding?*

He discussed his decision with Porter and with Porter alone. Only his half brother, a man so unfaithful to his marriage that his advice would be useless, also knew of the affair. Porter didn't offer counsel. He sighed and complained about his own miserable child-ridden, sex-starved marriage.

Enrique phoned Sally in Santa Monica two days later. He told her that he loved her, that she was good for him, but that he had made a mistake. He had had a son with Margaret, and although he didn't love her and never would, he believed it would be worse for everyone—Margaret, Greg, and himself—if he left.

She argued, of course, but was frustrated by Enrique's lack of a defense. He agreed that he was miserable, and that he would be miserable for the rest of his life. He agreed that Margaret would be happier in the end if he left. He even conceded that it was possible a divorce would be better for Gregory. "I just can't do it" was the only explanation he gave, and it was the complete truth of what he understood of his feelings.

It took more than a week of daily wretched, painful conversations before Sally gave up. She was suffering, of course, but he never comforted her during those agonized calls by telling her how forsaken he felt by the loss of their romance. After a few more dishonest sessions of counseling, Enrique announced to Goldfarb and to Margaret that he was going into individual therapy, that he had problems he needed to resolve before his marriage could improve. He didn't think that was entirely a lie, or even mostly a lie. He was unhappy about every aspect of his life. It couldn't be that his marriage was the sole cause. Margaret and he resolved to keep the hour they had set aside for therapy as a regular date, an oasis of intimacy in their crowded marriage. They also arranged for a regular babysitter on Tuesday nights to spend an evening alone together. Their relations, including their sexual relations, became friendlier, although without passion.

And he began his own therapy, the sole relief in his private mourning for what he had sacrificed. He told no one besides his new shrink of the affair and swore Porter and his half brother to secrecy. Acute loss blackened his days for a year. He trudged to his office at eight-thirty every morning and returned at five o'clock every afternoon, back and forth in echoing steps of despair, his head aching with longing, his heart wincing in pain. With every step he was certain that he was doomed to live without love, and without the hope of love, for the rest of his life.

chapter nineteen

Love Interrupted

EVERYTHING ABOUT Margaret's disease seemed to have been designed to occur with malicious timing. The crisis struck while Natalie Ko was away for twenty-four hours at a conference in Atlanta. Dr. Ambinder, a young doctor on call, was diligent. He returned Enrique's message promptly and consulted about Margaret's condition over the phone at length, but the multiple social connections they had with Dr. Ko would have led her to check things out herself. Although she no longer saw patients in the hospice service directly, a consequence of her administrative duties, she had made an exception for Margaret when she came to their apartment to discuss how she could die. Ko's exceptional coverage of Margaret was an example of the special privileges granted to them because of people they knew through Enrique's career, and had been of considerable use and comfort during the fight to preserve her life: gaining after-midnight admission to hospitals, leapfrogging waits for procedures, obtaining doctors' cell phone numbers and e-mail addresses. Those extras had been reassuring and helpful and had let Enrique feel useful, but they had not saved his wife's life.

"She's got shaking chills and she's delirious," Enrique reported in the neutral tone that he had learned to maintain no matter how panicked he felt, so that medical personnel wouldn't lose confidence in him.

"What's her temperature?" the young Ambinder asked.

"I haven't taken her temperature. She goes from shaking uncontrollably and feeling cold to kicking off the covers. Half the time she feels like a furnace. She's also incoherent or asleep, so it's obvious that she's running a high fever. I don't think it makes any difference how high, given that she doesn't want to live, but if you really think the degree is significant, I'll take it. Right now that's going to make her very uncomfortable. She's buried herself under blankets and gets upset if I uncover her at all." There was a time when for him to make so mildly disobedient a speech to a doctor of any age would have been unthinkable.

"No, that's okay, we don't need to know her exact temperature. You've given her Ativan to control the chills?"

"Yes, two milligrams by mouth."

"Okay . . ." Ambinder said slowly and fell silent, stumped. Enrique understood his dilemma. The source of Margaret's fever wasn't supposed to be treated. Therefore no antibiotics. She had already received a sedative to alleviate the fever's effects. What else was there to do except add more palliatives, which would send her into unconsciousness?

Enrique's half sister, who had turned around from heading home on the Long Island Expressway at the news of Margaret's abrupt decline, was standing helpless over the bed. Rebecca looked up from watching Margaret's huddled shape tremble beneath two heavy quilts in June to ask, "Should I get another blanket?"

Enrique shook his head no and said to the phone, "I gave her the Ativan by mouth, not by IV."

"Oral dose is fine," the young doctor answered.

Enrique argued without arguing. "Um, it isn't clear how much of the Ativan her stomach can absorb because of her PEG."

Ambinder contradicted him confidently: "Her PEJ wouldn't make any difference—"

Enrique interrupted, "Her stomach PEG. Not her enteric PEJ. I understand her enteric PEJ wouldn't affect the oral dose, but the stomach PEG drains it immediately. I just don't know how much of the Ativan she can absorb that way." He was being conscientious in pointing out that perhaps she ought to be getting the sedative intravenously. He wished he didn't feel so obliged. Margaret was delirious, and it was impossible to communicate with her. That might be reversible; Enrique might yet have a chance to talk with her if he could diminish the fever. But if Ambinder ordered him to infuse Ativan, she could easily become so sedated that she would remain unreachable whether the fever abated or not. Unfortunately, that was his Margaret-given task: she had asked him to help her die at home and with as little consciousness of what was happening to her as possible. If that meant sacrificing his urgent desire to have a true good-bye, then so be it.

"She has a stomach PEG. Right." Ambinder absorbed this fact. As Enrique suspected, he had forgotten. "To make her comfortable . . . ," he trailed off. "What hospital are you near?"

"She wants to die at home. Dr. Ko promised Margaret that she would do everything she could to make that happen. What are you considering?"

"Giving her an antibiotic to help bring the fever down. But if she needs it IV, I have to admit her—"

"I have two IV doses of cefepime here," Enrique interrupted. "I can give them to her. You can send more bags down. I can also give her the Ativan IV."

"You have cefepime?"

"Yes. Two bags left over from an infection in March."

"You've kept it refrigerated?" Ambinder asked.

"Yes. I can give it to her, but she doesn't want anything done to prolong her life."

"Antibiotic won't prolong her life if she's not getting any hydration."

"That's my question," Enrique said, looking at the small shape of his wife quivering under a mound of blue quilts. "Is there any harm in trying to get this fever under control so she can die peacefully?"

"It may not be an infection," Ambinder said.

"What could it be?" Enrique asked, although he could guess what Ambinder was going to say. He sat down in Margaret's desk chair, where she liked to work with Photoshop on her computer, playing with the images she had taken years ago—the present altering the past for the entertainment of the future. "It's fun," she'd said a year ago, when she was in remission and had returned to photography with a happy grace, the gratitude of the pardoned. He was exhausted. Here was another diagnosis, another remedy: the catacombs of her illness seemed to have no outlet. She wanted the struggle to end. How could giving up be so arduous?

"Could be toxins released by her kidneys as they shut down."

That was what he'd been afraid the young doctor would say. Natalie Ko had warned Enrique that while a body dehydrates, in a small percentage of cases, the kidneys or the liver may release poisons in the final days that they would normally process, toxins that cause delirium. She had prescribed a bottle of liquid Thorazine to relieve that reaction should it occur. He was looking at the minifridge where it was stored only a few feet away, along with three spare bags of hydration, the cefepime, a month's supply of IV Ativan, and a pump to provide continuous dosing if necessary to keep her fully sedated. Enrique had been under the impression that Thorazine was exclusively used to treat schizophrenics. Suspicious of why Dr. Ko wanted to add an antipsychotic to deal with his wife's final days, he had asked her how Thorazine, presumably used to alter brain chemistry, could possibly deal with toxins released by the kidneys or liver. She'd supplied an answer that Enrique had often heard from doctors, and whose vagueness he didn't like. "We don't know why it works, but it does." Does Thorazine actually destroy the toxins or diminish their effect? Enrique wondered. Or is it simply so powerful a sedative that it paralyzes the patients and convinces the beleaguered caregivers that their charges feel better when actually they are only easier to manage? He suspected the latter.

"I have Thorazine here for that," Enrique volunteered.

"Yeah, I see that in Dr. Ko's notes," Ambinder said. "Maybe you should give her a dose of Thorazine and see if that helps," he added with a tentativeness that didn't inspire confidence.

Enrique proposed his own course of treatment. "Shouldn't I start some cefepime and give her another dose of Tylenol suppositories and see if that makes her comfortable before resorting to Thorazine?" He was pushing his own agenda, proposing a treatment most likely to restore Margaret to lucid consciousness. So they could talk. Not for long, just a paragraph or two of farewell. Enrique finally felt able to explain what she had come to mean in his life. He was ready to articulate that in their twenty-nine years together both of them had been transformed, not once but three times; that he had come not only to need her but to love her more profoundly than ever: not as a trophy to be won, not as a competitor to defeat, not as a habit too long to break, but as a full partner, skin of his skin, head of his heart, and heart of his soul. That was his secret objective, but he also believed that his course of treatment would be best for Margaret. She wanted to be comfortable while she died but not frozen by drugs into a quiescent torment.

"Why not do both?" Ambinder asked, as if Enrique were the senior doctor.

The lump of Margaret under the covers had stopped trembling. Perhaps she had fallen asleep. "This feels to me like fever, not toxic delirium," Enrique said.

"Difficult to tell the difference," said Ambinder, assurance returning.

"My father had an infection of the brain casing from a defective heart valve, and I took care of him for a shift until I could get a private nurse," Enrique informed the young doctor. He paused, wondering why he was bothering to go into so much detail. Am I complaining? "Anyway, that seemed different. Dad was moving his bowels uncontrollably. He was thrashing about, saying crazy things. Margaret's just shaking and not talking except to moan or ask for water. Right now she seems to be asleep."

"You're giving her water?" Ambinder interrupted.

"She has a stomach PEG. So yes I am."

Again the doctor on call had forgotten. He covered by adding, "Well, it does pass through her stomach. Like with the Ativan, she may be absorbing some of that water. It could prolong things."

"By what? An hour? I don't want her throat to be parched if it doesn't have to be. Is it really necessary for me to stop giving her water with a stomach PEG?" Why am I arguing? He's not here. I can do what I want. In fact, I could kill her. I should kill her. I should put a pillow over her head and end it. Or pump all the Ativan at once into her veins and stop her heart. That's what she wants. If I truly want to do her bidding, that's what I should do.

"Okay," Ambinder conceded. "Give her cefepime. I'll send a full cycle down. And the Tylenol suppository. If she doesn't improve in three hours, call me and we'll discuss our options."

Enrique went into the bathroom to wash his hands. While drying them, he called out to Rebecca detailing how she could help him. He donned gloves, removed the antibiotic packaging from the fridge, broke the seal, and hung the bag of cefepime. Unfortunately, Margaret was disconnected from all her IVs, and in order to reach the port on her chest, he needed to lift the two quilts. He might have to take off her top; he couldn't remember whether she was wearing something that could be unbuttoned. He hoped he wouldn't have to disturb her to that extent. Before pulling back the covers, he also readied the Tylenol suppository, handing it and the lubricant to Rebecca to have at the ready, since he would have to expose Margaret's bottom half for that and he didn't want to subject her to the painful air twice.

For months these nursing tasks had distracted him from terror. There had been times when dealing with tubes and needles and invasions of his wife's body had repelled him, but the tactile job of caring for her, knowing that he could bring relief to her dread of what was ahead, or supply nutrients to keep her alive to say farewell to their sons, the distraction and comfort of these practical tasks, after a lifetime of doing so little that was useful to anyone, helped to suppress his own wild incomprehension at what approached.

That illusion of usefulness as his motivation was stripped away as he prepared these last desperate measures. The truth was that his nursemaid duties supplied more than mere busyness. There was the unacknowledged magical thinking: as long as he was doctoring her, she would live. His brain had understood for nine months that Margaret would soon cease to talk and respond, her body would get cold and stiff and be taken away, hidden in the earth; but standing over the bed armed with these futile palliatives, he knew that his heart didn't understand this irretrievable finish, could not comprehend that within three or four days something other than argument, infidelity, boredom, or hatred would, no matter what he said or did, end his marriage forever.

He handed Rebecca the Tylenol suppository and a packet of lubricant. "When I ask for it, give me the lube first, then the suppository."

His sister looked anxious and squeamish. She wasn't accustomed to this hands-on nursing duty. Though she had gotten used to seeing the contents of a stomach PEG, she had never witnessed the rest of Enrique's chores. But she maintained a brave front, and he was confident she wouldn't fail him should Margaret resist.

He hesitated for a moment, studying the stilled, small curlicue of a lump under the quilts, and felt stupid for disturbing her oblivion. She wanted the agony to end; why couldn't he leave her alone? I am trying to ease her suffering, he reassured himself against the worry that giving her these remedies was for his sake, so they could talk. He held the end of the IV connection to the cefepime and lifted a corner of the covers to see her upper torso. Her eyes were shut tight, her narrowed face as still as a death mask. She didn't stir or complain. He saw her chest rise and fall very slightly. She was alive, which relieved him, although he supposed that was selfishness. Luckily, the neck of her T-shirt was low enough for the three brightly colored baubles of her ports to hang outside. He put his forehead under the tented covers, unscrewed the blue port's top, cleaned it with the antiseptic swipe he had already opened, and connected the antibiotic. He backed away gently, the covers burying her again, then adjusted the rate of the drip on the pole and started the antibiotic flowing.

He had just defied Margaret's wishes. He was treating her for a possible infection though she had asked him to cease all treatments. He told himself that she wouldn't object if she were conscious and not delirious, since the cefepime, though it might relieve her symptoms by fighting an infection, wouldn't prolong her life, as long as he didn't, in addition, give her hydration.

He paused before taking the next step, inserting the suppository. "Everything okay?" Rebecca asked. He nodded. A sinful thought had come into his head. He had given the antibiotic against her wishes, why not connect a bag of hydration? She was running a fever. A liter might make her feel better, and it wouldn't add more than half a day to her life, he guessed. Would she really begrudge him twelve additional hours?

He couldn't give up. That was the truth, wasn't it? These maneuvers were selfish. He couldn't stop grabbing for more of her. That's why he had failed to say good-bye. It wasn't the hordes of visitors or the evil arrival of this infection or toxic assault, whatever was tormenting her. He had told himself over and over: she is dying, my wife is dying, Margaret is dying. The other day she had spoken of herself in the past tense. "Remember how I loved to get lost in the car with you and the boys? I loved it when you called me Adventure Girl, remember, Enrique? I was your Adventure Girl," she said, as if she were a ghost visiting him. "Help me do this," she had begged him in the hospital. "You're so strong, Enrique," she had said. "I want to die at home in peace. You can do it for me." He couldn't disobey her. The antibiotic wouldn't prolong life, but the hydration would. Over the years he had learned to protest her autocracies, and she had been gracious enough, occasionally, to let him think he could prevail. Although she was unconscious and dying and incapable of resistance, it was nearly impossible to disobey her. "Okay, you ready?" Enrique asked Rebecca and slathered the suppository with lubricant.

His sister lifted the quilts from the bottom. Margaret's feet pulled up at the air but only a few inches. He parted her buttocks with one hand and invaded his wife's body with his right index finger. "I got used to losing all my dignity as a patient a long time ago," Margaret had commented when Dr. Ko proposed the fever-relieving suppositories as a way of circumventing the fact that Margaret's stomach was being drained. She clenched at the assault and moaned, but Enrique was out and the covers back within a second. She immediately quieted and didn't stir again. He leaned over and kissed the hard top of the lump where her head was hidden. Feel better, my love, he thought and looked at the clock. Three hours from now would be nine o'clock. Around then, he hoped. Perhaps then she would shake the delirium and come to consciousness. He wouldn't hesitate the next time. My wife is dying, he said to himself, in a scolding tone. Your wife is dying, he chided. Say what you have to say or she will never hear it.

◆

Enrique woke up in Margaret's bed. Scared, he nearly jumped right out. Her big eyes were open, staring at him. They were inches away and filled his vision. He pulled back to gain distance on her, but his skull bumped into the wall. "Ouch," she said, as though she sympathetically felt the blow. But he noticed something chilling in her eyes—an absence of affection, an evaluating and cold attitude.

Waking quickly, he understood. Of course. She hated him because of his failure. His pathetic sexual failure had disgusted her. He had fallen asleep like a lamb, a romantic fool, trusting that after sleep he would find their love intact, and instead, in the brilliant crosshatched sunlight flooding through the blinds of Margaret's studio apartment, last night's carnage was revealed:

Enrique and his ineffective cock had disappointed her beyond all hope of recovery.

What would she say? The truth? I want you out of here, you wimp! Or a polite lie: I have to get ready to go to my New Year's party; let's talk after the holiday. And when he called, she would be busy for the rest of the century.

She opened her mouth to speak. He had a desperate thought: kiss her, silence her, and take her, take her fast and make her come hard and his miserable performance would be erased. He didn't do that. In fact, he had no idea how to do that. He waited, dreading her words. At last she said, "I'm going to make coffee. Want a cup?"

Was this her way of telling him that she didn't want to try to have sex again? Or her way of signaling that he was welcome to linger and have breakfast, that there was all the time in the world to prove he was man enough for her? Or her way of getting him up and out of her bed, and then up and out of her life? Or maybe this was her way of telling him that she wanted a cup of coffee.

He said, "Sure," and contradicted the request, or at least its immediacy, by draping an arm over her shoulder, sidling closer, and moving toward her lips. She waited, neither resisting nor opening to him. He kissed her tentatively, lips hardly touching, with a wariness more appropriate to bussing a shark than embracing a woman you had lain with all night.

Her lips were cracked and dry from the New York City winter and her apartment's heat. So were his. They both tasted of stale cigarettes and coffee. His eyes lit on the radio clock beside her bed; it was eleven-thirty. They had slept for less than four hours. It was no wonder their tongues were furry and his body ached all over, and not from lust's yearnings. There was no sense attempting a longer exploration under these circumstances. He did anyway. Her breasts were firm and warm on his skinny chest. His left hand roamed down her smooth, strong back. His right cupped the side of the smooth column of her neck. He was hard. As hard as he had ever been, although every other part of his body felt exhausted and weak. He pressed against her while they kissed, each time deeper and longer, familiar with each other's rhythm from last night's explorations. The stale tastes dissipated, replaced by something sweet from inside her that he decided was her essential goodness.

He was like a horny dog, feeling stupid about his eagerness, his left hand grabbing a globe of her behind, squeezing urgently. I need to do this now. Get it over with. Prove to her I'm worthy so I don't lose her. Because that would be a disaster. He had slept beside her in utter trust. Her smell, something between the spray of a lemon and a warm bagel, infiltrated his skin. While looking at her and listening to her, he wasn't aware of his own awkwardness, of the world's obstacles, of the ceaseless competition of his gender, and best of all, the puzzling feeling of being adrift all the time. Despite Enrique's identifying labels—Jew, Latino, New Yorker, high school dropout, novelist prodigy—and despite all the large presences in his childhood—bullying, passionate father; needy, intelligent mother; greedy, gregarious half brother; fearless, righteous half sister—he felt that he was without someone who knew his real self, that he was without a place to rest, without, in a word, a home. He had been unaware that he felt unknown and lost in the world until he met Margaret. The feeling didn't make sense to the twenty-one-year-old Enrique, but he did know that while gazing into Margaret's eyes he felt safe.

So he pushed his cock at her, to get inside, to unite with this heart, this spirit, this body, to be lost in her beauty and her certitude. He bumped and ground against her and felt her spreading moisture and an opening in what moments ago had been sealed. He thought himself unpleasant and disgusting, but longing overwhelmed that judgment and pulled his muscles so tight he felt they could snap.

"Wait," she said.

He withdrew as if shot.

"I have to reload my diaphragm." She skipped out of bed, and he saw the lovely sight of her breasts bouncing free as she disappeared into the bathroom. He had forgotten all about birth control. What the hell was the matter with him? And he had a thought so crazy that he discounted it, namely that he wouldn't care if she got pregnant. He had never wanted a child. For a literary novelist, having a baby would be a particular disaster—he could never hope to support a family. Besides, when the hell had she put in a diaphragm last night? The answer came to him: the bathroom visit at three in the morning. She wanted him. It was obvious. Even Enrique had to admit, this woman wanted him.

When she returned, scooting back under the heavy quilt in a flash of white and a black triangle of sex, he smelled the residue of spermicide on her right hand as she pulled him toward her. He was, of course, no longer hard, but he assumed a few minutes of kissing and they would be back in business, especially now that he understood he was welcome.

He was wrong. The same kisses, the same smells, the same touch, the smooth and sweet of her skin did not return him to the oak-hard readiness to be inside her. This was more severe than last night's nervous impotence. This was being a eunuch. He felt like a little boy who had no concept of an erection, for whom this warm and fertile creature was alien and terrifying.

She reached down and tugged at his infant member. Dimly he could feel her fingers, but the tiny, shrunken, useless thing didn't seem to belong to him. The look on her face was worse than the numbness. Her great eyes stared through him, picturing the failure below, dismay welling like sorrow. She let go.

"I'm sorry," he said.

"Don't worry about it," she answered in a clipped tone that did worry him. "I'll make coffee." She slid out of bed, grabbing discarded panties and bra, and disappearing into the closet next to the bathroom. She reappeared in jeans, T-shirt, and sweater, only to vanish again around the corner of the L, heading toward the kitchen.

Despair didn't overwhelm him. He suspected that would come later. He had failed her, that was clear from the haste of her departure. It was a sad fact that at twenty-one he was accustomed to failure. His novels weren't bestsellers, why should he be a man? He stumbled around on her parquet floor, assembling his black armor, trying to get his legs into the black denim and his arms through the black cotton of his turtleneck. It was odd that he did not feel suicidal, knowing he had met the woman of his dreams and had lost her. He had confirmed through long conversations that their connection was profound and had managed to succeed in convincing her to take him to her bed, and then he had thrown all that away with his dismal lack of masculinity.

A rational response would be to defenestrate himself. He could do it there. Get a running start, jump over the glass dining room table, and shatter her wall of windows, falling through the frigid air to be impaled on the scrawny tree below, his entrails sizzling from its sad Christmas lights. When *The New York Times* interviewed Margaret for a brief news item noting the passing of this peculiar adolescent novelist, he was confident that, out of respect for him, she would suppress the information that his cock didn't work, and it would be supposed by readers that he was a rejected suitor, a much more respectable cause of death. Possibly the publicity would help his forthcoming novel. Hanging around for publication date wasn't necessary, since his fucking publisher never got him any interviews anymore. He certainly didn't have an idea for a fourth novel, and he doubted he ever would, now that he was facing a lifetime of being unable to have sex. How had he managed to become a Hemingway hero without fighting in a war?

"Do you want a bagel?" Margaret asked, reappearing from the kitchen. Her manner was efficient. Not cool, but guarded. Of course, he thought, she's creating distance so that we can both pretend it isn't about the fact that I'm a lemon, a car whose engine sputters out when it should hit cruising speed. He admired her for this, the grace and elegance of her rejection, her valiant attempt to ignore his humiliating failure.

"No, I'm fine. I should go, get showered and shaved for this New Year's party." He leaned toward her, and she looked alarmed by his movement. She's probably afraid I'm going to kiss her again, inflict my false promise of a body on her. "Listen"—some part of him was behaving with a weird confidence, bringing up the unmentionable—"I'm sorry about my not being able—"

Margaret stopped his apology. "Don't worry about it. I'm not."

He didn't believe her, but a self-assured Enrique burst through his skepticism, an Enrique that he didn't know and couldn't access at will, an Enrique who took hold of her with an easy confidence, leaning down to kiss her once, twice, three times, lingering to whisper, "I really want to make love to you. I've been so nervous about it. I guess I'm scared because I love you."

She pulled back enough to turn on her searchlights, blue and bluer as they bored into him, as if he were a riddle she had to solve. After a long pause, she spoke in a conspiratorial whisper. "Don't say that. That's what's making you so nervous. We're just getting to know each other. Relax." She lifted her face to his, kissing him once fast and then longer, staying with it. He hardened below. She pushed him away. "Let's not get you revved up again," she said with a sly smile. "What are you doing New Year's Day?"

"Nothing," Enrique said, infinitely relieved that she seemed to want to him see again.

"Want to have brunch with me and three other women?"

"Sure," he said. He would have said sure if she had proposed brunch with the Gestapo.

"No men," she added. "Just you and the girls. Sure you can handle it?"

"I like my odds," he said and moved in for another kiss.

She pushed him away, both hands on his chest. "Go. We both need a rest."

He was exiled to her street, the oasis of beautified Ninth in the wasteland of bankrupt New York. He trudged past the homeless, the strung out, and the odd wary, respectable worker, too poor or powerless to get New Year's Eve day off.

His brand-new apartment looked tiny and soulless. The sight of his Selectric typewriter atop his oak desk made him feel like he was a secretary, not a novelist. He was so exhausted he undressed, flopped onto his narrow bed, and tried to sleep. He couldn't. He couldn't shake a vision of Margaret and her white form hurrying to get beneath the sheets with him. He masturbated as an exorcism more than anything else, annoyed that his cock seemed to work just fine when there was no one around to impress. He showered and shaved and put on black jeans and a blue work shirt and made coffee and waited, drearily, to attend a New Year's Eve party at a friend of Sal's where he had been told there would be eligible women. He couldn't see the point of meeting anyone else. He had found the girl of his dreams, and, in reality, he couldn't sleep with her.

chapter twenty

Grief

ENRIQUE HAD NEVER looked at a dead body. Not a fresh one. He had been able to tolerate no more than a glance before he shunned his grandmother's embalmed remains, appalled by her eighty-five-year-old face smoothed to marble: lips sealed, eyes shut like iron doors. That mortician's sculpture of his father's mother, his storybook *abuela,* had no life in its death. No hint of the ebbing human, of the soul just fled.

This dead body, lying in a Beth Israel hospital, this six-foot-three stillness, cheeks gaunt, jaw slack, this flesh of his father, although cool when he kissed its brow, still possessed the temperature of its life. And the lines of Guillermo's face, the sag of his neck, the slight parting of his bloodless lips, did not seem thoroughly absent the life of his spirit. Enrique's father was not there, but he was not gone from the room.

Enrique whispered to him, in case the nurse at the station could overhear. "I'm sorry, Dad. I'm sorry I wasn't here." He couldn't say more, dismayed that there would be no reply. All his life Enrique had cared deep into his bones, and resented that he cared deep in his blood, what his father thought of how he spoke, how he looked, what he hoped, and what he wrote. Not a quarter of an inch of Enrique had escaped his father's assessment. No habit, no taste, no ambition had formed in Enrique without either surviving the gauntlet of his father's condemnation or marching in the parade of his approval. He had lost his compass.

It was sixteen minutes after three o'clock in the morning. Even the hour evoked his father. "In the dark night of the soul," Guillermo liked to quote Fitzgerald, "it is always three o'clock in the morning." And Enrique found himself thinking about the fact that his father believed Fitzgerald was overrated, and wondered whether that opinion was envy or aesthetic, or both—and then he was back, standing at the foot of a hospital bed, staring down at the gray lips of his dead father.

The Beth Israel hospice nurse's phone call had startled Enrique out of a deep sleep at 2:37 am. "I'm sorry, Mr. Sabas, but your father has passed," she said and added that the body had to be moved to the morgue in two hours. If he wanted to spend time with his father, he would have to come over right away. Enrique phoned his half brother and half sister to tell them the news, and Margaret held and kissed him in their bed while he stared at the two boxes of light, the Twin Towers, centered in the windows of their dark bedroom, stunned that his father's death, which for a year he knew was coming, had actually happened. He didn't want to see his father's dead body, but he felt compelled to go. Was he merely obeying a convention? Or was there something to see in death?

He dressed quickly, and Margaret walked with him downstairs. Eleven-year-old Max appeared from his room, asking if something had happened to Grandpa. Both he and his older brother were very close to Guillermo. Their grandfather babysat for them at least once a week and spoiled them shamelessly, filling their heads with his praise and big ambitions and wit. Max hugged his daddy, squeezed him tight in his small arms. Enrique asked, "The call woke you up?"

Max said, "I always know when there's something wrong in the family." He added with the confident solemnity of the prepubescent child, "Grandpa loved you, Dad."

Margaret smiled ruefully at Enrique and proudly at Max, then took her younger son by the hand and led him back to bed. Enrique thought of that sight, his wife and his son, safe and waiting for him to return, while he stared at Guillermo's body, lying faceup, large, hairy hands folded across his chest, his strong features not asleep, because sleep is full of animation, but still as stone—and silent. More silent than even those angry months of Enrique's early adolescence, when they lived in bedrooms ten feet apart and his father refused to speak to him.

He wanted to tell Guillermo about Max hearing the bell of the hospice phone call and claiming to be the family guardian. "You have played perfectly the role of the Latin son," his self-conscious father had said to him three months ago, when ceaseless pain from the spread of his prostate cancer into his bones began to overwhelm his doses of morphine, and their conversations increasingly acknowledged that they were reaching the final curtain of their drama. "You know that, don't you? You've done everything a Latin father would want a son to do." The grandsons Enrique had given Guillermo were part of that achievement, and just as great a part was the mother he had provided for them. Margaret pushed and protected her boys with ferocity and tenderness and an absolute sense of what was right that Guillermo cherished. "Your grandsons will grow up to be fine men," Enrique had said in answer to a regret Guillermo expressed that he wouldn't get to see them in full maturity. "Oh, I know that," he said. "I have no worries about the success of my grandsons. Margaret will make sure they conquer the world." He laughed. "Or else."

"I'm sorry," Enrique said to the dead body, a second attempt at apology. "I'm sorry I wasn't . . ." This time he couldn't manage the entire sentence. While Guillermo had been comatose for the previous three days and nights, Enrique had failed to keep a vigil. On the first day, he left after three hours. He stayed for two on the second. Before going on the third day—yesterday—Enrique had leaned over the bed, kissed his father's wrinkled brow, and listened for a while to the rapid breathing that he had been told was a consequence of the ascites, cancerous liquid created by the prostate tumor, filling Guillermo's abdominal cavity and pressing on his lungs. Eventually he put his mouth to his father's left ear and whispered, "It's okay, Dad. You can go now. Everything is taken care of." He listed all the things his father had told him that he was worried about: confirming that the deal with a university press to reissue all his novels had been closed; that Enrique would look after his half sister, Rebecca, and her children, and last, "I'm fine, Dad. Margaret is well. Your grandsons are well. You can go. It's okay for you to go." He was following a hospice booklet's advice about what to say to a dying comatose patient. He didn't believe for one second such speech was recommended for the patient's sake. He knew in his own heart, as he spoke the odd words, that they were comforting to him. They provided a lovely illusion that Enrique was willing to let his father go.

Why not? he had thought walking back home to dinner with Margaret and his sons, only hours, he now knew, before his father's last breath. It was time for Dad to go. Guillermo had lived a successful life, he had caused more than enough trouble and more than enough inspiration. He had brought the Sabas name a great distance from the obscurity and poverty of his fatherless childhood in Tampa among the cigar makers. I'm forty-two years old, Enrique thought, I am happily married, I have two sons, I have published eight novels and written three movies. I am ready for my father to die.

Brave thoughts, but at the reality of the end, Enrique sagged at the foot of the hospital bed, dropping to his knees, ashamed that he had abandoned his father to hospice workers, that he had gone home to cheerful Margaret and his energetic boys and let his father die alone among strangers. I wasn't the perfect Latin son, he felt. He tried to apologize for the third time to a dead body. "I'm sorry I wasn't here, Dad." He heard nothing back, no sarcasm, no forgiveness, no rage, no bitterness, and no love from that great slab of a father; the apology was worthless. He had failed at the very last moment, in a lifetime of striving to be fairer to his father than his father was to him; he had scurried away, too frightened by death to take a last look at life.

He spent another ten minutes of awkwardness with Guillermo's body, like a shy man at a cocktail party of strangers. Having no words of good-bye, he kissed the cold forehead of what used to be his father, told the empty vessel that he loved it, and walked home through the same streets that he had walked after the birth of each of his sons at Beth Israel, the same streets he would walk five years later, when Margaret, late at night, would be diagnosed and he had to hurry home to pretend everything was all right while waking up Max for school. In that predawn twilight, returning from his father's death to the life of his wife and children, he had a dim consciousness, saw a faint outline of the rampless bridge between birth and death, and death and birth, that people traverse all their lives convinced they are on a highway to somewhere new.

The telephone rang all day. Margaret, as she had throughout his father's illness, took over many of the errands of his father's death. She and Rebecca went to the funeral home and made arrangements. Margaret answered most of the phone calls. Enrique listened to her tone of regret, leavened with kind sentiments. "Poor Guillermo," she said with genuine affection, "he was suffering so. It was very hard to see him in pain. He was such an enthusiastic man, he enjoyed being alive so much, and he wanted so much to have a good time. It's better he's out of it." She had organized the mess of his father into these easy sentences, bundling into a neat and soothing package all the crazy things his father had done in old age—divorcing Enrique's mother after forty years of marriage, stubbornly living alone, although many women would have been glad to take care of him in exchange for the pleasure of hearing the booming music of his personality.

He'd moved into a studio apartment two blocks away, becoming a daily adjunct, and sometimes a burden to Enrique's life. For the last five years, Enrique had had lunch with his father once a week; Guillermo babysat for the boys another evening each week, which always entailed a debriefing. Father and son spoke on the phone nearly every day. Following Enrique's adolescence, which had been a daily war of fighting or not speaking at all, of wariness at his father's demands and longing to meet his expectations, they had become almost a single individual. Listening to his wife effortlessly sum up the long columns of Guillermo's irrational numbers was comforting, and annoying.

The day of the funeral Enrique found himself alone in their bedroom while downstairs Margaret supervised the dressing of her sons and also, tirelessly and in good humor, made calls to his extended family, raising their ragged sails to make sure they would arrive in the correct port at the correct hour. At last she came up to check on Enrique.

The middle-aged Margaret was, as always, put together.

Although dressed in her grimmest outfit, gray skirt, white blouse, gray jacket—almost a business suit—she was light on her feet and still as pretty as a girl with her thick black hair, round white face, lively blue eyes, and welcoming smile. She inspired confidence. She was suffused with brilliance and spirit, imbued with matchless good cheer.

"How's this?" Enrique asked about his Armani suit, black and elegant. He had chosen a maroon tie. "This too much? Should I wear a black tie?"

"You don't have a black tie, " Margaret said with her usual precision. She adjusted his knot. "You look great," she said. "Guillermo would be proud. He liked you to dress up. He once told me I always dressed you perfectly. That until you met me you were a slob."

"You hated his taste in clothes," Enrique said.

"He had terrible taste," she said and laughed as though that was one of his charms. "Remember that suit he bought for you!" Twenty years ago, to make up for a last savage argument, a disagreement, of all things, about a movie, Guillermo had bought Enrique a three-piece suit at least two sizes too large for Enrique. The forty-six long fit his narcissistic father to a T, and was cut in a boxy shape that didn't flatter the skinny Enrique. Besides those flaws, it was a strange green color that Margaret said made Enrique look as if he were suffering from a stomach flu. "Hysterical!" She laughed gaily at the memory. Guillermo was vain about his taste in clothes. Margaret was sensitive to that and never mocked him for his working-class affection for colors that were too loud, or his yearning for a WASP dowdiness in style that, at its best, ended up with the Latino Guillermo buying peacock colors at Brooks Brothers. In them he looked not so much like a man who lived in Westport as like an exiled Latin American dictator who had found refuge in Greenwich Village.

Margaret's prompting of that memory didn't evoke for Enrique the comedy of his father's sartorial sensibilities. It brought back ugly words from that last fight, unrestrained verbal abuse, like all their battles. With Greg's birth, they had agreed to a cease-fire. They had never made a true peace. Rather, they had decided not to kill each other and formed a strategic alliance for the greater good of the Sabas name. He had never told his father he loved him without a trace of irony, or without the excuse of a good-bye or the farewell of a letter. He hadn't understood, or truly believed, that one day such an opportunity for Dickensian earnestness would be forever lost.

"I'm sorry, Puff," Margaret said, presumably seeing that sadness in her husband. She stroked his cheek and got up on tiptoe to kiss him softly and add in a whisper, "I'm sorry your daddy's gone."

The surging tide of all that he was holding down rose up, pushing out of him through his eyes and squeezing his chest in its hurry to escape. He jackknifed over, as if someone had whacked him in the stomach with a two-by-four. He felt Margaret's hands on him, trying to gather him to her. He pushed her away, hiding his face, angry and ashamed. He felt it was her fault: his betrayal of his family, the mockery of them in his head, the fake peace that Margaret had demanded he sustain with his father, his half brother, and mother, so that family gatherings with her children wouldn't be even crazier. It was all her doing, including that he had failed to stay by his father's deathbed. It was Margaret who told him that there was no point in sitting up all night at the hospital, that it would worry Greg and Max, and exhaust him and make no difference. "He's in a coma," she said. "He doesn't know who's there."

He curled up on their bed. She hovered above him, trying to get into his arms, to hug him to her, but he rolled his six-foot-four frame up into a ball so tight that she was longer than he. He felt her breath on his cheek as she tried to get her lips near his and instead kissed his brow, whispering, "Baby, poor baby," desperate to console him. But it was her fault, all of it, the betrayal of everything his father wanted him to be—a great artist, a bold teller of truth—all thrown away to live in the bourgeois squalor of endless purchases and the cowardice of security. The truth, the bitter truth:

"You don't love me," he blubbered, a grief-stricken and vicious animal. He poked his head out from his fetal hiding place to snarl: "You don't love me!"

"What?" His wife looked bewildered.

He tried to run away from the storm of confusion in his head, stumbling out of the bed without getting to his feet first, and staggered—he heard Margaret cry out as he flopped onto the narrow oak floorboards. Somewhere in the middle of that clumsiness he yelled, "You don't love me."

She touched him on the back and hooked his shoulders, trying to help him up, asking, "Are you okay? Did you hurt yourself?"

He jerked away and stood up, moving to the windows, fleeing to the cityscape, to get away from himself, get out of this head that never left him alone. I'm mad, he decided, a clear judgment cutting through the thicket of disorganized thoughts crowding his skull. I'm losing my mind.

Margaret appeared in his vision, ducking under his arms, her happy face shattered into lines of confusion. "Enrique," she pleaded, "what are you talking about? I love you. Don't you know I love you?"

"No, you don't," he said, sobbing, no longer able to keep his brain in charge. He bawled and listened to himself repeat, "You don't love me, you don't love me," as if he weren't speaking those words but overhearing a mad stranger.

She held him, declaring, "I love you so much." She leaned back in his arms to look him in the eyes and confront him: "How could you not know I love you?"

He sagged onto the couch under the wall of windows. She sat beside him, caressing his hand, kissing his cheek, trying to soothe him while he trembled like a leaf in the wind. For a moment he was still. Then he shivered again and moaned. "Shhh," she said. He put his head on her chest and shut his eyes and tried not to listen to himself whimpering. The shaking stopped. When his brain also stopped its frantic noise, its wild attempt to crash out of his skull and flee into the sky, he thought: *Where did that come from?*

Once he was quiet, Margaret lifted his head, kissed him on the lips, and asked softly, "You know I love you. Right, Enrique? You know I love you more than ever?" She looked at him, only inches away, with the Pacific Ocean of her eyes washing him clean of the craziness. "You know that. Right?"

"No," he said. Just as a fact.

"How could you not know that?" Wonder filled her voice. Her lips parted in astonishment.

"I'm crazy," he said. "Your husband is crazy."

"It's okay to be sad about your father."

He grabbed her, and it came right out, although he'd never formed the thought before. "I'm scared you'll stop loving me. I'm so scared you won't love me anymore."

"I'm never going to stop loving you," she said as easily as if she were ordering a meal. "You're my life," she said simply.

He squeezed her small frame as hard as he could. She grunted at the pressure and mumbled, "Unless you break my back, then I'll stop loving you." But he didn't relax the tension in his arms and she didn't squirm or complain again. He wished he could push her inside himself and incorporate her spirit. He felt relief, a long sigh of gratitude that the race had been run, that for all his mistakes, for all his failures, for all the wear and tear he had doled out, for all that he had smashed and given away of love and good intentions and grand ambitions, for all his errors there had been an unexpected mercy, and he had not been punished. Life had given him Margaret to make him whole.

chapter twenty-one

At Last

THE FEVER ABATED. Margaret wasn't in a coma, but she didn't rouse to full consciousness. At nine o'clock Enrique removed the quilts and checked to see if she needed another Tylenol suppository. She responded with a slight shake of the head when he asked whether she felt cold or hot, and mumbled a sleepy "Okay" when he offered water. She opened her mouth greedily for the cup, keeping her eyes shut, as if determined not to see or hear the world. She barely lifted her head off the pillow to drink, expending as little energy as possible. As soon as she could, she curled back into a fetal position and a stillness that resembled hibernation.

She wants to go in an oblivious peace, he thought, looking down at the profile that appeared above the sheet's edge. That morning an alert Margaret had announced that she had completed her last chore, choosing her burial clothes. He understood now that when she had asked to go to her grave wearing the earrings he had bought for her birthday, she meant that to be her good-bye to him, her last words of approval and gratitude. She had spoken and he had not answered. He looked up at the June evening sky, streaked from the west by Homer's rosy fingers, and felt a premonition of what would soon be his life. This feeling of aloneness was quite different from loneliness. This was a kind of solitary confinement in his own skull and heart that he had not known since he was twenty-one. He had been walking blithely in the world all these years, believing that he was an independent creature who just happened to be married to Margaret. The true nature of this separation was revealed to him as they neared final departure. Part of his self belonged to her and so would travel with her. Abandoned. That was the word. Enrique, watching from the dock without waving a good-bye, was being left behind by Margaret and also by himself, the man she had created out of her love.

He hung the second bag of cefepime, able to disconnect the old dose and add a new one without disturbing her because the line hung outside the sheets. He couldn't waken her to life with these human remedies. She wanted to diminish like a summer's day, a gradual and lovely vanishing into the blue-black night. Something much larger and unfathomable was calling her. His eyes strayed to the forbidden bags of hydration lying in a brown box next to the small refrigerator. Sleepiness was part of the dying process, he had been told. A liter might act like a cup of strong coffee and bring her back to indulge his selfish need for her. And he was a greedy man, wasn't he? Hadn't he taken and taken from his wife? Hadn't he and his sons drained her life? Hadn't he bullied her into putting up with his useless parents and his grasping half brother? Hadn't he let her languish in the pessimistic pragmatism of her own family instead of nagging her into the confidence to produce her art? And what little she had been allowed to create in between his self-important, endlessly discussed novels and scripts—her frank photographs of people going about their lives with friendly and brave determination; the paintings of children with their heartbreaking bravado in the face of a world too big and cruel to satisfy their naïve ambitions; her last paintings of elegant cattle awash in brilliant reds and yellows—had a spaciousness and generous acceptance of life which didn't exist in Enrique's competitive and angry head.

He honestly didn't see how his poverty-stricken heart could afford to lose the currency of her loving nature. Was there any buoyancy to his spirit without the elevation of Margaret's azure gaze and the confidence of her belief in his strength? He wasn't strong really. Without her he was simply confused. Look at what was happening to him at that very moment—deprived of his task as appointment secretary and losing his job as nursemaid—without her as his conduit to the world, a way of being, he had nothing to do but stand stupidly and watch the sunset over Manhattan with sadness rather than amazement at its grace. How could he delight in its beauty? He knew the city's buildings, no matter how tall, were not permanent, and he knew the tastes, the sounds, the touch of life were not forever. His head was always in the future or the past, whereas Margaret resided in the present. She was life, so life was dying.

He resolved not to attach a bag of hydration. He could justify what he had done so far, controlling the fever with an antibiotic, but not prolonging life. The process was probably irreversible anyway. Without hydration and nutrition for four days, she was drifting into the weakness that would precede a final coma. He decided to hope that if he stayed by her side for every second, he would be granted a break in her sedation, that she would be sufficiently conscious so he could tell her, not these fears about his future without her, but how great the gift of her time and her affection had been, and how grateful he was to have had her, not only for all of his adult life but even for a single day.

And if not, if he had lost his chance to say a proper good-bye, at least he had not been pointlessly cruel to her. She would die without knowing that he had betrayed her with one of her friends. Sally had gotten back in regular touch with Margaret after she fell ill, e-mailing or calling every few weeks from London, where she lived with her English husband and blond twin girls. She had crossed the Atlantic for a visit a year ago, spending a couple of hours alone with Margaret—and then Lily had joined them for lunch, the trio reunited. Enrique had made sure to stay away. Not to minimize awkwardness; he and Sally had been in groups at a landmark birthday or two, and those encounters had been friendly and easy. He wanted them to enjoy recapturing their manless youth.

Sally was an awkward artifact. In the deepest sense, their affair was irrelevant to his marriage. Yet he had no illusion that Margaret, if she found out, would still be keenly hurt and enraged. He could never have explained that the unfaithful Enrique was deader than the affair itself. As for Sally, content in her twenty-year marriage, the episode was a profound embarrassment that she would have gladly forgotten. He had no fear she would talk of it.

Lily had reported to Enrique how heartbreaking it had been to help Margaret pick out her ensemble for the grave, and also how sad to bring Margaret her laptop so that she could compose a farewell e-mail to a few other friends to whom she couldn't say good-bye face-to-face, Sally among them. It was a shocking reminder to Enrique of how weak and stupid he had been, how close he had come, for example, to not creating their son Max, to not discovering the true love of his mature married life, or to failing to become the man he now was. And there was relief, for once, that Margaret was at the brink of death, that his fear she would one day unnecessarily learn of his betrayal could be buried as well. There was something good in this finality.

He went downstairs and informed Rebecca of Margaret's status and thanked her for agreeing to sleep over in Greg's empty bedroom in case he needed her. He reached Max on his cell phone. He was out with Lisa and told Enrique that he wouldn't be coming home tonight but that he would be sure to return by noon in case his father needed him. Enrique checked in with Greg, who would be returning tomorrow to keep vigil, and gave him a report on his mother's condition. "She's comfortable now," he said accurately, although he felt false saying it. He repeated that strange statement to Leonard in his daily report to Margaret's family, gathered in Great Neck. Leonard said they would be coming in tomorrow after having kept away for two days. Enrique was unable to muster the courage to ask them not to. What if she became lucid just when they decided to be at her bedside? He resolved that he would ask Rebecca, or whoever else was around, to keep Dorothy and Leonard busy downstairs.

He inflated an air mattress because he was afraid of becoming entangled in either the tube draining Margaret's stomach or her IV lines. He pushed the mattress to within an inch of the foot of their bed, so that while he slept he would be sure to hear any distress. After a few minutes of trying to read, his head hit the page. At nine-thirty he turned out all the lights and lay in the dark, listening for the sound of Margaret breathing.

He woke with his heart pounding. Moans were rising from Margaret's bed. They were strange, unhappy sounds. He turned on the light. He didn't understand what he saw. A large green and white snake was undulating sideways across the mattress. It seemed to be dragging something that it had killed. He stood stupidly for a moment and rubbed his eyes. He looked again. Margaret was tangled in the top sheet and a green blanket that he didn't remember spreading across her. She twisted in discomfort, towing the thick tube and the stomach drainage bag.

He had trouble locating her head. Although her legs were uncovered, her torso was in a confusion of sheet and blanket. While he unwrapped her carefully, he worried that she was being strangled. She didn't seem to know what he was doing or where she was. She moved blindly, eyes firmly shut, although she seemed to be seeking something that she expected to find in the bed, since she was crawling all over its surface. He couldn't imagine what, even in a delirium, she might hope to find in between the sheets. He asked her, "Margaret, what do you want?" and got no reply. He tried to cover her, but she crawled away, toward the foot of the bed. "Do you want to go to the bathroom?" he asked, not knowing why he was making so unlikely a guess, and then realized he was smelling excrement. He pulled the top sheet off her, and the mystery was solved.

She had soiled the bed with a pasty diarrhea. Her movements had mashed it into her panties, the back of her T-shirt, and most of the middle of the fitted bottom sheet. She was trying to get away from the discomfort and smell, probably, but wanted to go on sleeping. "Margaret, I'll be right back. Don't move too much," he said, worried that she might fall out of bed, a useless admonition, he assumed, because of her semidelirious state. Maybe it would sink into some part of her unconsciousness. He had little choice but to desert her in order to clean things up. "Margaret, I'll be right back, okay? I'm here. Don't worry."

He ran down the stairs two at a time, forgetting that he was barefoot and the steps were slippery. Where the staircase turned ninety degrees, his right foot shot into the air. He was about to be upended when his left shoulder whacked into the wall. That smarted but gave him a chance to regrab his lost hold on the banister and stop himself from tumbling down the remaining five steps. He landed on his ass, which jarred him right through his skull. Nothing felt broken. From the scare of thinking he was about to fall headfirst, his heart raced and thumped, hard enough for him to feel it through the wall of his chest. He scolded, "Don't have a heart attack now. Wait until next week." He called out, "Rebecca?" in case she had heard him smack into the wall, half-hoping she was awake to help him. He could see the kitchen wall clock. It was only twelve-forty-five am, and she might not have gone to bed yet.

There was no response. He had to hurry to return to Margaret. He got to his feet. His back and right thigh were sore. Touching his leg hurt so much that he wondered if he had broken something, but he had no trouble walking to the hallway outside the boys' bedrooms. Rebecca's light was out. He opened the squeaky linen closet door as quietly as he could, removing two complete sets of fitted and top sheets. Based on previous experiences with infections, he had become adept at anticipating trouble. If one accident had occurred, another was likely.

He didn't wonder about how there could be was anything for her bowels to move since she hadn't digested food since February. That mystery had been answered months ago by one of Margaret's doctors. The lining of the intestines shed every few days; in addition, little bits of food could manage to get past a stomach PEG and into the thoroughly blocked digestive tract. During the past week, she had chewed and swallowed all of her favorite foods. From the kitchen he gathered two plastic garbage bags, two rolls of paper towels, an extra box of wet wipes, and carried them up the stairs, his back and thigh aching.

Margaret was still struggling to get away from the smell and the smears. He turned on all the lights to see what he needed to clean up. Her eyes remained shut. "Margaret, I'm going to strip the bed and clean you, okay? You can't get out of bed, right?"

No response. He put on latex gloves. He removed her panties and T-shirt. She made sounds but didn't react otherwise. He was dismayed to discover that the sticky excrement covered most of her buttocks and lower back, hence her feeling that she couldn't escape it. "Margaret, the wet wipes may feel cold. I'm sorry, but—" An alternative had occurred to him. "Wait," he said pointlessly, since she continued not to react to him. He rushed to the bathroom, found a pair of washcloths, and soaked them in warm water in the sink, peering out to check on her. She looked perilously close to crawling off the far side of the bed under the windows. He hurried back.

The warm washcloths didn't disturb her at all. They weren't sufficient, however. There was too much shit wadded, and it had dried into a resistant spread. He had to use the wet wipes. He held them briefly in his hands to warm them. Although he was wearing latex, they still felt cold. Margaret moved at their touch and made a guttural noise, but she wasn't conscious. Her insensibility was at least as depressing to him as the smell, the mess, and the indignity of what was happening to his beloved's body. Why was this disease making it so hard for her? he wondered, baffled by its cruelty. "She's beaten," he said aloud, as if cancer were standing at the door looking on with pleasure at its work. "Leave her alone."

Once she was clean, he rolled the fitted sheet on one side up to her body, nudged her over its speed bump and onto the mattress pad. He removed the soiled sheet and checked whether diarrhea had leaked onto the pad. Fortunately not. He lay down a new fitted sheet, repeated the technique of rolling it up to Margaret's body, pushed her onto it, and then spread the sheet the rest of the way. He checked her again—she seemed to have fallen back into deep unconsciousness—found two spots that he had missed, cleaned them, and put fresh panties and a new T-shirt on her. He did the latter awkwardly, losing her head for a while before getting it through the hole. Even those clumsy maneuvers didn't seem to bother her. He checked the quilt, saw that it was soiled in one corner, cursed that fact, and found that the other quilt was clean. She wasn't shivering, so one would suffice. When he spread a laundered top sheet over her, followed by the spotless quilt, and kissed her on the forehead, he had a deep feeling of satisfaction and relief. She lay quietly and comfortably. He had fixed it. He had understood her mute distress and made things better for her.

The pleasure of that achievement didn't last for long. He was exhausted, and his back hurt. He put the soiled linen, washcloths, and clothes in one plastic bag to be washed; and the used wet wipes and latex gloves in another to be tossed. The dirty quilt was too large for the bags he had on hand. He went downstairs to fetch a larger one. When he returned, she hadn't moved.

This is probably a coma, he thought. Her lack of awareness of him and of the world was total. She had reacted only to what the skin of her body felt. She was gone. The Margaret he needed to speak to was gone.

◆

Enrique tried to be cool about it. Although he was up at the ungodly hour of eight-forty-five, he waited until eleven am on New Year's Day 1976 before he lifted the heavy black phone to dial Margaret's number, got as far as the first two digits, and then replaced the receiver with a thud that provoked a single muffled chime from the base's internal bell. Something about the unnatural quiet outside his windows on the usually loud Eighth Street convinced him that it was way too early to call and ask whether he could pick her up for brunch, thus making sure that he was still invited.

Doubt had crept in as to whether he was welcome to join Margaret and her girlfriends in their first meal of the year because he realized—nearing midnight at a dreary New Year's Eve party, while dreading that awkward moment for singles when they have to kiss someone to celebrate the new year—that he didn't know when or where this brunch was taking place. She had invited him without providing those details.

By the next morning, Enrique had inflated this omission into a suspicion that Margaret had shrewdly failed to supply the location because she intended never to see him again. He pictured himself waiting by the phone all day until eventually he broke down and called, only to be told by a cheerful, yet somewhat chilly Margaret that she and her friends had been out until dawn and had slept through their intended brunch; that she was sorry and they would make another date soon. And, of course, he would never hear from her again. He became convinced that last night, at the fun, loud, sweaty dancing party where Margaret had celebrated the advent of 1976, she had met a man with a working penis in whose arms she now languished while she realized with horror that she had to deal with sad Enrique and his pathetic expectation that he would soon be enjoying nova and bagels with her. When he lifted the receiver and put his index finger in the hole to dial, he imagined what could happen if he completed the call. He vividly heard the pleased laughter his triumphant rival would enjoy after she hung up, having explained that their brunch was off because two of her girlfriends were suffering from botulism. He saw this Lothario cupping her lovely breast and kissing her nipple while she giggled with naughty glee. It was too much. Don't call, he told himself. As awful as it would be to sit all day by the phone, that humiliating vigil would be so much better than making an idiot of himself by pressing an unwanted pursuit. This resolution not to phone calmed him—albeit settling into an embittered and hopeless feeling of doom.

At eleven-fifteen he lifted the receiver again. He got as far as rotating through five of the seven necessary digits before dropping it like a hot potato from so great a height that this time the bell jangled loud and chimed twice before it settled into an ominous silence. "I can't stand this," he cried out, as nervous and as miserable as he ever remembered feeling or imagined that he could ever feel. "I can't see her anymore," he mumbled, accepting the fact that he didn't have the strength to live through this sort of torment. I'm too sensitive, he told himself, I don't have the capacity for this kind of emotion. That's why I'm a writer, he realized, I can't deal with the real world. That's why my cock only works when I'm writing sex scenes, he decided, forgetting that he had lived with Sylvie for over three years and managed to make love to her hundreds of times.

I should go, he decided. Not be here at all. But where? Or to what? He had no notion. But he should leave. Ignore her rejection. He got as far as the closet to put on his green Army coat before he was stopped by the simple fact that he might, after all, be mistaken. Perhaps she would call. Very, very unlikely, and probably only to cancel politely, but she might.

He smoked five cigarettes. He made a four-cup pot of coffee and drank all of it. At eleven-thirty he decided never to call her again. At eleven-thirty-four he dialed, got through six digits, and then replaced the receiver so gingerly that this time there was no forlorn bell decrying his cowardice.

By eleven-fifty-two, he was seated on the edge of his bed, keening back and forth, moaning aloud, "Oh my God, I'm losing my mind, oh my God, I'm losing my mind," when his phone rang. He stared at it for a second, astonished. It's someone else, he warned himself, heart pounding as he leapt up and walked to his desk, staring at the black thing, its bell blaring. Waiting through all of its second ring was agony. What if she hung up? How could he stand to talk to anyone else? Imagine if it were his father calling. Imagine if it were Bernard. My God, Bernard was right, had been right all along. He wasn't in her league. He wasn't even in Bernard's league. He wasn't—this was the awful truth—he wasn't in any league at all.

The start of Ma Bell's third ring was so harsh that he jerked the receiver up just to silence it. "Hello," he demanded, prepared to yell at whoever was on the line.

"Happy New Year," Margaret said. At the sound of her brisk, gentle, amused, and sly voice, relief was all-encompassing: Novocain vanishing a throbbing toothache, the heat of a bath enveloping aching muscles, or, most accurately, the embrace of a loving woman.

"Happy New Year to you," he said, and if you had heard his voice, you would have thought him the calmest and most confident young man on earth. "How was your party?" he asked with a tone of ease and pleasant curiosity while inside he was prepared to hear that she had met someone better.

"Boring," she said. "Kind of boring. I didn't really know what I was doing there. How about yours? Was it the most fabulous fun you've ever had?" She laughed gaily.

"I was ready to kill myself it was so boring," he said. "So—are we on for brunch?"

"Yes. Sure. I mean, me and the girls are having brunch and it'd be great if you came. Are you sure you want to join us?" Her doubt worried him.

"I'd love to come. But if you really need to see them alone, I mean if it's weird for me to crash it, I understand. Maybe you and I can have dinner later?"

"Sure, we can have dinner later if you're not bored with me, but I'd love it if you came to brunch. It'll get the girls all excited, and that'll be fun."

"It'll get the girls all excited?" Enrique asked, wary and skeptical. What was exciting about him? His inability to penetrate? His harmlessness?

"Sure. A strange new man on New Year's Day? They'll be all atwitter."

"Let's twitter them," Enrique said, and Margaret laughed, again with that odd and inexplicable merriment. Where did she get her good cheer? And how could he afford to live without it? "When and where?" he asked, praying that he had enough time to reconsider his wardrobe. He was in black jeans, of course. Maybe today was the day to switch to blue.

"Guess where we're going," Margaret said and added, "The Buffalo Roadhouse. Can you stand going back there?"

"Definitely. I love the Buffalo Roadhouse. I think we should have dinner there too. We should never eat anywhere else."

Margaret didn't laugh at that joke. "Oh my God," she said. "That would be horrible. Okay!" she announced. "I have to get myself together. My friend Lily and I will come by at twelve-fifty and ring your bell and we'll walk over there together."

"Okay," Enrique said, and he was alone again, only this time a great surge of excitement and happiness flooded him. He danced around the living room in goofy ecstasy. He checked himself in the mirror, changed his blue work shirt to a black turtleneck and his black jeans to blue, realized that was wrong, then went back to black. He noticed that the black turtleneck and black jeans gave him a severe appearance, but that there was something oddly right about his forbidding look. I am, after all, quite insane, he thought with dismal pride. I should dress as if I were institutionalized.

He did his best not to be downstairs waiting for Margaret and Lily before they arrived, but he was on the sidewalk by twelve-forty. He waved like an imbecile when he spotted the two girls half a block away, talking in an intense and earnest manner to each other. What were they discussing so seriously? It wasn't him, he decided, because when they saw him, they unself-consciously broke into smiles and waved back with equal energy as if they were all old friends, reunited after a long separation.

Margaret and Lily were giddy during the walk to Sheridan Square, repeatedly praising him for his bravery in attending an all-female brunch. At the third mention of it, he commented, "I'm beginning to get worried that you're so impressed. I'm just *attending* this brunch, right? I'm not going to be cooked and eaten, am I?"

The girls giggled at that and exchanged a look which had some sort of meaning. He wasn't worried by it; they clearly approved of him. Considering how much ammunition he had handed Margaret for her to mock him, he felt reassured—almost. Two women he hadn't met were joining them at the Buffalo Road-house. He remained somewhat nervous about how they would react to him, since he supposed that Margaret was displaying him for some sort of approval from her girlfriends. It was clear, however, that he had Lily's okay, and she, according to Margaret, was her best friend.

The two others were waiting for them just inside the front door. Penelope, a curly-haired redhead whose skirt and blouse—the others were in jeans—and formal manner made her seem older than her years, didn't seem surprised to see him. But a blonde named Sally, with startled eyes and a general look of discombobulation, goggled at him. "*You're* coming to our girls' lunch?"

"Isn't that brave?" Lily insisted.

"I'm brave," Enrique said as he took Sally's hand. "In fact, I'm fearless. On our way here, I got these two to cross against the light and run across Sixth Avenue. Exhilarating, wasn't it?" He turned to Margaret, who didn't skip a beat in answering, "Yep. We're outlaws now."

They were seated at a table beside the one where he and Margaret had had dinner. "Our table," he commented. Sally asked what he meant. Margaret explained that their first date had been only the night before last, a fact which Penelope seemed already to know from her solemn nods. It was news to Sally. She cracked up the table by commenting, "Wow! And she invited you to brunch! And you said yes! That must have been some hot date." The laughter put everyone at ease. Enrique asked how the girls had all met, and they hurried in their answers, talking over each other. Sally, Lily, and Margaret had gone to Cornell. Lily and Penelope worked as assistant editors at a publishing house, and Penelope's husband, Porter, was the movie critic for a start-up weekly magazine, rumored to be on the verge of folding. The latter possibility had put him into a state of hysteria—that was Penelope's disapproving characterization. After making it, she turned to Enrique and added, "Oh, Porter read your novel. He liked it." She chuckled. "And that's rare for Porter."

"You published a novel?" Sally asked, the fluted lips of her mouth parted, green eyes bulging, a look of astonishment that was so broad Enrique laughed. He said, "Presumably," and didn't elaborate. The last thing he wanted to perform for this audience of pretty young women was the dismal ballad of his career. He asked Penelope how she got her job, and when she first met Lily, and how she met her husband, Porter, and soon he was safely in the background, listening to the girls talk about their holidays, their families, and, in Sally's and Penelope's cases, their men. He enjoyed eavesdropping on their complaints and enjoyed even more overhearing their heated discussion about their hair cutters and the styles they were trying to impose on them, and was also surprised by the sincerity of their interest in William Styron's forthcoming novel, *Sophie's Choice,* which three of them had read in manuscript. They actually seemed to care whether the book was good for its own sake, unlike members of his family and Bernard and every other writer he had ever met. They didn't twist the experience of reading into a byzantine reference to their ambitions or their complicated opinions of the world. In general they displayed a charming democratic leveling of worries: they moved effortlessly, and with equal concern, from whether it was worth having your toenails painted in winter to whether Jimmy Carter's presidency meant we'd have peace in Jerusalem.

"You're being so good," Margaret said at one point. "Isn't Enrique being patient?"

"He's great," Penelope said. "Porter would rather shoot himself than listen to us gossip."

Enrique smiled at the women, a demure smile that he hoped would imply he was being kind to tolerate them, when in truth he was relieved and grateful to be surrounded by all this femaleness, by their fragrance, their tousles of red and black and blond and brown hair, and to listen to the quartet of their musical voices—Margaret's briskness, Sally's bafflement, Lily's warmth, and Penelope's doubtfulness—and to steal glances at their white necks, their young breasts, their small hands, and their heartbreakingly fragile wrists and delicate fingers. They got bored with the brunch sooner than he did. After three hours they were ready to leave and graciously credited him for making the gathering so entertaining. That was a transparent lie since he had been quiet almost the entire time, but they did seem reluctant to split up, all agreeing to walk to the West Fourth Street subway station before Margaret and Enrique would peel off.

The group turned east outside the restaurant, and Enrique, without giving it any thought, put his arm around Margaret's thin shoulders and tugged her close to him. She snuggled within the crook of his arm, presumably grateful to have the tall shield of his body against the January wind. When he glanced at the others, he saw they were all staring at him instead of walking toward Sixth Avenue. Before the trio got going, they smiled, all three at once, as if an announcement had been made. Didn't they realize I was with her? he wondered. He thought the story of their date had made that clear. By the time they separated, they had gotten over their surprise and were chatting merrily again about how their hair, their jobs, their men were all disasters. Each one kissed him on the cheek, and Lily gave him a firm hug and said, "You're so tall!" He felt as if he had been welcomed into a friendly foreign land.

Without any discussion of where they were going, Margaret remained in the shelter of his arm on the way back to her apartment. She talked the whole way, explaining this and that about Sally and Penelope and Lily, and he listened, soaking in these details because they mattered to her and so they would matter to him. He did his best not to think about what was looming. They got past her disapproving doorman and upstairs into her parquet-floor studio and shed their coats and she made another pot of coffee and settled beside him, with her flouncing hair and her welcoming smell and her white neck and happy breasts, and for the first time since puberty he fervently wished that there weren't such a thing as intercourse.

◆

He woke with a startle at the sound of her unhappiness, heart pounding, eyes gritty with sleeplessness, head in a fog of despair. He turned on the lamp he'd placed on the floor next to the air mattress. She was crawling again, tangled in the quilt and sheets, undulating in misery across the surface of her bed, desperate to escape while also desperate to sleep. It was an exact replay. He leapt up and said soothing things. "I'm here, Mugs. Wait a second, I'll help you." He prayed that it was the Ativan wearing off, not her bowels again.

He saw light brown stains on the fitted sheet. Some looked nearly green, a sicklier hue. He sighed. A slow, heavy sigh. He longed to walk away. To trudge down the stairs and out the front door and let strangers find her and clean her and watch her die. Why do I have to do this? I'm a selfish man, he thought. Why am I being forced to be good?

All that, the loathing of her dying, passed through his body and soul with the inhale and exhale of his despairing sigh, and seemed to evaporate. He moved fast and without thinking. He had to hustle downstairs for more washcloths because the diarrhea was sticky again and difficult to wipe from between her buttocks. His aching thigh and back reminded him not to run this time. After a stop in the kitchen for garbage bags, he moved to the hall linen closet. Margaret had soiled the last clean quilt. He fished down a light cotton blanket from the highest shelf. He noticed that Max's door was shut. He had come home after all. Did he have a fight with his new girlfriend? Enrique couldn't speculate about that with Margaret, the first of many things they would no longer share about their children. Rebecca's light was out. He should wake her. But for what? Company? He had the cleaning up under control.

Once he was back upstairs, however, the chore proved not as simple as before. This time she fought the process. The touch of everything on her skin distressed her. She squirmed away from the warm washcloths, she grunted and ducked her head when he tried to get her soiled T-shirt off. "Mugsie, I'm just trying to clean you up. You'll be cozy again in a few seconds." Cozy? He sounded stupid beyond belief. That must be why so many nurses end up speaking like dolts—how can you intelligently reassure someone cast into the darkness of this struggle? Or worse, explain your tedious and hopeless tasks?

It took longer because she struggled. He had to get two additional washcloths and soak them longer, and use one hand to hold her in place while scrubbing away all of the sticky mess. He studied her face for a sign that she was conscious, but through it all—and it took almost twenty minutes—she kept her eyes shut and didn't respond to any of his questions. She seemed closer to delirium during this episode. Once he had her back in clean clothes on clean sheets and under a clean cotton blanket, she ceased her audible noises of complaint.

Enrique turned out the lights, got back in bed, and waited for his eyes to adjust. He heard her rustle the sheets and blanket. When he could see, Margaret didn't appear to be as disturbed. It was two-forty-five am. He could call Dr. Ambinder and ruin the young man's sleep, but what could the doctor propose other than giving her Ativan IV and Thorazine? That would be Enrique's good-bye then: not words, hanging a bag of plastic.

The next thing he knew his head was throbbing and his heart was pounding. Someone was there in the dark. "What?" he cried out and reached for the person next to the air mattress. He fell out, smacking his chin on the oak floorboards. It was a drop of only a few inches. He staggered up and turned on the light.

No one was beside him. He gasped anyway. Margaret was sitting up. Her eyes were shut. A hand reached blindly at a mirage in front of her. He sat down on the bed, facing her. "What it is, Mugs?" She slid down and over, returning to her snakelike maneuvers. He lifted the covers to see if she had soiled things again. The answer was no, but that negative was not a relief. He watched her twist and turn restlessly. He lifted her stomach drainage bag like a wedding train so its tube wouldn't be strained by her movements. She slithered to the foot of the bed and then around again. "Margaret, do you want water?" he asked. No answer. "Margaret, do you want to go to the bathroom?" No answer. "Mugsie, are you awake? Can you hear me?" She moaned and mumbled gibberish, but not in time or in answer to his questions. In despair, he called Ambinder's service. After giving his number to the operator, he held the cordless receiver in his hand, watching his wife's dance on the marital bed. Even in this choreography with death, Margaret remained full of energy, fighting the misery her life had become.

Ambinder sounded like a man trying to keep his head above water. Enrique gave a dispassionate account of the sequence of events. "No fever?" the doctor asked.

"She's not hot. I don't think she has a fever. Anyway, I can't keep her still long enough—" At that moment, as if to illustrate, Enrique had to pause and put out a restraining hand as Margaret launched her head and shoulders past the bed's left side, about to topple out. "She seems delirious," he admitted.

"Yes," Ambinder agreed and floundered, "um . . ."

Enrique couldn't wait. "Should I knock her out with IV Ativan?"

"You don't want to try Thorazine?" Ambinder suppressed a yawn.

"No," Enrique said firmly. "If the IV Ativan doesn't relieve her, I'll go to the Thorazine, but I'd like to try Ativan first."

"Okay."

"Giving it to her on the IV pump will put her out permanently, right? She won't come back to consciousness, right?"

Ambinder sounded more awake. "No, she's out of it. Won't hurt her."

She's out of it. Those words echoed in Enrique's head while he assembled the pump that would deliver a continuous dose of Ativan, enough to keep a healthy person fully sedated. Once everything but the connection to her IV was completed, he carried the pump, the size and weight of a portable cassette tape recorder, to the bed and sat on its edge. Her dance had left her sitting up, eyes shut, head turned to him. "Margaret?" he said into the uncharacteristic blankness of her face. "Margaret, I'm going to give you Ativan on the pump. We talked about this, right? Once I give you this, you'll be fully sedated. You won't be able to talk and maybe you won't know what I'm saying. So this is our last conver—" He stopped. "This is the last time we'll talk," he managed to say. "I love you," he said. His scratchy eyes were awash. He thought he was going to sob if he attempted another word. He took a deep breath. Margaret hadn't moved. Her head was pointed in his direction, but he didn't believe that she could hear him. She was seeing and listening to another world. Her hand reached into the empty air, trying to grasp something that didn't exist. When he tried to take hold, she touched his fingers for only a second and then reached past, as if his presence and his touch were a distraction from her real goal. "I don't know if you can hear me, Mugs, but I want to tell you that you're what made my life work. I know when I was young or when I got angry and moody I said things that hurt you. But the truth is that you and the boys are the best people in my life and that you made it worth living." This is dreadful, he thought. Empty words drained of feeling. So odd considering that his head was drowning with emotion. He wasn't articulate, after all. The labor of his life, self-expression with words, the language of his heart were proving to be banal and useless when he most needed them. "That's all," he said, voice fading in humility. "Thank you. Thank you for everything you've given me."

He wanted to convince himself that she had heard him, but she gradually collapsed onto her right side and went back to slithering and twisting. He found the IV line and attached it to the pump. Before starting the machine, he tried to gather her in his arms. She quieted for a moment, and then pushed at him as if he were an obstacle, not a person. He kissed her lips, but they were dead in response, motionless and cold.

He rose from the bed, placed the pump on the floor beside it, and pressed the large green start button. The LED readout came to life. He watched white fluid begin a halting climb toward her chest port. It took about five minutes before her snake dance stopped.

He arranged the sheet and cotton blanket so they were no longer tangled around her legs. He kissed her cool forehead. After ten minutes, all movement, except for the rise and fall of her chest, ceased. He had said his paltry good-bye and she was deaf to it.

◆

He kissed her. He didn't want to face the disaster that the kiss would lead to, but he couldn't help himself. Margaret had just drained a cup of coffee and aptly described her group of friends. "The Disaster Dames. Isn't it hysterical how they're so happy about everything that's going wrong in their lives?" She noticed the odd look on his face, which was passion laced with fear, and misinterpreted. "They were okay, right? They didn't drive you crazy with all that talk about publishing?"

He kissed her. She was startled at first but then opened to him, and moved into his arms. Her lips were warm, her tongue was hot and wet, and her hands were cool and soft on his neck. He wanted, so desperately wanted, to be inside her. She pulled back at some point and asked, "Did they?"

"Did they what?" he mumbled, kissing her vulnerable neck.

"Drive you crazy . . ." She moaned softly when he found the crevasse, the shadowed place, behind her ear. After a beat, she added in a whisper, "About publishing?"

Enrique asked with the wonder of a child, "What is publishing?" He maneuvered to find her mouth.

She reached down and placed her hand on the denim-encased bulge at his groin. She opened her eyes and looked, from only an inch away, right into his soul. "Shall we?" she mumbled.

"It'll just go away."

"Why? You seem to want me," she commented with a sly smile.

"I'm terrified."

"Of what?" She rubbed the bulge as if to soothe it.

"I don't know!" he cried out, frustrated.

Margaret leapt to her feet with characteristic energy. "Don't think about it. Just fuck me," she said and tugged him up, leading him to her bed as if he were a lost child. She sat on the edge and pulled at his belt. He started to take off his turtleneck. She stopped him, saying, "No. Just fuck me. Don't make love to me. Just fuck me."

She pulled his jeans and underpants down to his knees, then opened her jeans and pushed them off along with her panties, the white and black of her sex flashing as she kicked them away. He sat and tugged his bottoms off. His cock poked and bobbed in the air as if trying to launch away from his body, and it all seemed so right, just perfect, as, their bottom halves naked, their tops fully clothed, wool sweater to cotton turtleneck, penis to vagina, he got on top of her, mouths hungrily opening to each other. She reached below, spreading her thighs, and guided him toward her.

It seemed to him that he was hard in her hand as she brought him close to entering her, but no. His mind split off from the tactile pleasures of her scratchy sweater and the hot embrace of her thighs. A part of his self abandoned them both and he thought, It isn't going to happen. I can't do it.

She tugged at him to push inside her, and he obeyed, but his cock did not, instead collapsing like an accordion.

"I can't," he cried out and wanted to weep. He was so close. So close to finding what was missing in the universe. He had treasure inches away, in his arms, in his heart, and his body wouldn't let him. He wanted to throttle himself.

"Shhh," she said. "Relax," she whispered and rolled him onto his side. Her fingers caressed his cheek. "It's going to happen. There's no hurry." She kissed him. "We have all the time in the world," she promised him.

◆

The third time her moaning wakened him, he saw light at the edges of the blackout blinds of their bedroom windows. He checked his watch. With the early June sunrise, it was still only a little after five-thirty in the morning. This was Margaret's third incident in eight hours. He stared at the bed. She was crawling again. Most of the covers were off, and he saw right away, in the better light of the summer dawn, the greenish brown paste seeping through her panties and spreading across her legs.

"No!" he protested aloud, as if the author of all this were able to hear his complaint. "There's nothing left," he said, meaning both that there shouldn't be more in her bowels and that her body oughtn't to be able to move at all considering the quantity of sedation. No matter how strong the smell and her discomfort, she should be insensible. "This is impossible," he cried out.

Margaret responded. She pushed herself against the wall and managed to sit up. Stranger and more astonishing, her eyes were open, and she was reaching for him. He was frightened by this impossible show of energy and alertness. Am I dreaming? he wondered. "Margaret?" he called to her. He didn't sit on the bed. Her stool was loose, almost liquid, and he noted in dismay that the sheets and cotton blanket were soiled. There were no more blankets and only one set of clean sheets. He'd have to wake Rebecca for help. I can't be dreaming, he calculated. These thoughts are too boring to be anything but real.

Margaret's eyes were odd. Objects seemed to register, but she didn't appear able to focus on him, although he was in the line of what ought to be her vision. She made a sound. It scared him. There was more grunt than word to the sound, but there was a lilt to it, as if it were a question or a demand. She was struggling to speak.

"What?" he asked, stupidly.

Her right hand lifted, in a blind way, without her eyes moving from a fixed point. She did appear to see something. She stared into the middle distance and touched her lips. "Dree," she said and he knew she meant drink.

"You want some water. Okay." He poured bottled water into a plastic cup and tilted that into her mouth. Her lips were cracked and dry. She gulped at the water and swallowed hard. "Unhh," she said, which sounded like gratitude. Then she slumped over, so intent on sleeping again that she put the side of her face into one of her smears.

"Oh, Mugs," he said, sorry for her. He lifted her gently by the shoulders to move her head onto a clean portion of the sheet. She groaned in protest but settled quietly when he had shifted her.

He hurried downstairs with the bag of soiled linen and knocked on Rebecca's door. She appeared, half-asleep but dressed, while he explained the situation as quickly as he could and asked her to load the two sets of sheets into the washing machine.

He fished down the last set of queen-size sheets and went upstairs. This time the looser and heavier concentration of stool in one area of the bed had soiled the mattress pad as well. Rebecca arrived just as he made that discovery. He paused in despair, trying to remember if they had another somewhere. At the sight of what he was dealing with, his sister came to a halt and said, "Oh."

"Any trouble with the machines?" he asked. She shook her head. "The mattress pad is soiled," he said. "Wait here while I look for another." He found one on a shelf near the sheets. Margaret had reorganized all the closets while in remission, throwing out some of the accumulation of their married family life while saving memorabilia and making their photo albums current. He'd suspected at the time that part of her motivation was to recall the span of her life as an accounting of what she had to live for, and that another part of her wanted to curate in case it turned out that she had reached the end of her journey. She had faced her death. Why couldn't he?

With Rebecca's help he was able to finish up quickly, and soon Margaret, or her body, since that was all that seemed to be left, was peaceful under a sheet and a blanket his sister had brought up from Greg's room. He double-checked the pump to make sure that she was receiving a steady dose of the sedative. She was. How she had managed to be conscious at all was remarkable. The distress inside must have been tremendous. Was he really soothing and helping her depart, or was it all just a show at her expense so everyone else could feel better about what was happening? Whatever the truth, he believed he ought to raise the dose and end her torment now, not oblige her body to breathe for a few more insensate days.

He didn't go back to sleep. He made himself coffee and poured a bowl of cereal, but had no appetite. He did want to take a shower. When he mentioned that to Rebecca, she asked, "Can I knock on the door if she wakes up?" which meant that she was too scared to be left in sole charge. The visiting hospice nurse would be coming at eight am to check on Margaret, so he didn't say to his sister: She can't wake up, and yes you can knock on the door. Instead he said he would wait until the nurse arrived to wash himself. To wash himself clean.

◆

Margaret was laughing. She tilted her head back and blew out the puff of smoke she had just inhaled from her cigarette.

Since she was enjoying it, he continued with his absurdist vision of their future. "We could spend the rest of our lives together and never have intercourse, right? I mean, I can take care of your needs without my penis, and I know I can masturbate."

Her head snapped to look at him. Exquisite blue eyes enveloped him with their curiosity. She demanded, "Did you masturbate on New Year's Eve?"

Well, he was telling her everything, he might as well continue to fess up. "Right after I saw you. I was so pissed off that it worked."

Margaret pressed out her Camel Light, turned on her side, tenting the lower half of the sheet, which provided a thrilling view of her slim hips and the patch of her sex. "Me too," she said with a sly smile. "What a waste." She pulled the bedsheet off him to expose his lower half. "Let's see you do it now."

"What?" he stammered.

"Go ahead," she said, nodding at his equipment, which, oddly, was halfway there already. "Show me."

She moved her round, merry face to within an inch away, kissing close, her great blue searchlights blinding him. "Here," she whispered, her cool fingers snaking around his growing manhood. "I'll get you started."

◆

For an hour and a half Enrique waited for the hospice nurse to arrive. Margaret didn't move other than the rise and fall of her chest beneath the blanket. He left her side only when her mother called to announce they would arrive before noon, which really meant eleven. Enrique found himself, in the tradition of his wife's family, downplaying the events of the night. "She had some fever, but she's comfortable now," he reported. "Oh good," poor Dorothy said in a voice taut with sadness and dread. After hanging up, Enrique lowered his head, shut his eyes, and breathed slowly until the desire to run and scream and bang into things passed. He had worked so hard to make this ending as graceful for everyone as possible, and he liked to believe that he had succeeded for the others. But not for himself and Margaret. Their indirect good-byes in between her heartfelt farewells to the rest of the world weren't what he wanted, and the mess and agony of last night felt like a great failure, a failure to which he would never be reconciled.

He returned to her bed, nodding when Rebecca whispered that Margaret had stirred while he was downstairs on the phone. He could see that she had shifted from her right side to her left. Her face was exposed. The lean angles of her starved features were beautiful. The translucence of her skin, the blue and green veins, the whiteness of her forehead, were otherworldly. Her eyes were shut, her mouth set, lips sealed. There was something embryonic and intense beneath the surface peacefulness of her pose. She looked as if she were being born into another life, but he didn't believe in that comforting illusion. He checked the Ativan pump.

It was functioning properly. He wondered how she had managed to move at all.

He discussed that with the hospice nurse when she arrived ten minutes later. "Really?" she reacted with surprise after he reported that Margaret had managed to sit up and sip water despite the heavy dose. "I've never seen that happen before," she claimed. Enrique wasn't all that impressed by her being impressed. Although medical people were supposed to be ruled by science, in his experience they were often hyperbolic in their statements. If you were to believe Margaret's doctors and nurses, she had displayed at least a dozen exceptional symptoms and reactions to medications. The superstitious and histrionic side of Enrique's personality was vulnerable to that sort of talk. As he undressed in the bathroom, he warned himself not to be mystical about what lay ahead. She was astride the doorsill of death, and everyone, including the medical personnel, was likely to find meaning in banalities. He shed his clothes, got under the hot water, soaping himself up, glad to be scrubbing off the memory of last night's dreary horror. He put his head under the cascading water, shut his eyes, and lectured himself. The Margaret I know is gone. The Margaret I love is gone. All that remains is the husk of her physical body. The light inside her no longer shines and I can no longer feel its warmth or bask in its illumination.

The banging on the bathroom door wasn't comprehensible at first. He thought something might have fallen in the upstairs apartment. Then he heard Rebecca, her voice frantic. "Enrique! I'm sorry! Enrique! I'm sorry!"

She's dead, he thought.

"Margaret's upset! I'm sorry. We can't deal— Can you come out?"

He stumbled out of the shower stall and grabbed a towel. Margaret was awake!

He jerked the door open. Rebecca and the hospice nurse were attempting to prevent Margaret from rising to her feet. She had somehow managed to sit on the edge of the bed. She was nude but for her black panties. Her head was pointing in the direction of the hospice nurse, but her eyes were shut.

"Margaret, I'm just checking your port," the nurse said in the unnaturally calm monotone of the caretaker of a deluded patient.

"No!" Margaret said in a clear, loud voice. She reached blindly into the air.

Enrique moved toward them awkwardly on his wet feet, holding the towel at his waist. "She started fussing—" the nurse explained in a defensive tone. In the background, Rebecca was adding some piece of information, but he couldn't hear over the nurse, who continued, "And I noticed her shirt was stained, so I started to lift it off—"

"I think we need to leave her alone. Just leave her alone," Rebecca said, also with an unnatural calm, hers layered over anger and agitation.

Margaret lurched forward. Alarmed, the nurse took her hands. "Margaret, do you want to get up?"

And then it came. Loud and clear, as though she were fully alive. *"No!"* she shouted. She opened her eyelids, but her eyes looked unfocused and wild. She pulled her hands free and slapped at the air. *"No!"* she announced again, a statement of identity, more than an argument.

"I don't know what you want," the nurse cried out. Enrique let go of his worry about slipping on the floor and losing his towel. He managed to reach his wife, both of them more or less naked, her body, like his, wrinkled and wan from the fight. He took hold of her heartbreakingly small wrists in each of his hands and knelt on one knee, so that his face would be exactly on her level. "Margaret," he said to her roving and angry eyes.

She stopped trying to stand. She looked through him, as if she were blind, as if she were searching for something or someone else. He didn't know what she wanted, but he gave her what he had to offer.

"I'm here, Mugs," he said and moved close, putting his lips to hers, although they were not ready for a kiss. "I'm right here." He pressed his mouth on hers, touching teeth as much as anything else.

Her face relaxed. Her shoulders subsided. Her cheeks widened in a smile, and she brought her lips together, puckering them, eyes shut, searching—it was clear even to the doubting Enrique that she was searching for him.

He kissed her, and while their lips met, she hummed. When he moved off, she made a contented noise, "Mmm," and puckered again. He kissed her again, his arms going around her thin shoulders, and she hummed throughout, vibrating with pleasure.

After he broke off contact, Margaret sighed with relief and leaned back onto the bed. He helped her down, easing her onto the mattress, arranging the IV line so that it wouldn't tangle beneath her.

She didn't return to her fetal position. She lay on her back, eyes shut, mouth closed, stretched out to her full length as if going to her final rest. He pulled the sheet up to cover her and then grabbed the towel to cover himself. Her breathing had changed. It had become rapid and shallow, as the hospice had told them it would when the final phase began. Soon she would lapse into a coma. He glanced at his sister, whose face was awash in tears. "She wanted you," Rebecca said with a gasp. The hospice nurse touched him, a light tap on the shoulder as if she were knighting him.

He had been wrong all along. Margaret had meant to say good-bye. She had made certain to say good-bye, an eloquent good-bye.

She had managed to tell him, despite all the obstacles nature and the human world had put in their way, that her love and his love had survived.

◆

Soon, so soon, within a minute, within less than a minute, in seconds, in a single second Enrique was plunged into excitement. His head was drunk from her touch and his heart was full of her sea-blue eyes, drowning him. He no longer remembered that it was January first, the start of a new year. He no longer remembered that the sun was shining or that he had had a scallion omelet for brunch. He no longer knew her name or remembered the parquet floor. He no longer remembered to be afraid.

She was underneath him. He didn't understand how she had managed to get him on top of her without lifting him. Her smiling face filled everything he saw and became the world. He followed it like a compass or a hypnotist's wheel. She never let go of his sex. She aimed it at herself and before he had a chance to think about what could go wrong, she spoke.

"You're not going to be able to do this," she said.

"I'm . . . not . . . ?" he stammered in surprise.

"Because if you go inside me, you'll never get away."

"I won't?" he asked with the wonder of a child.

"No, you never will," she said and tugged. He felt warmth at the tip and was terrified that he would disappear. "After this, you'll be trapped."

"I will, won't I?" he said with a grin.

A hand landed on his ass and urged him on and there was no wall, there were no obstacles, there was only the sea of Margaret, the hot bath of her enveloping love. She put her lips to his ear and whispered warm while cool hands pressed on his back and steered him all the way into her. "You'll never get away. You'll move in with me, we'll get married, we'll have children. You'll be here forever," she whispered, and in the ocean of her being, he let go of the frightened air trapped in his heart, he exhaled the despair of his soul and he thought with glee: *I'm home! I'm home! Thank God, I'm home!*

acknowledgments

I wouldn't have made it past the opening chapters of this novel without the forceful and consistent encouragement of Tamar Cole, Susan Bolotin, Ben Cheever, and Michael Vincent Miller. And I would not have managed its revision without the kindness and understanding of Donna Redel. Writers habitually thank their agents and editors for helping them. That seems prudent but obvious. However, *A Happy Marriage* would not be published at all, and certainly would not make me proud, if it weren't for Lynn Nesbit and Nan Graham. They went far beyond their usual and widely known excellence at their work, extending themselves and their considerable skill to help me in vital ways. The value of Nan's meticulous editing can't be overstated. Also consistently helpful with every phase of editing and publication has been the thoughtful and careful Paul Whitlatch. Last, the spare bits of medical information were vetted by Kent Sepkowitz, a superb doctor and graceful writer. All mistakes, of course, are mine.